ANGELUS ASSIGNMENTS

By

Jeannette Haley

Hidden Manna Publications

ANGELUS ASSIGNMENTS

Copyright © 2024 by Jeannette Haley

ISBN: 979-8-9893588-3-0

Except where otherwise indicated, all Scripture quotations in this book are taken from the King James Version of the Bible.

Hidden Manna Publications
P.O. Box 3572
Oldtown, ID 83822
www.gentleshepherd.com

Facebook:
https://www.facebook.com/HiddenMannaPublications/

DEDICATION

To my faithful co-laborers
in the Gospel,
Rayola Kelley and Carrie Seaney.

ACKNOWLEDGMENT
AND RECOGNITION

To all the saints that the Lord has so graciously
brought into our lives through the years. Your
faithful love, prayers, encouragement and support
have not only greatly blessed our hearts and lives,
but the lives of others as well.
Great is your reward in heaven.

Contents

INTERVIEW IN HELL

A Novel

Book One

INTRODUCTION

We all have ideas and inspirations at some time as we travel through this life. However, only those ideas and inspirations which originate from an eternal source continually occupy our thoughts until we are prompted to action.

The book which you now hold in your hands began in such a way. I compare it to the obscure and humble beginnings of a great, flowing river. In the beginning, from outside of myself, came trickles of ideas, then rivulets of inspiration. Soon these developed into fast moving streams of thought which eventually grew into something far greater and deeper than myself. At that point, I knew this book had an eternal purpose.

You will meet Caree Collins, a young, single woman who, until she became confused over the reality of hell, planned to marry and serve Christ with Lance Lyons. You will travel on an unforgettable journey with her and her angelic guide into the recesses of the blackness and horrors of hell. There you will encounter various demonic beings and experience the agonies and torments of the lost. You will hear their stories and explanations of their lives prior to death.

Throughout this book you will gain instruction and insight with Caree as she learns exactly what the Bible has to say about heaven, hell, and life on earth. You will read information regarding such subjects as the New World Order, the occult, spiritual warfare, and the end times as well as graphic illustrations of what actually occurs when a person has an out-of-body death experience, taken from documented and real-life experiences.

Interview in Hell is a teaching novel with overtones of romance, loaded with valuable and challenging insight regarding the Christian life and the great God whom we serve.

1

BECKONED
FROM BEYOND

Thunder rumbled ominously through the dark, mid-afternoon sky over the small Montana town of Homedale. Gusts of wind whipped leaves, dirt, and miscellaneous litter into swirling masses resembling miniature tornadoes. Anxious shopkeepers ushered scurrying customers into the safety of their humble businesses seconds before torrents of rain descended from the angry, black sky.

Squeaking in protest, the rustic sign, which proudly announced the Lamplighter Café, swung wildly in the ruthless wind. The Lamplighter was by far the most popular eating establishment in Homedale. In fact, it was the favorite gathering place for folks from miles around, and usually Sunday afternoons found happy churchgoers gathering in the warm and inviting dining room to enjoy the twin pleasures of food and fellowship.

Several small apartments had been built above the busy restaurant, which served as humble living quarters for a few of the cafe's employees. The tenants enjoyed one another much like a well-adjusted and happy family—that is, until recently. There were picnics in the summer along the picturesque and peaceful river. Swimming, boating, fishing, hiking, horseback riding, camping, and open communication contributed to happy, and lingering memories for years to come. During those times Caree Collins always seemed to be the one who brought sparkle and cheer. That is, until lately.

Streetlights began flickering in confusion as the usual late afternoon light succumbed to the storm's threatening darkness. Above the

Lamplighter the outline of a petite figure stood motionless in the narrow window. No one was left in the vacated street to notice the thoughtful young woman. It wasn't as if people didn't appreciate Caree Collins' pleasant personality and sense of humor. But lately, ever since she was assigned to write those bizarre magazine articles, she had seemed strangely distant. Most folks assumed she just needed a little space and concluded that in time Caree would be her bubbly self again.

Caree turned away from the scene on the street below, moved methodically to a rather worn oak office chair and sat down with a sigh. Her dark blue eyes lingered for a few moments on the pile of paper strewn across the desk before her. A series of lightning flashes illuminated Caree's slender five feet, four inches while, casting eerie shadows in the dusky room. Her flowing blonde, shoulder-length hair seemed almost white in the fleeting seconds of dazzling light. Her flawless complexion and delicate features resembled carved ivory. But there was much more reflected on Caree's oval face than the light from nature's show.

Even the most casual observer, had there been one, would instantly realize this twenty-three-year-old woman had something on her mind. Something which demanded an answer.

It had all begun when she agreed to write a series about life after death for a popular women's magazine. She could still recall her enthusiasm as the editor spelled out the benefits of taking on such a job. It didn't seem like a difficult assignment. After all, all she had to do was read a couple of books, interview a few people, and make a report. Little did she know what she was getting into or how it would change her life—forever.

Loud knocking on the sturdy wood door jarred Caree's wandering thoughts back to the present. "Who is it?" she called in a tense voice as she groped in the darkness for the light switch.

"It's Lance!" A deep masculine voice boomed through the closed door and seemed to fill the small, conservatively furnished room with vibrations of life. "Caree, are you alright?" His voice sounded anxious.

"Yes, yes, I'm fine, Lance. I'm trying to find the light." Brushing her fingers across the Victorian wallpaper, she felt the switch, flipped it on and swung the door open.

The tall figure quickly stepped inside. Raindrops glistened on his rich umber hair and long eyelashes. His soft brown eyes searched Caree's uplifted face. "Caree, what are you doing? I mean, why are you sitting here in the dark in this terrible storm?"

Caree shrugged her shoulders. Ignoring his question, she countered with one of her own. "What are you doing walking around in the pouring rain? You're soaking wet!" She gestured toward a round, antique oak table and two chairs. "Come in and sit down. I'll make us some coffee." Before her guest could reply, Caree gingerly slipped into the small kitchenette where she busied herself with this simple chore. What Caree wanted was a few minutes to rouse herself from the intense concentration of the past hour and force her mind into the present. Suddenly she felt a hand on her shoulder. "Lance! You startled me...I didn't hear you..." Her voice sounded strained, unfamiliar. Caree felt awkward. What was happening to her? Was she losing her mind?

"Caree," his voice was low, warm, loving. "I'm sorry. I didn't mean to intrude on you, but the storm was so severe and I haven't seen you all week. I had to know you are all right."

A loud peal of thunder cracked overhead and the lights flickered momentarily as if to emphasize Lance's concern. Caree forced a smile in an attempt to be lighthearted. "I'm the one who should apologize. I guess I have been rather vague lately. Please forgive me. I'm glad you came. I really am."

Lance's handsomely rugged face broke into a grin. Dimples accentuated his smile, giving him a boyish appearance. His dark eyes seemed to sparkle with life. Truly, he was what Caree often called "model material."

The aroma of freshly brewed coffee soon filled the air. Lance carried two steaming mugs of the hot liquid to the small table. Gallantly pulling out a chair for Caree, he gave her a sweeping bow and said, "For my lady fair."

"Oh, Lance, really! You're too much!" Caree felt silly being treated like a member of the royal court. "Let's face it, Lance," she laughingly responded, "we are in a small, western Montana town and I look a mess!" She glanced down at her purple sweatshirt and faded blue jeans.

"Well, you look like a queen to me." The tone in Lance's voice had turned serious. "Caree, you know how I feel about you."

He placed his strong hand gently over her fingers. "Caree, I believe it's God's will that we make a team. I've prayed a lot about it. I want you to be my wife and work with me on the mission field."

Caree stared into her coffee cup. How could she tell this man what she felt? How could he understand? It was too much for her to handle right now. She needed answers to so many questions.

"Lance," she slightly squeezed his hand, hoping this small gesture of affection would somehow soften what she was about to say. "I know…but, I can't give you the answer you want right now. It's just not the right time. I can't explain it, but there are certain things which must be resolved in my own mind before I make such an important decision."

A strained hush descended on the young couple as they finished their coffee. Each seemed to be lost in their own world. Finally, Lance stood to his feet and walked slowly toward the coat rack. His six-foot-two frame seemed slightly stooped with an invisible weight. "Thanks for the coffee," he said with forced cheerfulness. He reached for his coat, "I think the worst of the storm is over and I best be going. Pastor Munson asked me to preach tomorrow as he'll be out of town."

Caree had risen and silently followed him to the door. Her heart thudded inside her chest like a caged bird. How she longed to feel his muscular arms around her, holding her, sheltering her from all that assailed her weary mind. How she yearned to tell him how much she loved him, needed him. Instead, she heard her voice weakly say, "Thanks for coming. I hope you don't get wet going home."

Lance turned and put his hands on her thin shoulders. His somber eyes searched her uplifted face as he tenderly brushed a runaway, strand of blonde hair from Caree's brow. "Caree, his voice was gentle, yet determined, "I'm going to pray until you give me an answer. I must have a definite 'yes' or 'no'. God will help you; you'll see. He never fails." He slowly turned, stepped through the doorway and disappeared down the narrow, shadowy hallway.

Caree locked the worn door, switched off the light and walked as if in a trance toward the twin bed. She kicked off her shoes and slowly lowered herself onto the blue and white quilt. "Oh God," she buried her

14

head in her hands, "God, oh God, You've got to help me! I have to know the truth."

Unexpected geysers of emotion surged from deep within her innermost being. Sobs shook her shivering body. "Show me, God. Show me if it's real. If there really and truly is such a place as hell! I've got to know! I must know now! I can't become a missionary's wife if I don't believe myself what we tell the people! Is it true what Marietta Davis saw in the mid 1880's? Lord, do You hear me?"

Caree's breath came in gasps. She remembered the quotes from Marietta Davis's eye-witness account of her "trip" to the nether world. It read in part, "Suddenly a sable veil of nether night appeared...I fell as one precipitated from some dizzy height. The moving shadow of a more desolate abyss arose like clouds in dense masses of tempestuous gloom; and as I descended, the ever-accumulating weight of darkness pressed more fearfully upon me."[1]

Caree shuddered. Most of her life she had attended Sunday school and church. She considered herself a genuine Christian. Hadn't she accepted Christ when she was twelve years old? "But what if there is no such place as hell?" she asked herself aloud. "What if the people I interviewed who are not Christians and who died and saw a great light and experienced great love and peace instead of hell are true?" She wiped the tears from her eyes with the back of her hand. "But what if the accounts I investigated are a hoax? And what about the discoveries of Dr. Elisabeth Kubler-Ross and Dr. Raymond A. Moody, Jr.? They didn't confirm there was such a place as hell, or heaven either, for that matter!"

Caree's mind spun in a whirl of confusion. "How could a God of love allow people to suffer so horribly forever?" Her voice sounded scratchy, strained. "What if I do marry Lance," her mind fleetingly pictured a bride and groom, pledging their love and lives to one another, "and we go to the mission field and risk our lives...what if we spend our whole lives telling people they have to get saved or they'll go to hell when they die if it...if it isn't really true?"

The bedsprings squeaked in protest as Caree wrestled with the quilt. Once settled under its comforting warmth, Caree continued her pursuit for answers. "Oh Lord, I've asked you before, but never like this. I must know, I have to know! Show me!"

15

Caree's last words seemed to be eerily suspended in the very atmosphere. It was as if somehow the Spirit of God was confirming that He had heard, that He knew, that somehow something was going to happen.

Caree pressed her face into the pillow and listened to the muffled sounds of the retreating storm in the distance. The low moaning of the wind melded with the intermittent higher pitched whistles of air in a cacophony of nerve-jarring sound as it forced its way through unprotected cracks around the windowpane.

Overwork, tension, and emotional exhaustion finally overcame Caree's restless mind. Submission to both the luxury and necessity of rest forced itself upon her taut muscles. She felt as if she were suspended between two worlds—consciousness and unconsciousness. Her thoughts formed themselves into strange abstractions, which somehow resembled the ebb and flow of lapping waves gently caressing sloping shorelines. She felt herself surrender to the peaceful current.

"Caree." The voice was gentle, sweet, celestial. "Caree, come. You will see, Caree. Come with me."

2

TWO WORLDS, OR THREE?

Bands of brilliant color suspended within beams of shimmering light vibrated with Heavenly melody. Crystal-clear colors of the rainbow gently swayed as they emitted sounds Caree had never dreamed of. Every fiber of her being responded in ecstasy to this rapturous experience.

"Caree." The beautiful Voice wrapped her in an eternity of pure love. She felt no fear, no anxiety. Only peace. Sweet peace.

He spoke again, "Caree, you will see."

Deep within her spirit she knew she had heard those words before, but where? It does not matter now, she thought. All that matters, all that exists, all of eternity is here, now. Peace, love, joy, radiant and pure, holy, glorious beauty.

"Caree. Come with me." The voice was different, yet it somehow harmonized with the other Voice, like different instruments in a magnificent symphony.

Then she saw him. He was at least ten feet tall and he walked right through the dazzling light; his countenance glowed from within; his hair was soft, flowing; his eyes gold and pure; his lips sweet and smiling; his robe sheer and white. He came toward her with arms outstretched.

Caree swooned but he caught her. She felt herself instantly strengthened.

"Fear not, Caree. I am Maschil, giver of wisdom and understanding; an angel, and your instructor and guide."

Joy and thoughtfulness radiated from his intelligent eyes. "You asked. Now you shall see, know, understand, and believe."

17

Caree's mind raced back to a small, lonely room in a place called Homedale, Montana. She looked with wonder at her guide. She was afraid to speak, afraid he would disappear at the sound of her voice, afraid it was all a dream. But it wasn't a dream; she knew if she was ever alive, ever fully awake, it was now.

"Caree, you are not dreaming." Maschil's voice hinted of laughter. Then, in a more serious tone, he added, "The time has come. Do not fear, for they cannot hurt you."

Instantaneously the brilliant light grew in intensity, compelling Caree to shut her eyes. She felt herself, light as a feather, being lifted into the air as the heavenly music gradually faded as if receding into the hollow and soundless echoes of a tomb.

With a knowledge not her own she knew they were traveling at incalculable speeds through a vortex of thick blackness. Its suffocating reality pressed against her, but at the same time she was conscious of Maschil's presence. Caree was not certain if her eyes were open or closed, the darkness was so great.

Then, without warning, fear, like a well-aimed missile, exploded inside her mind. Caree helplessly succumbed to its paralyzing grasp. Instantly she heard Maschil's powerful voice, "Caree, have no fear. Do not allow it. Jesus has overcome."

As the realization of this simple, yet profound, truth flooded Caree's being, she experienced the sensation of total deliverance from the tentacle-like grip of this unseen enemy. She dimly perceived Maschil's hand pointing at a black, shadowy figure. She couldn't quite make out its appearance, but it was there all right. It cringed under the angel's steady gaze and vanished, leaving only a slight vapor suspended in the ebony atmosphere.

"Praise His Majesty on high. Praise the Lord God Almighty!" Maschil's praises to God vibrated through the airless void. Maschil then addressed Caree. As he spoke, Caree thought of golden honey, dripping with goodness and health. "Caree, we are nearly there. We will begin our descent into the bottomless pit." Sensing that panic was about to again strike her heart, he reminded her, "You requested that the Master show you the truth. Remember, I am your protector, guide, and instructor. Do not fear."

18

Instantly, before Caree could reply, Maschil enveloped her in the folds of his gleaming robe and plunged into the fathomless depths.

This was no dream, no vision. She was more alert, more alive than she had ever been. Caree's five senses seemed to be unusually fine-tuned. She heard the swish of Maschil's garment; felt his powerful arms holding her; saw the concentration on his angelic face. This is real, she told herself. This is really happening.

Within a time-frame of split seconds, Caree pragmatically organized her thoughts. At the same time amusement at herself ran parallel to her orderly conclusions. "I asked for it and I'm getting it. But will I survive this? What will happen to me if I can't take it?"

Caree wasn't surprised when Maschil broke into her mental questioning. She knew he could read her mind. Without a hint of impatience, the angel repeated, "Caree, you will see. You will be safe." He let go of her body and placed her alongside him. Caree turned to look full at this angel who had been particularly assigned to this unusual task.

"Why, you have wings!" Caree's startled exclamation clearly amused Maschil. "I was told angels, if they did exist, didn't have wings!"

"Yes. We do have wings except when we take on human form and walk among men on earth." Maschil's lips parted into a broad grin. "Have you not read in the Scripture, 'entertained angels unawares'?"

Caree's brilliant blue eyes widened. "No! I mean, you've actually been to earth," she stammered, "in the flesh?"

"Yes, I have, Caree. Many times, on different missions."

"You actually stayed with people...I mean you were 'entertained' in homes?"

A look of sadness overshadowed Maschil's beaming countenance. "Twice. Only twice." Sorrow, and something akin to weariness and longing, intertwined into one explanatory communication—a communication which penetrated Caree's heart with spiritual perception. Many of God's people had been given an opportunity and had failed. How many she did not know. But within her spirit she knew it was too many. And to our loving Heavenly Father how many were too many? She distinctly heard the answer, "One".

Caree saw Maschil turn slightly and look downward. She followed his gaze and at the same instant felt his strong hand under her arm. She gasped and tried to step backward, but her body would not respond. "No! It can't be, it's, it's..."

"Hell." Maschil's grip tightened on her arm. "Heaven, Earth, and Hell. Three worlds." His voice was soft yet intense. "Come." Caree knew she could not resist, could not run, could not escape from this interview in hell.

3

FOR OF SUCH IS THE KINGDOM OF HEAVEN

The nauseous odor of sulfur and putrefying gases rose in visible columns of swirling vapor from somewhere within the slimy chasm. A curtain of this odoriferous haze seemed to hang suspended like a veil immediately in front of Maschil and his young charge. Maschil extended a hand and the hazy curtain parted, allowing them to continue their descent.

Suddenly they appeared, hideous and grotesque; the army of demons advanced on every side. "Maschil! They're awful, oh ugh, they're jeering at us!" Caree's throat felt constricted and dry. The atmosphere was tinged with a repulsive greenish color and she fought to breathe. Remembrances of eye-witness accounts she had read describing these beings raced through her mind. Caree vividly remembered Howard Pitman's description in his book *Placebo*:

As each type of demon was pointed out to me, I quickly discovered a social order, or rank, that existed among them. Those at the top of that order were revealed in forms similar to humans. As we moved down the order, or rank, I saw demons in shapes or forms that looked like half-animal and half-human. I saw demons in forms resembling animals we know in this present world and I saw demons in forms and shapes so revoltingly morbid that you cannot possibly imagine them.[1]

"Jesus is Lord! Praise His Holy Name! Glory to God on high! All power and honor and glory belong to Jehovah!" At the sound of

21

Maschil's loud praise the detestable beings fell back. Some were hissing, others muttering and chirping, their gleaming eyes bulging with evil and maliciousness.

Caree watched with a mixture of horror and fascination as Maschil expertly ushered her into a small chamber where she detected the presence of a miserable prisoner. The figure gasped and moaned as the couple drew near. Caree peered through the thick darkness, straining to make out the appearance of the solitary figure. Eerie lights flickered far below them, and occasionally the sound of screams and shrieks reached her ears. "Who are you?" The sound of her own voice startled Caree, but she asked again, "Who are you? Why are you here?"

"Water. Did you bring some water?" The voice was that of a woman. "I hate you, I hate H..." The venomous tirade stopped abruptly as Maschil stepped forward, hand raised, in front of Caree.

"Answer her question, and no more." Maschil's command was stern and forceful. "Now!"

"Aaugh!" The woman's voice rang out in agony, then she turned toward her interviewer. Caree sensed without seeing the warped features of this miserable sinner. What she could see, however, was enough. The woman's hair was hopelessly snarled and tangled and stuck to her bony face like clods of dirt in a newly plowed field. Her eyes glowed with a strange reddish tint, and her pale lips, cracked and fissured, sounded like the crunch of dry autumn leaves as she spoke.

"Children! When I lived in the world, on earth, you know," she stopped, wheezing and choking in the rancid air. A dreadful stench issued from her contorted mouth. Then she continued, "I had money. Ah, yes. I was extremely wealthy!"

Caree watched as this pathetic creature's eyes lit up with greed and avarice. "I worked in a school—a school for impoverished children. They were so miserable, so detestable to me. Then, this Christian," she spat out the word 'Christian' with a hatred that could literally be felt, "this little believer came to work in that school. I hated her, despised her. She always did good things for those puny children! She gave them pencils and clothes and her own lunch! That stupid, insipid Christian had no money...nuthin'. But she gave and gave and gave. I ordered her to stop it. But she wouldn't. She gave them pennies and took them home when they should've been made to walk. I saw to it that she was slandered, ridiculed, and mocked. I made sure everyone knew what a dysfunctional family she had." Her voice had risen to a shriek. "When I finally asked her why she kept loving, and giving and being kind to me, she told me about Him!"

Caree blurted out, "Why didn't you come to Christ? How could you not see His love and..."

She cut Caree off with a howl. Her blistered lips drew back into a vicious sneer. "I couldn't stand it! I didn't want to hear about that One! I had money and power and didn't want to give any away! If I believed in Him, then I would lose what I had! I was better than her, better than the whole lot of them. They were so stupid! I knew better than to believe what she told me! I was educated, intelligent. I knew there was no such place as thisssssssssss!"

Scripture flashed like a neon sign in Caree's mind concerning Jesus' words about little children:

...forbid them not to come unto me: for of such is the kingdom of heaven. See that you do not despise one of these little ones, for I say to you, that their angels in heaven continually behold the face of My Father who is in heaven.[2]

The doomed soul began to loudly boast, "I was highly trained and handpicked to bring atheism, communism, gender identity, social justice, and globalist New Age philosophy and beliefs into the American educational system. I turned many of those brats away from the Christian God in spite of that insipid Christian! I had my ways."

Caree gasped. More words from God's Word paraded through her mind like tickertape:

...but whoever causes one of these little ones who believe in Me to stumble, it is better for him that a heavy millstone be hung around his neck, and that he be drowned in the in the depths of the sea.[3]

Caree squinted through the shadowy prison. Her eyes detected heavy chains binding this eternally lost captive to something which appeared to be alive. Then she saw them—tormenting demons. Caree counted four squat, scaly devils lurking in the corners of the filthy compartment. Their malevolent eyes were on Maschil, and somehow she knew as soon as she and her angelic guide departed, they would continue tormenting their prisoner.

Caree watched as pride, like a living, evil mask, overshadowed the woman's distorted features as she threw back her head and opened her mouth. Pure visible hatred foamed from her lips and slowly oozed down the tortured chin. Caree turned away. She had seen and heard enough.

"Maschil, please, take me out of here. I've seen. I believe."

4

CHILDLESS

Caree lifted her somber face and gazed expectantly at Maschil. Impatience surged through her like an exploding geyser. "Maschil! Oh, please get me out of here! I believe!"

His kind features glowed from the reflection of distant fires. "Caree, it is in God's order that there must be a witness; that is, two or three. And, in your particular case..." He paused for a moment and surveyed her uplifted face intently.

Amazement mingled with alarm caused Caree's strained nerves to tingle. Was this powerful angel actually uncomfortable? For a split second this question somehow made Caree's confidence in Maschil to waver, but she heard herself ask, "Yes?"

"In your particular case," the angel continued, ignoring Caree's discernment, "God is granting you an interview in hell."

Caree gasped. "What? Why? I..." She began choking uncontrollably as the acrid air filled her lungs. Maschil quickly covered her face with his hand. She closed her eyes and felt sweet, cool air penetrate her nasal passages and lungs. Instantly her throat cleared and Maschil removed his hand.

Caree stood silently, eyes closed, and concentrated on rounding up her runaway thoughts. Her mind seemed to be going in a thousand directions at once. How could she handle this situation? How could she remember everything? Would she be able to understand what was happening? How could she tell others? Would they ever believe her? Was she losing her mind?

Maschil's amiable voice abruptly subdued Caree's jumbled thoughts. "That which is decreed by God will be accomplished by God. Caree, there is nothing about your nature God doesn't understand. You, like Thomas, need proof. Did you not read dozens of books about life after death, near-death experiences, and interview many people?" Maschil's eyes and words penetrated to the depths of Caree's soul. Before she could answer, Maschil continued. "For every person you interviewed on earth, that many people you are also assigned to interview in hell."

Caree's mind spun crazily as pinpoints of light began whirling and spinning within her inner view. She felt herself falling headlong into a whirlpool of helplessness and horror. Instantly robust angel arms lifted her up and pressed her gently against his chest. "Child, it is all right. You are safe with me. No harm will come to you. Fear not."

Peace, like liquid gold, effused through her entire being. Strength returned and Caree secretly wished she could stay forever in this safe, blissful state.

"No, Caree, we must continue our journey." Maschil calmly stood her beside him and extended his hand. "Come."

Caree obediently took her guide's outstretched hand. Maschil led her down a narrow, sloping path. At first, she could dimly see great chasms and towering walls of rock. Steam and smoke rose from various fissures in the jagged cliffs. Flickering reflections from hidden fires periodically lit up portions of the rocky scene in a strange kind of tantalizing dance of hellish light. Caree's grip on Maschil's hand tightened. Was it her imagination or was it becoming darker, blacker? Her eyes felt strange in this wretched place and she wasn't sure about anything, including what she saw, heard, and smelled. All she knew was that this was real and she was here, and even if she couldn't rationally explain everything and quite trust her senses, her mind was more alert than it had ever been.

"Yes, Caree Collins," she reprimanded herself sternly, "You did ask for this. You always have to have 'proof.' Look what you got yourself into this time!"

Without warning they were plunged into total darkness. Caree stiffened and clung to Maschil's muscular arm. "It's all right Caree," he reassured her. "Remember the account you read of missionary evangelist Lorne F. Fox?"

Yes, she remembered it vividly, even though, at the time, skepticism had quenched the importance of missionary Fox's testimony. Fox's spirit had been taken down into the nether world and with an angel at his side he was permitted to see the fate of a lost soul.

Fox's account in part rambled through her mind.

"Everything was wrapped in total darkness, but eventually faint, strange lights and shadows became brighter. It was up to this point that the atmosphere had been warm, now it took on an oppressive, almost unbearable sensation as the descent into the bowels of the earth ceased.

"Just below him was a lost soul that was joined by a weird creature. It was a demon from the lower regions. This entity's job was to take this soul by force on the remainder of the journey to the abyss.

"Once the descent began again, things began to take on form. A huge orb or sphere that was bathed in flames of liquid fire that proved to be the source of the mysterious light. However, the sphere was so large that it was impossible to see around it.

"The descent stopped at the vast orb where he witnessed the fierce struggle between the demon and the lost soul. Accompanied by a loud shriek, the lost soul was plummeted head long into the vast wall of fire.

"At first, everything was clothed in total darkness, and then after a time there began to be faint, weird lights and shadows, like a flickering firelight, which gradually became brighter.

"At this point, the atmosphere, which had been warm, became stifling, finally almost unbearable, and then the descent ceased for a few moments.

"The lost soul was just below, and by now it was possible to discern that he was joined by a weird creature, which arose from the lower regions. It was a demon, sent from Hell to take that soul by force on the remainder of its downward journey.

"The descent began again. Far below us, things now began to take a definite form. There appeared a huge orb or sphere, which was bathed in flames of liquid fire. At closer proximity, the sphere was so large that it was impossible to begin to see around it. This had been the source of the mysterious firelight.

"Finally, the descent stopped as we came close against this vast orb. I saw a fierce struggle for just a moment between the lost soul and that demon, and suddenly, with a wild shriek the soul was plummeted headlong into the wall of fire that covered this huge sphere."[3]

Caree's eyes stared without seeing into the ebony atmosphere. She felt Maschil turn slightly to the left and as he did so, she stepped into the place where he had been standing.

Her heart skipped a beat and seemed to catch in her throat. There it was! Just like missionary Fox described. Far below a lake of liquid fire of gigantic proportions pulsated and writhed as if in an orgy of private agony. Waves of heat and steam, hissing and whining eerily from within the boiling cauldron wafted upwards in spiny columns which resembled disfigured skeletons.

Caree couldn't tell how long she stood, transfixed, engrossed in the hideous scene far below when suddenly she felt her skin crawl. Someone or something was definitely behind her. She knew she was being watched and felt her body shudder in spite of the heat.

"Maschil, wha, what's behind..." Caree's quavering voice was drowned out by an earsplitting scream. Maschil quickly pulled Caree closer to himself and in the same move turned both of them around. Something heavy and ugly stood before them. It towered above Maschil by three or four feet and its huge eyes bulged from its grotesque head. Its broad mouth bared, revealing two rows of sharp fangs.

Sheer terror gripped Caree's heart. The ledge upon which they stood was narrow. One misstep backwards and they would plunge into the lake.

"Caree!" Maschil's voice brought instant reassurance, although Caree sensed a slight reprimand, "Do not fear! Jesus is Lord and I am here with you."

At the name of Jesus, the enormous demon grunted and stepped backward. He watched Maschil with wary eyes, as if waiting for orders. "Bring him out. Now!" Maschil's demand brought instant action. The hideous beast seemed to vanish for a split-second, then returned with a pathetic, emaciated man. In spite of his bony appearance Caree could tell he was rather young.

"All right, Caree," began Maschil, never taking his gaze off the demon, "here is your second interview. His name is William and he's someone you once met on earth."

Caree squinted through the hazy atmosphere at this sad wreck of a human being. Yes, he did look familiar. There was something she seemed to recognize, but she wasn't sure just what it was.

"Hah!" spat out the young man. "You goody-two-shoes religious celibate, you could've had Jack if you..."

"Stop! You will not speak to her that way!" Maschil took a step forward and both the man called William and the demon moved backward. "You are being interviewed and you will answer the questions she asks, but you are not allowed to verbally assault her!"

At the mention of Jack, Caree slightly stiffened. Jack had been the best looking, but wildest boy in high school, and girls literally threw themselves at him. But Jack had a strange fascination with Caree. He always seemed to manage to "accidentally bump into her" in the hallways and to show up at different events which involved Caree. But Caree steadfastly resisted temptation, knowing full well Jack's intentions and reputation. Girls who dated Jack were usually the talk of the town. And now, in this wretched place, Caree was face-to-face with one of the boys from her high school days who chided her then and even now with the fact she had remained pure.

"William! Oh, William!" Caree felt tears sting her eyes. How she remembered! William had dated Francine, one of her best friends, about five years ago. The young couple had been going steady for a few months when Francine became pregnant.

"Well, what do ya wanna know?" William nervously eyed Maschil. "What can I say, Caree, I'm in hell, if ya hadn't figured that out by now."

"William," Caree began, "about the baby, you didn't have to, you could have. . ." Caree was an expert at interviews, but that was on earth. She wasn't prepared to practice her business expertise in hell.

"Look, Caree," William shrugged his emaciated shoulders and gestured helplessly. "I told Francine to get that abortion, okay? But she is just as much to blame as I am!" His voice began to rise in anger, "Francine is just as guilty as I am. She didn't have to kill the fetus if she didn't want to."

"William!" Caree's emotions were churning. "You know why Francine did it! She wanted you to love her—she didn't want to lose you! And then, afterward, she went through her own hell on earth with guilt, and self-loathing, and depression and you left her anyway!" Caree stopped short of reminding him that his next girlfriend also got pregnant.

"So, I suppose I'm a murderer too?" William's face began to twist and distort as if it was having convulsions separate from the rest of his body. "After all, everybody knows it's just a bunch of tissue, not a ba..." His head dropped and wagged back and forth but he kept his angry eyes on Caree. The demon beside him seemed to enjoy watching his captive's misery and stood with its greenish arms folded.

Caree wanted to forget this whole scene, forget the past, forget the interview. But she knew she had to follow through, to find out, to know. William and Francine had renewed their relationship after his second girlfriend, Jana, aborted her babies. She had been pregnant with twins. Caree remembered it vividly. As soon as Jana had the abortion, William worked his way back into Francine's life. Shortly after that, on a cold and dark night, William and Francine were together in his car when they hit a patch of black ice. The car slid off the highway into the frozen river. They both drowned.

"What I want to know, William, is why didn't you accept Christ? You were given the gospel by many of the young people at school, including myself." Caree waited for his reply.

"Why should I? You Christian kids never seemed to have it together as far as I was concerned. I wanted to have fun, to try it all—drugs, sex, and...and, to really live! I didn't want to be a stick-in-the mud like, uh, well," he glanced up at Maschil, lowered his voice and continued in an even tone, "Ya know, I didn't believe in all that stuff from the Bible!" He

30

waved his thin arm as if to indicate the words of life shared by Christian acquaintances were less than nothing to him.

"What I want to know, William," Caree's voice was low, deliberate, "Where is Francine? Is she, is she..."

"Here?" William's mouth shaped into a wry grimace. "Francine, here? Are ya kidding?" He threw his head back and tried to laugh, but all that came from his parched throat was a maniacal scream which ended in a gurgle. "Didn't ya know? Ha! Ya didn't know? She received Christ as her Lord the Sunday before the accident. She ain't here!"

"But you are, and you're all mine!" The demon sprang into action, ferociously grabbing William by the throat. Its long claws viciously ripped at the terrified victim's head.

Maschil threw his robe around Caree's face and she felt them again traveling at a tremendous speed. She had no concept of time or space in this ghastly place, but she knew they had suddenly come to a standstill. Maschil loosed his hold and gently stood her to her feet.

"Oh, Maschil, how awful...how beyond description is the hopelessness, the horror of this place!" She began to weep uncontrollably. "Can't we leave here? Please, oh please? I really believe, really! I want to go home. I want to see Lance, to tell him, to...to marry him and forget all this!"

"Child of God," Maschil's voice somehow reminded Caree of a sweet, spring breeze softly caressing boughs filled with apple blossoms. "Caree, do you not realize that God is teaching you many things which you will share with others? You will be His excellent witness!"

Caree looked up at her magnificent guide. "Then tell me, please... oh, I hope I can bear it, but I must know anyway, please tell me, are there any, um, are there any..."

"Children here?" Maschil finished the question for her. "No Caree, hell is childless."

5

MINDSET

Maschil was taking on the role of teacher as he reiterated, "No Caree, there are no children here. Upon death, aborted babies and young children are escorted by the angels to heaven. You see, all people have been given the power to choose whom they will serve, but babies and little children are unable to make that choice until they reach an age where they comprehend." A soft sigh escaped his lips before he continued, but his hesitation was not lost to Caree who raised her eyebrows questioningly. "And, you need to know something, else, Caree. People's names are not written in the Book of Life when they are born again, as most churches teach, because everyone's name is already in the Book of Life from their conception."

Caree's eyes narrowed as she stared at her heavenly escort. Her mind spun as it frantically chased a dozen questions that she tried to organize into one comprehensive whole. However, the only word she found herself uttering was a feeble, "But…"

"Caree," Maschil's piercing gaze had a paralyzing effect, "you remember all the Bible verses you have read about God blotting names out of His Book?" Before she could choke out the answer, he continued, "When a person dies who has rejected Christ in their earthly life, it is then that their name is blotted out of the Book of Life."

Caree shuddered as hot tears filled her eyes. She began to softly moan. Maschil laid a hand on her shoulder, as if to calm her raging emotions. "Caree, do you remember the book you read by missionary H. A. Baker?"

Caree nodded. She loved that little book which had been given to her by an elderly saint. The book was hard to find in the marketplace. It was called *Visions Beyond The Veil* and recounted the events which took place at the Adullam rescue home in China many years ago.

Maschil continued, "Remember what missionary Baker reported about the children in the home being visited by the Holy Spirit in power and might and how they saw both angels and demons?"

Caree nodded without looking directly at her angelic instructor. She was becoming fascinated with their present surroundings. What seemed like only moments ago she had been greatly shaken by her "interview" with William. They had been in the presence of pure unadulterated evil and darkness. However, at this time, nothing could be seen, heard, or felt except Maschil's presence.

They both stood in a small circle of light. She wondered at the source of this illumination in hell and finally came to the conclusion that it was somehow emanating from Maschil himself.

"Excuse me, Caree, are you with me?"

"Uh, oh, I'm sorry!" A faint smile played around the corners of Caree's lips and momentarily replaced the tension which had gripped her lovely features.

"I'm in school now, right?" Caree's sudden sense of good humor caught her off guard. She had always been witty, but in a place like this? What was the matter with her, she wondered.

"Caree, God's Spirit keeps us in all situations and the hope He has given anchors the soul. You are who you are, no matter where you are, so guard against condemnation."

Maschil, as usual, communicated her thoughts before she had time to sort through them, or answer him, for that matter. "Yes, you are 'in school' and I'm going to quote portions of H. A. Baker's writings. You are going to learn valuable lessons for use in your ministry with different types of people."

Caree carefully folded her hands in front of her and dutifully looked up at this tall heavenly being. "I'm ready," she said quietly.

"Remember the boy who was dragged from Adullam to Hell?"

Caree could feel her heartbeat increase, and she frowned slightly. "Sort of, but didn't you just say children go to heaven?"

33

"That's what I want you to learn, Caree. Innocent children who have no opportunity to understand good and evil and make a choice are saved eternally. But now let me share a particular tragic example of a younger person who did know the difference and made the wrong choice."

Maschil began summarizing the incident recorded by missionary Baker's testimony about a boy who was dragged to hell.

This boy had been exposed to the message and benevolence of the Gospel at the Adullam Rescue Home in China that was run by Mr. Baker, but showed his real intentions when he was caught trying to sell various articles that he had stolen from the home. He had promised to reform and made an outward show of it, but he continued to stick to the ways of his old life.

This young thief was put out of the home. Eventually, he was discovered back on the streets, begging for meager handouts. Even though this young boy had witnessed the powerful manifestations of the Holy Spirit and supernatural revelations, as well as given a second chance by those at the rescue home to embrace a new and better life, he would not allow his encounter with God to transform his inner person. He later ran away from the transforming power of God's Spirit and Word, and joined himself to a street gang of beggar-thieves.

A few months later he fell and broke his arm. Infection set in, and when he was finally discovered by a hospital worker, he was close to death. Even in the hospital, he was hopelessly disobedient and once again thrown out into the streets.

His death became inevitable, and he came to the rescue home making empty promises. However, the claws of death were not about to release their grip on this rebellious boy. As death began to claim the last moments of his life, the young boy came face-to-face with his foolish ways as hellish demons gathered about to take his soul. His screams and shrieks for the missionary to help him as these demons bound him with chains to drag him off to hell would never be erased from the ears of those who heard the fear and the harsh reality of the spiritual consequences that has been prepare for fools such as this young boy.[1]

Caree's widened eyes met Maschil's somber gaze. She wanted to weep, to run, to somehow escape this heavy reality, but all she could do was stand motionless and wait for Maschil to conclude this special lesson.

Even though there were a only a few seconds of silence before he spoke again, it seemed like time stood still for Caree. She held her breath, stunned by the fact that sometimes younger people who understand accountability, yet remain in rebellion, do not automatically gain Heaven.

"Daughter, know that all over the world Christian workers who minister to people such as this Chinese boy, street people, gang members, inmates, criminals and, yes, even other members in the social order such as 'respectable' business people and," Maschil hesitated, then continued, his words distinctly sorrowful, "even church people, experience defeat."

"I just don't understand why..." Caree began. Maschil took both her hands in his.

"Let me give you another example. This is also a true story. Two single Christian ladies with a heart for the lost and hurting became involved in a small jail ministry. In time, one of the women prisoners, Peggy, who had received Christ as her Savior during a chapel service in the jail, was set free. Because she had lost her home, family, and possessions due to a heroin addiction, she had no place to go. The Christian women took her into their home and began to lovingly disciple her. Peggy loved church, read her Bible faithfully day and night, became baptized and witnessed many wonderful manifestations of the Holy Spirit. She went back to the jail and shared her testimony with the women during chapel services. Peggy had a healthy fear of hell and prayed for her lost children."

Maschil looked at Caree. She stood straight and silent, intent on absorbing whatever wisdom this resplendent instructor wished to impart.

He was still holding her hands in his and tenderly tightened his clasp. "Caree, today that poor woman is back on the street, prostituting for drugs."

"Why? How?" Caree felt as if her entire body was wilting like a piece of lettuce on a hot day. She wanted to drop to Maschil's feet, curl up in a ball and disappear. But he was firmly holding her up and all she could do was yield to his will.

"Caree, receive strength." His voice was clear, calm, and confident. Instantly she felt waves of power flow up her arms and flood her body. A familiar scripture streamed through her mind: *Are they [angels] not all ministering spirits, sent out to render service for the sake of those who will inherit salvation?*[2]

Caree wanted to somehow thank her ministering spirit, but finding the right words eluded her. How does one say "thank you" to an angel without sounding trite? While she struggled within herself, Maschil's amused and silent communication entered her mind, "Caree, it is all right." Then aloud he continued, "God wants you to gain wisdom and insight into these types of people. As you work for the Lord, you will find yourself laboring to understand how they can be set free from destructive cycles. You see, Caree, these people have a determination of the will. This determination of the will can involve a person not being willing to submit to any authority, including God's. So, they 'play the game', outwardly conforming without inwardly transforming. Sadly, this includes people who call themselves Christians."

Caree heard Maschil deeply sigh. She wondered how awesome the scene must be in Heaven every time a Christian failed to overcome. Do the angels, who rejoice over every sinner that repents, also mourn over every one who does not?

Her superb teacher continued the lesson. "These people are the ones who greatly fear being vulnerable. Therefore, they will not submit to authority because it makes them vulnerable. Remember, Caree, they are greatly motivated by the need to survive. They must be in control, which ultimately puts them in a position to be god of their world."

The first commandment flashed in Caree's mind. There were to be *no other gods.* She tried to absorb every word that her heavenly instructor spoke.

"Because these people cannot submit and be vulnerable, which they consider a weakness, they continue in pride and fear." Maschil was watching Caree closely, making sure she was following him. Satisfied that she was, he continued. "You already know pride and fear are open doors for Satan."

Caree sucked in her breath. Different people she had met in her lifetime began popping into her mind. She was beginning to understand why some of them could never fully surrender to the Lordship of Christ.

"Caree, let me further explain. When a person opens the door through pride, fear, or rebellion, for whatever reason, Satan has the right to come in and put them in further bondage. Remember, it is written *'the just shall live by faith.'*[3] When a person refuses to allow Christ to be Lord of their life, they are unable to live by faith. What such individuals are saying and demonstrating is they have faith in their own standards, perceptions, and determinations. This makes them god of their own world."

Caree's thoughts were racing. God wasn't to blame if people played games and refused to submit to His lordship. Once a person heard the gospel, then they were responsible for their decision to either surrender to Christ's love and to love Him with all of their heart, soul, mind, and strength or to go on living their own way. Passages of scripture from *Matthew chapter 13* flashed through her mind. Had not Jesus warned of different heart conditions when he told the parable of the seed and the sower? Some people who heard God's word are like seed sown beside the road. These individuals do not understand the word and Satan snatches away that which was sown in the heart. Others, who receive the word with joy, but have no root in themselves, fall away when persecution arises. Then there are those who, even though they have received the word, are like seed sown among thorns, for the worries of the world and the deceitfulness of riches choke out that very word and these individuals fail to bear fruit.

"You are beginning to understand, Caree." Maschil seemed pleased with her progress.

"But," Caree interjected thoughtfully, "How do you minister to such people?"

"An excellent question!" Maschil's face beamed. "Caree, I am going to say one word, and I want you to remember it." He paused as if waiting for her full attention. Then, in an even tone which was somehow tinged with a note of sadness, he said, "mindset!"

"Mindset?" Caree mused. "What exactly do you mean by mindset?"

Maschil folded his arms and leaned slightly forward. Caree was standing very erect now, alert with anticipation. Somehow, she sensed this information was being deliberately laid out for her, step-by-step. She must not disregard the wisdom which God had ordained for her to know.

"People who minister to those with such mindsets,"—his knowing look silently communicated to Caree that she would one day be such a minister— "must be able to recognize them as strongholds which have to be brought down. People can only be set free by recognizing their stronghold, with God's help. You see, Caree, the person with the mindset must give God permission to bring it down. In other words, for people to be set free, there must be an exchange. While it is true that criminals, street people, and such have these mindsets, I want you to realize that Christians have these mindsets too. That's why they suffer defeat in their Christian life."

"I see," Caree murmured more to herself than to her tutor. There was so much to learn, so much to understand. *Mindset!* she thought to herself. *Hell was full of people with mindsets—strongholds for Satan—erected through pride and fear. Hell was full of people by their own choice.* Caree's eyes met Maschil's.

Finally, he spoke, "Come. Your next interview awaits."

6

THE WEAKER VESSEL

Maschil took Caree's hand and positioned her close to his side. She felt his great strength and power and wondered if all the heavenly angels were like him. He responded to her unspoken questions by tightening his hold on her and with a mighty surge of energy descended straight into the dark abyss.

Caree's heart fluttered with excitement. What was she about to see, to smell, and hear? As they continued their descent, Caree began to hear a low moaning sound. Gradually the moaning became louder, punctuated by intermittent shrieks and howls. She wondered if they were near that place documented by missionary Baker. Bits and pieces of his written testimony crisscrossed her mind. He not only recorded the darkness of hell, but also the lake of fire that was approached through a region of stygian darkness. Clouds of smoke arose out of the semi-dark pit of the great lake of molten fire. However, when the clouds of smoke lifted, the lake with red and greenish flames along with its occupants could be clearly seen.

Missionary Baker admitted that it was a horrifying site as the lost were falling into hell. Some simply walked over the brink, while others were bound by the chains of demons and cast into hell. Groups of wicked individuals were actually bound together, ready to be cast into the furnace of fire. When the fire abated and the smoke somewhat cleared, the moans of the miserable wretched souls of the lost could be heard, while in the lake of fire oceans of hands reached up for help.[1]

"We're here!" Maschil's exclamation snapped Caree's mind to attention. Where was "here?" This place was so dark, so black one could only assume it was mammoth in size, indescribable in composition and structure, as well as laden with innumerable labyrinths, canyons, and pits. Even if it were well lit, Caree mused, one could probably never navigate its complicated configuration without getting hopelessly lost—unless, that is, one was a devil or an angel.

Maschil gingerly set Caree on her feet and stepped directly behind her. Startled, she stepped backward and bumped into him. Her heart raced wildly. "Oh, Maschil, I thought for a second you had left me...I mean, that you were far behind me!"

"Caree, rest assured. I am not going to leave you here! I want you to meet Mr. Wright."

Caree strained to see through the inky atmosphere. She could still hear the muffled sounds of moaning and shrieking, but nothing else could be seen or heard.

"Maschil, are you sure? I mean, is there really someone here?"

"Hah! Spoken like a true woman!" The voice screamed so loudly Caree instinctively stepped back, only to bump into her guide once again. "Women! So stupid! Never believe whatcha tell 'em! Women! It's all their fault!" The shrill voice ricocheted off the ebony walls and rattled Caree's eardrums.

Suddenly she saw them—a pair of red eyes, venomously glaring at her. She squinted slightly, straining to make out some form. She heard Maschil say something, but she couldn't make out what the words were. They were in a language she had never heard. A faint light began to shine overhead, lighting up the adjacent surroundings.

Caree gasped in horror. Before her stood a shriveled and twisted figure which barely resembled a human being. His skull was covered with dreadful bumps with tufts of scraggly hair sticking out between them. It reminded Caree of an unkempt graveyard, the bumps representing tombstones and the hair, weeds. His unblinking eyes were set far back within the sockets and stared at her maliciously. His mouth was small, disfigured, and hung open unceremoniously displaying two uneven rows of needle-like teeth. There were holes where his nose and ears should have been.

Caree's gaze lowered from the grotesque face to the rest of his body which was basically a skeleton. What appeared to be pieces of flesh hung from the bones and a terrible stench issued forth from his small cell. His entire appearance reminded Caree of what she had read in one of her research books that gave some vivid descriptions of hell.

"Yeah, I'm Mr. Wright!" he hissed. "And I was right too! I know I was right. I should be rewarded for being right! I instructed hundreds, maybe thousands of people RIGHT!" He was shouting now. "I was right about women! It's all their fault I'm here. If it wasn't for females, I'd be on top, outa here!" He poked a spindly finger up in the air, jabbing it up and down to indicate the earth above. "Why should I talk to you? You're a stinkin' woman and..."

Maschil interrupted and his booming voice filled the small cavern, "Because God has decreed it and I am here to make sure you do it."

Mr. Wright's glowering red eyes seemed to retreat further into their sockets as he shuffled backward. "What do ya want to know?" he questioned warily.

Maschil was definitely in charge. "Tell her exactly what you taught while on earth and where you taught it."

The cowering figure struggled to stand somewhat erect. His mouth opened and shut several times and made funny clicking sounds.

Caree shifted her weight, cleared her throat and asked, "Just what did you teach, Mr. Wright?"

"Hum," he seemed to be looking past his two visitors now as if seeing into the distant past. "I taught it right; about women I mean. I was a religious leader." His words were filled with pride. "Yessiree! Real religious, that I was. I taught those pathetic church people why women are to blame. Started with Eve." His red eyes lit up with hatred. "I hate her. And she was supposed to be a gift from God. Ha! Some gift she was! Poor, poor Adam. Why do you think in many countries of the world baby girls are fed to pigs and alligators and are aborted and suffocated and sold as slaves and..."

He watched Caree's horrified reactions with malicious glee. Obviously motivated by pride and hate, he persevered, "You see, if only people could understand that women should have no say in politics or religion. It was the latter I concentrated on. I taught all over the country

41

that women were to blame for the problems in the world. Women should never be allowed to teach, preach, prophesy or do anything other than serve the men and have children." He clicked his mouth shut and glowered at Caree and Maschil, then continued with malicious delight, "I married a woman once. She wanted to serve God." His voice was a wild shriek. "She! Wanted to serve God! I taught her who she was to serve all right! Women are for men! She was to serve me! So, Mrs. Wright had to be taught, trained! Ha! I fixed her good in the bedroom. Did things to her she wouldn't dare confide to anyone! She was ashamed, ha, ha! But she never learned," his weasel eyes glowed with evil satisfaction and foam bubbled out of his mouth like a rabid animal. "So, so I took a hammer to her head. Had them all convinced it was an accident! She was still in a coma when I came here. I shouldn't be here. I'm a MAN!"

Caree gasped. What a wicked, evil, horrible, base creature. How could a human being conceive of such reprehensible thoughts and actions?

The sight, sound, and smell of this pathetic individual sickened Caree. She wasn't sure why Maschil had felt it important for her go through this particular experience. It was no mystery why this lost sinner was here. And furthermore, lots of people, both men and women, shared Mr. Wright's opinion about women in the church and, after all, everyone had the freedom to make up their own mind on such matters. Of course, Caree knew no person filled with self-love and sheer hatred for God and others would ever make it to heaven, but, just the same, what was the point in all this?

"Caree, let me explain. "Faithful Maschil, always reading her thoughts. She should've known he wouldn't let her drown in her own misgivings. "You are a woman, right?"

"Well, yes, but I don't see what diff..."

"It is important that you be prepared for this exact spirit to continually attack you and try to destroy your freedom in Christ when you enter the ministry. Furthermore, you will be ministering to all kinds of women, some who are abused by their husbands, or other people, and some who are discouraged from serving Christ because they are told they are women!"

"Oh, I see," Caree replied thoughtfully. "There are lots of 'Mr. Wright's' out there being used by Satan to abuse their wives and destroy God's handmaidens, or at least discredit them."

"Exactly! That's why I want you to learn a valuable lesson, Caree. You personally need not fear the 'Mr. Wrights' of the world, but you do need to have discernment, knowledge, and power when you meet them. Of course, God's word is the final authority. Abuse of any kind to anyone for any reason is strictly forbidden. Furthermore, remember, concerning Eve, it is recorded in Genesis that she actually repented, but Adam did not. She told the truth when she confessed that she had been beguiled and ate of the forbidden fruit. Adam, on the other hand, blamed both God and Eve, which is definitely not repentance!"

The lone prisoner began nervously growling and whining like a dog. Caree watched him in amazement as he shifted his gaze back and forth, obviously agitated by the presence of truth.

"Wow!" exclaimed Caree, "I have so much to learn! It's obvious why this person is here! His delight in torturing and trying to murder his wife, causing trouble among the believers by spreading heresy, not to mention his hatred. But there is so much I don't know about this particular argument—I mean about women serving the Lord!"

Maschil placed his hands on her shoulders. "Caree, you have more in your heart than you know. What does the Bible say about the Holy Spirit? Who received Him?"

"Well," Caree began, "the Holy Spirit was poured out on Pentecost to all those waiting in the upper room, and that included both men and women. Even Mary, the mother of Jesus was there."

"And, why was the Spirit given?"

Caree remembered well her Bible training. "He came mainly so we would be empowered to be witnesses of Jesus Christ."

"Didn't that include women as well as men?"

"Yes! He gave women the same gifts of the Spirit as men!" Caree felt a surge of happiness, even in this miserable place. She distinctly recalled the encounter she had had with the Holy Spirit and His call on her life. Until recently, when she investigated all those stories about life-after-death experiences, she knew without the shadow of doubt that she had been called to be a missionary and Christian worker. She even had

43

certain gifts of the Spirit and shared in church what the Lord revealed to her on occasion. People in her church were like-minded and loving. No one had questioned her right to speak, prophecy, or give a word of knowledge as the Spirit moved upon her. Pastor Munson was a humble man who continually studied and searched the scriptures. Surely if she were out of line, he would've told her so.

"Caree," Maschil was driving his point home. "In the New Testament, whose four daughters prophesied in the church?"

"Phillip's?"

"You are correct." His gentle smile was calming. "Who was a prominent teacher and instructed Apollos?"

"Priscilla!" Caree was gaining confidence.

"Right. Who was the first evangelist to the Jews, the Samaritans, and the disciples?"

Caree hesitated, and Maschil answered for her. "The first one to give the good news to Israel that the Messiah had come was the prophetess, Anna. The woman at the well shared with the entire Samaritan village and many were saved, and Mary Magdalene was commissioned by Jesus to announce the resurrection to His disciples!"

Caree had never taken her eyes off Mr. Wright. He had retreated to the farthest recesses of his filthy cell. An occasional growl escaped his gaping mouth, but his former boisterousness had evaporated in the presence of truth.

Maschil continued his quiz, "Who was the first to anoint Jesus for His ministry, the first to anoint Him for his burial, the first to visit the empty tomb? And, who was with Him when he died on the cross?"

"Women!" Caree announced triumphantly. "And," she added on her own, "women outnumber men about seventeen to one on the mission field where they serve as apostles, evangelists, teachers, prophets, and pastors! And, are also martyred."

"Very good, Caree!" He seemed pleased with his student.

Mr. Wright suddenly shouted in a high-pitched voice, "Bah! I know that book. I read it a lot and Paul told the women to shut up! I was forever telling that old bat I married to shut up!"

"Well, Caree, what do you say to that?" Maschil waited for her to answer.

"The Bible can't contradict itself. If you don't understand something, then you are either judging it by your own warped perception, taking scripture out of context, or you haven't studied the original manuscripts or considered the culture and the times in which those people lived. In First Corinthians Paul was quoting from a letter he was answering, not laying down new rules. On the contrary, Paul repeatedly defended women and even ministered with many of them. In fact, he established the Philippian church in Lydia's home!"

"Stop! I can't listen to this—this—slop! I wouldn't be in here if it wasn't for women! Men are superior!" Mr. Wright sat on the stony floor and began rocking back and forth. "Women are the weaker vessel," he howled. "Stupid, dumb, brainless, idiots!"

Suddenly, something inside Caree snapped. Much to her surprise, she heard herself stoutly reprimanding the doomed soul. "You're taking that passage of scripture out of context altogether!" she admonished. "'Weaker' doesn't mean spiritually or mentally. Perhaps physically, but 'weaker' can be compared to how weak the church is compared to Christ! Furthermore, 'weaker vessel' refers to married women because of their position of servitude, but they are to be loved and exalted by their husbands. It's by Jesus' sacrificial and undying love that we, the church, live and overcome the very gates of hell! 'Weaker' in this context means that women are more susceptible to monsters such as yourself and they need to be protected!" Caree's brilliant blue eyes flashed with righteous indignation. Mr. Wright seemed to be fading into the musty atmosphere. Transfixed, Caree watched as the once belligerent soul all but vanished. Only a grayish blanket of vapor could be seen where the obnoxious and hateful personage once stood.

Maschil spoke, his voice like a gay melody from the Irish countryside, "Well done, weaker vessel."

45

7

THE LIGHT AT THE END
OF THE TUNNEL

"You are going to find the next interview most interesting." Maschil looked knowingly at Caree. "In fact, the individual you are about to meet wrote one of the books you researched for the magazine series you were asked to write."

"Who?" Caree was bursting with curiosity. Maschil had a way of almost making her anticipate these bizarre encounters. One thing was certain—she was learning far more than she had ever thought possible. How was she going to explain all this to Lance? Factual, fearless, and faithful Lance. A warm, tingling sensation raced up and down her spine and she felt a knot in the pit of her stomach. How she longed to see Lance, to be in his arms.

"Caree?" Maschil had stooped over and was studying her intently. "Are you with me?"

"Oh, yes, of course. I was just..."

"Daydreaming about a certain love?" His voice was level, yet unmistakably infused with teasing.

Caree blushed. "Well, since you do know everything, and since it wouldn't do me any good to say otherwise, yes I was." Even though his face remained serene, Caree knew beyond the shadow of a doubt that she heard him laugh.

"To answer your question, remember the famous eye-witness account about the light at the end of the tunnel?" Before she could answer, he reached down and scooped her up as if she didn't weigh an ounce. "Trust me, it will not be long!"

She heard a rush as his mighty wings carried them through the stuffy atmosphere at an inestimable speed. Maschil had deliberately placed Caree close to himself and well within the folds of his garment. She wondered at the softness of this mysterious, heavenly material which never seemed to get soiled as clothes on earth do. Nor did it retain any of the sulfuric stench of this gruesome place.

"It will not be long!" Caree's mind replayed Maschil's statement. Did that mean it wouldn't be long until she was with Lance? Perhaps it meant it wouldn't be long until they reached their next destination. He may even have meant the interviews wouldn't take long and she would soon be whisked out of this terrifying and hideous place.

Between the protective covering of this awesome angel and the intense speed at which they traveled Caree was unable to discern the tortured sounds which were all around them; nor was she able to view the demons which quickly retreated as Maschil passed through their territory. Try as she might Caree could not keep a sense of time. She had no idea of how long she had been "missing" from her humble lodging place in Montana; no idea how long she had been with this angelic host; no idea how long each interview had taken. All she knew was both this experience and the overwhelming longing for it all to end were real beyond description.

Caree felt Maschil come to a complete stop. She stirred slightly, thinking he was about to release her for the next encounter. He tightened his hold, however, and whispered into her mind, "Not yet, Caree. I will tell you when." The next thing that happened caused Caree to momentarily panic. She was sure something had gone wrong, terribly wrong with this angel in whom she had completely come to trust. Twisting and turning, he plunged straight down through a narrow chasm in the inky tunnel. Caree felt her throat constrict in a silent scream. Hysteria became a living, tangible creature which clawed and stabbed at her eyes, lungs, heart. "Oh God! Oh God! Help! Help me!" The silent shriek from her dizzy mind escalated until all she heard was a shrill crash, then blackness.

Something was floating, hovering in a small dark room. Caree saw herself lying motionless on the ebony rock floor. Somehow, she had become that floating, hovering thing. Momentarily puzzled, she tried to sift through her fragmented thoughts. Where was she? What had happened? Oh, yes, there had been an accident of some sort. Yes, that was it, an explosion or impact. She remembered now, calling out to God for help.

She looked down again and studied her still form. "Funny," she thought, "I don't feel any fear or pain, but..." Without warning a brilliant burst of dazzling light at the far end of a black tunnel appeared slightly above her head to the left. A strange force began drawing her up, up and into the mouth of the tunnel.

For a brief moment Caree hesitated. Perhaps she should resist this irresistible pull. After all, she hadn't had time to test it out. But then, where else was she going to go? Obviously, the light meant it was of God, that it was the right thing to do.

Higher and higher, closer and closer—the inky blackness of the tunnel was disturbing, frightening. But that light! Oh! How beautiful it was! As Caree floated up toward it's beckoning beams, she began to feel warmth and goodness flow through her in waves of ecstasy. This must be what the others had experienced when they had died and come back to spread the news. Death is nothing to fear, death is a wonderful, satisfying experience. The light, so magnetic, so compelling, so...

Caree was close now. She could faintly discern the figure from which the light emanated. It was going to be so wonderful, so peaceful, just to enter that light, to be engulfed by it, to be one with it.

He spoke. His voice literally oozed with a kind of celestial sweetness which seemed to reach beyond the senses, beyond the soul, beyond the spirit. "Hello, little one. I am so glad you are here. I am so glad you have come to me." The sound echoed down the dark tunnel and ricocheted off the lifeless rocks. "Do come closer. I have something to show you."

A shiver of fear rippled through Caree's nerves, followed immediately by guilt. "There is no fear in love," she reminded herself sternly. "Christ is the light of the world. Do what he says!"

Before Caree could initiate a move toward the being of light, an irresistible force pulled her forward and into his immediate presence. Caree gasped and stared wide-eyed with shock and utter dismay. This being wasn't the Christ. She knew he wasn't her Lord, yet there he stood, bright and radiant, powerful and compelling.

"You know I am the one whom you must worship, do you not?" His veiled features were becoming clearer and Caree watched with fascination as his face subtly changed images. Finally, the moving and shifting stopped as one image sharpened into focus. It was that of a rather young man, perhaps in his thirties. The skin tone was bronze, the hair and beard light brown and the eyes of darkest velvet. He smiled, and his beautiful white teeth shone like expensive pearls. "Worship me, Caree! I am god! I am lord! I am the king!"

"No!" Caree's voice was barely audible. Her heart pounded wildly like a caged bird. Never, never in a trillion years...not for eternity would she bow to this fake...this imposter...this anti-Christ!"

"Worship me, NOW!!!" His handsome face suddenly contorted with hatred and rage. "You came through the tunnel, remember? You came to the light . . . to my light . . .you must bow before me!"

Caree stood as if frozen to the spot. "This can't be happening, can it?" Her mind demanded an answer but got none. She watched in horror as the once beautiful face became overshadowed by another visage, a visage so macabre and ghastly she tried to force herself not to look. But her eyes refused to obey and stared unblinkingly at the gruesome scene before her.

The smooth bronze face had become disfigured with pure hate; the formerly soft hair and beard were matted and filthy; the deep velvet eyes had turned a murky swamp green and the sensuous lips sneered mockingly. The perfect white teeth now resembled those of an old hag.

From deep within her heart scripture began surging through Caree's mind. "It is written," she loudly exclaimed, "'You shall worship the Lord your God and Him only shall you serve! It is written, 'The Lord our God is one God!' It is written, '...I have given you power to tread on serpents and scorpions, and over all the power of the enemy; and nothing shall by any means hurt you.'"[1]

Caree took a deep breath and continued to look straight at her opponent. Amazingly, it appeared as if he had imperceptibly diminished in size. Encouraged, Caree forcefully continued, "It is written, '...even Satan disguises himself as an angel of light.'"[2] A ghastly hiss emanated from between his distorted lips. He began to sway back and forth and seemed to be struggling to keep upright. Caree eyed him grimly and drove the point home. "It is written, 'And they overcame him by the blood of the Lamb, and by the word of their testimony; and they loved not their lives unto the death.'[3] It is also written 'that at the name of Jesus *every knee should bow*, of things in heaven, and things on earth, and things under the earth, and that every tongue should confess that Jesus Christ is Lord, to the glory of God the Father.'"[4]

At first it began as a low growl—then it erupted into a roar that sent pulsating waves of shock through Caree's body. "Lord help me! Give me overcoming power against the enemy!" Immediately she felt the sweet presence of the Holy Spirit. She raised her arm and pointed her finger straight at the beastly form. One more verse, one more... "It is written 'Submit therefore to God. Resist the devil and he will flee from you.'[5] Satan, in the Name above all names, I resist you!"

Faster than lightening he crashed to the stone surface and began writhing. Horrified, Caree watched as his form began to dissolve and then merge into the form of a gigantic black snake. For a moment Caree nearly gave in to sheer terror. But the presence and anointing of the Holy Spirit stayed her and she remained calm. "God's word is the final authority, it always has been and always will be," Caree whispered into the thickening darkness. She watched as the once beguiling but now defeated serpent withdrew and disappeared into the murky shadows of hell.

8

DEADLY DELUSION

Caree stood motionless for several moments, her eyes fastened to the barely visible jumble of slate rocks under which her adversary had vanished. Then it dawned on her—she was alone in hell! A trickle of fear began making its way up her spine.

"Caree." At the sound of her name, she visibly jumped. Whirling around she saw Maschil, relaxing on a huge bolder about three feet from her.

"Maschil!" She sounded both relieved and somewhat angry. "Where were you? What happened? You said you'd never leave me! Why weren't you here?"

"I was," he answered calmly.

Relief surged through Caree like an incoming tide. Tears came to her eyes and began rolling down her cheeks. Futilely she wiped at her flushed cheeks with the back of her hand. "You said," she whimpered, "you said I was going to interview the author of that famous book!"

Maschil quickly came to her side and took her in his strong arms. "You just did." His voice was smooth, peaceful, almost apologetic.

"What?" she choked, and tried hard to compose herself. Why was it people like her literally fell apart after a great victory? She'd have to meditate on that someday when she had time. Right now, she just wanted an explanation from her angelic, and sometimes unpredictable, guide.

"Caree, you encountered the real author—that great deceiver of all mankind, Satan himself." Maschil stepped back and studied her face. His eyes were both serious and joyful at the same time. The richness of

51

his wisdom enthralled her; the love of God she felt pulsating through and from him drew her like a magnet.

Caree tipped her head to one side as if to better scrutinize him. She did fully trust him, didn't she? Of course, she trusted him! Then why did these little doubts and questions keep surfacing in her mind? One thing was sure, she certainly would never escape from this loathsome place by herself!

"God assigned me to this mission, Caree," his gentle rebuke cut through her mind and heart. "I told you not to fear, that you would be protected."

"I'm sorry, Maschil! I really am!" she began to cry again. "But that last encounter, it was...it was such a terrifying and horrible experience."

"Through Christ you were more than a conqueror. Now," he admonished, "be strong and of good courage and He shall strengthen your heart. We must be on our way to your next appointment!"

In one swift movement he picked her up, cradled her against himself and began traveling through the smothering atmosphere. Caree felt the tension drain from her body. She tried to imagine what wisdom the forthcoming scenario would hold.

Caree's heart suddenly fluttered wildly as she felt Maschil abruptly change direction and then plunge downward. For a brief moment she imagined he was going to allow her to repeat her last experience. But relief swept over her mind and body when she felt him hold her closer.

As they continued their downward journey, her ears began to pick up strange and eerie sounds. At first it sounded like hundreds of violins, in the distance, playing off-key, screeching and whining violently. Then it became closer and louder until the discordant noise assaulted her hearing and frayed her nerves. Painful tingling crept up and down her spine. "Maschil," she screamed silently in her mind, "I can't stand it, make it stop! Oh, please, make it go away!" Instantly the crescendo ceased and Caree could make out bits and pieces of conversation. Maschil was moving much slower now, but he retained his hold on his young charge.

"Stand aside!" She heard him sternly warn someone or something she could not see. "Special angel...you're not..." the voice was hissing and wheezing profanities.

Caree wished she could see who or what was withstanding Maschil. On the other hand, she was glad he had carefully shielded her from most of the sights, sounds, and smells of this place called hell.

The verbal battle continued for a few moments and then she felt him stiffen. In the same instant bolts of electric energy surged through his body and discharged in a powerful blaze of Biblical pronouncements from the book of Isaiah. "'Those who contend with you will be as nothing, and will perish. You will seek those who quarrel with you, but will not find them, those who war with you will be as nothing, and non-existent.'"[1] Maschil paused, then, in the name of Jesus, concluded, "God is 'confirming the word of His servant, and performing the purpose of His messengers!'"[2]

Caree wanted to shout "Hallelujah! Praise the Lord!" Instead, she inwardly praised God for His almighty power and strained her ears to catch the slightest sound. But there was nothing but silence. Maschil stood so still she felt like she was in the arms of a colossal statue. Then she felt the opposing "it" wordlessly shrink back and pull away. No further utterance was made by either Maschil or this murky presence of evil. It simply shriveled up and silently slunk into the blackness of the pit.

Maschil carefully slid Caree to her feet. She blinked into the heavy darkness, trying to make out her new surroundings, but it wasn't until Maschil miraculously produced light, as he had on other occasions, that she could see.

"Wow! What a strange place!" Caree turned slowly in an attempt to absorb and somehow memorize every jagged pinnacle and curved obsidian cliff. Bands of the polished and lustrous volcanic glass shimmered in reflected light, emanating a bold and brilliant form of beauty while at the same time vibrating with horror and evil. Caree's memory flew backwards in time to long-ago visited places in Arizona and Utah; great canyons and chasms in the earth with breathtaking vistas of giant red and orange rock and cliffs with infinite variations in shapes and bands of colors. But even these mind-boggling and soul-thrilling monuments to a great Creator's handiwork didn't compare with the staggering scene before her. She swallowed hard. "I, oh Maschil! I can't believe my eyes! What a formidable and dreadful sight!" They

53

were standing on a narrow ledge and she leaned slightly forward, curious to see the bottom. Maschil's arm shot forward, protectively.

"No, Caree. You will not find the bottom, nor the summit either for that matter." He firmly took her arm and guided her along the crooked path which was barely wide enough for the two of them. "In here," he indicated a small dark opening along the cliff wall.

Caree reluctantly flattened herself against one side of the smooth rock wall and inched her way through the narrow passageway. Maschil, still gripping her arm, guided her from behind. When she felt the tip of her toe bump into something that moved, she let out a shriek. "Ugh! What was that? Maschil?" Before he could answer, hellish laughter rang out from somewhere in the thick blackness of the cave. "E-e-e-e-e-a-w! H-e-e-e, h-a-a-a-h, e-e-e-e-o-w!" Caree's body stiffened with fear. She wanted to turn, to run, to escape from whatever was in this place, but Maschil blocked her only escape route.

"Look, Caree," he ordered softly, "Do not be afraid. Look."

As Caree obediently peered into nothingness, strange forms began to emerge. At first they were abstract and disconnected, but as Caree continued to stare, the images took on shape. She saw something about the size of a bulldog which resembled a bat with four legs. Caree concluded it must have been what her toe had bumped into.

Finally, Caree could make out their surroundings. The cave was round and small. The ceiling hung quite low and was punctuated by pieces of jagged rock. But it was the floor that fascinated Caree. It was perforated with hundreds of small holes about the size of golf balls. Molten lava and fire could be viewed through each hole and occasionally smoke or steam wafted up through these vents and lingered in the stuffy air.

"E-e-e-e-e-a-w!" There it was again! Caree's eyes searched the recesses of this miserable confinement and finally landed on a small figure crouching in the darkest area. Caree could tell that the woman's hair had once been long and blonde, but now it was a mass of knots and filth. Her eyes and haggard face vibrated with sheer hate and glowed from light reflected from the hissing fires below. Caree noted the woman's mouth could only be described as vulgar.

"Mrs. Voyager?" Caree paused. This woman couldn't possibly be the same woman who had written the book; the same woman who had calmly and confidently talked with her over the phone and even volunteered to help write several articles for the magazine. Caree had some photos of her, but never had an opportunity to personally meet with her before the murder. She had been a beautiful and rather famous woman, making millions from her bestseller about her life-after-death experience.

"Yeah, ya got it." She tried to spit, but only fine, dry particles of matter drifted out from between her parched and lips. "Wish ya had brought some nice, cold water." She held herself and began to sob but only spurts of dust sifted down the cracked and parched cheeks.

"Mrs. Voyager," Caree interjected. "What exactly . . .?"

"Happened?" She screamed vehemently. "I'll tell ya. I know whacha wanna hear. I know He sent you here and I know that, that angel with you will see to it ya get whatcha want and protect ya to boot. Ya won't get any argument outa me. After all," she tried to spit again with the same result, "what do I have to lose? Hah, hah. I'm a better writer than you are anyway. I made millions of dollars! What do ya think you're gonna get? Hah!"

Caree felt Maschil stir behind her. The pathetic soul she was facing suddenly sat on the floor and folded her bony arms in front of her. "I was doing good until that nut shot me to death. The world is full of nuts ya know. He was such a religious freak. Some weirdo who had the world convinced he was a Christian! The best part is," she began to cackle, "even though he may have killed me, people blame the Christians! Oh, it's too good!" She began laughing hysterically.

Caree glanced over her shoulder at Maschil. His face was emotionless as he gazed at this miserable prisoner of hell. Finally, he spoke, "Tell her the truth. What was it you really saw at the end of the tunnel, and why did you write that book?"

Caree looked appreciatively at this comely being and then turned back to the famous author.

"Okay, okay." She looked straight at Caree. The bulging eyes had suddenly narrowed to slits. Little blue flames sparked out from between the pink eyelids like pieces of ice. Her voice took on a different tone, a reptilian tone. "As you know from my book, I really did die in that hospital. I actually did float up above my body and see those robed figures. They were intelligent, wise. I really did hear those chimes and experience an awesome power. I did go into that thick black mass, into the tunnel. I know I felt love, security, peace, and tranquility." She shifted uncomfortably as waves of heat and steam rose up through the floor vents where she sat. She moved slightly closer to Caree, and continued. "Yeah, I saw firsthand that pinpoint of light. I actually experienced traveling at a great speed toward it. And then," she lifted her gnarled hand and waved it in front of her face. Her eyes followed the movement of her fingers as if trying to recapture a lost memory. "And then, I saw him. He was brilliant! Dazzling! Brighter than the sun! I knew it was Jesus. I knew from experiences I had gone through. I knew from my feelings. I just knew!"

Caree waited anxiously for this deluded and lost soul to finish. Looking disdainfully at Caree, she went on. "He told me, you know, that Jesus and God aren't the same. I had to pitch out my religious upbringing. I also found out that we all pre-existed and that we all took part in the creation."

Caree gasped. She had not read Mrs. Voyager's entire book nor had she discussed theology with her. In the beginning she had mistakenly assumed that the woman was a Christian because she talked about Jesus as if she knew Him personally. All she had done was report on segments of Mrs. Voyager's testimony about her death experience, the light at the end of the tunnel and how much love and peace she had found. Caree, however, began to feel strangely uncomfortable when talking over the phone with Mrs. Voyager. And when she was shot to death, Caree had to admit she had no peace concerning the woman's salvation.

Mrs. Voyager's testimony had been one of the things which brought considerable confusion into Caree's mind concerning death and the after-life. Caree began experiencing doubts about the reality of eternal punishment for people who didn't exactly agree with the Bible shortly after communicating with this woman and others whom she had interviewed with similar experiences.

Mrs. Voyager stared at Caree as if trying to manipulate her into agreement. Instead, Caree heard herself boldly ask, "Just why are you here, Mrs. Voyager?" Caree was unprepared for the sudden explosion of anger which violently erupted in hellish frenzy.

Jumping to her grimy feet, Mrs. Voyager shook her fist in the putrid air, screaming blasphemies against God. Caree covered her ears with her hands and shut her eyes. The woman was as evil, as wicked as any devil in this place, she thought to herself. There was a stir behind her, and Maschil pulled Caree backwards into his arms. His strong voice uttered one command, "Enough!"

Hell's captive stopped in mid-sentence. Finally, she slumped down on the floor and curled up in a tight ball. "He was," she wheezed, "he wasn't Jesus. He was the angel of light, the deceiver. But," she raised herself on one elbow and squinted at Caree, "but, it was fun ya know. Yeah, it made me feel powerful. For once in my life people looked to me. People wanted to talk to me. I was the expert! I wrote a bestseller! I had a name! I was on television! I had riches!" Then with a twisted smile, she concluded, "Maybe I was deluded, but remember, thanks to my book, thousands, maybe millions of others are deluded too!" She threw back her head in laughter, but her glee was cut short by spasms of coughing.

Caree turned and looked up into Maschil's solemn face. "There's so much I need to know about these after-death experiences!"

"I know," he said tenderly. "Come. I will explain it to you on our way to your next interview in hell."

9

THE DOCTOR
WHO DARED

Caree was glad when they exited the small dungeon and retraced their steps to the narrow ledge. She glanced back over her shoulder and shuddered. Fire and molten rock bubbled and boiled up through the sieve-like floor, converting the small chamber into an inferno of heat and smoke. Caree couldn't see Mrs. Voyager or the small, bat-like demon, but as she turned to follow Maschil, a shrill scream behind her pierced the heavy air. Icy fingers of fear stabbed at Caree's body, threatening to overcome her.

Maschil instantly took her arm and she felt fear's icy grip loosen. He quickened his pace, and once they stepped outside the narrow opening, he turned to the left and followed the precarious path. Caree wondered at his casual demeanor. She was becoming accustomed to being escorted from interview to interview at dizzying speeds.

"We are going to talk for a while." Maschil's communication came wordlessly. He rounded a sharp corner and stopped. "Over there." He pointed to a jumble of rock.

Caree looked in the direction he was pointing and saw that the rugged trail had widened into an alcove along the side of the cliff. He led her to a flat rock and motioned for her to sit down. Caree dutifully obeyed. It was surely going to be classroom time again she told herself. She leaned forward, elbows on her knees, and her chin cupped in her hands. Her long blonde hair swung forward, framing her feminine features.

A wisp of a smile played around the tall angel's lips as he watched Caree. "You have many questions, doubts, and opinions." He stated matter-of-factly.

Ordinarily Caree would have grabbed this verbal ball and run with it. But she was quickly learning Maschil's stringent rules of conduct while attending his "school" of facts. She remained silent.

"First of all, questions are good for they show an eagerness to learn." He paused, and she knew he was amused by her thoughts—amused because she silently appreciated his graciousness in not discussing her insatiable curiosity. Surely being teachable and being curious weren't quite the same thing.

"And," he continued, "doubts can be the result of inexperience, misunderstanding, ignorance, or lack of the knowledge of God and His Word which can cause confusion. Doubts can also be the work of Satan and his demons." He studied her contemplative features. "Caree," he said kindly, "it is natural for your particular nature to be curious and to desire proof. And it is also natural for you to be opinionated. But as you offer yourself up as a living sacrifice to God, the Holy Spirit will change these natural tendencies and conform you to the image of Christ."

Caree sat upright and slightly stretched. She waited for him to continue. "Remember Gideon, King David, John the Baptist, the Apostle Peter, and Mary Magdalene? And Thomas? They were all like you. God understands, for He made you, Caree. It is His desire that you seek His Son, Jesus Christ first, then all these other things will fall into place."

Choking back tears she finally spoke. "Yes, I know, I do let my curiosity get the best of me. I don't mean to run ahead of Him, but I know I do!" Hot tears flowed unabated down her cheeks. "I know I have allowed doubts to come in about hell because many of those people I interviewed were really nice people who really thought they had met Christ! It was so hard for me to believe they had encountered the devil because they talked a lot about God and Jesus, and most of them lived better lives after their experience. I knew they hadn't really been born again, but I began to doubt what I had learned over the years about the Bible and its teachings. So," she nervously twisted a strand of hair in her fingers, "so I formed my own opinions about the whole thing. Now," she looked up at Maschil almost pleadingly, "Now I believe in hell. Now I understand. Please take me out of here!"

"In time." Maschil smiled reassuringly. "But there is more you need to learn." He tilted his head back and stared up through the oppressive darkness as if seeing straight into the throne room of God. Caree watched, spellbound, as his lovely countenance began to mirror an invisible, heavenly light. She instinctively knew he was receiving instruction directly from His Creator and hers.

Caree couldn't guess how long he remained in this position, but finally the light faded and Maschil returned to his original position. "Caree, He wants you to understand."

"Understand what?" Caree felt suddenly embarrassed. She hadn't meant to sound so all-wise.

Maschil graciously overlooked his flustered pupil. "God wants you to understand the plan and power of Satan, both in the lives of individuals as well as nations."

Caree's eyes widened. She was accustomed to life in a small western town and most of the articles and stories she wrote centered around everyday people.

"To begin with, you must always remember Satan desires to be worshipped as God. He will use any means he can to accomplish this end. Remember, Satan is a fallen angel, and both he and the other fallen angels are religious! They have great power to deceive."[1]

Caree shifted her weight. Up until now she hadn't noticed just how hard the rock was upon which she was sitting. "Maschil," she stated in a no-nonsense tone, "the bottom line is people who go through the tunnel and are not saved by the blood of Jesus run right into a counterfeit—the angel of light!"

He beamed approvingly at his "A" student. "This experience is happening frequently now upon the earth because time, as you know it, is short."

Caree sucked in her breath. More than ever she wanted to marry Lance and head for the mission field. Jesus was coming soon, very soon…and so many had never heard the gospel.

"Satan's reign will be established on earth through the anti-Christ, Caree. The devil has been working throughout the centuries to accomplish this goal. You can see this desire of his in the Garden of Eden and again at the Tower of Babel. Many times, through the ages, he nearly succeeded in establishing his one-world government, such as through Hitler, but God brought it down because it was not the right time." Maschil paused momentarily, and then went on. "Through these numerous after-death experiences, which are widely publicized, Satan hopes to overthrow God's plan of salvation through repentance and faith in Jesus Christ. This way he gains worshippers for his wicked kingdom."

"I see," Caree interjected. "Satan deludes people through their experiences because humans are so experience-oriented. Rather than believe the plain teaching of the Bible, they rely on their experiences, feelings, and stories others tell in books and on TV." She dropped her head for a moment and stared at her shoes. She knew at times she had been guilty of these things herself. And hadn't it been her own emotional makeup which had allowed her to be swayed concerning the reality of hell? She saw it all so clearly now. People had free will; they had a choice. Tragically, the majority chose eternity without God. Hell was prepared for Satan and his angels, not for God's beloved people. But if one chose to follow the devil, then that very choice would be honored forever.

Maschil's eyes were filled with understanding. Quietly he said, "Caree, you are learning well. Now, before we go further, I want to make something quite clear. Satan does not dwell here in hell."

Caree quickly stood to her feet. "What? I just had an encounter with that..."

"What you had," he said, "was indeed an encounter with Satan, but it was for your instruction. Satan has not yet been cast into the lake of fire; he spends his time walking around on earth seeking whom he may devour and trafficking heaven so he can accuse God's people. Remember, he is 'the god of the world' and the 'prince of the power of the air.'"

Caree returned to her uncomfortable seat and sat down with a sigh. She would just have to be content with what limited knowledge she had, she told herself. When was she ever going to stop trying to understand the entire universe? Only God had all knowledge.

"There is one author you neglected to investigate, Caree. Satan deliberately steered you away from his books."

She looked up, startled. She had searched long and hard to find credible evidence, especially about the tunnel and the light. "Who?"

"Dr. Maurice S. Rawlings." He folded his arms.

"Dr. Rawlings?" she queried.

"Yes. He was a physician and specialist in cardiovascular diseases who witnessed the terror of patients who literally died and were escorted to hell."

Caree's mind raced backwards in time to the interviews she had had with people such as Mrs. Voyager. All of those "witnesses" of the "light" were full of peace and love and they absolutely had no fear of death. True, none of them talked about Christ's sacrifice on the cross or of their need for repentance of sin in order to enter heaven. It began to dawn on Caree how clever and powerful Satan was, and how eager to steer innocent searchers in the wrong direction.

Maschil interrupted her musings. "Caree, let me quote several passages from one of Dr. Rawling's books:

> Light of all sorts is presented in near-death-experiences and out-of-the-body experiences reports, more often in those without clinical death. This unidentified, beautiful figure could conceivably represent the imitator, the one whose name in most monotheistic faiths means "light bearer." It comes from the Latin lucis-ferre, or Lucifer. Lucifer is so beautiful that he is also known as "the morning star." Could this be the same "Angel of Light" seen by those of little faith and the uncommitted?[2]

Maschil paused as if waiting for this information to take root in Caree's mind.

She sat quietly, waiting for him to continue. "Caree, I am going to quote one of his patients:

> "…You started shoving on me with both hands and then I was out of it. I was floating, pitch black, moving fast. The wind

whistled by and I rushed toward this beautiful, blazing light. As I moved past, the walls of the tunnel nearest the light caught fire. Beyond the blazing tunnel a huge lake of fire was burning like an oil spill. A hill on the far side was covered with slabs of rock. Elongated shadows showed that people were moving aimlessly about, like animals in a zoo enclosure.

"An old stone building was on the right, mostly rubble, with different levels and openings crammed with people trying to move about. Down the hall I saw an old friend who had died. The last I recall, they were dragging the river for him; he had been involved with gambling. I yelled to him, 'Hi there, Jim!' He just looked at me. Didn't even smile. They were taking him around the corner when he started screaming. I ran, but there was no way out. I kept saying 'Jesus is God.' Over and over, I would say, 'Jesus is God.'

"Someway, somehow, I got back as you were putting in the stitches. I loved every one of those stitches. Only God could have gotten me out of a mess like that. I'll never forget it."

Maschil stopped his recitation and looked around as if detecting some unseen being. Nothing seemed to be visible to his keen powers of observation, and he smiled at Caree. "Dr. Rawlings later described the change that took place in the patient:

'When I saw this patient later in the office, he wasn't the shy young man I had known. He told the nurses about the positive experience of the miraculous recovery, but never mentioned details of hell nor the reason why he was there.

"Like so many negative experiences, this patient had no recall of scenes or activities that occurred in the room. He saw the being of light at the end of the tunnel, but the light soon turned into blazing fire, igniting the tunnel walls as he went by. He called it the "fire of hell." Several other people saw the heavenly light turn into a foreboding ring of fire."[3]

Maschil extended his hand to indicate it was time to go. Caree stood to her feet and stretched. She murmured thoughtfully, "I'm sure Dr. Rawlings has suffered mocking and rebuke by many of his colleagues as well as others."

"Yes," replied the angel. "He truly is the doctor who dared."

10

THE GOAL
IS GLOBAL

Maschil and Caree left the small alcove and resumed their journey along the edge of the steep cliff. She wondered why they weren't traveling in the usual manner. Perhaps the next encounter would only be a short distance.

Abruptly the confining trail ended and Maschil stopped. Ever curious, Caree positioned herself as close to him as she could and attempted to catch a glimpse of what lay ahead of them.

"No! Caree!" But the command came too late. Caree recoiled in sheer terror and at the same time lost her balance. Falling backward she swung her arms wildly, trying to grab something, anything solid. But only slippery and crumbling rock met her frantic search. A blood-curdling scream tore from her throat as she felt her body fling into space and plunge through the nightmarish blackness.

In the split seconds between consciousness and unconsciousness wild, hideous laughter ricocheted through her mind. Its deafening clamor was the last thing she remembered.

At first, she heard his voice as if from a far distance, barely audible. Then it became clearer, louder. She moaned.

"Caree, you are safe. Wake up. Look at me.

"What? Where?" Caree gasped weakly. "Where am I?"

"You are with me, Maschil. You are safe."

Caree opened her eyes and tried to focus on this exquisite being. Everything was blurry. "Oh, Maschil! It was awful, dreadful!" She closed her eyes as if to shut out all memories.

He gently touched her face and she felt life-giving warmth flow from his hand. Her mind began to clear and she opened her eyes again. This time everything was perfectly clear. Caree took a deep breath and sat up. "Ugh. I hate that awful stench. It's like rotten eggs down here!"

Maschil laughed softly. Caree was back to herself, praise the Lord. She suddenly stiffened at the recollection of what she had briefly seen. "What were those horrible creatures doing here? I mean, those Martians from outer space?" The memory of spindly grayish green beings with huge, slanting eyes flashed on the screen of her mind. Involuntarily she grabbed Maschil by the arm.

"They are not from Mars, or outer space as you have been conditioned to believe, Caree." He spoke in hushed tones. "They are Satan's special agents, like the ascended masters."

"W-h-a-a-t?" Caree wondered for the first time if this celestial being had momentarily taken leave of his senses. But of course, God's angels don't "take leave of their senses" so therefore this must all be just a bad dream. Some things were just too far-fetched to believe. Yes, that was it. She was dreaming and soon she'd wake up and life would be normal again.

"You certainly are not dreaming, Caree." Maschil's quick response to Caree's undisciplined thoughts abruptly snapped her back to the present. "Oh, Maschil!" She buried her head in her hands. "I'm sorry, but I just don't understand what's going on!"

"You will. Come." He smiled and extended his hand. "The next interview will only be an overview, but it is important for you to understand the mysteries and the end times."

Caree gulped. If God wanted her to know some of these things which she had deliberately avoided most of her life, well, then she would just have to go through with it. Prophecy, the New World Order, and even the book of Revelation were subjects which made her uneasy. Life in the Big Sky Country seemed far removed from politics, economics, wars, plagues, famines, and international struggles which appeared day

66

and night on the "fake news," or even from other, more trustworthy, "digital soldier" sources.

Maschil once again pulled Caree close to himself, and, protecting her in his glowing robe, he ascended straight up between the steep canyon walls. Caree was thankful for this brief respite, thankful she hadn't experienced what Clyde Christensen had on his brief tour of hell when, escorted by Jesus, he "...felt creatures like snakes slithering over his feet and around his ankles, but he could not shake them off. Whether they were lost souls or demons, Christ did not say, but Clyde had never before known the utter revulsion he felt in his heart as when those things touched him."[1]

Maschil stopped in a long tunnel. He helped Caree stand to her feet and held her hand, knowing it would take time for her eyes to adjust to the darkness. The heat was suffocating and the stench nearly unbearable. Wisps of smoke curled and hung in the heavy air, making abstract patterns which resembled floating, transparent reptiles.

"Where are we?" As soon as the question escaped Caree's lips she felt stupid. Hell was hell. It didn't matter which part one was in, it was still hell.

Gracious as always, Maschil side-stepped her question and asked, "Are you ready to proceed?"

"Uh huh." She still felt small and pathetic. *Oh well*, she told herself, *this should just about do it. Soon I'll be back in beautiful Montana, planning a wedding.*

Still holding her hand, Maschil began moving noiselessly forward. Caree, obliged to follow, struggled to tame her wandering thoughts so she could concentrate. Just what had he meant by "mysteries"? And where had she heard "ascended masters" before?

"The Plan! Yes, save the Plan!" Caree visibly jumped as the voice boomed through the dark tunnel and then repeated itself several times in a series of echoes. "I am a member, an important member. I am one of the future rulers of this planet!"

Maschil turned to his right and began walking down crude, narrow steps which had been hewn from the black rock. Caree felt apprehensive, yet her feet seemed to safely glide down each step as she closely followed her guide. Her eyes strained against the thick, heavy darkness hoping to make out an outline or catch a glimpse of something. What: she did not know. Everything she had seen so far in hell was black, grotesque, miserable, and frightening beyond description. The molten rock, sulfur, and fire was, as some had reported, unforgettable. And, the wretched lost souls and hideous, evil demons, and other terrifying creatures, well, if only she could somehow tell people . . .

"H-e-l-p! H-e-l-p! H-e-l-p me!" The terrified screams came from the same individual who had boisterously announced he was going to rule the planet.

Maschil came to a halt so suddenly Caree bumped into him. He quickly reached around and pulled her to his left side, positioning her under his arm for protection. Startled, Caree looked to his right and saw six warrior demons. Tall as Maschil, with huge muscles bulging under their bronze-toned skin, they marched toward him. Six pairs of protruding luminous eyes blazed with unadulterated hatred. Each wore a Roman-type helmet and suit of armor. As they advanced, one took the lead; behind him two marched abreast and likewise two behind them with the sixth bringing up the rear. She gasped as she saw them draw sharp, two-edged swords. The leader's thin lips twisted into a cruel grin.

"Ah, so it's Maschil...again!" His metallic voice vibrated on a frequency which hurt Caree's ears. "This time..."

"Save the Plan! I am from the Age of Aquarius!" The unseen voice boomed and reverberated through the heavy air.

"Shut him up!" The leading commander ordered, beckoning toward the devil bringing up the rear. He never took his penetrating eyes off Maschil. Caree watched breathlessly as the sixth warrior stalked off through the darkness. The piercing screams which followed sent shivers of revulsion and fear through Caree's tense body. She gripped Maschil's robe in both hands and clenched her fists. "Oh God!" Her voice was hoarse, squeaky. "Save us!"

Time seemed to stand still as Maschil and the demonic commander faced one another. Neither moved nor spoke. Caree buried her face in Maschil's soft robe. Her ears strained to catch the slightest sound, but all she heard for what seemed like an eternity were muffled curses followed by shrieks of terror. Finally, the commotion ceased and Caree correctly identified shuffling sounds as belonging to the sixth soldier who had rejoined his comrades.

"This time," the leader repeated, ignoring the interruption, "we win!" With bloodcurdling shouts, they raised their swords in unison and began advancing toward Maschil.

Caree felt icy fingers of sheer terror grip her throat and seize her heart. So, this is how it would end. Wild thoughts crisscrossed her mind like exchanged rounds of gunfire in some senseless war in which she was forced to participate. "Oh Lord Jesus!" the cry tore from her constricted throat. Never had she uttered a more sincere plea for help.

Then it happened. Up until this time Maschil hadn't moved a muscle, but unexpectedly he simply stretched forth his right arm while continuing to shelter Caree under his left. Light, indescribably brilliant and dazzling, shimmered between Maschil's outstretched arm and that of the attacking warriors. Blinded and confused the startled enemy fell back. Caree kept her face buried in Maschil's garment, knowing her eyes could never endure such brilliance. Her mind swiftly rehearsed events recorded in Genesis chapter nineteen when the homosexual Sodomites pressed against Lot because he would not turn two visiting angels over to them to use wickedly. Those angels also struck their enemies with blindness.

"It is all right, Caree." Maschil reassured her. "They cannot see, for their eyes are only accustomed to the darkness. The light is something they cannot bear." Caree grasped the spiritual significance behind his simple words. Darkness cannot overcome the light, and praise the Lord, Jesus is the light of the world.

Caree finally opened her eyes, not knowing what to expect. But the menacing warriors were nowhere to be seen. She sighed in relief and looked up at her guide. He studied her for a moment. His golden eyes seemed to penetrate into the very depths of her mind. Finally he spoke, "You will be meeting a man who, when on earth, was one of Satan's key people for ushering in the New Age and the One World Government. Satan sent six of his most powerful demons to prevent this next interview."

"It's the man we heard yelling, isn't it? I mean the one they just tortured?"

He nodded. Then, taking her hand, he began moving along the narrow, twisting tunnel. Caree's eyes darted back and forth watchfully. This eerie place was somehow different from the other tunnels they had traversed. "This is a maze." Maschil's voice interjected into her mind. Then he spoke audibly, "We are here."

Caree noticed the usually jet-black rock highlighted by a mysterious greenish light. Everything inside of her recoiled from the overwhelming evilness which permeated their surroundings. Then she saw him. He was tall and proud even though shackles and chains around his neck, wrists, waist, and ankles held him fast against the jagged rock wall. She wondered at his ruggedly handsome and compelling demeanor. Something began rising up within Caree over which she had no control. She stood as in a trance, unblinkingly returning his steady gaze. Waves of emotion pulsated through her body and mind, drawing her deeper and deeper into his beguiling image. She felt as if she were floating on a sea of exotic pleasure. All remembrance of who she was, where she was, lost within this unfathomable magnetism. Caree felt herself reaching out to become one with his force.

"The blood of Jesus Christ, God's only begotten Son!" Maschil's deep voice thundered through the hypnotic atmosphere, startling Caree back to reality. Visibly shaken and confused, she looked up at her angelic protector. "What's happening . . .?" her voice trailed off. Maschil's countenance had taken on an entirely different look than she had witnessed thus far during their brief acquaintance. His eyes, focused on the prisoner, resembled translucent amber, and his face and jaw looked like cast bronze.

Caree quickly looked back at the chained figure. An involuntary scream burst from her throat as she hurriedly stepped backward. "Oh, how awful! How gross! I don't understand..."

The once sensuous figure now had the appearance of a partially decomposed, giant bat. His beady eyes pulsated with sheer hate while his blood-red lips curled upward in a sneer. Caree noticed that a faint greenish light seemed to pulsate through his horrible body.

"Caree," Maschil put his hand reassuringly on her shoulder, "meet P-I-9, one of Satan's master deceivers who worked long and hard on earth behind the scenes for the global New Age."

Caree stood speechless, shocked, and dismayed, more at herself than anything else. How could she have been nearly seduced by this ugly, corrupt being that was chained in hell? Revulsion and nausea swept through her. She wanted to run, to escape, to vomit.

"Child," Maschil spoke firmly yet with tenderness, "what you experienced was a beguiling spirit working through an image. Countless people are beguiled by images which certain individuals have. But that is another lesson for another time. Right now, you are here to interview P-I-9, which, by the way, stands for Positive Image. And the "9" means finality. Have no condemnation, Caree. Remember, the Holy Spirit is the supreme teacher, and He uses experiences which we will never forget."

Caree nodded silently. She wouldn't forget this experience as long as she lived. It was humbling, too, knowing how easy it was to fall into a trap even when you have no intention of doing so. She made a mental note not to judge others too quickly for the messes they found themselves in.

"I won't be here for long. You'll see. I am going to be reincarnated." P-I-9 finally spoke up. His words literally oozed with pride and self-love.

"Reincarnated?" Caree couldn't believe her ears. How could he possibly conceive of such a thing, especially in his present condition?

"Ah! You obviously are not one of the Initiates, one of the Insiders, or you'd understand. Soon all the inhabitants of Satania will be loosed to ascend to the earth plane where we will set up our global reign, the Age of Aquarius. The Masters of Wisdom, that is, the Ascended Masters have come to guide us."

Caree looked apprehensively at Maschil. Could this wretched being with the suave image be serious? Maschil, never taking his eyes from P-I-9, quietly replied, "Yes, Caree, he knows what he is talking about—and much more. For this time, however, you will simply hear parts of the whole."

Caree turned back to P-I-9. Shock and surprise crashed in upon her like an unsuspecting avalanche. He had totally changed back into the image she had first seen. His masculine body seemed to pulsate with inner delight known only to himself. But Caree was fully aware of what lay just beneath the surface of P-I's powerful image.

"Please explain this New Age business," she stated matter-of-factly while trying to focus on a point of rock which protruded slightly above his head. This energy, beguiling spirit, or whatever it was, wasn't going to suck her in again if she could help it. Inwardly she prayed, "Lord Jesus, help me get through this. Give me your strength."

"Ha! You are most ignorant, madam!" He teased, still trying to be debonair. "Perhaps if I explain, you will want to join us." He glared at Maschil who stood motionless, then returned his playboy gaze to Caree. "Let me begin by telling you we have been around for thousands of years, many of us hidden in underground tunnels that span the globe, yet few still believe there is a powerful, world-wide conspiracy.

Carrie was somewhat amazed at the great pride P-I-9 was taking in gushing forth his so-called "wisdom." He began to rattle off the names of different secret societies, while Caree furtively hoped this interview would somehow be abruptly terminated. "To name a few organizations and secret societies under the headship of the Cabal, which is under Satan," he bragged, "there is the Illuminati, Freemasonry or Knights Templar, Rosicrucian's, Theosophical Society, Lucis Trust, Club of Rome, Knights of Malta, the CFR, Skull and Crossbones, the United Nations as well as hundreds of secret, and even public, revolutionary groups in your own country, many funded by George Soros. They are too numerous to mention, unless, of course," he puckered his lips and pretended to give Caree a mock kiss, "you want to be here for a very long time."

Caree turned away in disgust. She wanted to beg Maschil to escort her away from this unclean spirit of lust. Instead, she turned back to P-I and stated, "Just give me the facts!"

"Yes ma'am!" P-I-9's lustful eyes slowly appraised her shapely figure. He tried to lick his lips, but his dry tongue refused to obey. Grudgingly he continued, "With the help of certain ruling powers, the Freemasons and the International Bankers, we have staged endless wars, some of which are very impressive I might add, along with countless revolutions, pandemics, medical genocide all over the world . . ." Caree gasped in horror as she recalled three close friends who had suffered terribly and died from the snake venom, horrible parasites and a host of other poisonous substances in forced vaccinations.

P-I was watching her closely, and when he saw the sorrow in her eyes, he instantly took advantage of it. "Aha!" He spat at her face. "Your friends suffered so exquisitely, along with millions of others. It was so delightful!" Carree felt as if everything in her was about to explode in a burst of anger, but before she could vent her rage, she felt a calming hand on her head, and knew that Maschil was in control, not only of her, but this beyond-repulsive entity as well.

"Think about how powerful we are!" P-I rambled on proudly. "Everything we do is to bring the nations of the world together to form a one-world government, especially after centuries of wars—they will beg for a peaceful solution. That's our goal. Yeah, it's already there, but few know it. What a Plan!" He threw back his head and laughed lustily. "Oh, it's so good! Like taking candy from a baby. We are expert at causing distrust, division, and dissention between rich and poor, black and white, young and old, male and female, opposing political parties and even churches. The way it works, honey..." he paused as if waiting for Caree to weaken. When she remained steadfast, he continued, "The principle is simple: cause a major problem which results in the populace demanding relief, then present a solution—our solution!

"We planned and created in our hundreds of bio-labs the 'Spanish Flu,' cancer, AIDS, that so-called 'Covid-19' and a host of other non-curable diseases, and then blamed your God for world-wide disasters. We rule the world by controlling the weather through bio-engineering and HAARP machines. We cause extreme weather disasters, floods, deep freezing, earthquakes, tsunamis, and use direct energy weapons to incinerate whole cities and forests." He began to writhe and pant heavily. A guttural snarl gurgled through his twisted lips as his eyes widened with increasing madness. "We've known how to control the weather for over a hundred years, and nobody even noticed!" he hissed.

"Maschil, please, please take me out of here!" Caree begged.

"Soon," he said without moving.

The hideous, demented wretch rolled his eyes, then blurted out vehemently, "You stupid girl! You're typical of all the ignorant dreamers who think your government cares about you! You have no idea how far technology has advanced, thanks to Tesla and the Reptilians. You have no clue what is coming on the face of the earth. You stupid 'Christians' will forsake your God in order to save your skin! When will you ever catch on that we, of the great global order engineer and plan crop failures, food shortages, and starvation, and you are helpless to stop us! We plan to reduce the world's population to a tiny fraction of what it is now. How? Oh baby! Can't you see it? No more overpopulation! We've seen to that! Murder the unborn, and kill the children! Sacrifice them by making them weak, sick, and mentally impaired with unending toxic vaccinations, toxic prescriptions, toxic drugs, toxic and genetically altered food. We advanced chemical warfare to lower people's immunity and cause disease and early death through not only poisoned air, water and food but by mutilation so you stupid people can never reproduce. I love that one!" he began to giggle, then burst into roaring laughter. "Then there's euthanasia of millions of old people—you know, people over 50!" Caree's mind was spinning, and her eyes filled with tears. *This is unbearable! I can't stand anymore!* Maschil put a hand on her shoulder, and she knew that he would help her get through this. But, oh! If it could only end!

P-I-9's voice rose in excitement. "By promoting and supporting homosexuality we knock out huge numbers of people you know. Fewer babies are born and more people die of AIDS. What a plan! And abortion! What a wonderful invention! By convincing people that the human baby is nothing but a fetus, nothing more than a little bit of tissue, we've managed to destroy millions and millions of babies. Excellent!" His voice was electrifyingly dramatic; his features filled with venomous loathing and pride.

"We created and promoted two of the most powerful, and successful deceptions in the history of the world—psychology and the theory of evolution. Both are now the foundation for indoctrination throughout the entire public school system so kids will believe they are nothing but animals, thereby destroying their true identity and self-worth. We simply tossed God out, and now kids are instructed to worship Satan through humanistic teachings, relaxation therapy, Tantra yoga, and courses in witchcraft and how to contact spirit guides. What's really exciting is when a suicide takes place because of it!

"Evolution is one of our most powerful weapons, even though that dupe Darwin didn't believe it himself and was sorry in the end for what he had done. It's taught as a fact even though it's not even a good theory! Oh! It's so easy to deceive people! And, psychology has replaced fear of God and wisdom while promoting self-love and pride. How incredible is that? He burst out with loud, uncontrollable laughter. After a few minutes passed the sickening laughter subsided. Drawing a deep breath, he squinted at Caree. "Innocent, naive. If I weren't chained here until the takeover, I'd personally teach you a few things!"

Ignoring Caree's discomfort, P-I-9 rolled his eyes toward the dingy ceiling of his prison, and resumed his dialogue. "'Evolution!' It causes people to lack purpose in their lives and helps set the stage for leaders such as Hitler. Get the students! Get the very young! Instill in them mistrust and hatred for authority. Instill in them hatred for God. Incite them to lawlessness and violence. After all, aren't they just 'evolved' apes? We have had a plan for even the most brilliant student— Dungeons and Dragons! It introduces them to the underworld and causes the most intelligent to kill, destroy, and commit suicide! What a Plan! Kids are buying it hook, line, and sinker! And, speaking of the powers of darkness, Harry Potter is one of our biggest successes to seduce, and destroy the souls of both young, and old. Sex, pornography, 'rock n' roll,' drugs, abortion, homosexuality, crime, suicide! Oh, Lucifer is excited. He's drunk on their blood!" P-I-9's body began to shake uncontrollably with excitement. He frantically thrashed against the chains which bound him. After some moments, however, he became somewhat subdued.

Caree could tell P-I-9 wasn't through with his spiel. He glared at her, and hissed, "One of hell's most successful schemes is hard metal rock and what you call 'paganism' in music. Through rock n' roll kids have a direct line into hell and hell has a direct line into them. We can't be stopped! Music is powerful—powerful in possession! Kids are wide open to possession—they love the beat! They love the sex, drugs, anger, hate, rebellion, and lewdness. They're addicted to it and will even kill to keep it! Sex, sex, sex! It's destroying whole cultures!" P-I-9 seemed drunk with perversion. "Sex is what they want. So much for 'higher education!' So much for the noble and wise. So much for good character and integrity! O-o-o-h-h-h, Satan is a master at robbing kids of their innocence.

"And the education! We have introduced death classes and Hinduism through yoga and certain holistic teachings such as relaxation therapy. We teach 'higher education' now, and mysteries of the occult. We've banned real history, along with that insipid Christianity and love for God and country from the classroom, and have replaced it with hatred for the flag, founding fathers, capitalism, success, freedom, and critical thinking. Islam is one of our most powerful weapons to destroy America and all of western society…and…and…Israel!" His body began to vibrate as if sheer hatred somehow infused a bizarre form of torturous delight into his very being.

"Even experiments in psychic phenomena are encouraged. As our secret societies and other underground forces distorted and drastically altered the history books, we managed to remove all references to *Him!* We changed it to suit our needs." His eyes fastened on Caree's face as if trying to suck her into his very being. Pressing her lips together, she blinked hard, and kept staring at the point above his head. His repetitious tirade was torturous to her frayed nerves and spinning mind. She inwardly cried out to God for help.

He glowered at her, as if reading her mind, and continued his dissertation. It seemed to Caree that suddenly some unseen force compelled him to finish his spiel. Rolling his eyes in frustration, his voice suddenly rose in pitch and frustration. "Kids are so easy to brainwash! And even more so now that we have successfully destroyed most family life. Oh, how Satan hates families!" He began to pant. His lips curled into a hideous sneer. "You know," he screamed, "he's a master planner. Destroy the family structure, destroy the nation. Of course," he sneered, "Hollywood has been one of hell's most powerful tools. And, movies like Star Wars help promote pure Hinduism and the occult! Harry Potter introduces multitudes of curious kids to witchcraft, and The Lord of the Rings reverberates with the occult. Shall I go on?"

Suddenly his visage reverted to the hideous bat-like creature. Caree sucked in her breath and tried to step backward. Maschil didn't budge, however, and she found herself leaning on him for support.

P-I wasn't finished with his tirade, and slurred, "Initiation! They are so ripe for initiation. You can't be part of the New Age if you aren't initiated into it, you know. Initiation must come through an altered state of consciousness! Aha! And, guess just what can cause this wonderful altered state?" he paused briefly, not really expecting Caree to answer, and went on, "drugs, hypnotism, transcendental and Eastern meditation, tantra yoga, trance-like states, mind altering drugs, and special initiation rites performed in such places as the Masonic temples. You wonder why? Because it's time people became aware of the Christ-consciousness, the Christ within them. In short, that they are all gods. In order for the golden age to dawn, everyone must believe that they are a god." P-I-9 was on a roll and as long as he had an audience, he was determined to 'spill his guts.'

Caree felt numb. P-I-9 was gripped with an urgency to use up every second granted to him to finalize his dissertation. It was as if the curtain had gone up and his time to perform had come. She wished with everything in her that he would shut up, that there was an "on" and "off" switch that she could flip to silence his repetitious tirade.

"Destroying children is Lucifer's specialty. Between cannibalism, removing their organs, ritual sacrifices, abuse, torture, pedophilia, adrenochrome, molestation and gene therapy to dehumanize them, he's having tremendous success. And, surely you must know that pornography is one of the most powerful tools we've ever had. Remember, little lady," he slurred disgustingly, "Pornography is protected by your 'free speech' laws. Porn takes out people of any age or sex! To make it even better, the Brotherhood, and New Age groups working within governmental systems are ripping kids away from their homes. "And," he added with glee, "they are going to belong solely to the United Nations. People won't have a thing to say about their kids! They will be global citizens!"

P-I-9 sucked in his breath. His beady eyes seemed to focus on both Maschil and Caree at the same time. His appearance was so revolting Caree forced herself to continue focusing at the spot above his head.

"Oh well. They are ready to be global citizens anyway. By the time they reach the first grade they are already worried sick about the environment! Ha, ha, ha. The environment! They are being prepared to help rule in the New Age. They will put people like you, Miss Priss, to death—you and babies, and the elderly and the sick, the retarded-anybody who doesn't measure up to being a god! They are willing to crawl around the equator on their hands and knees to save one insect, or—ha ha ha—get this—one little fish in California even if it causes food shortages!" His hideous laughter turned to howls of delight. Finally, he began to calm down and added, "Yeah, the new children of the planet will chain themselves to a tree and starve to death to save it, but they couldn't care less about the human race. Satan loves for people to worship nature. That way they won't worship Him!" P-I-9's lips drew back in a snarl. A low growl rumbled from deep within his throat.

"Are you finished?" Caree said sharply. She was anxious to be done with this long, tedious and sometimes repetitious session. Even though it was only an "overview," it seemed to drag on for eternity.

"All right, all right. Here's some more good news for you." His grin reminded Caree of pictures she had seen of sharks just before they attacked their prey. She grimaced and resumed staring at the place on the wall above his head.

"You know, don't you, that the economic collapse is very close at hand? A cashless society, and real soon too. Imagine all the panic, all the rioting and suicides! People worship money. It's what they depend upon! They lust after it and will do anything to get it. Soon every person on earth will have a transponder in the form of a chip injected into their forehead or hand or they won't be able to buy or sell. Just watch how they'll knock one another down to get one! Of course, within this one-world government there's going to be a world bank, along with the World Health Organization, a world food controller, the World Court, the one-world military, and other world powers, controlling every little thing. The wonderful Age of Aquarius is at hand! And, this means," he rolled his head, laughing gleefully, "good-bye Christians! Good-bye Israel! Oh, the bloody slaughter that is about to begin! I can't wait! Then we of the Brotherhood will rule and re-establish the ancient religion, the great Babylonian mystery."

Caree knew his predictions were true. The Book of Revelation made it plain for all who would read it that such times as these were coming on the earth. The Bible repeatedly warns that when the wrath of God is poured out upon this world, men will not repent of their sorceries. And sorceries literally means "drugs." She waited quietly for P-I-9 to finish.

Several moments passed before he spoke, and this time his alluring image reappeared.

"Oh, dear little lady," he cooed, "Lucifer is the god of this world. You must admit this to be true because your own book, the Bible, says so!"

Caree finally spoke. "If you are referring to Second Corinthians chapter four verse four," Caree retorted, "in context, it reads, ...the god of this world has blinded the minds of them which believe not, lest the light of the glorious gospel of Christ, who is the image of God, should shine unto them.'"

P-I-9 ignored Caree's contribution to the facts. "I've saved the best for last," he said. His voice was smooth, hypnotic. "The wonderful, enlightening one-world religion!" He paused, as if waiting for this bit of news to sink in. Finally, in the same monotone he continued. "The morning light will have come and I'll be reigning with him. Even now, as I speak, powerful forces which have infiltrated churches on earth are succeeding in deluding thousands, maybe millions of religious souls. People are tired of waiting for a Christ to return for them. They are seeking signs and wonders in the here and now...and they are getting them! Ha, ha, there are so many ways to deceive! People are so starved for the supernatural they will believe anything you tell them, especially when accompanied by a few miraculous events!"

"The mind science religions have infiltrated most mainline churches in the guise of positive confession along with our masterpiece, Freudian and Jungian psychology. Even metaphysics, magic, and other Satanic practices are used. And," he winked coyly at Caree, "you'd be surprised how many of those good church goers play around with astrology, Ouija boards and the occult. You'd be amazed at how many Christians buy into demonically "channeled" books that are supposedly the words of God or Jesus "calling" to them! Oh yesss! There are so many ways to dull down discernment and deceive to death. You'd be shocked to know the kinds of kinky sex so-called 'Christians' practice! Yes," he hissed, "Satan is ecstatic! Oh yes! I must not forget, our grand Plan. We've been working on this one for centuries, but now, thanks to many strong and popular movements, it's actually happening! The names for this are," he paused dramatically, "ecumenism, humanism, and social justice!" Today's theme for the organized church is unity and tolerance, seeker-friendly, and relational." He roared with uncontrollable laughter.

Caree shifted her weight uncomfortably and yawned. She knew full well what he was talking about for she had discerned over recent years, within the church, a subtle shift from focus on the Person of Jesus Christ as the way, the truth, and the life to powerful movements touting "unity" and "tolerance" as their "politically correct" theme.

"Just one more thing, sweetheart," P-I-9 sarcastically interjected. "UFO's! Bet you don't know what they are or how they are going to help bring the entire world together overnight."

Caree's eyes widened. She remembered the "Martians" she had just recently encountered. Curiosity hit her full-force. Every nerve was suddenly wide awake, alive, and straining to hear what her informant had to say.

"I see you really want to know. How cute. Well, let's just say that even the United States has had anti-gravitational flying devices since the 1930's. There are secret underground bases in such places as Nevada, Australia and the North and South Poles. And Satan is the master planner." He snickered with delight. "Satan has such great ideas! Some UFO'S are physical, as you would say, 'real,' while others are produced by holograms. But they certainly aren't from outer space as people have been led to believe. And, some UFO'S are purely, ah, shall we say, of Satanic, spiritual, design. What a plan! We are the ones who were given the technology to make material things, such as commercial passenger planes totally vanish into thin air with all aboard. Terrifically terrifying, isn't it? Ouuu! I love that one! Just think, the world's population, what's left of it that is, will be terrorized into submission by thinking they are being conquered by aliens!" P-I lapsed into uncontrollable, mocking laughter. "Instead, they will actually be conquered by armies of well-programed clones and robots that are equipped with incredible artificial intelligence. Whoo-hoooo! A-I, A-I, A-I!!!" he shrieked at the top of his voice. "The Reptilians will win the war and defeat God!"

Suddenly Caree felt Maschil stir for the first time since arriving in this sordid place, and she knew that, as far as he was concerned, enough was enough. He said one word which Caree thankfully understood quite well, "Come."

He took her hand, turning her so she faced away from P-I-9, and began ushering her back down the cramped tunnel. Caree detected a buzzing sound behind her followed by ear-splitting screams which filled the morbid air. A shadow projected itself onto the wall in front of her—the shadow of a warrior demon stabbing a helpless figure in chains behind them who had proudly given far too much information.

11

IMAGES

As Maschil quickly ushered Caree to the maze's entrance, her thoughts churned and crashed against each other like waves on a stormy sea. There was so much to learn! So much she didn't know! Her mind was thoroughly preoccupied and she barely noticed where he was leading her until he slowed to a halt. "Up there!" Maschil's short exclamation caused Caree to automatically look upward. All that met her questioning gaze, however, was that ever-present hazy darkness punctuated by puffs of sulfuric gases and steam.

"Are you ready?" Maschil looked down at her uplifted face with kindness. She felt like asking, "Ready for what?" but before a sound could escape her parted lips, he picked her up and flew straight up the side of the gigantic rock wall. She wondered at this magnificent creation of God. She would certainly never doubt the reality of angels again, she told herself. And that meant good ones or evil ones.

Maschil lightly landed on what appeared to be a high precipice within the chasm of hell. Giant slabs of rock jutted upward in crazy disarray while in other places boulders balanced precariously upon rocky pinnacles. A faint light from some invisible source illuminated the ghostly configurations.

"This is amazing!" Caree whispered breathlessly. "If this place wasn't so overwhelmingly oppressive, dark, and evil..." her whispered words faded as she swallowed hard, and groped for the right words, "I mean, if this wasn't hell, and if this scenery was on earth where the sun could shine on it and bring color and life, it would be a natural masterpiece!"

Maschil smiled as if pleased with himself for bringing her here. "Yes, all of creation tells of God's power and majesty, but without His presence, it truly is hell. Remember, Caree, God never created hell for mankind, but rather for the devil and his angels."

"I know," she replied softly, then asked, "What did you mean about the mysteries?"

Maschil, who had been standing alongside his inquisitive pupil, motioned for her to sit on a nearby rock. Caree gratefully followed his instructions. Even though she had been standing alongside a powerful angel from heaven, the dizzying heights were making her tense. She laced her fingers around her knees and waited.

"Even though there are basically two mysteries," Maschil began, "within those mysteries are countless intricacies. But for now I am going to simply explain the basics to you." Caree squirmed a little. Whenever Maschil took on the role of instructor, he reminded her of a professor. But here there was no way to take notes. Instinctively she knew she would be tested, and she fervently hoped she would pass. "There is the Mystery of the Ages and the Mystery of Iniquity. The last interview gave you some insight into the Mystery of Iniquity, or..." he waved his arm as if including the surrounding terrain, "Satan's grand plan to rule and reign as supreme lord of all." Maschil looked straight at Caree as if examining her comprehension. Satisfied she understood, he continued, "Always remember, Satan wants to be worshipped as god above all else and he craves attention. He deceives many by appearing to be religious, because the liturgical religious lack relationship with Christ and are, therefore, devoid of discernment. Satan has devised a master plan which has proceeded through the ages like a continuous thread of deception. This thread has always been skillfully and powerfully interwoven into the tapestry of ruling nations and governments, and has succeeded in infiltrating the religious institutions. Secret societies and esoteric teachings have played a major role in propagating Satan's devices. Volumes have been written by brave men and women who have authenticated the historical and present polices of these diabolical activities.[1] But the majority of the world's population is either unaware or ignorant of Satan's schemes. This master plan is not to be underestimated, but many do not believe it even exists. God does, however, have His remnant who are wise and understand the Mystery of Iniquity. This mystery is intended to counterfeit the true Mystery of the Ages."

"It's Jesus, isn't it?" Caree couldn't help herself. "He is the mystery of God who came to bring reconciliation, even to the Gentiles."

Maschil looked approvingly at his young charge. "Yes. Christ is the mystery who is returning in great power and glory to reign over all the earth. And, there are many other things which we angels long to gain a clear glimpse into."[2]

"But what about the New Age and all its plans to take over the world?" A small frown creased Caree's brow. "Are they really going to succeed?"

Maschil's voice was somber. "Yes, it is prophesied throughout the Bible. Remember the information P-I-9 shared with you? He knows the anti-Christ is on earth today, waiting for the stage to be set. War and turmoil in the Middle East, as well as catastrophic happenings in other places, will cause people to cry out for a world leader who can bring peace and stability."

"Jesus warned us in Matthew 24!" Caree couldn't hide her excitement. "He told us that if possible, even the very elect would be deceived."

Maschil nodded in agreement. "Remember, the Holy Spirit through Paul warned the church that there would be an apostasy or the falling away from truth. Now, there are different reasons people fall away from their first love. Reasons such as prayerlessness, lack of faith, ignorance of God's word, idolatry or love of self and the world. And in these last days many will be deceived by lying signs and wonders. But there is something of utmost importance you need to understand so you can share it with others."

Caree suddenly became very alert. Whenever her instructor spoke in such terms, she knew what he was about to say was vital to her and her future ministry.

"Caree," Maschil began slowly, "do you understand what happened to you when you first met P-I-9?"

Caree felt her cheeks flush with embarrassment. How could she have been seduced so easily? P-I-9's magnetic pull had totally overwhelmed her, body and soul. A trickle of guilt forced its way into her heart and then bubbled to the surface of her mind with an ugly insinuation—how could she have felt the way she did, even if for only a few fleeting seconds, when she was in love with Lance? She stared at her feet. "Uh, well, I'm not sure." She said sadly, overcome with a feeling of uncleanness. She buried her face in her hands and began to cry.

Maschil quickly knelt down beside Caree. Putting an arm around her shaking shoulders he kindly admonished, "Do not weep. You are human, Caree. You are not perfect, but you are forgiven because you were beguiled and you are humble and repentant. Jesus understands. Remember, the lessons you learn by experience are the ones you will not forget."

Caree wiped at her eyes. Yes, she told herself, it would all be over soon. How she longed for blue skies and sunshine, for green grass and trees, for flowers, mountains, valleys, rivers and lakes, for birds and animals, for people, and especially for Lance. She saw him in her mind, at their last picnic, tall and handsome, walking toward her with a handful of wildflowers, laughing and smiling, his heart full of love.

"Caree!" Maschil's rich voice was tinged with concern. "It will not be long, I promise."

A long sigh escaped Caree's lips. Everything inside of her longed to escape from this place of eternal suffering and separation from light, love, and life. Suddenly, sorrow and mourning overshadowed her like sackcloth. Doubling over she began involuntary convulsing with loud wailing and sobbing. Her body shook uncontrollably from an indescribable inner agony. Long minutes passed as Caree, overcome with the sorrow of the Almighty for lost souls, mourned unashamedly in the spirit. Portions of scripture tracked through her mind, "For God so loved the world, that He gave His only begotten Son…God has sent His only begotten Son into the world so that we might live through Him…In this is love, not that we loved God, but that He loved us and sent His Son to be the propitiation for our sins…He who has the Son has life; and he who does not have the Son of God does not have life."[3]

She had no idea how long this overwhelming sorrow and mourning engulfed her, but slowly the heavy burden lifted and Caree, weak and shaken, looked at her angelic friend who was still sitting beside her. His face was clean, holy. His eyes warm with heavenly love. "Now," he whispered, "now you understand the heart of God for all men."

"Yes." Her voice was husky, and she swallowed hard. "I think I understand more—more than ever what it means to enter into the sufferings of Christ. And," she added, wiping tears from her cheeks, "I want with all my heart to truly be a co-laborer with Him."

"Then," Maschil stood to his feet and turned to face her, "we need to proceed with this lesson on images." His smile brought the kind of warmth to her soul that she felt from the sun on fresh spring days after a long cold winter. "You may wonder what this has to do with the mystery of iniquity, but you will understand when we are through." Caree smiled to herself. She perceived he made this statement in anticipation of the question already forming in her mind. "Almighty Creator God always has an order," Maschil began. "He does all things well and with a purpose. Often the purpose is known only to Him, but you must believe nothing is by accident."

Caree nodded in agreement. Mental pictures of God's perfect creation as opposed to the theory that everything beautiful was the result of an "accident" darted through her mind. *Nothing has ever been improved by an "accident,"* she told herself.

"In recent years God, by His Spirit, revealed to one of His servants some precious truths which His people need to understand in these last days." Maschil looked pleased. Caree tipped her head as another question formed in her mind. Automatically, Maschil answered, "No, Caree, angels do not know everything. Only God is all-knowing. Do not forget we are created beings ourselves and are delighted when God chooses to reveal His wisdom to us."

"God will be instructing us throughout all eternity, won't He? I mean, He is going to continue to reveal the wonderful mysteries of Jesus Christ, isn't He?" Caree's inquisitive mind began bouncing like a ping pong ball.

"Yes, Caree. God has much for you to learn. But for now," Maschil's demeanor suggested it was time to concentrate on the main subject, "I must teach you something about natures."

"Natures?" Caree wasn't sure she heard him correctly.

"Yes, natures. For centuries mankind has been trying to figure out himself. Some have come close by suggesting there are four types of people, but have not been able to understand the whole truth and why God did make four distinct kinds of people. Most of the time those who are searching for answers stop with personality and do not understand the nature which God created."

Caree looked puzzled. Whatever did this have to do with the mystery of iniquity and the last days? Well, she told herself, Maschil had said it would all make sense.

"God is a God of perfect order," it was obvious he wanted to drive that point home, "And when He created mankind, He made them in His image. That means, in part, that just as God is identified by certain unchangeable characteristics, so are each of these natures." He paused then added, "In God's economy even numbers are of extreme importance."

"Yes, I remember some of them," Caree interjected, "number one stands for unity and primacy, and the worship of one God; two is union, division, witness, and double portion; three stands for that which is solid, real, substantial, complete, and entire." She rubbed her forehead as if trying to activate her memory. "I know! Number four is His creative works. It stands for material completeness and works associated with the earth!"

"Creation points to the Lord Jesus Christ and mankind is no exception. Remember, Caree, the 'four's' in the Bible?" Before she could answer, he continued. "Four rivers flowed out of Eden. Four consonants form God's covenant name, YHWH. Four women gave birth to the twelve tribes of Israel. The prayer shawl has four corners with four tassels. The Israelite camp was divided into four parts when camped around the Tabernacle. The Bible has a four-fold division of mankind: lands, tongues, families, and nations. There are four living creatures in Ezekiel and Revelation; four gospels; four sides to the tabernacle and the alter; four cups at Passover; four kinds of flesh. Concerning nature: earth is the fourth planet from the sun; there are four divisions of the day; four seasons of the year; four directions; four elements; four-footed beasts and other examples too numerous to mention."[4]

"So, what exactly is the point?" Caree asked eagerly.

87

"Back to four natures, Caree." Maschil's face lit up with joy. Caree knew the knowledge he was about to share gave him great pleasure. "God has revealed Jesus Christ through these four natures and totally disproved the satanically inspired theory of evolution. Let me briefly explain. Each nature has their own need, their own type of fear, their own way of seeing themselves and others, and their own way of responding to situations or crisis." A shadow seemed to momentarily cloud his usually beaming features. "Sadly, each nature has their own form of pride, but humans are quicker to see it in others than in themselves. But the good news is once people learn about their particular nature and recognize their form of pride, then they are able to repent and come into a relationship with God through Christ."

"That's what you meant! I mean, when we began this journey, you said something to me about having to have 'proof' for everything! You were referring to my nature, weren't you?" Caree clasped her hands with delight. She was pleased at making the connection by herself.

Maschil laughed softly. "Well said, Caree. Some Bible characters you may recognize with your nature are curious such as Eve, emotional King David, persistent Nehemiah, the weeping prophet Jeremiah, and impulsive Peter."

"This is incredible! It's simple, yet profound." Caree felt overwhelmed. "I want to know all I can about this so I can understand people and be able to help them. Tell me all about these four natures and how they reveal Christ and what these natures have to do with the four Gospels and..."

"When you return to earth, someone will give you a book and you can read about them.[5] But for now, I want to tell you the secret behind the most puzzling of the four natures—the one with images."

"Images?" Caree echoed. "Doesn't everybody have an image of some sort?"

"No, Caree. Of all four natures only one has an actual image of themselves. This image is made up of concepts about the way something should be and standards of how something must look or operate. These people not only have an image of themselves, but an image for those around them. They expect a person to live up to their images, which, of course, is impossible." Maschil took a deep breath and studied Caree's face for a long moment. "What happened in P-I-9's compartment was that you were attracted to his image."

Caree sucked in her breath. Quietly she murmured, "It was a mighty powerful one."

"You needed to experience it for yourself so you will understand. I want to take you back to the Garden of Eden. God made Adam in His image. Adam had an image because he was created with this particular nature. It was his responsibility to protect Eve and the Garden from Satan, but Adam granted him entrance. Satan, remember, was subtle and beguiling. He also comes as an angel of light, or as very religious. Adam, when he fell, simply exchanged the image of God for the pseudo religious image Satan portrayed. This way, Adam could still appear to be "religious" outwardly, but independent of God at the same time. Remember, Caree, sin is independence from God, or doing it your own way."

Caree's mind struggled to comprehend just why Maschil was going to such great lengths to explain all this to her. It must be true or he wouldn't be relating it, but on the other hand, she was shaken to the core. It had always been hard for her to believe new information at first.

Maschil seemed to understand the conflict raging in Caree's mind. He stepped closer and placed a hand on her shoulder. "After you have worked with many people, you will experience these things for yourself, Caree. You need to know that this particular self-assured nature has certain characteristics such as keeping a list of petty wrongs committed against them. They also have strong attitudes and a reservoir of anger and difficulty in making decisions. Adam, for example, could have chosen the Tree of Life and lived forever. But people with an image want to protect it, and never be in the wrong. Unless they have integrity in their hearts, they usually sacrifice the other person."

"Eve." Caree whispered. "He justified himself at her expense, plus, he blamed God for giving her to him, didn't he?"

"Yes, that is true. He was responsible to protect Eve. She was deceived, he was not." A moment passed in silence. Finally, Maschil spoke, "There is not much time left, and I want to tell you about the second Adam."

"Jesus!" Caree exclaimed. She looked up at her guide. Her eyes were moist. *Jesus! Emanuel, God with us!* Warmth and love flooded her heart.

"Yes, Jesus, the Son of God. Do you know why He is called the second Adam?"

Caree pursed her lips. "Well, because He came in the flesh and was tempted in every way Adam was except, He didn't sin. Therefore, He was the perfect example and the perfect sacrifice for sin." A slight frown creased Caree's brow, "I suppose, then, that is why we are told in Romans chapter five that Jesus is the second Adam, not the second Eve, and repeatedly that through one man, not one woman, we all die."

"You are right. But there is more to it. Jesus in His humanity was also the same nature as Adam. Remember when Jesus was asked by His disciples to show them the Father? He said, 'You have seen me, you have seen the Father.' And in another passage, it says that Christ is the express image of the Father."

"Oh, my, oh!" Caree's hands flew to her mouth. "Oh, He so totally identified with us, and especially Adam. No wonder it is written that Christ saves to the uttermost! I see! What great lengths He went to! We will never be able to comprehend it all!"

"Finally," Maschil began, "there is another individual with an image whom the Bible warns about—that is, the anti-Christ."

"Yes! I get it!" Caree jumped to her feet, forgetful of her whereabouts. "The image so beguiling, so religious, so seemingly wonderful he will, if possible, deceive even God's people. And he will demand everyone worship his image! The counterfeit Christ!" She seemed frozen to the spot. "Maschil," her voice was squeaky, tense. "That P-I-9 had a powerful beguiling image. It was hypnotic, compelling, awesome. It was…" She sat down and buried her face in her hands.

"Caree, you needed to learn about beguiling spirits operating through images. Time is short, and the anti-Christ will deceive many." His tone was dead serious. Startled, Caree looked up. He stood regally; arms outstretched. A long two-edged sword seemed to appear in his right hand before he changed his stance. His eyes searched Caree's as if hesitant to utter his next words. Finally, he spoke. "Warn the church."

12

PREACHER POSITIVE

Caree felt as if her blood had turned to ice. Maschil's admonition to warn the church brought a dull ache to her heart. As much as she loved church and loved being accepted by others, Caree loved the truth more. Both her love for truth and her tendency to be verbally blunt had caused problems for her in the past. Memories of different confrontations flashed across her mind.

"Caree? Are you alright?" Maschil's gentle probing brought a faint smile to Caree's lips.

"Yes, I suppose so," she said rather pensively. "I was just thinking..."

"Of all the times you have stood for the truth and been persecuted," he finished amiably.

"Well, yes, I suppose so. I sort of made up my mind to try and keep an open mind and a shut mouth!" she confessed.

"And, did that work?" he queried.

"Um, well, I suppose that depends on how you look at it."

"In other words," he countered, "it depends on whether your stand for God's truth caused problems for you, or whether being silent saved you from problems but not the other person, in an eternal sense."

"Excuse me, but I don't quite understand what you mean!" Caree shifted her feet uncomfortably.

"Caree," he admonished, "I think you do know what I mean. You can either speak the truth in love for the sake of another person's soul, or you can remain silent for your own sake."

"Yes, but," she stammered, "there are times when it's best to remain silent."

"Of course, there are times when wisdom dictates a person say nothing. But, if the Holy Spirit prompts you to confront for the sake of truth, then you must be obedient."

"Well, I have been!" Her voice began to rise defensively. "You know, if you were watching, about the time I confronted that pastor who misquoted the Bible nearly every Sunday. I was ridiculed, mocked, and gossiped about all over town for months."

"Caree, you will not know until you reach heaven how many lives were touched and challenged by your stand for truth." He lifted his eyes upward for a moment before continuing. "Little one, may I ask you, what did Jesus do? Did He avoid persecution?"

Convicted, Caree hung her head. "No, He didn't." Then she added, "I'm sorry, Maschil. It's just that—it's just kind of overwhelming for me right now. Nobody is going to listen to me, so how am I going to warn the church?"

"Caree," he countered, "why did Jesus send the Holy Spirit on the day of Pentecost?"

She hesitated, then quoted a portion of scripture. "...but you shall receive power when the Holy Spirit has come upon you; and you shall be My witnesses..."

"Very good!" He reached for her hand. "Come! Your next interview is with someone you once knew."

Caree momentarily wondered at this abrupt conclusion to their conversation. *Probably,* she told herself, *this next interview will shed light on the subject.*

Maschil once again held Caree close to himself. His robe's soft and flowing material pressed gently against her face. Occasionally she caught glimpses of molten rock and tongues of fire as Maschil flew across what appeared to be a broad crater of some sort. The stench of death and decay caused her nose and eyes to sting and burn, while the ear-piercing screams of the damned assaulted her eardrums. Even though she knew God was honoring her cry for understanding and even though her angelic guide was wonderful beyond description, she wanted to kick and scream and be freed from the overpowering depression and misery around her.

She sensed they were nearly beyond the rim of the crater for it had become darker and quieter. Suddenly Maschil turned to the left and began descending down a long corridor. Here the darkness was thick and heavy. The rising temperature caused Caree to feel uncomfortable and weak even though she was within the protection of her heavenly escort.

Maschil suddenly stopped, but didn't release her from his firm grip. She tried in vain to wriggle her face clear in the hope she could get a full view of their surroundings.

"Leave him!" Maschil's sharp command was followed by a flurry of activity. Caree's straining ears picked up eerie high-pitched squealing sounds as several demons retreated into the dark chasm. Finally, Maschil released his hold on her and took a step back.

Caree stared blankly into the swirling smoke. The heat had become nearly unbearable and the acrid air stung and burned her eyes and throat. She licked her dry lips and squinted. Something was moving toward her, but what or who she couldn't tell. She was about to turn and question Maschil when suddenly the shadowy figure lunged at her, screaming her name.

Startled, Caree tried to dodge the attack, but tripped over a rock and lost her balance. Immediately a strong arm caught her and pulled her to her feet. "You are safe, Caree," Maschil reassured her, "he cannot touch you." His words calmed her pounding heart.

"Well, I'll be!" the gloomy figure snarled. "If it isn't little Caree Collins, the Jezebel of the church!"

Although she still couldn't see this person's features clearly, Caree had no trouble in recognizing the raspy voice. "Pastor..."

"Positive!" he interrupted with scorn. His voice dripped with sarcasm and arrogance. "I believe that's what you used to tell people when you wickedly gossiped about me behind my back!"

Caree felt sick with shock. Pastor "Positive" Schroeder had actually been cast into hell! Memories of him drifted across her mind like torn wisps of newspaper floating in a breeze; memories she had tucked into the recesses of her mind several years ago after he had slipped into a coma and died.

"Ha! So, you are speechless, are you?" He advanced toward Caree until she could make out his features. Yes, it was the pastor all right. Even though she remembered him as being tall and lanky, here his appearance was stooped and bent. She readily recognized, however, his beady, hard eyes which seemed to penetrate to the very depths of her soul. His broad mouth and thin lips were fixed in a contemptuous grin. How often had she seen this very expression while attending his church. There was no doubt about it; the pastor was one of the most intimidating individuals she had ever met. Then she saw the chains that restrained him and sighed with relief. She knew if he hadn't been restrained, he would go for her throat.

Caree swallowed hard and mustered up enough courage to ask, "What are you doing here?"

"Well, lil' darlin'," he drawled seductively, "you, of all people, ought to know the answer to that!" Sharp pinpoints of light danced in his gleaming eyes.

He's running me around, she thought to herself. Quietly she prayed, "Lord, help me, give me wisdom,"

"Well, ain't that sweet! Prayin' in hell! You're quite the saint, aren't you?" Suddenly the mimicry stopped and he began screaming vehemently. "You did it, Caree Collins! I'll never forget you! It's all your fault! If it hadn't been for you and your little gossip group, I wouldn't be here! You negative, impudent, loser!"

Relief swept through Caree as Maschil stepped alongside her. He pointed his finger at Pastor Schroeder. "You!" His rich voice filled the deep recesses of the morose cavity and resounded against the harsh lava walls. "No more accusations. Answer her question."

Pastor Schroeder visibly stiffened. His penetrating eyes shot daggers at Maschil and his thin lips twisted into a silent grimace. Then, after a long pause, he unblinkingly returned his hateful stare toward Caree. "I preached the word. I was a word preacher!" His fingers tightened into a fist and he began beating the air as if pounding on an imaginary pulpit. "Thousands came to my meetings. Doesn't that tell you something? Thousands! Day and night I spoke the positive faith message. I believed it. I lived it." He lifted his arms and rolled his eyes upward. "No more dead, dry religion for me and my followers! No, no, no. I had an enlightened message and the people knew it! And," he glowered at Caree, "negative people like you just don't understand the new revelations." Before she could reply, he continued. "Take the Apostle Paul for example. What a fool! If he had known what I know, he wouldn't have had to suffer. That business about being beaten, stoned, left for dead, shipwrecked, imprisoned, hungry, naked, cold, tired, persecuted, and all that junk didn't have to happen. And all those martyrs! Didn't have to happen." He began to pace back and forth, dragging the two heavy chains which bound his feet. "And Job!" His voice rose angrily. "Job had it comin'. After all, the dummy put it on himself. Why, the word even says so!" He eyed Caree, hoping for a response. When he got none, he continued, "Ah, poor old Job. He even admitted that what he feared 'had come upon him.'"

"That does it!" Caree could contain herself no longer. "The Bible says Job was God's righteous, and I repeat, righteous servant! The Bible makes it clear that Job's trials were due to Satan's insidious and evil desire to torment him so he would deny God. But he didn't, and in the end, God rewarded him."

A low, barely discernable snarl escaped from Pastor Schroeder's lewd mouth. Then he threw his head back and attempted to laugh, but the only sounds he could utter were hoarse, hacking sputters. Finally, he looked down and slowly wagged his head from side to side. "Caree, Caree, Caree," he spoke in a monotone as if addressing a hopelessly incorrigible child. "You haven't changed, no, not one itsy bitsy bit!" His voice was full of rancor. "Wasn't it enough for you to be a genuine pain in the neck on earth, without having to come here to be an even bigger one?"

"Look here, Mr. Schroeder." A surge of righteous indignation surged through Caree like an electrical current. "God's Word, rightly divided, is the final authority. You are a genuine heretic and I had no choice but to expose your heretical teachings. You may call it 'gossip' all you like, but I was contending for the faith. You were preaching another Jesus, another spirit, and another Gospel. And," she pointed a finger at him, "you must admit you subtly brainwashed people into believing they were little gods and all they had to do was visualize what they wanted and then to confess it! That is nothing but witchcraft!"

"Negative! All negative!" he screamed. "I don't deserve to be here. No, I have been unjustly judged. I am a god! I have power! All I have to do is visualize my way out of here."

"Well, then, why are you still here if you are a god and you're so powerful?" She tipped her head and waited for his reply.

"Oh brother," he wailed. "You always did miss the point. God has gods like dogs have puppies and cats have kittens. We're all gods." He rolled his eyes toward the ceiling as if to demonstrate how hopelessly stupid Caree was. Then he looked straight at her, "Let's get to the point young lady." His tone was superior, threatening. "You had no right to challenge me in my church. The Bible warns people like you not to touch God's anointed. You had no business coming in with your divisive, Jezebel spirit and try to be an authority over me and talk about me behind my back, and believe me, you will pay for it!"

"Whoa! Wait just a minute there!" Caree put her hands on her hips. "Who do you think you are? For one thing, I had every right to warn God's people that there was a hireling shepherd behind the pulpit. Secondly, a Jezebel spirit is a spirit of idolatry and wickedness, which I do not have! Thirdly, all genuinely saved persons are anointed of the Lord, and if you really knew what the Bible says, you'd know that in Old Testament times God's warning not to 'touch' His anointed meant that they were not to physically kill the king, the priest, or the prophets!"

Pastor Schroeder stood motionless and silent as if gathering his thoughts for one final round. His harsh and lined face glistened with sweat and a faint hissing sound emanated from his throat. The corners of his mouth jerked upward in a ridiculous and inane attempt to convince his visitors that he was the victor. "Well," he cooed, "when Jesus descended into hell, he was tortured by the devil and had to be born again before rising from the dead."

"You blasphemer! The Bible says no such thing!" Caree shook her head. "You know, Pastor, if you had feared God, you would have had some wisdom." Shock and surprise registered on Pastor Schroeder's face. He stood speechless while Caree continued. "My only regret is that I didn't try harder to point out your error to you, then perhaps you would be in heaven instead of hell!"

"What?" He sneered. "Believe you? That would be the day! You negative fundamentalist! Not in a million years, baby!"

"Positive," Caree said firmly, "is not a criterion for truth! There is no such thing from Genesis to Revelation as positive or negative. But if you had received a love for the truth, then you would not have been sent a strong delusion, that you should believe a lie."[1]

"Oh, honey," he taunted, "Give it up. You just don't understand the deeper things of God."

Without warning a massive tongue of fire materialized between Pastor Schroeder and the two callers. Maschil quickly shielded Caree and at the same instant pulled her backward. Great gulping flames shot upwards before fanning out in all directions. Maschil, still holding Caree, sped upward and away from the roaring inferno.

The last thing Caree heard was the nerve jarring screams and curses of Pastor Positive.

13

TO SUFFER,
HERE OR THERE?

Billowing, white clouds resembling giant scoops of whipped cream pushed against the clear, azure sky. The distant hills of green and scarlet gave witness of new life. Birds flitted happily among the tree branches and chirped excitedly to one another. Spring was here and all of nature responded to resurrection's call to come forth from the cold death of winter.

Caree moaned softly to herself as scenes in living color flooded her weary mind. Lost somewhere between consciousness and the world of dreams, Caree allowed herself gently to enter the latter.

She saw him in obscurity at first and struggled to run to him, but her stubborn legs refused to move. Inwardly, mounting frustration at her helplessness became an instrument of torture until suddenly, in a fraction of time he was there, holding her, kissing her.

"Lance, Lance, I love you." She breathed into his ear. Holding her tightly, he smiled joyfully. "Oh, Caree, I've waited so long for this moment! I'll never let you go, never. I love you, darling!" Their lips met in a melody of ecstasy and tenderness.

Without warning the happy scene faded and much to Caree's horror the leering face of Pastor Schroeder loomed over her. "Suffering," the large mouth whispered hoarsely, "is not for Christians unless they have sin in their life. Suffering happens to people who do not know how to practice God's principles."

"Lance! Lance, help me!" Caree's screams echoed through the void.

"Where are you? Lance!"

Wretched, wicked laughter rolled over Caree until she felt as if her soul had shriveled up to a small pinprick of light. Somehow, she was now outside of herself, a casual observer watching as she became nothing more than an insignificant speck in the Universe.

"Jesus." His Name gently caressed the recesses of her mind.

"Jesus." In an instant Caree knew whose name she needed to call upon. *Quickly, before I'm gone, before I'm lost,* she told herself. *"Jesus! Save me!"*

Instantly she was back in the lush green meadow. The luminous clouds were directly overhead now, splashing abstract shadows across the hills and grasslands. She slowly scanned the peaceful scene. Yes, Lance was here, but this time he was sitting with a group of people under a picturesque shade tree.

Someone was preaching. She moved effortlessly closer to the crowd of outdoor worshippers. Yes! It was Evangelist Elizabeth Whitford. Caree had never seen an anointing like this evangelist had and eagerly awaited her yearly visits.

Past conversations with Evangelist Elizabeth came into sharp focus and replayed on the screen of Caree's mind.

It had been just the previous year when Caree asked Evangelist Elizabeth the question. At the time it had seemed like a dumb thing to ask, but she had to know. It went like this, "Sister Elizabeth, how did you get your ministry?"

What Caree meant was how did you arrive at this point where you have such an incredible anointing and power? She would never forget the answer, no, not if she lived to be a thousand years old. It came in one, softly spoken word—"Suffering."

Shaken, Caree had quietly slipped out. She needed to be alone to think, to pray. She wanted it all right. There was no doubt about that. The anointing! She had witnessed people touched by God in ways that were outlined in Bible stories, but seldom, if ever, in modern times. But God was very much alive, and He still did miracles. Caree knew, however, that there was a world of difference between the showmanship and hype she had all too often witnessed and the real thing.

But, suffering? Why did it have to be suffering? She knew Evangelist Elizabeth had gone through horrible experiences, losses, and physical challenges. Was that the price one must pay for such power?

Questions and answers tumbled through Caree's mind like agates in a rock polisher. Trying to get around the suffering issue meant bargaining with God for a shortcut, which, she told herself, amounted to shallow Christianity. And, Caree had a built-in disdain for shallow anything.

Three days later while agonizing in prayer, Caree made the choice. With trembling lips, she laid herself on God's altar and gave Him permission to do whatever He must to bring her to that place of power and anointing. "I want your fire, Lord. Give me the fire of the Holy Ghost!" Tears rolled down her cheeks. "Make me your servant! Oh God! Use me! No matter what it takes! Use me for your glory!"

For weeks and months after that pivotal moment Caree delved into the Bible and other writings of godly men and women. "Rejoice, inasmuch as you are partakers of Christ's sufferings," wrote the Apostle Peter. Caree soon discovered the teachings of Oswald Chambers. These she especially cherished, such as his inspired insights regarding suffering.

Mr. Chambers related how the sufferings of Christ are not those of ordinary men. He had suffered according to the will of God. It is only in identification with Jesus in His sufferings that believers can begin to understand what God is after when dealing with us. Even though the Christian Church has a tendency to evade being identified with Jesus in His sufferings, there are those who have sought another way of trying to carry out God's aim for their lives by taking a short cut. However, God's way often entails suffering and when a believer chooses to do God's will, he or she will do so regardless of the possibilities of suffering for the sake of Christ.

> Chamber's words filled her mind. "The sufferings of Christ are not those of ordinary men. He suffered 'according to the will of God,' not from the point of view we suffer from as individuals. It is only when we are related to Jesus Christ that we can understand what God is after in His dealings with us.

It is part of Christian culture to know what God's aim is. In the history of the Christian Church the tendency has been to evade being identified with the sufferings of Jesus Christ; men have sought to procure the carrying out of God's order by a short cut of their own. God's way is always the way of suffering, the way of the "long, long trail."[1]

"No healthy saint ever chooses suffering; he chooses God's will, as Jesus did, whether it means suffering or not."[2]

As Caree probed deeply into the word of God, she discovered three different responses to suffering; that is, one can despise it and treat it too lightly, faint under it and treat it too seriously, or be exercised by it and receive instruction from it. The Apostles Peter and Paul, as well as many Old Testament saints, advised to commit pain and suffering to God, realizing He is faithful to work all things out for good and for God's glory. Even James wrote in his epistle, "...count it all joy."

Caree concluded that suffering was a genuine test of one's faith. But she found there were other reasons for suffering. For one thing, it produces the fruit of patience, joy, knowledge, and maturity. It also silences the devil as in the case of faithful Job. One of Caree's favorite verses was Job 15:13, "Though he slay me, yet will I trust in him."

She also learned that sometimes suffering is for the glory of God such as when Jesus healed the blind man and raised Lazarus from the dead. If one wishes to be like Jesus, then undoubtedly that person will suffer in this life.[3]

Caree and Lance had many long discussions over coffee about the subject of suffering. "Honey," he had solemnly said to her one cheerful afternoon, "God must teach us dependence on Him and on Him alone. Sometimes He allows hardship to come into our lives so we will continually look to Him."

Caree sighed, "I'm afraid you're right. We all need to be refined and occasionally rebuked."

Their conversation that day turned to ministry and how personal suffering brought greater understanding and love toward others.

Later that evening they received the news. Pastor Schroeder had been badly injured while rewiring his home and was in a coma. Lance and Caree fervently prayed as he drove them to the hospital. Caree walked with Lance to the stricken man's room where she waited just inside the doorway while Lance walked quietly to the still form. Because Lance was a clergyman, he was allowed entrance. Kneeling beside the bed, Lance bowed his head and prayed in a low, but audible voice. Caree strained to pick up snatches of his conversation with God. "Lord, cause your Spirit to…bring Pastor to a full understanding…have mercy, oh Lord and…Jesus is the only way, the only truth, the only life…God help him to know the real Jesus."

It was nearly an hour before Lance turned towards Caree. He looked oddly pale and shaken. Taking Caree's arm he whispered hoarsely, "Let's head for the cafeteria and get something to drink."

Once settled at a small table for two in one of the large cafeteria's more secluded corners, Lance cupped his masculine fingers around a steaming cup of hot chocolate and leaned toward Caree. "He's not going to make it, Caree. I just know it."

"Not make it?" Caree questioned. "Not make it here or there?" Beads of perspiration dotted Lance's brow. "'Here.' I have no way of knowing about 'there.'" He took a sip from the steaming cup and quickly looked around the busy room as if making sure no one overheard their conversation. Satisfied no one was paying any attention to them, he leaned over the small red table toward Caree. "Hon, the man doesn't have a prayer unless he repents while in that coma."

"Wh-a-a-t?" Caree blushed at her impulsive outburst. Struggling to regain control of both her emotions and voice she pushed aside the tea she had been sipping, folded her hands on top of the table and leaned toward him. "Lance, what do you mean? Can people actually hear you talking to them when they are in a coma?"

"Caree," he said in a confidential tone, "let me tell you a true story." He repositioned his chair to the side of the table where he could be closer to her. "Remember when Pastor Munson and I were invited to Seattle to share at a pastor's conference?"

"Yes, I think so." She reached for her tea and brushed the side of his arm. It felt good being close to him and she secretly wished these private moments between the two of them could somehow last forever. As if reading her thoughts, Lance put a protective arm around her shoulders. She smiled at him appreciatively and he continued, "That was the time I went on the two-week missionary trip to Mexico. And then, after I got home, you went on another speaking trip to Wyoming. We didn't see much of each other that summer."

"I know." He gave her a slight hug. "I suppose that's one reason I neglected to tell you about Jo and her trip to hell."

"Jo? Who is Jo?" Caree tone was slightly tinged with jealousy.

"Honey, Jo Reynolds was a married lady I met in the church in Seattle. After the meeting some of us met for fellowship and..."

"Yeah, I know, you met for pie and coffee at one of those all-night restaurants."

"Well, yes you're right. But let me tell you what she told me about a death experience she had. It's really incredible on the one hand, but on the other, well, we both know that Jesus spoke more about hell than He did heaven...so we shouldn't be surprised."

"This is going to be interesting," Caree murmured. "Let me get some more hot water for my tea and I'll be right back."

"No, you sit still. I'll get refills for both of us." Lance stood and reached for their cups. His eyes met Caree's and for a moment neither spoke. Then he turned and walked toward the self-serve beverage counter.

Caree felt a faint twinge of anxiety. She loved real-life testimonies, but the subject of hell wasn't totally settled in her mind. Too many people she knew and loved had passed from this world to the next without receiving Christ. To believe they were in a place of eternal torment was unsettling and overwhelming. Caree was appreciative of all life and had great compassion on God's creatures, both great and small. How such a wonderful, powerful, loving Creator could allow any of His creation to suffer eternally was beyond her comprehension.

The light thud of cups being set on the table interrupted Caree's musings. "Honey?" Lance's deep voice reflected concern. "Are you all right? I mean, you seem rather pale and distracted."

"Uh, oh, no, I mean, I'm fine. Just a little tired I guess." She kept her eyes focused on her spoon as she pressed it against the teabag. "What was it you were going to say about this Jo lady?"

"Perhaps another time would be better. I can take you home if you like and..."

"No. Please, I want to hear what you were going to tell me." Caree was reluctant to go home just yet. She enjoyed being alone with Lance, a privilege they seldom had. Most of his time was taken up with his studies and ministry.

"This Christian woman," he began as he put his arm around her again, "asked the Lord a question. That's how it all began." He smiled more to himself than to her. "And, God answers questions!" She silently nodded. Lance continued, "Jo was involved in evangelism and one day asked the Lord just what they were saving people from. Then sometime later she had a bad bout with multiple sclerosis and ended up in the hospital."

Caree shuddered inwardly. Her least favorite place was a hospital, unless, of course, it was being secluded in a hospital cafeteria with someone you had fallen in love with.

"And, I believe," he smiled and gave her a quick hug, "you asked me about comas. Jo went into a coma and in that state, she heard every word that was being spoken around her."

"No kidding! You mean she heard all the doctors, nurses, and visitors while in a coma?" Color had returned to Caree's face and she suddenly looked alert.

"Yes, it's true. Not only Jo, but many others who have been in comas have stated the same thing. That's why I shared scripture with Pastor Schroeder and prayed with him."

"Oh, I do hope he is saved!" Caree whispered.

"So do I, Hon. Let me go on with this story the way Jo told it to me. While in this coma, she actually left her body. She said she had a falling feeling. She just kept going down, down, down. When she hit the bottom, she landed on her hip in some dirt. It was very dark and extremely cold."

"Cold?" Caree retorted. "I thought hell was supposed to be hot."

"Let me explain," Lance gave her a quick kiss on the cheek. Caree blushed and looked quickly around the cafeteria. Thank goodness, she thought, it's nearly empty in here.

"Caree, in ministry I have experienced incredible coldness when Satan walks in on the scene. I remember one incident in Idaho where a married couple was having difficulties and the wife feared for her life. One of their Christian friends stopped by the house and became quite terrified as she felt a presence enter which was like a blast of cold air. Her hair even stood up and she knew there was a murdering spirit in that house! But, that's another story; let me finish, okay?" He put his hand protectively over hers and continued.

"In front of Jo was a huge rock 'sort of thing.' The way she described it was that this rock had a little red bump on it. Then a big door swung open and two large figures came alongside her, one on the left and the other on the right to protect her. She knew they were angels. Then they began going down a long sloping path and it became terribly hot and humid. She said the heat was terrific and she felt light headed. At this point, the beings held her up. Afterwards, she recovered and they continued on the downward path. She saw tunnels off to the right and left and within those tunnels were little rooms, small cells."

Caree could feel the tension in her body and hoped Lance didn't notice. As long as she stayed calm, their evening together would be longer. She would think all this over later and make up her own mind about it. In the meantime, she would try to be composed, and act nonchalant.

Lance picked up his cocoa and studied her over the rim. He took a sip and slowly returned the mug to the table. "Caree, are you sure you're alright?"

Caree forced a cheerful smile. "Yes, I'm just fine. Do go on!"

"Ok, if you're sure you want to hear the rest."

"Yes, I'm quite sure. It's all very interesting."

Lance slightly frowned. Caree couldn't hide much from him and he suspected she wasn't in total agreement with Jo's testimony. Well, he reasoned, if she was truly God's will for his life, then she was going to have to accept the reality of hell as well as heaven. He took a deep breath and said, "Jo knew there were people in those little cells, but she couldn't see them; but she could hear them. She said it was awful, all the people screaming in torturous pain with horrible, ugly demons tormenting them."

He sipped his coffee thoughtfully for a few seconds, then continued, "She said there were countless little spiders everywhere and even they were laughing a horrible laugh and cursing and swearing."

"Oh, ugh! I hate spiders!" Caree snuggled closer to Lance for comfort, forgetful of their surroundings.

"Jo related that a light emanated from the angelic beings on her right and left so she could see. Then she told of enormous snakes all over the place and also huge spiders. But these creatures of darkness fled from the light." His voice held a note of triumph.

"Jo, of course, was feeling a terror she had never known. She said it was the most horrible feeling. She said that people who joke about hell as being a 'party' with their friends is certainly not true! Hell is no 'party' but indescribable loneliness and pain. Then she said they descended more and it got warmer and warmer. Her guardians pointed and she looked and saw the lake of fire. She said it was huge. She asked if that was what was talked about in the Bible. They told her 'yes' and that was their only communication. She said she saw the lake of fire to her left and off to her right were burning coals and it was even hotter. Jo told us the stench was awful and she smelled burning flesh. It made her sick to her stomach."

Lance took a deep breath and waited a moment before continuing. He liked the way it felt having Caree close to him. Her shiny, soft blonde hair smelled like fresh apples and her expressive face was a joy to watch.

"Where was I? Oh yes, Jo cried out 'I can't take this anymore' and they started up. As she listened to all the screams of the people, she thought to herself, 'I wish I could get these people out of here.' A voice within her said, 'This is not my choice, but their choice.' She wanted to weep; it was so devastating to her. Then they went on and came to the bottom of the shaft or tunnel. All the while, she said, things, demons, tried to grab her but the angels protected her. These demons looked like people but were grotesque. She said the pictures of demons we see on earth pretty much look like real demons but many of them are much worse."

He looked at Caree. "You alright, Baby?"

"Uh hum." She liked his closeness, his protecting mannerisms. Regardless of hell, she told herself, she could stay in this position forever.

"Jo related that they came back up the tunnel and the beings left her at the end of it and disappeared. She floated up through the floor and could see her body. She floated like a leaf and then re-entered her body."[4]

"What an experience!" Caree reflected, without moving.

"You better believe it!" Lance replied. "She said it changed her entire outlook on life."

"I suppose something like that would have a powerful impact." Caree whispered.

"Well, I hate to say this, but it's way past your bedtime." He lifted his arm from around her shoulders and helped her up. "Where's your coat?"

"Oh, Lance, I don't want to..."

"I know darling, but you'll be sorry tomorrow when you have to work on your project."

Good old Lance, she thought. Always so logical. She stood to her feet and let him help her with her coat. They walked slowly across the now empty cafeteria and into the long hallway. "I hope he makes it, Lance, I really do. I didn't mean to hurt him personally when I challenged him about his erroneous doctrines!" Caree choked back the tears.

"It's all right, Love. Don't cry." He reached for his handkerchief and handed it to her. "You did what was right. Pastor Schroeder needed to hear the truth. He won't make heaven without it! And when he stands before Almighty God on Judgment Day, he won't be able to say he never heard the truth."

They rode home in silence, each lost in their own thoughts. Lance walked Caree to her door. "Caree, let's just keep praying for him. I'll try and call you tomorrow. Pastor Munson and I have a full load." He pulled her close and kissed her gently. "Good night, Sweets."

That night, thoughts of Pastor Schroeder kept Caree awake well into the night. Was he still alive and if not, where was he now, she wondered. Hadn't he read the scriptural admonition that teachers would receive a greater judgment?[5] Why didn't he have fear of God? She tugged at her blanket and tried to relax but the relentless barrage of questions kept

107

marching through her mind. What if he went to hell? Suppose he really was sincere; would God damn him anyway? If so, what was hell really like? Was Jo Reynold's eye-witness account true? If so, was hell forever like the Bible said, or was there another interpretation? When Lance prayed the prayer of repentance and salvation in the hospital, did Pastor Schroeder hear him and repent in his heart? Why didn't people like him repent, even when they had heard the gospel time and time again? Why did some Christians lay down their lives for Christ while others would, or could not?

Somewhere between the tormenting questions and Caree's uncertain answers, sleep, soft as the morning mist, descended on her weary mind and gently carried her through the long night.

14

THE CROSS AND THE SEVEN SAYINGS OF JESUS

Caree sensed the cheerful light around her before she opened her eyes. She lay still for a few moments, trying to clear her foggy mind. Something stirred nearby, causing her heart to leap. Caree's eyes flew open but the brilliant light blinded her. "Wha ...where?"

"Caree, I am here. It is all right." The soothing voice was somehow familiar. "You had a little time out." Maschil chuckled more to himself than to her.

"Oh, no! Noooo! I'm still here! I was remembering in a dream!" Caree sighed and shut her eyes as if in so doing the present reality would fade and she would find herself in her own bed once again.

"You were asking some important questions, I believe." His glowing features reflected heaven's light. "And, God is faithful to answer them."

Caree stirred from her resting place and sat up. She ran her fingers through her disheveled hair, stretched her legs and frowned. "Maschil, I really want to go home," she commanded wearily. "Can you escort me there right now?"

"Caree, that decision is not mine to make." He was sitting on a long, flat rock opposite her. It seemed he reached behind himself and then extended his hand to her with a small golden vial. "Drink this."

Caree shrunk back suspiciously. "What is it?"

"It will strengthen and refresh you for the remainder of this journey." He replied calmly. His warm eyes never left her face and she felt herself reaching for the slender vessel. She raised her eyes to his as she tipped the container slowly to her lips. The pleasant liquid trickled into her dry mouth and brought instant refreshment. She wondered at this wonderful elixir which seemed to be an exotic combination of fruit, honey, water, and spice.

She handed the vial back to Maschil and took a deep breath. "Okay! What's on the agenda?" She nearly giggled and inwardly wondered at herself. Whatever was in that drink sure made her feel alive all right.

The corners of Maschil's masculine mouth curved into a slight smile. "The seven sayings of Jesus on the cross."

"What does that have to do with my questions?" Caree quickly checked herself. She should at least give him a chance to explain.

Overlooking her impulsiveness, Maschil explained, "When you understand this lesson, you will be able to minister effectively to all four types of people." Before she could interrupt again, he continued. "There are four responses to the truth, Caree. The first one is those who, when confronted with the truth, feel threatened. These are the religious. Some people are insulted because they are used to Jesus being a certain way. Many are fearful and afraid because the truth might cost them something. Then there are the truth seekers who are seeking the very person of Jesus."[1]

"Yes," Caree added, "this reminds me of the parable of the seed and the sower. Jesus talked about four kinds of soil."[2]

Maschil nodded with approval. As long as his student was open and willing, he would be able to impart many precious truths. "Now let's look at the seven sayings of Jesus on the cross."

Caree inwardly prayed that she would be able to remember what she was about to learn. To some extent she knew God desired for her to mature quickly for time was short, the harvest was great, and the laborers few.

"Father forgive them; for they know not what they do"[3] Maschil quoted. He paused for a moment as if in deep thought, then continued. "Caree, this relates to that part of the Christian's duty to love your enemies and pray for those who persecute you. The example of Christ's forgiveness on the cross demonstrates that if a person claims to be His follower, then he must obey Luke 9:24 which reads, 'For whoever wants to save his life will lose it.' Forgiveness is a command." Maschil looked at Caree who was deep in thought.

"Losing your life," she said slowly, "is easy to read about or even agree to. But the actual process is very hard indeed."

"Yes," he agreed, "It involves willingness to lay everything down at the foot of the cross. But the most difficult thing for human beings to lay down is their form of pride. There are three forms of pride you know."

Caree chuckled. "Why am I not surprised? Okay, what are they?"

"Conceit, selfishness, and pride itself.[4] But you will learn more about that when you return.

"The second saying was 'Today you will be with me in Paradise.' For the Christian this is a promise and means taking up your cross and following Him. To deny yourself, pick up your cross and follow Him requires faith in His promises.[5] And Jesus promised that He was preparing a place for you and will come back for you so that you may be where He is."[6]

Joy leapt within Caree's heart. No matter what happened, she thought, she had a promise, a hope, a future. Tears filled her eyes as she thought of the spotless Lamb of God, battered, bruised, and bloody, nailed to a cross in her place so she could inherit eternal life with Him forever. How wonderful to know she need not fear spending all eternity in the place of the damned. She wept unashamedly as she thought of all the lost souls who were hopelessly trapped in a Christless eternity. She looked up at Maschil and said, "It's so horrible—so tragic that millions and millions of souls have rejected God's plan of redemption and are forever lost."

"Yes, Caree. Truly, it is not God's will that any should perish. Now, remember the third saying of Jesus on the cross?" She slowly shook her head back and forth. He continued, "'Dear woman, here is your son,' and to the disciple, 'Here is your mother.'"[7]

Caree wondered how this particular pronouncement related to the Christian life. Maschil said softly, "The cost. Remember, Caree, there is a cost to be paid."

"Oh, I know!" Caree interjected. "Family can be a big cost. And, how beautiful that Jesus, as the eldest son, took care of His mother before he died on the cross. How broken her heart must've been! I know the cost can be a broken heart" she said softly. Tears formed in her eyes, and she continued, "Let me see, there is the scripture which tells us that we are to love Him so much that by comparison our love for our families would seem like hate. And Jesus warned that it would do no good to gain the whole world and lose our own soul. And Paul said that he considered everything as loss compared to the surpassing greatness of knowing Christ and he also said he never wanted to boast in anything except in the cross of our Lord Jesus Christ."[8]

"Very good! You are gaining wisdom." Maschil's face reflected perfect peace. He continued, "The fourth declaration on the cross was this, 'My God, my God, why have you forsaken me?"[9] This speaks of separation, and you can relate to this in your own times of desperation and depression. Jesus did ask the Father to take this cup away from Him if it was possible, yet He submitted to the Father's will. This is the determination each Christian has to make—the determination that even though you walk through the valley of the shadow of death you will fear no evil, but know that He is with you, and allow Him to comfort you.[10] Whenever you choose to follow Christ all the way, there will be different times of separation in your life."

Caree quoted Job, "Though He slay me, yet will I trust in Him." Her voice was barely audible. "Job had many separations, and basically suffered alone because his friends misunderstood him and the cause of his suffering."[11]

"Caree, remember, keep your life free from the love of money and be content with what you have, because God promised you that He would never leave nor forsake you."[12] He went on, "The fifth saying was 'I thirst!' Besides physical thirst, He suffered incredible agonies on the cross including bearing the sins of every human being who was ever born. He thirsted so that those who come to Him need not ever thirst again. That does not mean His followers will not suffer for the short time they live in their physical bodies. But you have been given the great promise that if you suffer with Him, you will also reign with Him."[13]

"I know," Caree said, longing to be with her fiancé. "Lance and I discussed this subject a lot."

Maschil looked at her with understanding. "It will be soon, Caree. Now," he went to the next point, "the sixth saying of Jesus on the cross was 'It is finished!' This speaks of the product."

"The product?" Caree asked.

"Yes. You see, whoever loses his life for Christ will save it. The product is having the life of Christ formed in you. But remember, before resurrection comes death."

"That reminds me of what Jesus told His followers when He told them that unless a kernel of wheat falls to the ground and dies, it remains only a single seed. But if it dies, it produces many seeds."[14]

"Here is the seventh and last utterance of Jesus on the cross, 'Father, into your hands I commend my spirit.'" *Maschil seems to enjoy these teaching times immensely.* Caree thought to herself. *Yes, even the angels want to learn more about Him and His plan.* Maschil looked at her and she knew he had read her mind. He made no comment, however, but continued, "This is the hope. Hope because God the Father raised Him from the dead, fulfilling scripture. Hope because Christians who have died in Christ shall also be raised to new life."

"'We are confident, I say, and willing rather to be absent from the body, and to be present with the Lord,'" Caree quoted triumphantly.[15]

"Yes," Maschil grinned broadly. "Jesus is the victor!" He sat down beside her. "You asked why people do not repent when faced with the truth. Here is the last part of this lesson. The Holy Spirit brings a reality check to people, but remember, He is a gentleman and will not violate a person's free will. He convicts of sin, or what people do will depend on their heart condition. He convicts of righteousness, of what people do not do, which is accountability. He also brings judgment of what people refuse to do—that is, change their hearts, minds, and conduct. These actions of the Holy Spirit are to lead people to the truth of Jesus Christ. Receiving the truth will bring changes to a person's life, but if people do not allow the Holy Spirit to convict of sin, then they quench the Spirit. If people do not allow Him to convict them of righteousness, then they grieve the Spirit. And, if they do not allow Him to convict them of impending judgment, then they can end up blaspheming the Spirit."[16]

Silence descended on hell's two visitors. Heaven's instructor had completed the lesson he had been entrusted to deliver, and earth's child sat in silent contemplation of his message. Slowly the truth of the wisdom of the ages began to penetrate her heart and mind. No one need be eternally lost. No one could say God had not sent His very best. No one could ever stand at the foot of His cross, hear His message, and deny His deity. No one, that is, except those whose hearts were closed to the voice of the Holy Spirit.

15

SUICIDE

The lesson had ended on a note of silence, but slowly, as if someone was turning up the volume from hell below, loud wailing and screaming began to intensify. Caree, still perched on the rock which had served as "schoolroom" furniture, involuntarily plugged her ears with her fingers in the hope of insulating herself against the now incessant commotion. It was a futile gesture, however, and she somehow knew if Maschil didn't get her out of here quickly she would surely teeter on the brink of insanity.

"Come." He extended his hand and she readily accepted. Quietly he escorted her across a narrow expanse of total darkness. Occasionally her ears picked up the clamor of countless voices crying out in agony, but she knew they were nearly out of earshot.

"In here," Maschil directed. Caree strained her eyes in the direction he was pointing. Finally, she made out the faint outline of a small cave opening within the side of a steep cliff. She stiffened and took a step backward.

"No, please! It's so dark! I can't, Maschil. I hate little dark places! What if there are snakes and spiders and rats in there?"

He stood for long moments gazing at her upturned face. Somehow it seemed he didn't see her even though he was looking directly at her. Finally, he said, more to himself than to her, "All right. We will do it this way then." He tightened his hold on her hand and with a loud voice called "Devils, loose her! Sasha, come forth!"

Caree's eyes were glued to the cave opening. Little puffs of dust began billowing out from the dingy entrance and floated aimlessly in the oppressive air. She detected a scuffling sound from somewhere deep within the cavern. What happened next caused everything inside of Caree to want to bolt and run. But run she couldn't, for the angel was holding her fast. The unearthly, bone chilling scream pulsated up and down her spine in waves of raw terror. She literally felt her hair stand on end as shocks of electricity shot through her captive body. Panic seized her heart and wrapped tentacles of hysteria around her throat, strangling the scream which rose in her throat. Her feverish mind demanded her muscles take action, but nothing happened. It was as if each brain impulse was systematically aborted by the enemy of fear.

Then she saw the eyes. They were greenish and slightly glowed in the darkness. Caree wondered at this creature, Sasha. Who or what was it? At this point, Caree's mind had reverted to tactics of self-preservation. Since she couldn't run, the next best thing to do was try not to panic, and to loosen up as much as possible while remaining alert. The thudding of her heart betrayed her, however, and she felt herself gasping for air.

"I still am holding on to you, Caree." Maschil gently admonished. "Remember, you are safe."

His reassurance seemed to snap Caree back to reality and she sighed with relief. She forced her set jaw to relax and managed to focus on the dark form facing her.

"What do ya want?" The voice belonged to the green eyes. "Why have you come here? To tell me I made a mistake?"

"Come forth!" Maschil commanded.

Caree blinked. She couldn't believe her eyes, for as the swampy-green eyes moved forward, they seemed to be somehow suspended in a skull which was partially missing. There was a small piece of bone at the top of the head from which strands of filthy, matted hair stuck out. One cheek, the nose and lower jaw seemed to be intact, but the rest of the face and head were transparent. The body, scrawny and grotesque, was draped with rotten rags.

Caree looked apprehensively at her guide. Why had he brought her here? What was she to say to this pathetic creature? Before he could answer, however, Sasha, shrieked, "They! They!" She swung her arm around as if indicating every demon in hell, "They promised me that they would take care of me! They promised me I'd be free of torment. They promised me I'd be in a better place!" Her eyes became round and strange. Caree was sure they were going to pop right out and fall to the ground.

"You don't even have a clue as to what I'm talking about do you!" Sasha kept her eyes on Caree's face. "You are not initiated, I can tell. You haven't been introduced to the deeper mysteries of the higher intelligences. Hah!" She ground her jagged teeth as if chewing invisible gum. "Look, Missy! I've seen things in the spirit realm you'll never know. When I was on earth, I did it once. I accepted Christ." She rolled her eyes upward and then fastened them again on Caree. "I did that stupid little sinner's thing—you know, went forward in a dumb little church in Arizona and 'got saved!' But," she grinned evilly, "the very next day I renounced Him! Yeah, I threw Him out. I said, 'Git out Jesus! I don't wantcha in my heart, no way!' And He left, just like that!"

Caree gasped. Scriptures flashed in her mind about going apostate.[1] She stood speechless. Sasha suddenly seemed to enjoy being the center of attention and continued. "Everybody thought I'd 'backslidden!' Ha! Ha! I didn't backslide, I just threw Him out! *Who needs this?* I thought to myself. If I had backslidden, then I would have to do that repentance thing until the next time. It seemed so stupid to me. Then after that I just did what I pleased. And I learned so much about the spirit world from that time on. I became friends with the invisible rulers of this world! It was a wonderful privilege, ya know."

Caree still wondered why Maschil had brought her here. Obviously, this person was damned from the moment she repudiated Jesus and the gospel. *But* she admonished herself, *Maschil knows what he is doing—just wait and see.*

"The wise rulers were my friends for many years." The green eyes had narrowed to slits. "They instructed me in the ways of the Ancients. I visited Tibet and India by astral-projection and received advanced knowledge. It was wonderful until those demons began playing tricks on me. They hate the wise masters. They hated me! They were jealous!" She stared unblinkingly at Caree and began to howl in a barely discernable note which escalated into a wild shriek.

Caree shuddered. "Maschil, let's go. I mean, what's the point?"

117

"You will see, trust me." Maschil gently squeezed her hand.

Caree watched as the strange figure began to twist and convulse from invisible tormentors. "See?" she screamed. "They're still here! They still torment me!" She opened her mouth as if to scream, but no noise escaped her parched lips. "Oh, oh, they are still doing it!" She gasped. "On earth, I asked those religious nuts to help me. Yeah, I had a shirttail relative who was a preacher. I even went to him and told him I needed relief from those demons. I told him I could talk directly to God, that I didn't need that Jesus Christ! And you know what? He couldn't help me get rid of those demons. He was no help at all!"

Caree sensed an inner urge to counter this miserable wretch with the truth. "Listen, here," she heard herself say, "For one thing there is no way you can come to God the Father without going through Jesus Christ![2] Secondly, the preacher had authority over those demons, but since you refused Christ, you refused the only remedy for your torment."

"Woman!" She pointed at Caree, "You listen to me! I couldn't deal with that stupid 'sin' idea. I was too smart, too intellectual to believe in that junk. All I needed was to be set free from those demons." She hunched over and began to pant. "They came in my room at night. They followed me into every room of my house. They went in my car with me. They went EVERYWHERE!" She began tearing at her mouth with her skeletal fingers. "The wise ones promised me if I did the ritualistic white rooster sacrifice, then they would deliver me from the demons! That's why I did it! That's why I shot myself in the head! Because they promised to take me to a better place—to a place of peace! But," she tried to stand erect and failed, "but, they will come. I just know they will come because I talk to the Father all the time!"

Caree's mind was racing. Now she understood why Maschil had brought her here. Ritual suicide! How often she had wondered about this terrible action. That explained why parts of this person's skull were missing!

Once again, Caree was speechless. Maschil, still holding her hand, began slowly leading her away from the dark cave entrance. "No! No! Don't leave me here! No! No! No! Come back, oh, please come back!" Sasha's voice began to rise uncontrollably. "Don't leave me here! They are tormenting me, they are...aaaauuuugh!"

Maschil quickly blocked Caree's view of the tormented woman. But he couldn't eradicate the sound of the flames as they boomed and crackled behind them. Nor could he muffle the agonized screams of Sasha as the eager flames licked at her bones. The stench of burning flesh stung Caree's nostrils.

"Oh, Maschil. I can't stand this anymore, please, please, get me out of here!" Taking hold of Caree, he swiftly rose to the top of the cliff wall and continued across a broad plateau. There he stopped and set Caree on her feet.

"You want to know," Maschil said, "what happens to people who claim to be Christians and who commit suicide."

"Yes, that's right," She replied. "At least I think I want to know. I'm not so sure anymore. I mean, I don't know if I can handle the answer."

"I know." He replied gently. "Some things God has not revealed to humans yet. But there are some things you do need to understand so you can help others." The ever-present light which seemed to be such a part of him dimly lit the area where they were standing. Beyond the perimeters of the light, however, Caree sensed evil presence's and knew demons abounded within the inky darkness.

"I do know," she interjected, moving closer to him, "that Judas Iscariot definitely did not make it to heaven."

"True," he replied. "He is in the lower regions which you will not see." Caree wondered at this revelation. She could not comprehend anything worse than what she had already experienced. He went on, "God is the author of life. Life is a precious gift from Him, and, as you know, people do not have the right to take a life whether it is their life or the life of someone else. God considers it murder."

"But," Caree quickly retorted, "murder is not the unpardonable sin."

"No, any sin can be forgiven except blasphemy against the Holy Spirit such as you just witnessed with Sasha. You see, Caree, God knows the hearts of all men and He knows why they do what they do. Sometimes people are driven to such actions by anti-depressants and mind-altering prescription drugs. God knows. But suicide is the ultimate act of selfishness, and selfishness is at the heart of sin. Besides being murder and sin, it is faithless, and without faith it is impossible to please Him!"

Caree's features were strained. Slowly she said, "Then, what you're telling me in a round-about way is that all Christians who kill themselves go to hell!"

"I did not say that nor am I at liberty to answer that question. You will know when you meet the Master someday. But in the meantime, Caree, God is calling you to warn people that only He has the right to take a life and they will stand in the judgment and answer to Him. Tell them, little handmaiden, that God is the answer for their despair and sorrow—not suicide!"

16

THE EMPTY COMPARTMENT

"Where are we going?" Caree quizzed Maschil. She wasn't sure he would give her a direct answer, but it was worth a try. Just maybe this time he would usher her up and out of the earth's terrible bowels.

"To the great gulf," he replied.

"The great gulf?" she repeated. "What is that?"

Maschil's eyes twinkled as he looked at his young charge. "Come." He took her hand and drew her into his flowing garment. As before, she knew they were traveling at a tremendous speed and thought to herself how impossible it was to even try to calculate, by human standards, how fast and how far they were going.

It was while she pondered these things that she began to experience strange sensations in her mind. One minute she felt totally alert and the next she felt oddly detached. It was almost as if she were bouncing in and out of two different worlds between the present and the distant past.

Caree tried in vain to dominate her out-of-control mental state. "I must hang on," she said aloud. "No, no, don't give in—don't! Stay awake, stay alert!"

Without warning the angel stopped. Caree found herself on her feet and was awestruck at what lay before her. It was an enormous tableland which was split into two distinct sections. She could see that one section was hot and dry. Flames and smoke covered the harsh surface. The opposite tableland was completely different, and seemed to be full of lush green plant life, and sparkling streams of crustal clear water. As fascinating as that was, what overwhelmed her the most was the enormity of the chasm itself. She had visited the Grand Canyon a few times, and each time had been thrilled beyond words, but it was nothing compared to what she now beheld. "Maschil, I..." Her voice trailed off as the slight buzzing in her head suddenly exploded into a medley of loud voices. Bright colors blazed abstractedly before her eyes and then quickly formed into costumes of Bible times. The lush, green tableland vibrated with activity. Caree was amazed to see beautiful flower gardens, palm and fruit trees, and cool, bubbling springs of water.

Unexpectedly, Caree found herself among the throngs of busy people. Even though she tried to communicate with them, they looked right through her as if she were invisible. Discouraged, she walked past a group of men who resembled the Old Testament Patriarchs. She was drawn to their conversation, and she moved silently behind the animated huddle and leaned nonchalantly against a nearby date palm.

The leader of the group spoke excitedly to those gathered around him. Somehow, she knew it was Abraham. His voice, rich and vibrant, rang with enthusiasm and life. "Jehovah promised to send a Savior through Isaac's seed." Several heads bobbed up and down in hearty agreement. "And," he continued, "when the Son of God establishes His kingdom, it shall be forever and ever!" Everyone started talking at once.

Caree saw a movement out of the corner of her eye and turned her head to see who was there. A young man about thirty years old walked briskly toward the group. She noticed his camel hair attire differed from that of the old Patriarchs. In an instant she recognized him as John the Baptist.

"Father Abraham!" the newcomer bowed reverently. "I am John, and I just arrived in this place! I bring good tidings from Jerusalem for all those who are here."

Abraham and the others crowded closer to him, eager to hear what news he had to share. Abraham smiled kindly. "Yes, Brother John, do tell us. We are anxious to receive word from above."

John looked upward for a moment, and then explained, "God chose me from before the foundation of the world to prepare the way of the Lord, just as the Prophet Isaiah, whom you know, prophesied." There was a low murmur among the men. John continued, "I baptized the people for repentance in the River Jordan. Then He came, the Lamb of God who takes away the sin of the world."[1]

The little group exploded into activity. They hugged each other happily while shouting praises to God. Caree watched with intrigue as one by one they began to joyfully leave one another and go separate directions, bearing the great news.

Before Caree could move from her vantage point, her surroundings became blurred and appeared somehow to melt into another scene. Without warning two angels flew past her and stopped in the place where Abraham, John, and the other believers had previously stood. She squinted through the misty air at their ivory visages. *I wonder what they are doing,* she thought to herself. *They seem to be carrying something or someone.* The air began to clear, and she noticed the figure of a man lying between them on the ground. An angel stood at each end of his body as if standing guard.

A lone figure appeared, walking toward the man and the angels. As he came closer Caree once again recognized Abraham. As soon as he approached the threesome, the angels rapidly rose out of sight. Caree's eyes were glued to the scene as Abraham knelt down beside the man. He tenderly lifted his head and then took him by the hand, helping him to sit up.

Caree sucked in her breath. She had never seen a person on earth in such a sad condition. By now she perceived that she was actually being shown a vision of the past and Abraham's bosom. She could tell that this poor man was covered with sores in his earthly life. His body was utterly emaciated. As she watched the scene before her, the man miraculously began to gain strength. Abraham helped him to his feet and embraced him. Tears stung Caree's eyes as she watched love in action. Abraham took off his outer garment and placed it around the poor man's shoulders.

A faint noise caused Caree to stiffen. She strained her ears, trying to determine from which direction it came. There it was again, this time louder. *It's a voice,* she thought. *It's calling someone from a great distance away.*

What followed froze her to the spot. Across the great gulf from Abraham and the new arrival, giant flames roared upward. Multiple screams rippled through the atmosphere, causing her flesh to tingle. She wanted to bolt and run, but her feet and legs refused to respond to her brain's command.

Then the screaming voice yelled out, "Father Abraham, have mercy on me, and send Lazarus, that he may dip the tip of his finger in water, and cool my tongue; for I am tormented in this flame."

Caree watched, dumbfounded, as fearless Abraham responded. "Son, remember that during your life you received your good things, and likewise Lazarus bad things; but now he is being comforted here, and you are in agony. And besides all this, between us and you there is a great chasm fixed, in order that those who wish to come over from here to you may not be able, and that none may cross over from there to us."

The agonized voice pleaded, "Then I beg you, Father, that you send him to my father's house: for I have five brothers; that he may warn them, lest they also come to this place of torment."

Abraham's voice rang with the authority of God, "They have Moses and the Prophets; let them hear them."

The man replied, "No, Father Abraham, but if someone goes to them from the dead, they will repent!"

But Abraham answered, "If they do not listen to Moses and the Prophets, neither will they be persuaded if someone rises from the dead."[2]

With that final statement Abraham placed his arm protectively around Lazarus' thin shoulders and escorted him away from the flaming inferno. Caree gazed after them until they were out of sight. She knew the scripture well relating to the rich man, who was now tormented in hell, and the poor man, Lazarus, who laid at his gate, longing to be fed the crumbs which fell from his table. Now, Lazarus was in Paradise.

Caree stood, transfixed, watching the hungry flames of hell recede into total darkness. She wanted to move, to go somewhere, but her legs remained cemented to the ground. She lost all sense of time. Was she awake or was she merely dreaming? She sensed that the scene before her had been fast-forwarded for about the space of three years. Suddenly loud proclamations interrupted her ponderings.

"Yeshua! Messiah! Jesus the Christ, the Son of the Living God!" Startled, Caree's mind snapped to attention. People were running from all directions toward the loud proclamations. Caree stretched her neck, trying to catch a glimpse of the figure who was the center of attention.

"Oh, Father Abraham!" the man shouted joyfully. "He is the Son of God! He forgave me, he forgave me!" he began to sob.

Caree saw Abraham emerge from the midst of the excited throng with a man who obviously had lived a rough life. His dark hair was shaggy and unkempt and his body bore the marks of cruel affliction. "They crucified me, the Roman soldiers, that is. I was a horrible sinner, but He was on the cross next to me. And He forgave me my sins. He said I would be with Him this day in Paradise!"[3]

Suddenly, the ground began to shake. The multitude of people looked upward as if on cue. Caree felt her legs weaken, and she swiftly moved away from her vantage point. The gigantic rock she had been leaning against split in two and crashed to the ground. The earth roared and shook violently. Caree watched as the people began to lift their arms in praise to Jehovah God.

Then she saw His form, as a Lamb that had been slain, as He descended into the midst of the multitude of worshippers. She stared, transfixed, until she knew in her spirit that three days and three nights had passed. Then, when the time was fulfilled, the earth shook with a violence she had never felt before, as a blaze of glory engulfed the rejoicing souls.

"Caree, Caree, look at me." The voice was firm, yet gentle. "Here," Maschil said as he lifted her head and helped her sit up.

Caree moaned. Where was she anyway? One minute she was traveling at incredible speed through hell and the next minute her mind went blank. She rubbed her eyes and blinked several times as if to clear her vision. Running her hands through her hair, she weakly managed to ask him what had happened.

Maschil smiled to himself. This particular assignment had been an enjoyable one for him. After all, his name meant "song of wisdom" or "giving understanding" and he had been doing his best to fulfill those titles. "Here, Caree, let me help you up." He leaned over and helped her to her feet.

Suddenly strengthened, Caree scrutinized the plateau and its great chasm. She peered into the depths of the bleak gulf and saw, far below

125

in the belly of hell, bright red, orange, and yellow flames. Cracks and fissures spewing lava and molten rock crisscrossed one another in an orgy of devastation.

"Now, little one, we will begin our journey upward!" Maschil's face beamed with joy. He opened his arms to her and she ran into them.

"Oh, praise God! Thank you! Oh, thank you! I'm leaving hell...at last!"

She felt the rush of his wings as he gathered her in his strong arms and lifted her up. She wanted to weep for all the countless souls trapped forever in this ghastly place and at the same time shout for joy at her deliverance. "Thank you, Jesus," she whispered, "that my name is written in the Lamb's Book of Life!"

They ascended rapidly and then the mighty angel stopped and hovered in midair over the great gulf. Caree looked below at the enormous expanse of land which she recognized as the place known as Abraham's bosom. Vivid memories of the dim past which seemed somehow strangely recent suddenly rushed through her mind and she cried out, "Maschil! Wait! This compartment, or side of the great chasm, is Paradise, isn't it?"

"Yes," the reply instantly came into her mind.

"But, where are Abraham and all the people? Where did they all go?" Before she could answer her own question, Maschil announced, "Jesus took them home."

17

ENLARGED BORDERS

At last, Caree whispered to herself, *I'm going home! Since it didn't take long to get here, it surely won't take long to arrive home!* She thought about Lance and mentally rehearsed how she would explain this visit to the underworld. Now she knew, without the shadow of a doubt, that hell was every bit as real as the Bible said it was.

Caree was totally preoccupied with her thoughts and just as totally unprepared for what happened next. Waves of shock and fear pulsated up and down her spine when she saw them. Too numerous to number they advanced in ranks, fitting the description given by Howard Pittman.[1]

Maschil had been holding Caree's hand as they made their way through the mysterious labyrinths of darkness. Now he quickly pulled her closer to himself and stood silent and motionless.

Caree didn't need to be told that the enemy meant business. Every evil, lewd and hate-filled eye was riveted on her and her escort. The first order of demons had forms like known animals and others had unknown forms. Murder, brutality, and sadism could literally be felt emanating from them. Their very appearance so repulsed her that she felt nauseated. Directly behind them came the second group which was more powerful. These had mixed shapes and forms such as human, half-human, and half-animal. The terrible dark countenances of these demons spoke of witchcraft, fear, self-destruction, and Satanism. Following this mixture of dreadful entities came the second most powerful of the demonic ranks. They looked like ordinary people except for their overwhelming and obvious features of greed, hate, and strife. Finally, bringing up the rear, were the tall, giant, bronze warrior demons which she had already met prior to interviewing P-I-9. Finally, out of the corner of her eye, Caree spotted the demons who were obviously responsible for sexual perversion of all kinds.

Hissing and snarling, the abominable army moved slowly toward them. Caree watched, wide-eyed with horror, as they inched their way closer. Still Maschil never moved a muscle. Sheer terror, like icy fingers of death, began numbing Caree's entire being. *Perhaps*, she thought, *I will never see daylight again, never hear the singing of a bird, never smell the sweet fragrance of a rose, never watch a blazing Montana sunset, never feel Lance's arms . . . No! She must not let that thought gain entrance into her stricken mind. No! A thousand times no!*

"There is no fear in love...perfect love casts out fear!"[2] The power and authority of her voice startled her. Love! It was love-God's love, Christ's love, Lance's love, and her love. A fire began to burn deep within her heart and surged upward, outward. It melted the tingling numbness which had threatened to paralyze her and drove out the fear.

The repulsive army wavered and appeared to become disoriented. Some of the smaller demons and those that appeared on the fringes of hell's army vanished. Encouraged, Caree shouted, "It is written, 'You are from God, little children, and have overcome them; because greater is He who is in you than he who is in the world.'"[3]

She watched as many of the demons in the first two ranks broke out fighting among themselves. Snarling and growling obscenities, they tore at one another with their claws and fangs. The last two orders of higher-ranking demons quickly moved around them, regrouped, forming a barricade between Maschil, Caree, and the fighting lesser demons.

She could hear savage outbursts and hideous screaming taking place behind the wall of towering warrior demons. *Surely,* she thought to herself, *Maschil will do something.* Suddenly she wanted to run—to hide herself from the cruel, vile, and repelling countenances of these powerful enemies. But Maschil continued to stand like a statute. It was if he weren't there at all. Caree could not remember a time in her life when she felt more overwhelmed. Somehow, she knew this was her final test in the pit of hell. And she had to pass it!

The Word, she told herself. *Use the Word! Your only weapon, your sword, is the Word!* Moistening her lips, she blurted "It is written, 'Jesus Christ, the same yesterday, today, and forever."[4]

The formidable army visibly reacted. Some curled their lips and sneered while others seemed somewhat shaken. They remained in rank, however, and Caree shot another well-aimed scripture at them.

"And being found in fashion as a man, he humbled himself, and became obedient unto death, even the death of the cross. Wherefore God hath highly exalted him, and given him a name which is above every name, that at the name of Jesus every knee should bow, of things in heaven, and things in earth, and things UNDER THE EARTH; And that every tongue should confess that Jesus Christ is Lord, to the glory of God the Father.[5]

I command you, in the Name of Jesus Christ, be gone!"

Caree watched, trembling, as most of the warrior demons quickly vanished into the murky shadows of hell. The tallest and most powerful of the warrior demons, however, remained standing, staring, steadfast.

Caree quickly glanced up at Maschil. What was he going to do? When was he going to fight back? She felt like a popped balloon and knew her strength was quickly ebbing. She clung to his arm and cried, "Oh Lord Jesus, send your warrior angels to help us. You are the Captain of the hosts of the Lord."

She looked back at the hellish warriors and gasped. With raised swords they wildly lunged. "Jesus!" she screamed, "Save us!"

Faster than lightening Maschil's arm swooped down and caught up Caree. As he lifted her high above the dazed demons, she caught sight of countless angels in pure white, swords in hand, pushing back Satan's best. What a wonderful scene it was! The hosts of the Lord, at His command, defeating the enemy!

"I know what you are about to ask me," Maschil spoke wordlessly to her spinning mind, "And you already know the answer."

"Well, it was terrifying back there! I felt all alone, even though you were standing there." She exhorted both tearfully and triumphantly. "I know, I know. It was another test. I sure hope I'm finished with this course!"

"Almost," came the reply.

"Almost? Oh, please, don't tell me there's more!"

Before he could answer the rumbling began. At first it was only a low roar, dull and far away. But soon it escalated into frightening and thunderous proportions. Caree watched speechlessly as the center of earth's cavity shook violently. Gigantic slabs of rock propelled through the air like mere pebbles. Solid rock walls split and cracked helplessly as if grasped by a colossal seizure. Smoke, steam, and ash spewed upward from newly formed craters deep within the belly of hell.

Her eyes and throat stung and her head throbbed from the reverberating din. Then, it stopped as suddenly as it had begun. Caree wiped her forehead with the back of her hand and blinked to clear her eyes. "Maschil," she began hoarsely, "what happened?"

"You have surely read," his voice was grave, "Therefore hell hath enlarged herself, and opened her mouth without measure."

"That's what happened? Just now? I mean, hell just enlarged itself?"[6]

"Yes. Come. What you will see next shall remain with you for the rest of your life. It will cause you to rise up and warn people, day and night, to repent." He picked her up and she felt the swiftness of his flight. It seemed they were descending, once again, into the lower regions of the earth. Joy and sorrow ebbed and flowed within her heart. Joy because this was her last visitation in this indescribable and eternal nightmare, and sorrow because of all the innumerable lost souls who were forever damned to remain here. And it was only because they refused to believe in the One whom God had sent; refused to repent of their pride and wickedness; refused to allow Him to be Lord of their life; in essence, refused His love and refused to love Him.

Caree heard the molten rock bubbling and hissing followed by loud screaming and wailing before Maschil pointed it out to her. She knew they were close to their destination. Finally, he stopped, positioned her close to himself on a large outcropping of rock, and waited.

"No! It can't be real...but I know it is!" Caree cried. "All those people—multitudes of people—falling into the fire, falling...Oh, God, no!" She turned away, trembling and weeping. Maschil laid his hand gently on the top of her head and slowly turned her back to the scene before them. She watched as the eternally lost, cascaded helplessly in one flowing, "river" of humanity into the hungry flames. Their cries of agony and torment were permanently etched into her mind. No, she would never—could never, forget.

As he gently lifted her to begin their upward journey, he spoke to her again, his voice low, the words measured, "Time is short—and hell has just enlarged its borders."

18

GLIMPSES OF GLORY

They ascended from hell's grotesque corridors without further incident. Caree began to relax as the oppressive atmosphere lightened. She knew she was sheltered by Maschil, whom she had come to love as well as respect. She wondered if she would miss him, but knew that even if he was out of sight, he wouldn't be far from her.

The shrieks and screams of hell's captives faded from Caree's range of hearing. All she heard was the rush of air as they rapidly rose toward the earth's surface.

"We are in the tunnel," Maschil spoke into her mind.

"You mean the one by which we entered?" she asked silently.

"Yes."

Caree's heart pounded with anticipation and excitement. Any moment now and she would be back in her own apartment. And then, Lance . . .

"Not so, Caree. We have one more little trip to make." Maschil's voice broke into her mental musings. She couldn't have been more shocked if she had been suddenly plunged into ice water.

"Wha-a-a-t? I thought..." She protested out loud.

"Trust me, little one. It is the Father's wish that you gain a glimpse of glory."

Instant shame and guilt tugged at her heart. Her ungrateful outburst served to remind her of how weak and human she was. Penitently she whispered, "Oh, Maschil! I am so sorry. I had no idea..."

"The Lord understands, Caree. He reads both hearts and minds you know." Maschil seemed to have accelerated his speed. "Caree, do not be alarmed," he warned, "but we must pass through the second heaven which is Satan's territory. You will see and hear many things, but there is no danger."

"This is the place then," Caree replied thoughtfully, "where the demonic prince of the kings of Persia withstood the messenger of God for twenty-one days until the angel, Michael, helped him."[1]

"This is true. The forces which would withstand God's messengers are many and mighty. Their goal is to hinder the work of God and the battle is fierce, but they cannot win, for God is greater."

"I remember! Pastor Howard Pittman, in his book, *Placebo*, outlined the ranks of demons and their activities in the second heaven."[2]

Before Caree finished speaking, she heard the advancing opposition. Maschil never wavered, but flew straight toward them, shouting "Blessed is the name of the Lord God Almighty who reigns forever more! All praise, glory, honor, and power belong to our God. Hallelujah!"

Caree watched as the enemy's forces halted, then scattered, making way for Maschil.

As they passed through the midst of the discomfited warriors, Caree grimaced at the loud cursing and swearing. *They certainly are unclean, the filthy things,* she thought to herself.

Suddenly Maschil veered to the right and then stopped. Caree squinted against the brilliant light, trying to determine the reason for this unexpected delay. Then she saw him and recognized him at once. The angel of light, dagger in hand withstood them. His beautiful yet utterly vile countenance radiated a false light and the surrounding atmosphere pulsated with strange and hypnotic magnetism. "So," he crooned soothingly, "we meet again."

Maschil eyed him cautiously, but remained silent. Caree, every nerve strained, wondered what she should do. It was her very nature to say something, do something. But part of her process of late was learning there were times when God did not require her to do or say anything. "Trust me, Caree." His melodious voice softly flowed into her mind like feathers floating lightly on a summer's breeze.

"You will stand aside, Lucifer." Maschil commanded calmly, not taking his eyes off the fallen angel.

God's chief opponent tipped his head mockingly. "Ha! Who do you think you are, Maschil? You know I am second in power to God. What does that make you? You're supposed to be the 'giver of wisdom and understanding,' so you tell me!" He began to laugh.

"The Lord God of all Creation has not been, nor ever will be, defeated. Neither will defeat meet those who are in His army," Maschil stated flatly.

"Oh really?" he conjectured snidely. "Have you not considered that most of earth's occupants worship ME? Or, have you forgotten to do your mathematical homework lately?" His reptilian eyes blazed with perversion and hate. "Listen, Maschil, and I'll remind you. Throughout earth's ages only a tiny bunch of fools followed Him! But billions have followed and obeyed ME!" He threw back his head and laughed savagely.

"Allow me to remind you, then," Maschil said evenly, "that only one-third of all angels rebelled with you. That leaves two-thirds who worship and serve the all-powerful, all-knowing, everywhere present, unchanging, Lord God Almighty. It is they who make up His undefeatable army.

Caree watched speechlessly as Satan's eyes narrowed into slits. His lip curled upward in a lewd sneer and a long hiss issued forth from his mouth. Finally, he spoke tersely to Maschil. "I will reign and rule. I will be exalted. I will take over the earth and its inhabitants. I will mark and seal them, and they shall worship ME!"

"Only," Maschil replied lightly "because God has allowed it—for a very short season."

Swift as lightening, Satan, dagger in hand, charged. Caree heard herself scream in her mind, but no sound escaped her parted lips.

Caree wasn't sure exactly what happened in the ensuing battle. She remembered Maschil expertly side-stepping the vicious attack while she stood, paralyzed to the spot, crying out to Jesus. It seemed like the two angels were locked for hours in the most ferocious battle she had ever witnessed. Time had no meaning, no influence in this spirit world. All she knew was that, without warning, the mighty hosts of God were on the scene. And then it was over and she was in Maschil's protective arms, shaking and crying.

"It is finished, Caree. Do not fear," he consoled her. "Come! Great things await you before you arrive safely home."

Her heart rejoiced over every word he uttered while her mind lingered on the words "arrive safely home."

"He was in heaven," Maschil instructed, regarding Satan, "accusing God's people. Your encounter with him in hell was unusual for he is normally walking to and fro over the face of the earth seeking whom he may devour or in heaven accusing the saints."[3] As he gazed at her upturned face, his golden eyes seemed to sparkle like fine jewels. His comely countenance shone with life and beauty and she suddenly felt overwhelmed and awestruck. Surely, she told herself, Abraham, Gideon, Daniel, John, Mary, and all the others who had genuine encounters with God's heavenly angels experienced what she was experiencing. *Sometimes,* she thought, *I still think I must be dreaming, but I know I'm not!*

Maschil slowly lifted his arm and silently pointed. Caree's wondering eyes followed his gaze and her heart skipped a beat. The panorama of the Universe spread before her with countless trillions of swirling galaxies and blazing suns. "The heavens declare the glory of God; And the firmament sheweth his handiwork." [4] Caree quoted reverently.

Then, as she stood transfixed, beholding the majesty of God's creation, a wondrous curtain of shimmering, colorful light began emerging from within the center of the panoramic view. Closer and closer it came until Caree found herself surrounded by glistening bands of both color and sound. Glorious, heavenly music like none she had ever heard filled her heart and soul. Like billowing waves of the ocean, she floated in a sea of glorious love, beauty, and joy. *No loud clashing here,* she thought. *No discordant, unnatural, nerve-jarring, blatant, disharmonious so-called "music" in heaven. No, a thousand times no! Everything here is clean, pure, upright, beautiful, and holy. Holy, because God is holy.*

She lost all sense of time and space, totally enraptured by the glories around her. Scenes of the heavenly city with its foundations, walls and gates of precious jewels and the golden streets passed before her eyes. Beautiful, lush gardens and parks with happy children of all ages and animals for their enjoyment thrilled her heart. Flowers of great variety and color filled the air with the sweetest and fairest of perfume. Never in her wildest dreams could she ever begin to imagine such magnificent beauty.

She was aware of countless multitudes of joyful people even though she was not allowed to actually see them individually. She knew the saints of all the ages were there in that heavenly city, walking and talking with one another in the presence of the risen Christ.

The light intensified and Caree shielded her eyes. *What a contrast to the black belly of hell! There was no way to adequately describe the light and glory of heaven,* Caree thought to herself. And the atmosphere of pure love! She felt her heart and soul softening, melting, yielding to the Holy Spirit. All thoughts and desires for earth had vanished.

"Caree, my child." The Voice of the Savior, compelling and loving, called her. She fell to her knees and bowed her head in worship.

"Lord! How I love You Lord!" she whispered. "Oh, Jesus! I am not worthy of all Your tender mercies! How majestic and wonderful You are! You alone are worthy to be worshipped and adored. Jesus, I want to stay here forever with You."

"That time shall come, Caree. I am sending you back to share my gospel with people who have never heard. And I want you to warn those who have heard."

Caree lifted her head and stared into the blinding light. Faintly, oh so faintly, she could see him. Pure love radiated from his eyes and face; his robe glowed from within; his outstretched hands bore the scars of man's hatred and pride. Overcome with love and wonder, tears poured down her cheeks as she uttered one word, "Jesus."

"Tell them, Caree," He said consolingly, "I am coming soon!"

"Come," Maschil moved toward her. "It is time." The angel's elegant robe engulfed her and she knew he was preparing to bring her back to earth. With everything inside of her, she wanted to cling to him and to push him away at the same time. Her only thought, only obsession was Jesus. Nothing, absolutely nothing on earth could compare to Him.

Suddenly she felt them swiftly descending towards the earth. She saw the demons who were yelling and cursing part as Maschil winged his way through the second heaven. Then she saw earth, resembling a wonderful blue and emerald gem, suspended in space, and amazingly upheld by Him.[5] Closer and closer, through the clouds, toward America, then Montana.

His words echoed in her mind as if spoken from a great distance, "Good bye, Caree-until later..."

19

SUNDAY MORNING

Shafts of sunlight streamed through the narrow window into Caree's bedroom. Birds chirped and warbled their melodies of cheer while an occasional dog barked in the empty street below.

Caree turned softly on her pillow and lazily opened one eye. Morning! It was morning and she was … *Home?* Her heart leapt for joy. *Home! It's true! I'm really home!*

Throwing off the quilt, she flew out of bed and ran to the window. The all-too-familiar scene lay serenely beyond her windowpane just as it had day after day. Nothing had changed except the sign in front of Brown's Bakery that hung lopsided, a victim of the previous night's storm.

Caree pushed her tousled hair away from her face and walked to the bathroom. Gazing into the oval mirror above the sink she stared at her own reflection. "It was real." She spoke in hushed tones. Then, as if trying to convince a stranger, she said aloud, "I know it was real. I was there!"

She hurriedly chose a smart two-piece powder blue suit and her best flowered print blouse. *Today, I must look my best,* she told herself. *This is going to be one of the most important days of my life!*

Once in the shower, her mind began to clear. "Oh Lord," she prayed aloud. "I know I was there; I saw it, I saw…" She stopped short. It was a word she wanted to forget, a word which represented the most vile, most reprehensible, most hideous place imaginable—a place she had tried to believe didn't exist even though the Bible confirmed it time and again.

She briskly dried herself as if trying to rub off anything that could have somehow clung to her from the abyss. But by the time she had blow-dried her hair and lightly applied makeup, she was fully awake and aware of everything she had witnessed and experienced. "Stay calm, Caree," she admonished herself. "Eat an egg, have a piece of toast, drink your coffee, and get to church on time!"

Each minute seemed like an hour to Caree. Oh, why did he have to preach this morning anyway? There was so much to tell him, so much to share. She wanted to call him, to go for a long ride in the mountains, to tell him everything that was in her heart. But Lance would already have been at the church for two hours, first praying for the service and then helping with the adult Sunday school. She walked as if in a daze to the small kitchen and mechanically made coffee, then glanced at the clock on the stove.

"Oh, no!" she mumbled, "I'll be late for church and Lance is preaching this morning! Impatient! That's the way you've always been, Caree," she scolded as she smoothed on light pink lipstick. She quickly chose pearl earrings with matching necklace and examined herself one last time in the mirror before grabbing her Bible and heading out the door. The pastel suit matched her eyes and complimented her skin, but there was much more to Caree Collins this Sunday than a young and attractive woman in love.

He was already seated on the platform when Caree slipped quietly through the double doors at the back of the small church. Caree watched his expression as she found a seat toward the rear. She hoped to catch his eye, to smile, to let him know she was with him, encouraging him. But if he noticed her, he gave no visible indication of it. Caree peered between the heads of the people, trying to read Lance's expression. He looked every bit like a clean-cut preacher all right. The casual observer would not discern the battle which raged just below the surface of Lance's confident demeanor on this warm, spring day. But Caree knew better. She had known Lance for nearly five years and she was keenly sensitive where he was concerned.

The announcements had been given and the offering taken. Lance took his position behind the pulpit. He was tall and handsome and Caree tried in vain to control her fluttering heart. She surveyed his features and felt a prick of sadness. Lance's face creased into a smile as he greeted the people, but Caree knew that an unusual seriousness lay behind his jovial appearance.

"Turn with me, if you will, to the book of Matthew 12:38 through 40." He looked directly at Caree and his eyes brightened momentarily, but then they suddenly grew somber. His gaze lingered for a moment on her smiling face as he tried to regain his composure. "Today, uh, we are going to talk about the 'sign' which Jesus said His generation would receive—that is, the sign of Jonah." Caree noticed he deliberately looked over her head as if trying not to focus on her.

Caree's trembling fingers turned the pages in her Bible to the book of Matthew. She listened to the sound of pages being turned as the congregation sought today's text. *If only they knew,* she thought to herself, *really knew how true everything is in this precious book!* She found the place and looked up at Lance. He was staring straight at her, she was sure of that, but he quickly cleared his throat and began to read.

> Then certain of the scribes and of the Pharisees answered, saying, Master, we would see a sign from thee. But he answered and said unto them, An evil and adulterous generation seeketh after a sign; and there shall no sign be given to it, but the sign of the prophet Jonas: For as Jonas was three days and three nights in the whale's belly; so shall the Son of man be three days and three nights in the heart of the earth."

Caree stared at the words in her Bible. "Three days and three nights in the heart of the earth," it read. Her mind became a jumble of thoughts and mental pictures. How well she understood the "heart of the earth!"

Lance's clear voice brought her back to the present, ". . . and here we see Jesus addressing the religious leaders of His day as basically 'evil' and 'adulterous." How would He address us today? Are we not always begging God for a 'sign'—for a miracle? What is Christ to you? Is He simply someone to whom you turn when your plans go haywire? Is He your Santa Claus in the sky and the sweet bye-and-bye? Who is He?"

Caree watched several members of the congregation squirm in their pews. She smiled to herself. *Dear Lance, he is a no-nonsense preacher. And, thank God for that! How many of those lost souls who I saw falling into hell's flames had been nominal church goers and pew warmers all their lives? For that matter,* she thought grimly, *how many of them had been ministers and evangelists?*

She turned her attention back to the pulpit and watched appreciatively as Lance verbally painted a picture of Jonah's great commission and his rebellion. *He's really fired up this morning,* Caree thought. Little did she know that Lance, after he left her apartment the evening before, went home and fell on his knees before the Lord. Lance was positive that Caree was God's choice for his life, and that she was the one he was to marry. But, lately she had nearly become a stranger to him and her behavior baffled him. There was only one solution—to pray it through! Agonizing in prayer, Lance wrestled with his own heart's desires and emotions. Finally, he groaned, "Oh Lord! You know I love Caree and want her to be my wife. You know, oh God, how desperately I need her. But Jesus, if it's not your will, if somehow I've made a mistake, then Lord, take this pain out of my heart and help me to follow you even if—even if I have to do it alone!" Tears poured down his face and in anguish he gasped out, "I'm placing her on the altar God. She is yours, not mine."

Lance waited silently in the darkness, listening for the voice of his God. Sporadic flashes of lightening illuminated the small bedroom followed by peals of thunder. But Lance knew God rarely spoke to his hurting servants through thunder and lightning, but rather through a still, small voice.

Then He came in His sovereignty, silently, with the gentleness of a dove. Peace descended upon the prostrate young man, the peace that passes all understanding. Lance knew whatever the outcome, God was with him.

"And," Lance lifted his Bible before the people, "Jonah's rebellion, borne out of pride, brought him down. Hear me, church! You and I have the same tendencies if we're honest with ourselves. Pride, pride, pride. We have to do things our way, have our way no matter what. Oh, we can obey God in the ways that don't cost us much, if anything, but just let the Lord ask you to do something that goes against your pride, and if you aren't careful, you'll do exactly the same thing Jonah did!"

Caree sat rigidly in her pew, as did the rest of the congregation. Lance was a good preacher, but she had never heard him more under the anointing than he was right now.

He replaced his Bible on the pulpit and walked to the front of the platform. "Let me paint a picture for you. The book of Jonah tells us that his rebellion affected others. Rebellion and sin always cost others, you know. We are told in the book of Jonah that his disobedience to God caused a great storm at sea which put the ship and its entire crew in jeopardy. The men on that ship knew God Almighty was against them, and who can stand, who can survive if God is against them?"

Caree watched a few heads nod in agreement. She wanted to shout, to scream at the people to believe, to repent, to press into God. Otherwise…

"…and so Jonah found himself in the belly of a great fish. You might be saying to yourself, 'Ah, God wouldn't do that to me. I'm a believer.' Let me tell you something, so was Jonah! God's word says he was a prophet, and not only that, but God spoke directly to him." He drew his handkerchief from his pocket and dabbed at his forehead.

Caree watched as one of the ushers got up and threw open some windows. The fresh, sweet air blew gently into the crowded room and she closed her eyes, silently offering thanks to God for saving her. It was so good to be home.

"Now, Jonah was a strong-willed man," Lance explained, "who always had to be in control. But, tell me, how much control do you have when you are within the confines of a fish's belly?" There was a low rumble of laughter. A faint smile played on Lance's lips. "Hell," he shouted, "is exactly that way!" A hush fell over the people. "Hell," Lance repeated, "is a place of desperation, a place of total hopelessness, of suffocating confinement, loneliness, and despair!"

You'll never know how right you are, Caree mused. She knew deep within that God, by His Spirit, had breathed this particular message into Lance's heart for this particular time. "How great you are, oh Lord," she whispered to herself.

"Jonah had lost control. Here he was in this miserable, dark, stinking hole. And brothers and sisters, if we insist on doing things our way rather than God's way, and if we think we can control our lives and our situations, then think again! Without a doubt we will meet the same disastrous end Jonah did." He looked straight at Caree and their eyes locked for a sweet, split second in time. "People," Lance looked down at the floor before continuing, "God is merciful. He is righteous in all His ways and His ways are pure. Remember what happened to this prophet? He repented! Repentance—the only way to get right with God is by way of genuine repentance. And, remember what repentance means. It means a total change of one's motivations, attitudes, and direction. It means you are lining up with God and His ways, forever forsaking your own ways. It means humbling yourself before Almighty God, asking for forgiveness and mercy. It means making Christ Lord as well as Savior, and, I might add, there are no people in heaven who don't know Christ as both!"

Caree fished in her purse for a tissue. Tears welled up in her eyes as the mighty presence of the Lord filled the small Montana chapel.

"Beloved," Lance implored, "Christ is the way for you and me to escape from a place that is by far worse than the belly of a fish, as terrible as that might be. God sent His only begotten Son to die on a cross to pay for our sins. He took our pride, rebellion, selfishness, perversion, and sin upon Himself so that through faith in His shed blood we might have everlasting life with Him!"

Lance stepped off the platform and began walking back and forth close to the people. Caree watched him with renewed respect and devotion. She wondered how she could have ever hesitated to say "yes." Everything inside of her wanted to stand up, to run to him, to throw her arms around him.

"Remember," Lance admonished, "just as Jonah did not cease to exist when swallowed by the great fish, neither do we cease to exist when we breathe our last on this earth. Our eternal destination is our choice, either heaven or hell!"

He turned and walked up the few steps to the top of the platform. "People, Jesus used this story of Jonah to illustrate that He would spend three days and three nights in hell after His crucifixion. But He went there

143

to preach the good news to the Old Testament believers who were in a separate compartment in hell called Abraham's bosom, or Paradise, and when those three days and nights were completed, He rose from the dead and set those believers free! Hallelujah!"

Caree quietly prayed, "Oh Father, grant that your Spirit move on the hearts of the people. Draw them to yourself this morning, Lord. Oh God! Don't let any who have heard this message perish!"

"Jesus is here to set you free, to deliver you, and to save you. If the Holy Spirit is moving on your heart to say 'yes' to Jesus, won't you do that today? We are going to close in prayer and then I'm going to remain at the altar to pray with all those who want to receive Christ into their lives. If you're here today and you have doubts as to your eternal destination, don't leave here without settling the matter with God. Today is the day of salvation for you."

Lance closed his Bible, bowed his head and prayed over the people. Caree watched as several people made their way toward the front. Her heart hammered against her chest like a caged bird. *If only people knew,* she thought, *how desperately important this moment is—how great the opportunity to meet with God and allow Him to save each one of them because He Himself has provided the way—the only way.*

Caree noticed two women and a teenage girl huddled together against a side wall. She could tell by the looks on their faces that they had been greatly moved by the message, but weren't sure about going forward. On impulse Caree found herself standing to her feet and moving toward the threesome. The next thing she knew, she was praying with all three of them to receive Christ. She was still rejoicing with them when she felt a hand on her shoulder. Spinning around, she found herself gazing into a pair of loving brown eyes.

"Thank you," he whispered, "for helping today at the altar, I..."

"Pastor Lance," Caree managed to stay outwardly calm, "I want you to meet Emily and her sister Susan and her daughter, Mary."

Lance shook hands with the joyful women. It seemed as if everyone were talking and laughing at the same time, and people continually approached Lance, engaging him in conversation. Finally, one by one the people drifted out the door and Lance found himself free to speak with Caree. He turned around to where he had left her but she was nowhere in sight.

He walked briskly down the aisle, through the hand carved doors and out onto the lawn. Where had she disappeared to? He fought the disappointment which began to rise in his heart. After all, he had given both himself and Caree to God. Perhaps it wasn't meant to be....

Then he saw her and his heart quickened. Her blonde hair shone in the warm rays of the sun and her blue eyes twinkled with joy. He studied her flawless complexion and soft pink lips. Even as she chatted amiably with one of the single young men, he couldn't help but notice how attractive and slender she was in her blue suit. He slowly turned and began walking toward his car. It was better to rein in his emotions now, better to leave it all with God.

"Lance?" was it her voice, or was he imagining it? "Lance, do you have a minute?" He hesitated before opening the car door. He had to get his emotions under control—he had to keep calm. But it was no use pretending. Better to get it over with now. He straightened and turned toward her. "Caree, there's something I must tell you."

"Oh good! Then we can have lunch perhaps?" Before he could protest, she added: "There's something I've got to tell you too!"

Caree's tone was urgent. Against his will, Lance found himself nodding in agreement.

20

TOGETHER

Caree was disappointed Lance hadn't offered to drive her to the Lamplighter Cafe, but perhaps he was short on time and needed his car. At any rate, they would have at least an hour and that would give her ample time to share what was on her heart.

Caree pulled her gray Nissan into a parking stall in the lot behind the restaurant. Sometimes, she thought to herself, life in a small town can be a rut, but then, city folks get into ruts too. All that really matters in this world is being right with God and having a relationship with Him through His Son.

"Hi, Caree! How are ya?" called Jim, the chef's son, as she stepped through the door. "I'm doin' the cookin' today. Dad's out of town." He turned with a wave of his hand and disappeared through the swinging doors to the kitchen. Caree located a small booth in a corner next to windows facing Main Street.

Lance should be here by now, thought Caree. *I wonder what he has to tell me.* Her mind began replaying their last visit in her apartment. *I just can't believe that was only last night. It seems like a hundred years have passed.*

The waitress brought two glasses of ice water. "I suppose Lance will be coming to join you?" Her eyebrows arched as she grinned at Carrie.

"Yes. Thanks, Marlene." Caree smiled, and then resumed her mental detective work. *Let me think, Lance was upset. Yes, that was it. He was upset because I didn't give him a definite answer. So,* she concluded, triumphant because the mystery was solved, *that is the problem. He's just moody because I didn't tell him "yes" or "no" last night.*

"Sorry to keep you waiting," Lance said as he slid into the seat across from her. Normally he would have communicated to her why he was late, but this time he said nothing and reached for the ice water. Little did she know he had pulled off the road to pray. Without a doubt he loved her, but letting her go was going to be the most difficult thing he had ever done.

Caree studied his face. He looked tired, she thought to herself. She reached across the table and touched his hand. "Lance, that was the best message I've ever heard!" He brightened momentarily, but forced himself not to return her gesture. Confused, she withdrew her hand and asked, "Are you all right? You look exhausted!"

Lance opened his mouth to speak, but just then the waitress reappeared to take their orders. "I'll have the patti-melt and a glass of iced tea, please." Caree forced herself to sound cheerful. Something was definitely wrong with Lance, and in a small town like this news traveled fast. No sense in airing their problems in front of anyone, anywhere.

"Umm, just a cup of coffee for me, Marlene," Lance said as he closed the menu.

"Are you sure that's all you want?" Caree spoke up. "How about some soup, at least or..."

"No, coffee is fine. I don't have much time." He played nervously with his spoon and avoided Caree's penetrating gaze. *She is gorgeous,* he told himself, *and you are a fool, Lance Lyons. But there is no other way.* The missionary board had given him a deadline to approve his application for Brazil and God's call was strong on his heart.

Caree suddenly felt strangely distanced from this man whom she had decided to marry and share her life with. She smiled absently at Marlene as she deftly poured coffee into Lance's cup.

"Thanks, Marlene," Lance said quietly. Once she had left the table, Lance looked at Caree. He cleared his throat, and began to speak. "Hon, uh, Caree," his eyes left hers and wandered up and down the windowsill behind Caree and finally focused on the bakery across the street. "I want to tell you..."

"Lance!" Caree interrupted, "What is happening? I mean, you are acting so strange and, I..."

"Caree, let me finish." His sharp retort brought tears to her eyes. She stared blankly at the checkered tablecloth. Her appetite had suddenly evaporated and she felt sick to her stomach.

"Oh, Caree, I'm so sorry. I don't ever want to hurt you, that's why..." his voice trailed off as he looked across the table at her downcast features. She had looked more beautiful this morning than he could ever remember her and now he had cruelly crushed her spirit much like an unappreciative child rips petals from a rose. *You're a joke,* the condemning voice hissed into his mind, *and you're a failure as a Christian and a minister.*

"Caree! Let's pray, right now!" Lance shoved his coffee aside and put his hand over Caree's which lay limply on the table. "Lord Jesus," he spoke in hushed tones, "I submit myself to you Lord and ask your forgiveness for failing just now. Lord, you know I love this woman and want the very best for her. And, Satan, I rebuke you right now in the name of Jesus Christ and notify you that I do not receive your condemnation!" He gently squeezed Caree's hand and finished, "Lord, give me the right words to say. In Jesus' name, Amen."

Tears began rolling down Caree's cheeks and she quickly removed her hand from Lance's grasp and wiped her face. *Thank goodness,* she thought, *Marlene hasn't brought lunch yet.* Caree fought the urge to run, to get away from this uncomfortable scene. Her greatest fear was rejection, and that very fear now pressed hard against her anguished heart. *If only I could go away, hide somewhere, disappear,* she silently groaned. Instead, she composed herself and glanced quickly at Lance. She tossed her head, bravely fighting against the tide of emotion which threatened to drown her. "What was it you wished to tell me, Lance?"

His soft brown eyes traced the outline of her brow, her brilliant blue eyes, her upturned nose and full lips. His heart felt like lead and his head slightly ached. *This just isn't going to work, Lord,* he silently prayed. *Why is this so difficult, why do I feel like I cannot do this? I gave her to you...* Lance was at a loss for words, and he wondered why the Holy Spirit didn't carry him through this. He felt like his nose was pressed against a concrete wall. Always, without fail, God had helped him through difficult situations, so what was the problem? Then, the sweet whisper of the Spirit spoke into his heart, "Listen."

"Lance," Caree's adamant voice broke the awkward silence after Marlene had delivered her lunch and disappeared into the kitchen, "I am sorry to take up your time today. I guess I was rather pushy and took it for granted we could see each other today after church." He took a breath and began to speak, but she continued. "This won't take long. I just want you to know God visited me last night." She watched his eyes widen. "He," her voice softened, then broke, "He answered both your prayers and mine, Lance. He sent an angel and you'll never believe what he showed me, or what I experienced! My whole life is His, like never before. So, no matter what God wants to do in your life, I know He must be first in mine."

Lance's expression changed from somber to surprise. Then incredulity and finally joy settled over his handsome features. "Praise the Lord! I want to hear about this. I mean, let's go somewhere and talk. This isn't a good place to be alone, is it?" He felt giddy, silly, and tongue-tied. No wonder the Spirit warned him to listen. His pride and lack of faith had totally blinded him this morning to the obvious change in Caree. He had been insensitive and self-centered. Convicted, he inwardly fell on his face before the Lord and repented. Why hadn't he believed that the great God whom he served would answer last night's prayer? It just seemed so sudden, so unexpected.

"I'd like that, Lance," Caree replied. "But you said you had things to do and didn't have much time. So, I'll see you when you have the time."

"Caree, I apologize for my behavior, but you see, I love you. What can I say? I do love you, you know that." His voice had risen and several customers looked their way, smiling. Everybody in town knew who Caree and this young preacher were. He blushed and lowered his voice, "Honey, I always have time for you. This is important—very important to both of us."

Caree leaned over the forgotten sandwich. "Lance, I love you too, you know that. Now, what were you going to tell me?"

He rose to his feet and signaled Marlene. "Can we have a doggie bag for Caree's lunch?" he asked.

"Certainly, Lance. I'll get it right away." She disappeared into the kitchen.

"Caree, my love," he said as he moved around the table and took her by the arm,

"Let's go out to the river. I'll explain there."

Caree tried to sort through her emotions. On the one hand, she wanted to be in control, to back off and lick her wounds; on the other hand, however, she wanted to rejoice in his affirmation of love and follow him anywhere. She quickly determined that she must humble herself, deny the flesh, and follow the Spirit. Having done that, all fear, hurt, and confusion fled. As they left the Lamplighter and headed for Lance's car, her heart rejoiced. At long last, they were together.

21

THE REMNANT

Little ripples gently lapped the sandy river bank. Delicate pale blue butterflies flitted among the multi-colored wildflowers. A refreshing breeze stirred the air and rustled the leaves of the ancient cottonwood tree. Lance and Caree reclined on a blanket spread beneath its sturdy limbs.

It was warm and Caree removed herself to shed jacket, stockings, and shoes in the car. Having done so, she rolled up the sleeves of her blouse, pulled her long hair up high on her head and fastened it into a ponytail. "There," she said aloud to no one in particular. "I feel much better now."

Lance watched approvingly as she casually walked toward him. She had already outlined much of her experience with him and he was anxious to hear her decisions. "Tell me, love," he smiled, "what conclusion did you come to?"

A far-away look came into her eyes. She gazed up through the leaves to the blue sky beyond. "Jesus is everything to me, Lance, like never before. I know now for sure that hell is real and that I must do everything in my power to preach the gospel and to make disciples."

Lance pursed his lips. This was exactly the response he had been praying for, except something was missing. And that was, of course, would she serve Christ with him or without him? "Caree," he began, "the missionary board pressed me for my decision to accept the opening in Brazil."

She looked at him for a moment and then asked, "And?"

"And, I accepted." He studied her face intently.

"That's wonderful, Lance! I know this has been what you've wanted for a long time. Praise the Lord!" She fastened her eyes on the river as it smoothly bubbled and gurgled its way around rocks and boulders. *Life, she thought, is much like a river. It just keeps going no matter what the obstacles—and one never knows what lies just around the next bend.*

Lance cleared his throat. *What is the matter with me,* he thought. *Now that Caree has totally committed herself to God, why shouldn't she want to marry me and go to Brazil? We are in love, aren't we? Well, then, why is she making this so difficult? Why doesn't she just tell me she wants to go with me? I might just as well make the jump,* he decided. He scooted closer to her, put his arm around her and looked at her for long moments. She continued to quietly gaze at the river as if it were the most fascinating thing she had ever seen. Finally in a surge of courage, he spoke. "Caree, will you marry me and will you come to Brazil, to the mission field, with me?"

Without answering, she laid her head on his shoulder for what seemed to him like an eternity. Finally, her voice choked with emotion as she answered, "Yes".

His throat went dry and his heart began to pound wildly. *Oh praise God,* he wanted to shout. *Thank you Jesus! I'm the happiest man in the whole world.* He looked down at her peaceful face, then kissed her forehead, her nose, her lips.

Later, as they strolled along the river's edge, they shared their innermost hopes and dreams. Lance pulled her to a large, flat rock. "Hey, darlin'. Let's sit here and dangle our feet in the water." She snuggled close beside him and sighed.

"Lance," she said thoughtfully, "I have a problem."

"What's that?"

"Well, the angel, you know, Maschil, he kept telling me to warn the church about different things. How can I do that when I have two strikes against me?"

"What do you mean? Two strikes against you?"

"Let's face it, strike one is I am a woman. You know how the organized church feels about women in general, and two, I don't have degrees in theology and all that."

Lance's brow furrowed into a frown and he stared through the clear water at the colored pebbles which lay on the riverbed. He lifted her chin until their lips met. "Oh Caree," he whispered. "You'll always be special to me. I, for one, am very glad you're a woman!" He chuckled, and then said, "Honey, if God is calling you, then God will open the door. All we can do is educate the people as to what the Bible really says about women and their place in the church. Most folks don't understand the culture or the times in which many passages of scripture concerning women were written. Also, many fail to understand God has mightily used women and with Him there is no difference. Secondly," he paused as if gathering his thoughts, "it isn't outlined anywhere in scripture that a Christian worker has to have 'degrees.' It does say we are to study to show ourselves approved unto God, not to men, and to rightly divide the word of truth.[1] And in First Corinthians chapter one the apostle Paul tells us that God chooses the foolish, weak, and base. God is no respecter of persons, Caree, so that should be no problem."

She wriggled her toes in the cool water and playfully splashed at his legs. "Hey! Just wait, lady, I'll get even with you one of these days." He jokingly pushed at her and then caught her lest she topple off into the river. The sound of her laughter echoed like music in his ears. He took her hand and gently helped her off the rock. "Seriously, Caree," his twinkling eyes looked deeply into Caree's, "I love the way God has given us the same mind and heart on so many matters. I need to share with you my concerns for the church, as a whole, in these last days. What do you say I take you to dinner and we can discuss this, along with," he raised her fingers to his lips and gently kissed them, "other things."

"Wonderful idea," Caree smiled. "I'm finally getting hungry. And," she squeezed his hand, "after what I witnessed in hell, there are many things which bother me too."

The Lamplighter Café, was dimly lit. Candles in the center of each table flickered invitingly and the young couple chose a small table in an obscure corner where they could be alone. After feasting on steak and trout, they relaxed, enjoying the warmth and peace of the cozy room. Lance took a deep breath and turned to face his bride-to-be. She was looking at him admiringly, her face an open book. He grinned at her.

"We have to get married rather soon," he said unexpectedly. "We have to be in Brazil in six weeks."

Caree's eyes widened. "Really? Well, that's fine with me. I don't want a big, fancy, expensive wedding, if it's all right with you. We'll just have a casual gathering of all our friends and family. My folks won't mind coming up from Texas. They were going to visit this spring anyway."

"Suits me fine!" His eyes twinkled in the candlelight as his thoughts turned to his parents. They lived in Idaho and belonged to a cult, but he knew they would attend the wedding. The idea of Lance and Caree going to Brazil wouldn't suit them too well, however. *Oh well,* he thought to himself, *when you follow Jesus you have to be willing to leave all else behind.*

"What do you think about the state of the church in these last days?" Lance said, suddenly changing the subject.

"I think," Caree said slowly, trying to collect her thoughts, "the organized church system and the church as a whole today is a far cry from what Jesus intended it to be."

"Oh?" he quizzed.

"Yes, and I'll tell you why!" She could feel the Spirit's fire welling up within. "People need a vision of hell! They need the experience I had so they would get real and stop playing church! The church is supposed to be the light and the salt of the world, not a place to entertain people or be a social center."

"Well said, Love," he nodded approvingly. "What else did you learn?"

"Most Christians don't have a clue as to the holiness of God or the depravity of man. Self-serving psychology has swept into the church and dulled people's senses and caused them to overlook or ignore Christ's repeated warnings about hell. Also, believers are basically ignorant of Satan's devices." She waited for his comments.

"I agree. The Lord has impressed on my heart that no matter where I am, whether here or in South America, I must keep it simple. I must present the Christ of the Bible, not the American, or Hollywood, version of Christ or the liberal and New Age version or any other thing, but the real Jesus. The modern, organized church has, for the most part, strayed far from obeying what Jesus called the first and great commandment and the second one also."

"You mean idolatry?" Caree interjected.

"Yes. People may confess with their mouth that God is first, but when put to the test, they don't really mean it, and especially in materialistic, covetous America. We need to return to our first love and to the love the early church had as outlined in the first four chapters of Acts! Instead of building bigger buildings, the church is to be the hand of Christ extended to the poor, the widows, which, by the way, include the single women, and the fatherless, such as the street kids." His voice rang with conviction and Caree was glad the café, was relatively empty.

Caree knew he was right and sat attentively as he continued. "Furthermore, if America is to be spared, God's people need to repent and call on His name in Spirit and truth." He picked up his spoon and began twirling it in his fingers.

"What do you mean, Lance?" Caree shifted her position and moved closer to him. She knew from her experience in hell that there were many well-intentioned people there who had attended church and considered themselves Christians, but who were flippant about sin. She wanted to hear Lance's viewpoint.

"You'd be shocked to know how much unbelief, immorality, witchcraft, and worldliness is within the church. But what really bothers me, Caree, is the church seems to be forgetting the great commission, to go into all the world and preach the gospel, make disciples, and equip the saints for ministry!"[2]

Caree studied the little flame as it bobbed up and down in its red glass on the center of the table. "I know," she declared sadly. "People just don't realize how very real Christ is and how vital it is to believe Him and obey Him. It appears all too often Christians are so busy building their little earthly kingdoms that they've forgotten about His kingdom. On top of that, Christians, like sheep, tend to follow the latest so-called 'Christian guru' rather than Christ." She sighed deeply and then thoughtfully concluded, "I guess what bothers me the most is the lack of genuine love among believers. I don't think they are even aware of it because church has become more of an entertainment center or social club than the house of God. People come in hurt, lost, and wounded, and they go out the same way."

Lance's bright eyes watched her intently. He loved it when she got "sparky." "Darling," she said softly, unaware of the appreciation in his eyes, "how can we ever 'bear one another's burdens and fulfill the law of Christ' if we are so continually self-centered, self-serving? How can we truly serve Christ if we don't serve one another? How can we offer Him that which costs us nothing? Our pathetic sacrificial acts are profane!"

Caree blinked back the tears. Lance put his arm around her, "Honey, you are a natural-born preacher. I pray we will always be like this, God first and each other second. Believe me, we are in the last days and scripture warns that there will be a falling away. All the big movements we see today to unify all denominations and beliefs are only the beginning of a world-wide sweep to establish the one-world religion. One thing I know for sure though," he ran his fingers through his hair, "Jesus is returning for a church without spot or wrinkle, and throughout the history of God's people that has always meant one thing— persecution!"

Caree remained thoughtful. *Time is short,* she silently agreed, *and we need to be redeeming the time.*

"Well," he said, taking her hand and standing to his feet, "are you ready to deny yourself, take up your cross and follow Jesus with me?" He helped her into her jacket and spoke low into her ear, "God has always had His remnant, those who choose the narrow way."

She stood facing him, eyes ablaze with holy conviction. "Yes, I'm ready." Her voice was soft but filled with resolve.

As they exited the restaurant and walked to the car, each was momentarily lost in their own thoughts. Frogs croaked secret messages into the twilight, while the evening star twinkled brightly on the horizon.

"Yes," Caree whispered into Lance's ear as he drew her close to himself, "I'm ready to be part of that remnant."

22

PEOPLE NEED TO KNOW

The muddy river slowly wound its way through the dense jungle on its voyage to the sea while lush tropical vegetation gave shelter to innumerable varieties of birds, insects, mammals, and reptiles. Primitive man was there, too, but for the most part forgotten, overlooked by a world of progress, technology, and commerce.

Caree and Lance, taking advantage of shade that the profuse jungle growth offered, reclined alongside the river's edge. "How different this river is from the one by Homedale, Montana!" exclaimed Caree. "And can you believe we've been married over a year and have been here in this village for several months?"

Lance smiled down at his wife and kissed the top of her head. "How are you feeling, Sweets?"

Caree put down the book she had been studying. It had been given to her by someone on the plane when they had flown to South America. Remembering Maschil's prediction, she was eager to uncover its secrets. She chuckled. "Ever since I told you God was blessing us with a little angel of our own, you've become a regular worry-wart!" She playfully reached up and pulled his face down toward hers. "Um, kiss me," she ordered. Lance began tickling her and then smothered her face with kisses.

Suddenly Caree knew they were not alone. She raised her eyes and met those of the chief. Lance followed her gaze and quickly sat up. "Hello, Chief," he saluted. Caree smiled at him and the stern, brown face crinkled. She knew he was laughing on the inside.

Naked, except for a light breechcloth, he stood regally, spear in hand. His adornment consisted of nature's treasure—bits of teeth, bone, feathers and leaves. Lance and Caree had worked diligently translating languages and painstakingly teaching him some basic English.

They waited in polite silence until he spoke. Finally, the chief pointed a finger at Caree. "Sis'er Caree," he began in broken English. "You say, die—after die Great Father, One who make people, uh, all—has a place?" Caree nodded. Every fiber of her being was alert, waiting, listening. The presence of the Holy Spirit descended like a mantle and she knew something eternal was about to take place.

The chief continued, his haunted, black eyes penetrating hers, "Evil spirits—we know, fathers know—many know—they have a place for people—very bad, very evil?" Caree's heart ached for these lost people who were tormented by the very gods they worshipped. She looked at the spiritual hunger and yearning registered on his weathered face.

"Yes," she respectfully replied. She drew a deep breath and waited.

The chief was in earnest now. Leaning forward on his spear he questioned, "What you call this bad place?"

Caree looked questioningly at Lance and she could tell he was silently praying. He reached over and took her hand. "It's okay, Hon. Tell him."

"Hell. Satan and evil spirits, demons, live there." She tried to read his face. She hoped he understood. "Hell," she repeated. Long moments passed in silence as Caree and the chief studied one another.

Finally, he sat on the sandy shore alongside the young couple. He sighed deeply and turned toward Caree. "Tell me again, about this God, who send Son to die as sacrifice. Chief need to know—the people need to know so not die and go to this hell place."

Palm branches stirred and rustled overhead as a warm breeze began to blow. Caree imagined she heard a voice, somehow strangely familiar, like that of an angel, whispering, "Yes, Caree, the people need to know."

NOTES

CHAPTER 1: Beckoned From Beyond
1. George Johnson and Don Tanner, The Bible And The Bermuda Triangle (Plainfield, New Jersey: Logos International: 1976), p. 90

CHAPTER 3: For of such is the Kingdom of Heaven
1. Howard Pittman, Placebo (Foxworth, Mississippi: Howard Pittman), p. 20
2. Mark 10:14.
3. Mark 9:42.

CHAPTER 4: Childless
1. Johnson and Tanner, pp. 87, 88

CHAPTER 5: Mindset
1. H. A. Baker, Visions Beyond the Veil, 12th ed., (Minneapolis, Minnesota: Osterhus Publishing House), pp. 69, 70
2. Hebrews 1:14.
3. Romans 3:11.

CHAPTER 6: The Weaker Vessel
1. Baker, excerpts, pp. 71, 72, 73

CHAPTER 7: The Light at the End of the Tunnel
1. Matthew 4:10; Isaiah 45; Luke 10:19.
2. 2 Corinthians 11:14.
3. Revelation 12:11.
4. Philippians 2:10, 11.
5. James 4:7

CHAPTER 8: Deadly Delusion
1. Isaiah 41:11b, 12.
2. Isaiah 44:26a.

CHAPTER 9: The Doctor Who Dared
1. Revelation 20:7, 8.
2. Maurice S. Rawlings, M.D., To Hell and Back, (Nashville,   Tennessee: Thomas Nelson Publishers: 1993), p.64
3. Rawlings, pp. 76, 77

CHAPTER 10: The Goal is Global
1. Rev. Lola W. Christensen, Escape from Bondage, (Auburn, Washington, The Christian Family of God Publishing House: 1984), p. 91

CHAPTER 11: Images
1. Suggested Reading:
   J. R. Church, Guardians of the Grail, (Prophecy Publications, P.O. Box 7000, Oklahoma City, Oklahoma 73153)
   Dave Hunt and T. A. McMahon, New Spirituality: A consumer's Guide to the Exploding Mystical Marketplace (Harvest House Publishers, Eugene, Oregon)
   Dave Hunt, Global Peace and the Rise of Antichrist, (Harvest House Publishers, Eugene Oregon)
   William T. Still, New World Order, The Ancient Plan of Secret Societies, (Huntington House Publishers, P. O. Box 53788, Lafayette, Louisiana 70505)
   Peter Lalonde, One World Under Anti-Christ, (Harvest House Publishers, Eugene, Oregon)
   Constance E. Cumbey, The Hidden Dangers of the Rainbow, The New Age Movement and Our Coming Age of Barbarism, (Huntington House, Inc., 1200 N. Market Street, Suite G, Shreveport, Louisiana 71107)
   A. Ralph Epperson, The New World Order, (Publius Press, 3100 South Philamena Place, Tucson, Arizona 85730)
2. 1 Peter 1:12
3. John 3:16; 1 John 4:9; 4:10; 1 John 5:12.
4. W. Bullinger, Number In Scripture, (Grand Rapids: Kregel Publications: 1894, 1967 First American Ed.)
5. Rayola Kelley and Jeannette Haley, Hidden Manna, (Mukilteo, Washington: Winepress Publishing: 1995)

CHAPTER 12: Preacher Positive
1. 2 Thessalonians 2:10, 11

CHAPTER 13: To Suffer- Here or There?
1. Oswald Chambers, My Utmost for His Highest, (New York, New York: Dodd, Mead and Company: 1935) p. 310
2. Ibid., p. 223
   3. Matthew 5:11; 10:22, 39; Romans 8:17, 28; 1 Peter 1:6,7; 2:20; 3:17;4:15, 19; 5:10; James 1:2,3; 5:10; Hebrews 10:36; 11:25; 12:5; Psalms 30:5; 66:10; 94:12; 126:6; Proverbs 17:3; Job 1:9-12; 2:3-7; John 9:1-3; 11:1-4; 15:1-5; Philippians 3:10; 2 Corinthians 1:3-7; 4:11; II:23; 12:1-10; Acts 9:16; 2 Timothy 2:12.
4. James 3:1
5. Mrs. Jo Reynolds, Seattle, Washington (as told to the author March 29, 1996).

6. James 3:1

CHAPTER 14: The Cross and the Seven Sayings of Jesus
1. "Threatened": Matthew 9:10-13; Luke 5:17; John 19:4-6.
   "Insulted": Luke 4:16-30.
   "Afraid": Matthew 13:18-23.
   "Truth Seekers: Matthew 8:5-13; John 4:1-32; March 5:27-34; Luke 19:1-10.
2. Matthew 13:18-23.
3. Luke 23:34.
4. Kelley and Haley, Hidden Manna, 1996, p. 515. Luke 9:23.
5. Matthew 16:24
6. John 14:1-3.
7. John 19:26:26, 27
8. Luke 14:26; 9:25; Philippians 3:7, 8; Galatians 6:14.
9. Matthew 27:46
10. Matthew 26:39; Psalm 23:4.
11. Job 13:15.
12. Hebrews 13:5, 6.
13. John 19:28; 6:35: 7:37; Romans 8:17; 2 Timothy 2:12.
14. Luke 9:24; 2 Timothy 2:11; Galatians 2:20; John 12:24, 32.
15. Luke 23:46; Matthew 16:21; 1 Corinthians 15:14; 2 Timothy 4:6-8; 2 Corinthians 4:8.
16. Bible Teacher Rayola Kelley, What Are You Doing With Jesus? Bible Study, 1996, (Oldtown, Idaho).

CHAPTER 15: Suicide
1. Hebrews 6
2. John 14:6

CHAPTER 16: The Empty Compartment
1. John 1:29
2. Luke 16:24-31.
3. Luke 23:43.

CHAPTER 17: Enlarged Borders
1. Pittman, Placebo, p. 20.
2. 1 John 4:18.
3. 1 John 4:4.
4. Hebrews 13:8 (KJV)
5. Philippians 2:11.
6. Isaiah 5:14.

CHAPTER 18: Glimpses of Glory
1. Daniel 10:12, 13.

2. Pittman, Placebo, pp. 16-19.
3. 1 Peter 5:8; Revelation 12:10.
4. Psalm 19:1.
5. Colossians 1:17.

CHAPTER 21: The Remnant
1. 1 Timothy 2:15.
2. Matthew 28:19, 20; Ephesians 4:12.

INTERVIEW

ON

EARTH

Book Two

1

LUMINOUS SERVANT

Bits of broken glass and gravel crunched under the soles of Luke's black leather shoes as he carefully made his way through the dark, deserted alley. The stench of rotting garbage assaulted his senses. A heavy blanket of oppression wrapped around him like a shroud. The shocking contrast of where he had been only moments before struck him like a physical blow. His mind tried in vain to cling to the fading brilliance and glory of the throne room of God. The worshipful music that had surrounded him now faded into nothingness. Only the Master's golden voice echoed through his mind, "Maschil, this is where you will go...who you will be...what you will do."

The scratching sound was muffled, but it caused him to hesitate momentarily. Quickly scanning the scene before him, his clear blue eyes finally focused on a shadowy form that dashed behind several overturned garbage cans before disappearing down a brick stairway. He sighed and quickened his step.

These assignments are never easy, Luke thought. His masculine lips curved into a half smile above his dimpled chin. His wavy golden hair seemed to reflect light from an unknown source as he abruptly halted at the end of the alley and leaned against the cold cement of an abandoned building.

It's so dark, so cold, so lonely here. He lifted his head, his eyes hungrily scanning the tops of the towering skyscrapers. Perhaps, just perhaps he could see the stars—even one star would do. But heavy clouds hanging low over the city intercepted Luke's eager gaze. Somehow in the oppressive darkness he sensed an evil, taunting

167

mockery. He shuddered and began walking briskly toward the street corner.

"Pssst—hey, feller, over here!" Luke's six-foot-two frame halted in mid-stride. "Here, here!" The voice seemed closer even though Luke couldn't find a face to match it. He finally saw him, huddled on the top step of an entrance to what appeared to be an Oriental market. The intermingled aroma of spices, rotten fish, and tobacco permeated the air. Luke's nose, which resembled that of a finely chiseled sculpture, wrinkled unceremoniously. Then he smiled.

"Wanna drink?" The words slurred together as the grizzled beggar stretched out an empty pint of whiskey toward Luke. "C'mon. Hava drink with me!" His bloodshot eyes tried to focus on Luke's kind face.

Luke knelt in front of the haggard drunk. "Who are you?" The gentleness in Luke's voice stunned the man. A look of surprise softened into sadness then abruptly hardened into anger.

"What do you care!" He spat contemptuously. "The question is," he slurred as he waved the empty bottle in the air, his eyes gleaming with malice, "who in the heh-heh-hic" he hiccupped loudly, "are you?"

"Luke." His honest answer was respectful, courteous. "Luke Obed Solomon".

The beggar drew back, shuffled his feet, and tried to straighten his tattered shirt. Luke watched him with curiosity as he set the bottle down with a resounding clink, stuck out his lower lip and folded his gnarled hands. "What kind of a name is that? Luke Obed Solomon? Are you some sort of a Jew, or what?"

"No, I'm not a Jew," he replied, raising a hand to silence the beginning of an obscene gesture. "My name means 'Luminous Servant Peace.' And, I might add, even though I am not a Jew, I am nevertheless one of the sons of God."

The foul air hung in heavy silence as the drunken man's thoughts struggled against each other. On the one hand, everything inside of him wanted to explode into a thousand angry pieces, but on the other hand, something in his broken and mutilated heart was responding to…to what? He didn't understand the sweet presence that threatened to reach beyond the tough, hard barriers he had erected to protect himself. It terrified him, and yet it wooed him. He wanted to scream, to cuss, to manifest all the anger and hate that seethed within his soul. At the same time, he wanted to melt, to weep, to surrender to the warmth that was somehow gently lapping on the shores of his barren heart. Tears found their way to the surface. All he could do was lift his head and look at this tall, handsome stranger who had somehow communicated volumes without speaking more than a few words.

Luke's penetrating eyes searched the man's soul. There was no place for him to hide, nowhere to run, and certainly no words to explain what was happening to him. An invisible yet powerful beam of light had pierced the thick darkness of his being. He began to tremble.

Luke held out his hand, his eyes warmly inviting the beggar to respond. For long moments the lonesome figure, now suddenly and strangely sober, sat as rigid as stone. Then as if some unseen force compelled him beyond his ability to resist, he slowly stretched his hand upward until his dirt-caked fingers clasped Luke's strong hand. Luke helped him to his feet and, putting his arm around his thin and stooped shoulders, silently led him down the street.

"Tim," the man whispered, his voice choking with emotion. "My name is Timothy!"

"Honoring God," Luke's voice sounded strangely like music.

"Honoring God?" Timothy questioned.

Luke laughingly explained. "Yes, your name, Timothy, means 'honoring God.'" There was a long silence. Luke led Timothy across an empty intersection, then turned and started down a broad boulevard toward the City Park.

"I ain't honored God, Luke. You've gotta know I've failed." He glanced up at Luke's face. What he saw there made his heart skip a beat. Luke's countenance was smooth as stone and pure as milk. But what held Timothy's gaze were his eyes and the set of his jaw. There was firmness, a resolution he hadn't noticed before. Luke's eyes seemed to be looking into another realm that Timothy could neither see nor comprehend. He could only later describe Luke's eyes as 'fire and light' dancing together.

"What's the matter, Luke?" His shaky voice was hoarse.

Luke's expression immediately softened. "Nothing, Timothy. I was just thinking about something."

169

"Something to do with me?" Timothy's tone was apprehensive. He didn't want to risk losing what he had found, or, more accurately, what had found him.

"Yes." They were nearing the park and Luke led Timothy in silence to a park bench under the protective arch of a giant maple tree. "Let's sit here and wait," Luke's authoritative tone amazed Timothy. He wanted to ask what they were waiting for, but somehow, he couldn't form the question.

Luke's strong voice broke the strained silence. "Yes, Timothy, I was thinking about you. I was thinking about your life." He sensed the fear that threatened to claw at Timothy's spinning mind and felt him stiffen on the hard bench next to him. "Do not fear, Timothy." At Luke's command the fear suddenly vaulted away from him. He literally felt it. Then warmth a thousand times greater than any liquor he had ever drank flowed over, in, and through his body. He nearly giggled.

Luke's lips hinted at a smile. He continued, "You were very young when you gave your life to Him." Timothy's eyes widened, but silence held him captive. "You did love Jesus." Luke reached over and gently squeezed Timothy's clenched fist. The hand relaxed. Luke continued, "You wanted to serve Him, to follow Him, to become a pastor." Timothy hung his head. Tears began to trickle down his wrinkled cheeks.

Luke's voice was compassionate. "Timothy, God understands what happened when your mother married Pastor Jones."

Timothy framed one word before lapsing into silence again. "How?" A faint breeze rustled the leaves of the great tree and playfully teased Timothy's matted, gray hair. He shuffled his feet and waited for Luke's response.

"God knows those who are His," Luke looked up. Pink and gold fingers of morning light poked into the retreating darkness of the night. He took a deep breath and looked at the man at his side. "God knows everything that man did to you. He knows why you ran away from home, and," he paused, "why you ran away from Him." Luke stood to his feet. "Look at me, Timothy. Listen to what I have to say, for the time is come." An unspoken question formed on Timothy's upturned face.

Luke smiled and Timothy subconsciously admired the even row of perfect, white teeth. His had been knocked out through a series of street fights over the years. "… and God loves you." Luke paused, letting the words sink in. "Timothy, the way back to God is to confess and repent of your sins and receive the salvation offered through the Lord Jesus Christ."

Timothy gave a curt nod. He knew that, but why was it so hard to do? His mind snapped back the answer, *pride, anger, bitterness, unforgiveness.* "I'll do it," he suddenly whispered.

"Good," Luke replied. "Then, surrender to Jesus. His arms are open wide to welcome you home."

Timothy nodded in agreement and closed his eyes. "I do love You, Lord," he whispered. "I do. Forgive me, oh my God!" A flood of fresh tears chased one another down his lowered face. "Forgive me and take my life! Make me into a new creation! Help me to forgive that man for all he did to me!" Great sobs shook his body, but when the emotional storm had passed, peace descended like a soft blanket, wrapping him up in the arms of God.

Finally, he lifted his head. He felt as if a thousand pounds had been taken off of his shoulders. Joy flooded his soul. A mysterious smile passed across Luke's features as their eyes met in silent communication.

Suddenly, Timothy visibly jumped as a woman's voice firmly said, "I will never leave you nor forsake you!" He whirled around to face a short, redheaded woman standing next to a rather chunky gentleman. The man's broad grin and twinkling eyes immediately put Timothy's doubts to rest.

"Who are you?" Timothy took a step back. . "What do you want?"

"I'm Gladys and this is my husband, Gerry." She smiled warmly and continued. "Gerry and I like to walk before dawn and pray. Well, this morning, as we strolled toward City Park, the Lord spoke to us and told us that we would be meeting one of His children right here, in this very spot!"

Timothy felt his jaw drop in surprise. Was he dreaming, or was this really happening to him? Ignoring Luke, she walked up to Timothy and extended her hand. Gingerly, he shook hands with her, then with Gerry. "I'm Tim, er, Timothy Jordan." Luke silently nodded his approval.

"We've come to welcome you to our home," explained Gerry. "That is, if you'll do us the honor of living with us. We can guarantee you a comfortable, clean room, meals and daily prayer, Bible study and fellowship. What do you say to that?"

"Oh, Lord Jesus!" He ran his fingers through his tangled hair, "Why me? Why do You love me so much?" A lump formed in his throat. "I don't have any money to pay you..." he said sorrowfully. Turning, he looked up at Luke. "What do you think Luke?" The couple stared at him quizzically.

"Uh, Mr. Jordan," Gerry began. He cleared his throat. "Timothy, who is Luke?" He glanced nervously at his wife.

Timothy began to pace in a circle. "Where did he go? He was standing right here beside me. Didn't you see him? He's over six feet tall and ... Luke, where are you?"

"Could you please tell us about Luke?" Gladys asked in hushed tones.

Timothy slumped onto the park bench. "It's like this," he began, "and I sure hope you believe me, because it's one of the strangest things that's ever happened to me." Timothy related how he had met Luke, what had transpired, and how he came to be in the park.

"This Luke fellow," Gerry asked thoughtfully, "you say he knew things about your life that no one else knows about? That his full name is Luke Obed Solomon?"

"That's right. And he disappeared, poof, vanished while you two were talking to me and ..."

Gladys and Gerry exchanged knowing looks. The broad maple leaves overhead began to sway as if performing a dance of their own choosing in the still air. Timothy whispered, "'Luminous Servant Peace.' Now I understand."

2

THE ASSIGNMENT

The sound of a thousand voices occasionally punctuated by raucous laughter reverberated through the windowless sanctuary. Several musicians and five worship leaders strolled onto the stage and positioned themselves behind the microphones. At a signal, the audience was plunged into darkness as bright lights illuminated the energetic music group. Words to a popular chorus flashed on a large overhead screen. The show was about to begin.

The worship leader stepped forward, microphone in hand. "Good morning, church!" He flashed a winning smile at the eager faces before him. Expectancy hung heavy in the air as he turned and nodded toward the keyboardist. An invisible current pulsed through the crowd as they stood as one to their feet, clapping and swaying to the beat.

The worship leader's voice soared over the thunderous music as he paced across the stage, urging the people into a hypnotic repetition of certain words and verses. The beginning choruses were upbeat, and most of the congregation jumped up and down while others waved banners. After nearly an hour of energetic clapping, stomping, shouting, and ear-splitting music, the people began to take their seats as the pastor walked across the stage and took his place behind the pulpit.

Pastor Rob, at age thirty-five, was a rising star in the mega church world. With looks that rivaled that of any Hollywood star, he had already secured a comfortable salary for himself that provided all the luxuries anyone could ask for. As he stood behind the custom-made pulpit, he pulled out a silk handkerchief and dabbed at his brow. Then he returned it into his suit pocket with a flourish and squinted through the now dimly lit room at his adoring adherents. He cleared his throat and indicated by a bowed head that it was time to pray. A hush settled over the crowded room. "Lord, You know," he began in a practiced tone, "we are your kids. In fact, we're King's kids!" A rumble of agreement rose to his listening ears. "We just love You so much, Lord. I thank You for everyone who is here in Your house this morning. Now Lord, we're gonna take the offering. I'm asking You to especially bless those who are faithful to tithe to the house of God. We know you bless, protect, and prosper those who tithe, and we know you can't bless those who do not. Oh, God," he raised his voice, "it's my sincere prayer that everyone here will be blessed today! Amen!" A chorus of responding amens echoed across the room.

The lights flickered on as several pre-appointed people walked toward the front with large baskets. Ushers took charge of dismissing rows in turn in order for the people to step forward with their money. Everyone seemed to know what was expected of them and followed it to a "T".

Several announcements were made of upcoming church outings, parties, and sporting events. There was a great deal of emphasis on a certain Prophet Black who would be speaking every night for a week and how important it was for everyone to attend because he would be expounding on God's judgments upon the nations. After this sobering announcement, six teenagers performed a skit, and while a few people laughed at it, most of them weren't too sure what it represented. Pastor Rob returned to the pulpit as the lights were once again dimmed over the audience.

The sermon that morning was gleaned from different portions of scripture as the pastor attempted to weave a picture of how wonderful it was to be a Christian. He interjected several small and humorous stories along with a few jokes, two of which leaned toward being slightly sexually suggestive. Everyone seemed to be spellbound, and totally caught up with his lengthy discourse—everyone that is, except the stranger.

No one among the enraptured congregation seemed to notice that Pastor Rob was beginning to act slightly unnerved. He glanced out of the corner of his eye at the tall, handsome man who sat with folded arms three rows from the front. The bright blue eyes seemed to stare right through him, as if he was invisible. Pastor Rob's mouth went dry and he reached for the tumbler of water perched on the side of the pulpit. His trembling hand nearly tipped it over. *Good grief!* He told himself, *Get a grip, man! Just look past this guy and pretend he isn't there.* The pastor cleared his throat, picked up the microphone and began striding across the platform. His lips curled into an involuntary smirk. *Who does that guy think he is, anyway!*

"Do you know what it means to be a child of God?" he thundered. "There's nothing, no nothing—no power in hell that can overcome you! As a matter of fact, right now, I curse anything or anybody who would dare to come against my anointing or me! I curse anything or anybody who would dare to come against this church! Ah!" He paused, as if a new thought had just struck him, "Yes, Jesus Himself said that He would build His church and that the gates of hell would not prevail against it!" He began stomping his foot, "Take that," he screamed, "Take that you devil." A thunderous applause shook the church. The pastor threw his head back and laughed. He suddenly felt powerful, invincible, and remarkably in control. Yes, everything was exactly as it should be— under his control.

He willed himself not to look in the direction of the tall stranger, but his eyes refused to obey. Finally, he glanced furtively toward the center of row three. The seat was vacant. The satisfaction of victory was short-lived as his triumph turned into a strange feeling of uneasiness that settled over him like a heavy blanket. Suddenly he felt tired, lifeless. He quickly concluded his message on the "Force" and offered a weak prayer in closing. It was over, at least for one more Sunday.

* * * * *

Luke stared absently through the canopy of jostling maple leaves. Taking time out to relax on the worn bench at City Park felt good. *These assignments are never easy.* The familiar words brought a smile to his lips. How often he had repeated these words to his God. He shifted his weight and watched as two young lovers strolled hand in hand through the thick, green grass. They definitely were in a world all their own. But so was Luke.

Luke's mind replayed the heavenly scene in vivid sight and sound. The sons of God had assembled before the throne. The angel, Maschil, was singled out. He sensed what was coming as he bowed in reverence before the Creator of the entire Universe. *Maschil, I am sending you on another mission to earth, to America,* the King of kings had said. *An angel unawares, you will take on the form of a man. Your assignment is to visit certain churches, witnessing to their faithfulness or follies. Furthermore, you will be a test and a testimony unto them, warning them of the judgment to come. The time of the end is at hand; I Am returning for a holy and overcoming church, and you will bear the message of warning and rebuke. My people are lukewarm and are perishing for lack of knowledge.*

God had even assigned Luke's name to him. He laughed to himself as he recalled the other times through the centuries he had been sent to earth. Most of the time he had come as an angel unawares to test individuals. On several other occasions he had come to rescue someone in dire circumstances. Once he had escorted a young, single, free-lance writer by the name of Caree Collins into the depths of hell so she could interview a select number of its captives, while teaching and instructing her at the same time. Yes, the Master kept him busy.

He watched two squirrels playfully chase one another as they scrambled up the trunk of the giant maple tree. Finally, he stood to his feet and with determination written on his face, he set off at a brisk walk. He had a mission to accomplish.

* * * * *

"Yes, Miss Daley?" Pastor Rob looked up momentarily as a rather breathless blonde woman in her early twenties cracked open his office door. "I'm sorry to disturb you, Pastor." Her voice sounded unusually strained. "But there's a gentleman here who says he needs to see you. Now."

Pastor Rob's eyebrows rose quizzically as he allowed his gaze to linger on the low-cut blouse his receptionist wore. "Um" he swallowed hard, "Who did you say was here?"

"A Mr. Solomon, Pastor. He …" her voice trailed off to a whisper as a tall, commanding frame filled the doorway behind her. Pastor Rob started in surprise. He had hoped to never see this stranger again. The color drained from his face, but before he could protest, the man had somehow bridged the distance and towered over him. Miss Daley had magically melted into the background and disappeared.

"Well, Mr. Solomon," the pastor drawled as he leaned back in his chair. He tapped a pen between his nervous fingers and pursed his lips. After all, this was his office, his church, and he was in control. So, why did he suddenly feel so weak, vulnerable, and intimidated? "How can I help you? You seem to be rather insistent on seeing me without an appointment."

Luke's sky blue eyes searched Pastor Rob's soul. He didn't like what he saw, but he held his peace. "I visited your church service Sunday." He continued to stand in front of the broad, oak desk.

"So, I noticed." He regretted it as soon as he said it. Why give this man any recognition? *Surely, that is what he is looking for,* Pastor Rob reasoned. *He's really a nobody who wants to be a somebody in the ministry, and I have nothing to fear.*

"Judgment begins with the house of God." Luke's words carried an authority that set the pastor's nerves on edge.

"So?" Pastor Rob reminded himself of a rebellious teenager arguing with a dominating parent. He couldn't believe he answered this way. What was the matter with him? Ordinarily, he was in control, measuring each word and tonal intonation to produce the desired effect on the hearer. He straightened in his chair, placed the pen with a deliberate and controlled motion on his desk, and smiled condescendingly. "Excuse me, Mr. Solomon, but just what are you driving at?" There! He had done it. He was in control again, or so he thought. He stared at Luke's immaculate white shirt.

"Just for the record," Luke replied, "let's go over some biblical criteria for God's church. For example, how many needy people and families receive financial aid from this church?"

Pastor Rob blushed. "What do you mean? That is, what kind of a salary do I get?" He could have kicked himself.

177

"No, Pastor. You see, I witnessed your church take in $69,853.27 in the offering." The pastor's face paled.

"How do you know—I mean, who told you the business of the church?" He swallowed hard and continued, "What business is it of yours how much money this church takes in on any given Sunday?" His voice had risen to a high-pitched whine. He was going to call a board meeting and lay down the law as soon as this intruder was out of his office.

"I'm waiting," Luke said calmly. "How many people does your church aid financially, and what does that aid total every month?"

"Well, it's like this." The pastor smiled weakly. "We have a separate amount set aside, um that is, alms, you know. Whenever there is someone who comes with a specific financial need that we deem legitimate," he paused at Luke's frown, then hurriedly added, "we assist them the best we can."

Luke raised his eyebrows. "Oh, really? How about the widow who came to you for help three weeks ago but was turned away because she had no way of repaying the church?" Pastor Rob's lips formed a thin line. He remained silent. Luke continued, "Then there was the time a blind woman came for help because her husband abused her and her children, and they had no food. You turned her away because she was not a member of your church!" Luke leaned over the desk. The pastor did not, could not move. He was held captive by Luke's penetrating eyes. "Remember this past winter when over a thousand children, and their parents, were homeless because of the economic downturn and subsequent loss of jobs in this community? Remember how families were forced to live in their cars? Remember how you and your elite board members couldn't settle on a solution to this problem because you couldn't bring yourself to ask the affluent members in your congregation to take these families into their own homes and care for them because that could be a threat to your personal income? There are more, many more cases like these, aren't there?"

Drops of sweat beaded on Pastor Rob's brow. His dark eyes narrowed to slits and his strained voice sounded like the hiss of a snake. "Lisssen to me, Mr. S-s-s-solomon! I don't know where you come from, but it's-s-s none of your business-s-s-s what I do with *my* church!"

"That's where you are wrong! You did not die for these people; Jesus Christ did. This church is His church, not yours!" Luke straightened his shoulders, took a step back, and then pointed a finger at Pastor Rob. "You are a hireling standing in danger of God's judgment. It will surely come, and on that day you will not have one excuse. As you have treated the poor and needy, is how you have treated the Lord that you claim to serve. He will recompense!"

Pastor Rob's trembling hands grasped the edge of his desk as if to balance him from falling out of his chair. His mouth opened and closed wordlessly, making him resemble a goldfish gasping for oxygen at the top of his bowl. Luke said with authority, "Your worship has no anointing. It is loud, hypnotic, vain repetition that glorifies the flesh, not God. You extract money in an unbiblical manner for your own gain. You place curses on the people who know better than to tithe to your ungodly institution. You preach heresy and unbiblical doctrines with no conviction of sin or call to repentance. No one gets truly saved in your church. You neither disciple the people nor equip saints for true ministry. You entertain them, thereby lulling them into spiritual slumber. You are a hireling and a heretic whose goal is to build your own little kingdom. You need to repent!"

Pastor Rob fell to the floor with a crash. His swivel chair slammed against the wall and tilted crazily against a mahogany cabinet filled with various trophies and plaques. He was fully conscious, but he had no control over his body. His mind spun dizzily as his brain told his arms and legs to move. He was totally helpless.

"Pastor Rob! Pastor! Are you all right?" Miss Daley knelt and lifted his head. "What happened?" She managed to help him sit up.

"Uh, I guess I'm okay," he said lamely. He struggled to his feet and straightened his rumpled shirt. "When did you come into my office?" he asked lamely.

"I heard a crash...I don't understand, Pastor," Miss Daley murmured. "Are you sure I shouldn't call 9-1-1?"

He ran his fingers through his tousled black hair. "No, I'm okay, Miss Daley. Thank you." He scanned the office as his receptionist retrieved his toppled chair. "Where is he?"

"Who?"

179

"You know. That Solomon guy?"

Miss Daley squinted at her pastor. "I think you might have bumped your head. I really think I should call for help."

"No!" Pastor Rob answered curtly. "I'm sorry, it's just that …" his voice faded.

"Um, Mr. Solomon, I mean, I never saw him at all. I thought he left when I told him you were busy today and couldn't see him."

Later that night after his wife and children were deep in sleep, Pastor Rob slipped through the double glass doors to the veranda. The serenading of frogs blended with the distant bark of a discontented dog. Occasionally, a car swooshed by on the road below his hillside home. He sighed, leaned against the railing, and looked up into the heavens. Countless twinkling stars met his searching gaze. "I may never know," he whispered to himself, "just who the real Mr. Solomon is. But I am beginning to think that I just could be in the wrong business."

3

ANGELS UNAWARES

Rising mist from the Green River captured the first rays of dawn, diffusing the soft light into various forms of movement. Somehow the gentle rhythm of each wispy figure reminded the teenage girl of floating ballroom dancers from years gone by. She sighed deeply as she curled her bare toes into the soft grass, and leaned against the mossy tree trunk. She closed her eyes and enjoyed the playful breeze as it teased her naturally curly red hair. Suzanne smiled to herself and let her imagination have its way. She saw herself being gently lifted by the handsomest of men onto the back of his prancing, white stallion. A magnificent castle loomed in the background. "Come away with me, my beloved," the prince whispered, his lips close to hers. "Yes, John," she said as her eager lips met his. It was the perfect daydream.

"Good morning!"

Startled, Suzanne jumped wide-eyed to her feet. Her shocked heart pounded wildly as she looked around the tree trunk, trying to locate whoever had spoken.

"I am so sorry." The intruder's voice was apologetic. "I certainly didn't mean to scare you."

The eighteen-year-old felt her face turn scarlet as she stared at the handsome stranger. Where was her tongue? Why didn't she say something, anything! Finally, she heard herself murmur, "Hi, um, I didn't hear your car, or are you on foot?" She suddenly felt silly, giddy, like one of the thirteen-year-olds down the road. She absently pushed at a clump of grass with her bare foot.

"Allow me to introduce myself," he said as he held out his hand. "My name is Luke. Luke Solomon."

"I'm Suzanne. Suzanne Shelby." She shook his hand quickly and looked away. *He looks an awful lot like the prince I was dreaming about,* she thought to herself. She felt thoroughly unraveled.

As if sensing her discomfort, Luke fixed his gaze on the river. The mist had vanished now. The brilliant rays of the sun sparkled on the shimmering water. He inhaled the fresh, clean air and smiled to himself. How much better it was here in the country than in the smoggy city.

"Where are you from, Mr. Solomon?" It was Suzanne's turn to interrupt his reverie.

If only you knew, he thought to himself, but replied, "The city." *Yes, I came from a City so high and deep and wide and so infinitely beautiful you could never comprehend it.*

"What are you doing way out here so early in the morning? Are you on a camping vacation or something?" She squinted up at him through the brilliant light.

His gentle smile seemed to have a calming effect on her rattled nerves. "Well, not exactly. I just wanted to enjoy God's beautiful creation for a while."

Before he could explain further, Suzanne turned toward the narrow, dirt road. "I have to go now." Then, on a strange impulse, she added, "Why don't you come to our place for breakfast? Mom makes the best breakfasts in the whole world."

"Oh, really?" he grinned broadly. "Do you always invite strangers to your home? I mean, aren't you afraid of whom you might be taking in?"

Suzanne felt the color rise to her round cheeks. "We've never had a problem before." Her voice was firm with conviction. "The Bible tells us to be hospitable, kind, considerate, and to take in strangers." Her pace quickened until she was a few feet ahead of Luke. He found himself watching her bare feet kick up little puffs of dust, and he thought of the time that the Lord of glory stooped to wash twelve pairs of dusty feet. And, one of those pairs of feet would run to shed innocent blood. He shivered involuntarily.

"Are you coming?" Suzanne called back over her shoulder.

"Are you sure your folks won't mind? After all, it's Sunday. Since you mentioned the Bible, doesn't your family attend church?"

Suzanne stopped dead in her tracks. Then she whirled and faced Luke, hands on hips, green eyes blazing with fury. Her lips were parted, but she said nothing.

"I'm sorry, Suzanne," Luke's eyes were filled with understanding and she felt herself melt under his searching gaze. It was as if he somehow knew everything about her, about her family. It was unnerving, yet strangely comforting. She began to cry.

Instantly Luke was by her side. Gently he led her to a fallen log by the side of the road and sat down beside her. She buried her face in her hands and tried in vain to stifle her sobs. But something had finally snapped deep inside her soul. It was as if everything she had bravely "stuffed" for weeks and months had finally reached the saturation point. Now it all threatened to erupt in an uncontrollable cascade of grief, despair, and sorrow.

"Suzanne," Luke's deep voice said, echoing the love of God, "the Lord knows all about it. He knows what happened."

"Then why, why," she stammered, "why did He let us go there? Why did He let me meet John and, and, ..." her voice choked with emotion.

Luke was silent for long moments before answering. "Suzanne, why don't you tell me exactly what happened?"

She lifted her head and met his calm gaze. "I guess that would be all right. I mean, I really don't know you, but for some reason, I feel like I've always known you. What I'm trying to say," she brushed at a runaway strand of hair with the back of her hand, "I feel like I can trust you. You see, I'm not sure it's okay to talk about what happened. Besides," she said as she jumped to her feet, "Mama will have breakfast nearly ready." She slowly turned back to the road. Luke followed.

He watched a baby sparrow try to balance on a thin branch. It fluttered its immature wings while its excited mother swooped and chirped. *Yes, Your eye is on the sparrow,* he mused, *and I know You are watching Suzanne and her family.*

"Okay," Suzanne interrupted his thoughts, "I'll just give you a real brief run-down of what happened." She tossed her head and smiled bravely through her tears. "We used to go to a little community church not far from our place. But then the pastor finally died and we couldn't find anyone else to come and be our pastor. Oh, some came and tried out, you know, different men mostly from the city." She wrinkled her nose. "Most of them were pretty young. You could tell they liked to preach." She gave a slight chuckle and Luke smiled at her, relieved to see no more tear-filled eyes.

"What do you mean?" he gently prodded.

"Oh, they'd get up in front of the church and strut around. They kinda reminded me of our rooster." She giggled, and then continued in a serious tone. "One of them told us if we just learned how to think positive and do something called 'positive affirmation' every day that we wouldn't be poor folks anymore. All we had to do was learn how to claim we were rich folks, even though we ain't. Seems to me that's akin to lyin'. Anyhow, he didn't get one vote, no sir. Nobody wanted the likes of him being our preacher."

Luke shook his head. He was appalled at what he had witnessed so far in the churches. It seemed like an insidious and heretical spiritual cancer was rapidly spreading throughout the organized church system. *The people are falling for Satan's wicked devices. And they refuse to be challenged, instructed, or corrected.*

Suzanne squinted up at Luke. "Did you hear what I said?" she asked quizzically.

"Oh yes, I surely did," he assured her. "I was just thinking about false prophets and such."

Suzanne's eyes widened. "We had one of those! He came every night for a whole week, shouting about damnation and repentance." She squinted at Luke's questioning gaze. "Oh, I believe in repentance. That wasn't the problem at all. It's just that this prophet was always angry and, well, um," she faltered, then found the word she was looking for, "dark! That's it—dark! In fact, his name was Prophet Black. A lot of people up and left the church. They said he was a false prophet. Others sold everything they had, gave the money to him and started following him around the world."

Luke slowly shook his head as mingled grief and anger gripped his heart.

Suzanne continued, "One after another they came and tried out, but none of them were really serious about us poor folks. They soon enough took off when they discovered we couldn't pay them a fancy salary with all kinds of benefits." She sighed. "Daddy says all we got were wolves, goats, and swine. He says that not one true, humble shepherd of the sheep came out here. So, the church is boarded up." "I'm sorry to hear that," Luke said. "I truly am."

"But that's not all." Suzanne's voice was strained. "Daddy decided we would all drive into the suburbs of the city and attend church there. We had heard about a certain church, so one Sunday we went there." She tilted her head and watched a woodpecker hammer noisily on the trunk of a tall pine tree. His antics seemed to amuse Suzanne. Luke politely waited for her to continue.

"We should've known it wasn't a good church the first time we went there. We should never have gone back!" Several moments passed before she spoke again. "You see, when we entered the church, the greeters looked us up and down in such a way that we got the message—we weren't dressed good enough. But Mama and Daddy just held their heads up and stayed for the service. They are such firm believers in Christian fellowship and churches that Daddy took us to a thrift store where we spent hours trying to find clothes and shoes that would be accepted by that church."

"That's not right," Luke retorted under his breath. "Go on, Suzanne; what happened then?"

"Well, we went for a while and the people seemed to be friendly. But that's where I met John."

Luke raised his eyebrows. "John?"

Suzanne eyes became fixed on nothing in particular and Luke knew the memory was a painful one for her. "John," she whispered. "He was the best looking and the nicest young man I've ever met. He really did love the Lord, and he felt called to be an evangelist. We hit it off right from the start, and," she faltered, "we became very good friends." Unbidden tears filled her eyes. "I have to admit," she glanced at Luke's serious countenance, "we were becoming very fond of one another ..." She lowered her eyes and focused on the dirt road.

"I understand," Luke said gently.

185

Reassured, Suzanne continued her story. This time the words seemed to tumble against one another like water gushing from a broken dam. "They were against us from the start! His family, I mean. I wasn't good enough for John because they are well off and we are poor. It didn't make any difference to his parents that we are Christians, that we love Jesus. All that mattered to them was their social standing in that— that church!" Suzanne spat out the words. "I really miss him!" She clenched her teeth, fighting back tears of frustration.

"I see. You don't see John at all then?" Luke gently prodded.

"No! His parents forbid it. We used to see each other on Sundays, across the sanctuary, but after Daddy confronted the next pastor ..." her voice trailed off to a whisper. "We're nearly to the house."

Luke nodded knowingly. "I think I know what happened." Before she could respond, he asked, "What do your folks say?"

"Well, it went like this." She wiped her eyes with her fingers, not wanting her folks to see she had been crying in front of this stranger. "The pastor of that church was promoted within the ranks to a bigger, richer church in another city. The first thing the new pastor did was campaign for money and tell the people that if they gave more to the church that God would automatically bless them. At first John thought he was wonderful, and the pastor flattered him and exalted him in front of the entire congregation—week after week! Then that awful pastor even came all the way out to our place to try to get more money out of my folks. That did it for Daddy. He pointed his finger at that pastor and let him have it!"

Luke watched a smile tug at the corners of her mouth. "I'll never forget what Daddy told him! He said, 'You are the lousiest excuse of a pastor I have ever seen in all my born days! You are nothing but a hireling that the devil sent in to fleece God's sheep just so's you can build yourself a big earthly kingdom!'" She giggled. "I've never seen a man's face get as red as that pastor's did! Then Daddy started quotin' from Jeremiah and Ezekiel—you know, real good scriptures about false shepherds such as, 'Thus saith the LORD of hosts, Hearken not unto the words of the prophets that prophesy unto you: they make you vain: they speak a vision of their own heart, and not out of the mouth of the LORD,' and 'Woe be to the shepherds ... that do feed themselves!

Should not the shepherds feed the flocks?' Then Daddy threw him out of the house, told him never to set foot on his property again, and we haven't gone to church since."

"And where does John stand now in all of this, Suzanne?"

"I ... I'm not sure. I pray for him all the time that God will give him a love for the truth so he won't be deceived and caught up in these terrible doctrines of demons!"

"Suzanne," Luke said after a moment of silence, "before we go into the house, may I tell you something?"

"Sure; what is it?"

"You need to know that what happened to you and your folks has happened to many of God's people. I know it's been a terrible experience for you and that you have gone through much turmoil, disappointment, rejection, shame, and loss." His eyes held her in their embrace. "Suzanne, God loves you and He knows everything you and your family have been through. You should never be ashamed of who you are or the fact that your family is not well-to-do. God looks at every person's heart. What matters to Him is that you love Him. You have to understand that while Christians are admonished to gather together, to worship, to pray, and to study the scriptures, that doesn't necessarily mean you have to go to a church. You see, the true Church of Jesus Christ is made up of individual members who love Him and who have given their lives to Him. Whenever you and your family fellowship or worship together, or pray or praise the Lord, then He is there in your very midst."

Suzanne's wide eyes surveyed him with interest. His skin seemed to glow with a light purer and brighter than the pool of sunshine in which they were standing. She watched him in silent fascination. Just who was this Luke Solomon anyway?

He smiled into her eyes. "Suzanne, God loves you and He knows the desires of your heart. What you and your family have experienced is foretold in the scriptures. In these last days there will be an increase in false teachers and teachings. In fact, there will be a falling away from the truth. God wants you and your folks to continue to love and worship Him in spirit and truth regardless of the church system."

Suzanne smiled at him. "I am so glad to hear that. Sometimes I feel so guilty that we don't go to church anymore. Sometimes I think we'll all go to hell because of it. But on the other hand, except for wanting to see John, none of us could really stand it anymore."

Luke laughed. To Suzanne his laughter sounded like a medley of wind chimes. He said, "Now, as for John. God is working in his heart, Suzanne, so he will be able to discern between good and evil. God wants his servant John to know the difference between the holy and the profane. In fact, isn't that him coming down the road right now?"

Suzanne gasped in disbelief. "No, it can't be," she said hoarsely. "How did you know?" Her step quickened as she began walking in the direction Luke pointed.

The dark-haired youth waved at Suzanne as he trotted up to her. "Suzanne, I miss you so much. Can we talk?"

"John, what happened?" Words suddenly failed her and she stood speechless.

"Oh, you mean my folks? It's okay, Suzanne," he took both of her hands in his. "I was confused, at first, but God showed me through His Word and by His Spirit that I had believed a lie because, well," his head dropped as he stared at his dusty shoes. "Let's face it, Suzanne; I fell because of pride. I let that hireling pastor feed my over-inflated ego. I wanted to be a somebody in the Kingdom of God, and so I turned a deaf ear to the Holy Spirit's warnings and listened to that man and my parents."

Suzanne gave a little gasp of joy. "Oh, John!"

His eyes grew somber, "Suzanne, you need to know something else. I have rededicated my life to Christ. He is truly my Lord, and this means that I have no more rights to my life, no hidden agendas. His will is all that matters."

"I understand," she said meekly.

He drew a deep breath, "God has brought the sword down between me and my family." Suzanne searched his face, but his steady gaze radiated peace and resolve. "I believe that in time all these things will work out and there will be restoration. But if I don't hold the line with them, they will never come to the knowledge of the truth."

"Yes, yes, I know," she said softly. "I understand that. You are so right about that! Now, can you join us for breakfast?" Suzanne's green eyes sparkled with joy.

"Of course, I can. I'd love to!" He reached out and took her hand.

Suzanne said, "Wait a minute. I want to introduce you to Luke Solomon."

"Who?" John's smooth brow crumpled into a question.

"Where did he go? Didn't you see him? He was right here, standing right there!" She turned and pointed toward the spot where she had left him.

"Suzanne," John questioned, "are you sure you're feeling all right? I honestly didn't see a soul."

"But, I walked all the way from the river with him. He was a stranger, and I invited him to breakfast and—" Suddenly her hand flew to her mouth. Eyes wide, she gasped, "Oh John! He must've been an angel sent from God. I knew there was something different about him, something unearthly, something heavenly! Now I know why he seemed to know everything already. He even told me about God's will for you!"

"There you are, darlin'! Breakfast is ready!" Suzanne's mother called cheerfully from the doorway. "I see you have a special guest this morning. Come on in, John. We have plenty to share."

Suzanne and John walked side by side in awed silence toward the house filled with good home cooking, and more than enough love to go around.

4

THE MESSAGE

He sat alone and motionless on the old wood bench in City Park, while deep brooding thoughts enveloped him like a shroud. Light from a full moon played hide-and-seek between drifting clouds. Overhead, giant maple leaves rustled in the spontaneous breeze. The wail of a distant siren rose and fell, momentarily interrupting the peaceful scene.

This next assignment is a tough one, Luke silently reminded himself. He glanced toward the sky. Traces of moonlight punched their way through the thick clouds that were forming into eerie, abstract shapes. Luke sighed and committed himself to obedience. *Your will be done.* He stood to his feet and turned absently toward the wharf.

The smell of brine mingled with the pungent aroma of seaweed, barnacles, and creosote hung heavily in the air. Luke turned onto a long, narrow pier. The worn wooden planks creaked in protest as he slowly made his way to the end of the dock. Fishing boats, yachts, and sailboats tugged at their moorings as they bobbed on the gentle swells. Suddenly the clouds parted as if at the moon's stern command. Brilliant light streamed to earth and joined the restless sea in its endless dance. Luke listened to the relentless waves as they swished and gurgled against the dark pilings under the groaning pier. His lips parted in praise to the One who walks on the wings of the wind, the One who once walked on the sea and who challenged His disciples to do the same. Luke's glowing face reflected more than light from a full moon; it reflected God's glory.

He leaned against the railing and focused on the symphony around him. The *tink, tink* of the sailboat rigging contrasted with the soft *thud,*

thud of the fishing boats as they fought against their bumpers. The docks replied with their own peculiar complaints as if insulted by the endless assault of both water and vessels. Somehow Luke found it to be peaceful and compelling while at the same time lonely and foreboding. Perhaps it was because he knew everything around him was temporal, including the earth and the sea. Even though it was originally created good and perfect, to be enjoyed by man and animals alike, sin had entered and forever altered the beauty, purity, and permanence of this special creation. Luke looked toward the city. In only a few short hours he would be at his first assignment for the day. It was time to leave.

The full moon silently retreated as dawn gave birth to a new day filled with heavy, gray clouds. A stiff south wind carried the promising scent of rain. Luke hurried across the wide parking lot of Faith Central Church and entered through the wide double doors just as the first drops of rain slammed against the building. He straightened his coat and tie while scanning the spacious foyer for a sign that would indicate the location of the pastor's office.

"May I help you?" a pleasant voice asked. Luke turned to see a stylish woman of about twenty-two smiling at him.

He returned her smile and answered with a question, "Yes. I need to know where I might find Pastor Williams?"

A slight frown creased her smooth complexion. "Do you have an appointment with him?"

"You might say that I do," Luke replied.

"Oh, well, um, that is ..." she stammered. She tipped her head and appraised him openly. It appeared that this tall stranger was properly dressed. He certainly looked "professional," and even though no meeting was scheduled in the appointment book in her office at that time, perhaps the pastor did have an appointment with this man. "I'll tell him you're here," she offered. "What's your name?"

"Luke Obed Solomon," he stated. "But, if you'll just be so kind as to tell me where I might find Pastor Williams, I'll ..."

"No, no," she interrupted. "Please follow me." She turned and led the way down a long hallway to a small but well-furnished office. "I need to let him know you're here," she called back over her shoulder. "It's very unusual for him to take appointments anymore, now that he conducts three services every Sunday." She reached the door and turned to admit Luke into her office where he could comfortably wait while she informed the pastor of his visit. Her eyes widened in surprise as she realized that Mr. Solomon was nowhere in sight. She was positive that she heard his footsteps dutifully following her all the way down the hallway to her office. "Well, that's strange," she said aloud to no one in particular. "Where could he have gone?"

Luke grasped the locked door to Pastor Williams' study. It gave way to his silent command with a solid *click* and he let himself in. Pastor Williams, a well-built man in his late thirties, looked up in surprise. "Who ... how," he started to ask, his voice rising in annoyance. "Who are you and how did you get in here?"

Luke extended his hand. "Luke Obed Solomon, pastor. I am glad to meet you." The pastor remained still and Luke withdrew his hand. Ignoring the pastor's second question, he continued, "I have been sent here with a message from God." He lowered himself uninvited into a plush chair facing the pastor.

Pastor William's dark eyebrows shot up in surprise. His steely gray eyes stared blankly at Luke for a moment, and then squinted suspiciously. Luke's calm appraisal was rewarded with caution and then contempt. The pastor rose from his chair and paced uncomfortably under Luke's steady gaze. He didn't like this unwelcome intruder. No, not one bit. He wanted him out of his office, but something in the back of his mind warned him to handle the situation with care. There was something different about this visitor. He didn't know what, but whatever it was, he knew it could mean trouble for him.

Trouble was something Pastor Williams wanted to avoid. He had worked hard through the years to acquire the position he currently held. He was loved, respected and, yes, even feared by most of his contemporaries. Church leaders looked up to him for advice on church growth, financial success, investments, and even political platforms. He trusted no one. His board consisted of submissive yes-men.

As for the members of his congregation, they saw him as their spiritual leader who told stories and pleasantly entertained them every Sunday. They had come to accept the fact that, because the church membership ranged into the thousands, their wonderful pastor had no time for them as individuals. Thus, they never had an opportunity to know or fellowship with him on a one-to-one basis. Rather, they were content to be herded into weekly cell groups led by under-shepherds of the pastor's choosing. In these small groups they were encouraged to discuss the pastor's messages. All conversations, ideas, complaints, and deviations from the designated outline were dutifully reported to the pastor. If anyone had personal or family problems that required attention, they were referred to one of the staff psychologists. The church ran like a well-oiled machine.

"Ah, yes," Pastor Williams said as a silent voice in his head seemed to be warning him to play along. Just listen to whatever "word" this intruder has, and then you can usher him out the door. He rubbed his pointed chin, and his thin lips curled into something resembling a lopsided smile. "So, you have a message from God, you say?"

"Yes, I do." Luke's penetrating eyes never left the pastor's face.

"Well, well. Of course, we're always happy when the Lord speaks to one of His children." His voice, condescendingly sweet, held an undercurrent of cynicism. He stepped behind his desk and sat down. "Now, Mr. Solomon," he began, lacing his fingers behind his head and nonchalantly leaning back in his swivel chair, "you must realize that any such revelations, as such, must be discerned by the board of this church as to their validity …"

"Excuse me," Luke interrupted, "are you or are you not considered a servant of the Lord? A person who has spiritual discernment?"

Insulted, the pastor's face reddened as any attempt to play along evaporated. "Mr. Solomon! Sir! Listen to me!" He leaned forward, folding his hands on the desktop. "In the first place, you had the audacity to barge into my office, unannounced. I don't know how you did it, but you have quite the nerve to pull off something like this. Secondly, you have the bad manners to flaunt yourself in front of me. You need to understand, Mr. Solomon, that I am the senior pastor of this church." His voice began to rise. "And that, Mr. Solomon, means," he said through clenched teeth as he tapped his finger on the desk, "that you must submit to my authority and the procedures established in this church."

"I see," Luke replied softly. He remained motionless, his gaze unwavering.

Pastor Williams fought to regain his composure. *What is it about this person that rouses such intense fear and anger*, he wondered. *Why can't I control my reactions? Why do I feel so terribly threatened?* He cleared his throat and forced a smile. Taking a deep breath, he asked, "Okay, uh, Luke, isn't it? Um, okay, then, why don't you tell me what church you attend, what your background is, and why you think you have a message from God?"

A strained silence hung between them for several moments. Finally, Luke said tersely, "I can assure you my background is unsullied in the sight of God. My church affiliation matters not."

Luke watched Pastor Williams' fingertips form a steeple in front of his pursed lips. The cold gray eyes squinted contemptuously at Luke, but he held his peace.

"The Lord God Almighty," Luke said with authority, "has entrusted me with this solemn warning."

"Warning?" The pastor sat erect in his chair. A sneer formed on his lips. "What do you mean, *warning!*" He spat out the words as he half rose from his seat. "We need no warning from someone who has the audacity to show up in my office without an appointment!" He pounded his desk with his fist. Before Luke could reply, he yelled, "Prophet Black has given us God's warning, and that is all the warning we need!"

Luke was instantly on his feet, his finger pointing straight at the enraged pastor. Williams lowered himself back into his chair. Icy fingers of fear began to crawl up his spine. He felt helpless, paralyzed.

"You," Luke's eyes blazed with the fire of heavenly power, "God is warning you ... repent of your idolatry, pride, and immorality else your sins will be exposed before the world. You are a hireling shepherd, Mr. Williams, one who has used God's people for your own worldly gain. You have oppressed the poor, the widows, needy children, single women, the jobless, and homeless by turning a deaf ear to their cries. The two people who fled for their lives from a satanic cult were turned away at the door to your church! You are a respecter of persons, flattering and conspiring with the rich to build your kingdom. You empty the people's pockets through curses and suck the life out of your blindly loyal followers in the name of Christ! You are an adulterer inside and out. Pornography burns within your soul, and unless you repent this very hour, it will consume you for eternity!"

Pastor Williams gasped in horror. His eyes appeared as if they would pop out of their sockets. His once haughty, guarded expression was now demonically disfigured. "You can't prove that! Get out, now!" he rasped. He tried to stand, but all strength had drained out of his shaking body. He fell back into his chair, swallowed hard, and pointed a trembling finger at the door. "Get out, I tell you!"

Luke's eyes left the man's face for the first time since he had entered the room. He stared at the floor and slowly shook his head back and forth. He had delivered the message. There was nothing else he could do.

"Lila! Lila!" Pastor Williams shouted into the speakerphone. He ignored Luke's towering figure as if he didn't exist. Eyes glued to the instrument, he yelled, "Get Fred, George, and Bernie in here on the double!"

Luke recognized the timid voice of the blonde receptionist. "Yes, Pastor. They'll be right there!"

"Good!" Pastor Williams bellowed. "I have a problem in here!" He closed his eyes for a moment, as if trying to collect himself. "You are leaving, Mr. Solomon," he said wryly. "You see ..."

The sound of a rushing wind suddenly swallowed his words. Startled, Pastor Williams lifted his eyes toward the place where Luke had been standing. All he saw, however, were Fred, George, Bernie, and a very shaken receptionist.

5

THE RESCUE

Thick fog drifted through the narrow chasm, threatening to suffocate the narrow bridge that connected two islands. If anyone familiar with the famous steel structure had dared to venture out onto the dangerous waters this moist morning, his or her only view of the bridge would have been a blurry likeness of delicate lacework. Occasionally, the muffled *hiss* of angry waves struggling against the incoming tide could be heard through the damp, gray shroud.

In the midst of this eerie scene, the angel, Maschil, surveyed with interest the solitary figure that shuffled toward the center of the elevated structure. His stooped shoulders looked as if they carried a great, invisible weight while his hands dangled limply at his sides. Once he reached a point directly above the rushing tide, he stopped, turned mechanically, and brought his arms to rest on the protective railing. For long moments he stared sightlessly into the dense mist. The man somehow reminded Maschil of a lifeless, detached robot.

Suddenly the man shifted his weight to his arms and jumped up in an attempt to catapult himself over the banister. Instead, he found himself balancing precariously on the slippery top rail. From this position he appeared to hesitate for a few moments before forcing his body to the outside of the cold railing. His fingers grasped the wire fence as his legs swung wildly in the gray mist. It was almost over. All he had to do was let go. "Yes," a sweet celestial voice hissed into his mind, "just let go. It is so easy. You will have no more problems, depression, or sorrow. Just let go. Let go. Let go-o-o-o."

Suddenly, an unexpected hot flame of indignation blazed through the weary man's spirit. "Satan ... no ..." he gasped through chattering teeth. Numb fingers began to lose their grip on the rough wire. *"Jesus!"* His tormented mind screamed in agony, *"Save me!"*

The attack was instantaneous. A thousand jumbled, deafening voices from the recesses of hell shrieked their way through the corridors of his panic-stricken soul. His tortured fingers surrendered to the stabbing pain and released their grip, flinging him into the misty air as the evil and relentless attack hammered his mind into the black abyss of unconsciousness.

Luke's strong arms lifted the limp form and carried him to one side of the empty bridge. He turned his back to the road and carefully picked his way through the underbrush, walking around the towering, dripping evergreens. His keen eyes came to rest on a soft expanse of moss. Here he gently laid the still body and sat down beside him.

Luke's compassionate gaze drifted from the damp, brown hair to the straight forehead and finely chiseled nose, neatly trimmed brown mustache and manly lips. Luke's orders had been to rescue this distraught, middle-aged human. He knew the Master had his reasons for salvaging this forlorn soul from the eternal fires of hell.

A full forty-five minutes passed before the man began to regain consciousness. A low moan escaped his slightly parted lips and his eyelids fluttered open. "What happened? Where am I?" His brown eyes stared blankly at the thick tree branches overhead. He tried to lift his head, but quickly lay back on the mossy cushion.

"You're safe. You'll be all right." Luke's deep voice was reassuring.

"Who are you?" The startled man succeeded in propping himself up on one elbow.

"Luke Obed Solomon." Luke's grin and casual manner brought a measure of comfort.

"Jewish?" He lay back down and took a deep breath.

"God is my Father," Luke said matter-of-factly. The rescued man closed his eyes as if deep in thought. Finally, he sat up.

"What happened out there ... I can't remember ..." He ran his fingers through his hair and then fixed his gaze on a collection of pinecones at the base of a tree as if by focusing on them his jumbled mind would come into order. A shaft of sunlight managed to penetrate the mist and find its way to the forest floor. The entire scene was transformed into varying hues of green and yellow. Wildflowers dotted the landscape with brilliant splashes color. A million drops of water balanced upon the delicate ferns, sparkling like diamonds in the sunlight. Suddenly the hallowed hush was interrupted by the raucous cries of seagulls fighting and diving at a newly discovered scrap of food.

"I'm not in hell," the dazed man whispered. He continued, "This isn't heaven, is it?" His questioning eyes tried to focus on Luke's solemn face.

"No," Luke said, "you are very much alive on planet earth. Remember, the place you tried to leave?"

The man pushed himself into a sitting position and slowly shook his head back and forth as if in denial of what he just heard. "I don't understand." He gave a short cough, then continued, "I mean, I could swear I remember hanging from that bridge ..." He buried his face in his hands. His square shoulders shook as great sobs tore through his body.

Luke instantly kneeled beside the tormented man. "What's your name?" Luke queried. "Talk to me!" He put his strong hands on the man's arms. Finally, the sobs subsided and the man looked searchingly into Luke's steady gaze.

"Caleb. Caleb O'Brian." He lowered his eyes for a moment and took a deep breath. "Whoever you are," he swallowed hard, "I know you saved my life out there. I don't know where you came from or how you did it, but I do know you rescued me."

Luke's blue eyes sparkled as he smiled at Caleb. "Caleb O'Brian, do you feel strong enough to sit on that log?"

"Sure, uh, well I guess so," he answered sheepishly.

Luke helped lift Caleb to his feet and braced him up as they walked a few feet to the fallen fir. The heavy fog had finally given way to the persistence of the sun. Warmth and light began to find their way through the massive trees to the living ground below. The fresh, clean air carried the scent of pine and damp earth. Birds excitedly chirped their joy to one another as they flitted from branch to branch. *It's almost as beautiful as heaven,* Luke thought to himself, *but not quite.*

Luke glanced at Caleb and knew a war was beginning to rage inside of him. The rescued man was caught in the middle of a fierce struggle between joy and sorrow, gratefulness and anger, hope and despair, between God and Satan. His fists began to clench and unclench as conflicting emotions collided. Luke watched in silence as a muscle began to twitch in Caleb's tightened jaw.

Caleb suddenly broke the silence. "I may never know how you saved me," he said gruffly, "but why … why? That's what I want to know."

"Did you not cry out to Jesus?" Luke's voice was firm.

Caleb's mouth dropped in surprise. "Well, yes, but …"

"Very well, then." Luke's reply was a dismissal and Caleb knew he would get no more answers on that subject from Luke Obed Solomon, whoever he was.

"Okay, okay," Caleb said sarcastically, "I know I should be thankful, grateful." He seemed to soften for a moment. "You know, Satan was there. I know he was. I suppose I would've ended up in hell if I had succeeded with it." He hung his head and stared at his folded hands.

You have no idea, Luke thought to himself, *what a battle I had with the enemy of your soul. No idea at all. Satan meant business and sent hordes of powerful demons to see to it you perished forever.* A replay of the rescue flashed through his mind. He wasn't the only angel involved in that conflict. The King of glory had dispatched a host of angels to assist Maschil. It had been a fierce skirmish. But, now here he was, back into his human disguise with the suicidal man. He knew the battle for his soul was far from over. "You have some decisions to make, Caleb," Luke stated firmly. "Do you understand?"

Caleb nodded his head. "I know, but you have no idea what I've been through."

"Have you suffered to the shedding of blood?" Luke asked.

"Well, no, but …" Caleb sensed his feeble arguments were no match for this kind, yet somehow intimidating individual. He sighed, threw his head back and stared up through the maze of crisscrossed branches. White, puffy clouds lazily floated in the pastel sky. Caleb wondered at the peaceful surroundings. It somehow made him feel as if everything was in harmony—except for him. It was almost as if nature's indifference mocked him. An insidious trickle of resentment began to manifest itself until he could no longer contain his anger. "Nobody gives a rip!" His voice ricocheted through the trees. Birds, startled by the outburst, flew to the safety of higher branches. "Where was God when everybody turned against me for standing for the truth?" He glanced sideways at Luke who remained erect, unmoving, and silent.

"I can't help it," Caleb's voice edged on hysteria. "I put my whole life into God's work! I knew He called me; there was never any doubt about it. I thought I had counted the cost, but nobody, nothing, not even Bible school told me about this!" He angrily stomped on an unfortunate spider. "Boy, was I ever a fool! A fool and a failure!" He moistened his lips with his tongue. "I know suicide is wrong. I used to preach against it. Thought I had all the answers when I was younger! Now look at me!"

Luke turned and appraised this frustrated man. Finally, he spoke. "Caleb! Yes, God did call you. He knew you before the foundations of the world, and He knew one day your heart would respond to His invitation to follow Him. But you never came to that place where you really understood for yourself the depths of Christ's sufferings, His rejection, loneliness, and sorrow. That is, not until lately." Something in Luke's tone made Caleb shudder. He covered his face with his hands as Luke continued. "You see, my friend, God never forsook you, but you forsook God when you tried to do everything in your own strength. You didn't leave God behind today when you tried to kill yourself. Oh no. You left Him behind months ago."

Caleb groaned an answer. This strange man who had somehow managed to rescue him from the jaws of death knew the raw truth. And the truth began to set him free.

"Caleb, you need to repent of pride and self-pity. Right now!"

Caleb knew it was true, but how would he gain the strength to go on living? How could he pick up where he had left off and continue to follow Christ when everything he had worked for was destroyed by the very people he had trusted and loved?

"Caleb," Luke's insistence was both annoying and strangely reassuring, "are you going to repent?"

Caleb heard himself say, "Yes."

"Then do it."

Caleb closed his eyes. *Don't be a fool.* The familiar voice crooned. *You know that as soon as you humble yourself you'll be at the mercy of God again. You'll never get ahead, never have anything, never succeed. Just look at how those Christians in your church treated you! After all, who do you think you are? What nerve to think you are a true servant of God!* Caleb groaned in protest. The voice continued, *You're nothing but a failure. You just tried to kill yourself, remember?*

"Resist the devil and he will flee from you!" Luke ordered. "Do it now!"

Caleb straightened. Yes, Luke was right. What a liar Satan was. With new resolve he nearly shouted, "Satan! In the Name of Jesus Christ of Nazareth I resist you! Be gone!" Then, in a penitent tone, he prayed, "Dear Lord Jesus, I confess to You my faithlessness, self-pity, and pride. Lord, please forgive me for my conceit! Forgive me for believing a lie. Forgive me, oh my God, for taking control of my life by trying to kill myself." Tears flowed down his face as he lifted his hands to heaven.

Luke raised his arms and joined in praises to the Lord Jesus Christ. It seemed to Caleb that the voices of a million angels echoed through his spiritual hearing. It was the most beautiful thing he had ever heard.

"Thank you, Luke." Caleb's eyes shone with joy.

"The Lord has never left you, Caleb," Luke replied.

"It's just that ... well, let me explain what happened. You don't mind, do you?"

"Go ahead, Caleb," Luke encouraged. "It's good for you to bring everything to the light. Let God put everything into the right perspective for you."

Caleb drew a deep breath and let it out slowly as he ran his fingers through his wavy hair. "Well, Luke," he said as his mind searched for a starting point, "I accepted Christ as my Savior when I was five years old. I always felt drawn to Him and I loved Him. The entire course of my life was set to serve Him, and I tried to stay pure though all my teenage years. Even though my parents weren't too keen on my wanting to become a pastor, my grandparents were godly and encouraged me all the way. I attended a popular Bible College not far from here, and it was during that time I began to see things that deeply disturbed me. I realize now, looking back on it, that the enemy had subtly infiltrated the school."

Caleb stood to his feet, brushed off bits of moss and leaves that clung to his clothing, and continued. "Oh, not everything was warped, but enough of it was to cause confusion. But I knew I had to stick it out if I was to become ordained." He grinned wryly at Luke. "Let's face it. Without that magical piece of paper, a man doesn't have a chance.

These days you have to be approved of men to pastor a church, whether you are called by God or not."

Their eyes locked for several moments. Caleb did not have to guess that Luke thoroughly understood the implications of his last statement. "Well, anyway, Luke," he said, "as time went on and after I had jumped through all the appropriate hoops, I became the pastor of a fast-growing church." He began to pace back and forth. "I poured my life into those people. I prayed for them, visited them, was available to them. I loved them." He suddenly stopped and faced Luke. "But the day came when God challenged me to get off the fence. I went through an intense period of fasting and prayer. God wanted to bring me higher, to commit to preach the resurrected Christ and the cross as never before. He wanted me to go against the grain, you know—to challenge the popular trend of the day. God wanted me to call the people to repentance of their self-indulgence, covetousness, complacency, pride and unbelief. He constrained me to preach the truth regardless of the consequences!"

"Yes," Luke said softly.

Caleb hesitated, but when Luke said nothing further, he continued. "So I did. I exposed the unfruitful works of darkness and that damnable heresy that gain is godliness. I came against the popular televangelists and others who preach the prosperity doctrine. I exposed the Manifest Sons of God and the New Age doctrines of positive confession, those who teach that we are little gods. I hit it hard. I even tackled the emergent church movement, and social justice! I preached against the sins of the mind, attitude, and body. I came against those sins that are an abomination to God and damn the soul."

He plucked a twig off a nearby bush and began nervously breaking it into little pieces. He glanced furtively at Luke, who remained attentive. Encouraged, Caleb proceeded with his testimony. "At first the congregation seemed to agree with my messages. But after a time, certain members began to talk behind my back. It was rumored that I was unrealistic and negative, that my messages were too hard. They accused me of bringing division among the brethren and of touching God's anointed." He looked at Luke, who was watching him intently. "Do you know what I am talking about, Luke?"

"Of course I do," Luke replied. "These are the end times when men cannot endure sound doctrine. They would rather pursue heretics and false prophets who tickle their ears."

"I guess I shouldn't be surprised at what happened," Caleb said thoughtfully, "but I became so absorbed in my own little world with my own overwhelming challenges that I fell into the same depressive trap that Elijah did. You know, I felt like I was left alone, that no one else in the whole country still stood for the true Gospel." He walked back to the fallen tree and took up his former seat beside Luke. "I felt like a drowning man. It seemed as if I was running in all directions trying to 'put out fires,' trying to educate people to the truth, trying to save a sinking ship. What made it so difficult was that my elders and board even turned against me. Then I began to wonder if everyone else was right and I was the one in the wrong. But the Word of God and the Holy Spirit confirmed over and over again that I was up against doctrines of devils and that the people loved to have it so."

Luke nodded in agreement. His strong features were grim, and Caleb could not help but notice the far-away look in his clear eyes. *I wonder who this person is*, he thought to himself.

"Tell me the rest," Luke prompted.

Caleb's shoulders slumped and he hung his head. The air suddenly seemed to become heavy, and oppressive. In a hoarse voice, he uttered one word: "Sarah."

"Yes." Luke's simple response was a statement. Caleb looked at him with raised eyebrows. *Why is it I feel that this person already knows everything I'm telling him?* Caleb mused.

"Sarah?" Luke prompted.

Caleb sighed. This was going to be the hard part. Sarah had been the final blow to his dreams of shepherding the flock of God. "She was beautiful, Luke. You wouldn't believe how very beautiful." His voice broke with emotion, and then, as if thinking aloud, he concluded, "She was my wife, my true love. She was everything a man could ever want in a wife. Everything was going so well, until she ..."

Tears began flowing down Caleb's ruggedly handsome face as her soft features filled the screen of his mind. His memory caressed her long, auburn hair, exulted in the scent of her perfume, relived a lingering kiss. Caleb's body, now aroused by vivid memories of Sarah, began to long for her touch. How could he live, now that she was gone? How could a God of love expect him to go on serving Him when He had allowed the love of his life to walk out on him?

"Caleb," Luke interrupted his thoughts, "you need to deal with this."

Caleb shot him an angry look. "Yeah, sure!" he snarled. "And just how do you expect me to do that! When I caught her with that deacon--right in our own house—"

"God never said it would be easy, Caleb," Luke admonished. "He never said it would be fun, comfortable, or predictable."

Caleb jumped to his feet and walked to the edge of the small clearing. He stood with his back to Luke, trying to regain some measure of composure.

"Listen to me, Caleb," Luke said. He was on his feet now, fighting for this soul that had just been snatched from the power of death. "You have to give Sarah to God. She belongs to Him, you know. You have no right to hold on to her, Caleb. And you must rid yourself of this anger toward both her and the deacon or God will not forgive you." He lowered his voice. "You already know these things, Caleb. Once you step over the line, once you fix your heart to obey the God you love, then He will give you all the grace, comfort, and power you need."

Caleb slowly turned and faced Luke. His features were contorted with a strange mixture of fear, anger, and sorrow.

"Trust me, Caleb, when I say that God knows, God cares, and that God means what He says. He promised to direct the steps of the righteous, and He has directed your steps. As long as you trust and obey, you will know the Father and be able to dwell in His presence and be in His will for your life. You may not always understand His will, but what human can understand the mind of the Lord?" Luke walked towards Caleb. "Only those who overcome shall stand in His holy presence. Are you ready to lay Sarah on the altar? Are you ready to let God be God? Are you ready to take up the challenge, put down your flesh, and be an overcomer regardless of the price?"

Caleb turned away. There was something about Luke that stirred him, drew him, yet made him afraid. Luke was unlike any person he had ever met before. Wasn't this the kind of confirmation and agreement that he had been looking for? Weren't Luke's words the truth? His words were like fire, and yet they were a balm for his aching soul. Hadn't he struggled for seemingly endless periods of time alone, with no one to stand with him in truth? Suddenly, it dawned on Caleb that Luke stood for everything he stood for, that Luke was not like his fickle, worldly congregation, that Luke confirmed that he had been right after all.

"I'll do it!" he stated. He whirled to face Luke. "Lord," Caleb cried, "forgive me for worshipping Sarah! Forgive me for standing in the way so she couldn't hear from you! Oh, God!" He clasped his hands and sank to his knees. "Forgive me for my hatred, vengeful spirit, and murderous heart! I forgive the deacon; oh Lord, help me to forgive that wretched, hell-bound sinner! I am just as wretched, Lord. If it wasn't for Your grace, I could be that man! Forgive me, precious Jesus!" He paused then added, "Lord, make me into an overcomer that I may stand in these latter days and declare your name through unprofaned lips. You alone are holy. Thank You, Lord God! In Jesus' name, Amen." He slowly rose from his knees and turned to Luke. Luke's countenance radiated joy. Caleb's throat constricted. He had never seen anyone glow with heaven's light like Luke did.

"Praise the Lord," Luke said reverently.

"Amen." Caleb echoed. "Luke, would you walk with me? I mean, back across that bridge? My car is on the other side, you see, and, well, I just really don't want to cross that bridge alone. You understand?"

"Yes," Luke said.

They made their way through the lush underbrush to the highway and then turned toward the narrow expanse of steel. A car swished past them, rumbled over the bridge, and disappeared around a corner on the other side. Now that the fog had lifted, Caleb's blue Chevy could be seen parked in a wide area provided for those who wished to view the breathtaking scenery. Silently they walked to the center of the bridge. Caleb stopped, leaned against the guardrail and peered over the edge. Hundreds of feet below several small boats battled against the strong current of the narrow channel. Whirlpools threatened to capture the straining craft and toss them helplessly against the steep, rock walls, but somehow each one triumphed over the massive opposition. *They look so foolish,* Caleb thought, *struggling against such overwhelming*

205

power. But they seem to enjoy the risks. He smiled to himself. *They're kind of like me, I guess. Going against the current.*

"Remember, Caleb," Luke interrupted his thoughts, "you're not fighting alone. Those on God's side may not be a majority, but God still has His people."

"I'm so glad," Caleb's voice broke as he looked over the railing for the last time.

"I know." Luke smiled warmly. "Come. I'll walk you to your car."

Caleb laughed as they neared the vehicle. "I lost my car keys when I ... you know. But I didn't lock it, and I have a key under the mat." He opened the driver's door and stooped to lift the mat. "Hey, Luke," he muttered as he tried to locate the elusive key, "how about a lift? Then you can explain to me just how you managed to rescue me in midair." He grinned triumphantly as he located the key. "I can drive you anywhere you want to ..." Caleb spun around. Luke was nowhere in sight. "Luke? Hey, where are you? Luke!" He shaded his eyes from the sun and looked toward the bridge.

What he saw made him gasp.

Hovering over the center of the bridge were three angels in a circle of light. The one in the center looked just like Luke.

Then they vanished from sight.

6

UPSTREAM

The small café was bustling with noisy activity when Luke pushed through the door. He glanced past a cluster of elderly ladies who were waiting for a table.

"Smoking or non-smoking, sir?" The middle-aged hostess smiled.

"I'm meeting a friend for lunch. And he's already here," Luke replied as he slipped past her and headed toward a booth in the back of the non-smoking section.

"Thanks for saving this place for me," Luke whispered hoarsely to the boyish young man seated opposite him. "I got caught in a major traffic jam."

"I know," his friend said with a twinkle in his eyes. He knew Luke wasn't referring to the mangle of vehicles crammed onto the freeway but rather to certain demonic forces trying to block his progress.

"What's happened so far?" Luke asked in low tones as the waitress hurriedly set two water glasses before them and left to take orders from three women seated directly behind Luke.

"You haven't missed too much, Luke," he whispered. He smiled warmly. "But I did hear one of the women say that she hasn't anything left to give."

"In other words," Luke muttered under his breath, "she's ready to give up."

"I have to leave, you know," his friend suddenly stated. "See you later." He got up and walked out the door. Luke watched him disappear behind a parked U-Haul.

"So, your friend didn't want any lunch?" The waitress stood over Luke, pencil and order tickets in hand.

"No, I guess he had something else to do," Luke replied thoughtfully.

"Well, what can I get for you then?" She was obviously feeling the pressure of too much to do in too little time.

"A large iced tea, if you will, and the salad special." Luke said politely.

"House dressing?"

"Yes, thank you." He glanced out the window to where he had last seen Pirathon. *What an angel,* Luke mused to himself. *Pirathon, Princely. How I miss seeing you lately around the glorious throne of God. I'm so glad to know you're working behind the scenes here on earth.* Luke sighed. He didn't really enjoy his role as a human; however, his radiant joy came from obeying and serving his Creator regardless of the task. It's just that this particular assignment on earth was weighing heavily on his heart. Through the centuries he had watched the struggles, trials, and tribulations of God's true people. Now, however, Luke realized that he was witnessing the fulfillment of the prophecy in 2 Thessalonians that states there shall be a falling away from the truth. Never before had he seen such widespread corruption, error, heresy, false prophets, lack of love, and subtle doctrines of demons within the church as now.

"Here's your ice tea, sir," the waitress announced cheerfully. "Your salad will be right up." He watched absently as she expertly poured coffee for a table full of businessmen.

Luke suddenly became alert as a woman's voice from the neighboring booth broke through his musings. "We've given everything to try to be faithful to what God has called us to do!"

"Well, I just don't understand, Casey, why God never allows you girls to have a break," replied an overweight woman in her late forties. "After all, God does promise blessings to his people. Are you sure you're in God's will?"

"Believe me, Georgia, we know we're in God's will. The problem is, most of the church people today are so consumed with religious works, they've forgotten the most important thing."

"Which is?" Georgia quipped.

"A relationship with Jesus, and obedience to Him!"

"You need to understand, Georgia," the third woman interjected, "that Jesus never promised His disciples that it would be easy to live for Him. But He did promise to be with us until the end of the world."

"Well, Ralene," Georgia argued, "I know scores of people who serve God, and they are rich. They are absolutely blessed." Her diamond ring flashed in a beam of sunlight streaming through the window as if to emphasize her last point. "You know what your problem is?" Without waiting for a reply, Georgia continued, "As I see it, you need a covering. You're out there running around, doing your own thing without any accountability." She sipped her latte and forced a weak smile.

The waitress set Luke's salad before him, but he had lost his appetite. He forced himself, however, to poke through the crisp lettuce looking for shrimp. The conversation behind him was becoming more heated, and he knew his moment was coming.

"Where do you find 'covering' in the Bible?" Casey asked bluntly. "There's no such thing, except for three coverings which are a woman's hair, an evil covering over nations, and, of course, the Holy Spirit."

Georgia waved her hand in the air as if swatting at a bothersome fly. "Oh, come now, Casey. Let's face it. You're never going to get anywhere in the churches if you don't have a covering to give you credibility."

Ralene shot Casey a warning glance. Casey lapsed into a reluctant silence. "Scripturally, Georgia," Ralene calmly explained, "we are required to submit to one another. Also, the Bible tells us that we do need wise counselors, which we have." She studied Georgia's taut expression before cautiously continuing. "You see, we believe that Jesus as our head is a far better covering than any fallen man."

"Um-hum," Georgia murmured. "Well, really, I do want to see your ministry succeed, but you know what Pastor Benjamin says."

"What's that?" Casey asked tersely.

"He has flatly stated that he has never seen an independent ministry make it. They need to be part of the church."

"System!" Casey whispered through clenched teeth. She thought to herself, *Man-made, man-centered, man-exalting, religious system that makes the Word of God to no effect through man-made doctrines, endless programs, and Hollywood-style entertainment.* She felt sick to her stomach.

On the other side of the booth Luke smiled to himself. If only Casey knew who was sitting next to them and that he could read her thoughts. He sipped his tea and motioned for the waitress to get him a take-home box for his salad.

Georgia finished her latte, dabbed at her mouth with a napkin, and reached for her purse. "I have to go, girls," she said, trying to sound apologetic. "Lunch is on me."

"No, that's not necessary," Ralene objected.

"No, no, I'm the one who suggested we meet today. I know you can't afford it." She opened her purse and drew out a ten-dollar bill. "Here's a little something for your coffers. It was an interesting conversation, girls. I hope you have a good day." As she began to slip out of the booth, her purse flipped over and emptied its contents on the seat. Casey briefly saw two crisp one hundred-dollar bills before Georgia snatched them up. "See you Sunday," she cheerfully called over her shoulder as she hastened to the cash register.

Ralene and Casey sat in silence for long moments, each absorbed in her own somber thoughts. "Excuse me, ladies." The compelling male voice stunned them out of their cheerless musings.

"Oh, hello," Casey forced a smile at the tall, handsome stranger. She recognized him as the person who had been seated next to them.

"Pardon me, but I conclude you are Christians?"

Ralene's face reddened slightly as she nodded. She had hoped that no one in the café could hear their conversation with Georgia. She felt uncomfortable and wished she was home watching the cooking channel. At least the activities on that channel ended in something being brought forth to a state of completion.

Casey, as usual, was delighted to see a friendly face. Georgia's comments and her own arguments left her feeling uneasy, guilty, and depleted. There were times when she hoped the earth would just open up and swallow her, but she replied, "Yes, we're Christians. Are you?"

"I am a believer, you might say, and I know the only true God." Luke's blue eyes seemed to communicate a secret joy.

Impulsively, Casey gestured toward the now-empty seat Georgia had vacated. "Won't you sit down and tell us about yourself?"

Ralene sighed. All she really wanted was to leave the scene of their latest put-down and go home. She forced a tired smile. "Hi," she said wearily. "My name is Ralene, and this is Casey."

Luke lowered his tall frame into the narrow booth. "My name is Luke Solomon," he said warmly. "I can see you are two battle-weary soldiers." He watched tears form in Casey's gray eyes as Ralene stared into her teacup.

Luke studied the two friends. They appeared to be about the same age, but he knew that Casey was twelve years older than the forty-year-old Ralene. Ralene's short, neat brown hair framed her soft features and flawless complexion. Her full lips were pressed together, betraying her obvious displeasure with the departed Georgia. Casey's face was also an open book. Her gray-blue eyes were filled with emotion beneath her reddish-brown bangs. The tip of her nose was a light tint of pink, betraying her efforts to appear as if she was far from tears.

After long moments, Ralene looked up. "It's that obvious?" She said quietly.

"I do understand," Luke's voice was compassionate. "God has many weary soldiers these days. Let's face it: The devil knows his time is short, and he is attacking God's people with great wrath."

"True," Casey stated. "God put us together twelve years ago in ministry. We both have the same love for Jesus and the truth and the desire to see people win." Luke nodded in agreement. She felt the tension drain from her body. It was such a relief to meet someone who didn't put her down for sharing her heart.

Ralene intently studied Luke's face. Casey knew she was trying to discern his spirit. As for herself, Casey had never felt so comfortable with someone she had just met in her entire life.

"More coffee?" the waitress smiled at Ralene. "Oh, yes please." She held out her cup. Casey relaxed. If Ralene was going to enjoy another cup of coffee, then they would be staying a while longer. She smiled at Luke.

"Would you mind telling me about your ministry?" Luke asked with genuine interest. Casey and Ralene looked at each other. How long had it been since anyone had truly been interested in them as individuals?

Even though they were kept busy helping Christians in crises, most of the time no one cared to enter in with them.

"It's a long story," Ralene said slowly. "We met over twelve years ago and became good friends. Even though there are multitudes of people in this world, only God can put together a team." Luke nodded in agreement. Ralene continued, "A lot of major things happened in our lives, and eventually God actually threw us into the same boat. We've been paddling upstream ever since."

"I gather you two don't go with the flow then?" Luke asked. His tone was serious, and both Ralene and Casey somehow knew he was not leading them on so that he could eventually reprimand them.

"No, we don't!" Casey interjected.

"Mr. Solomon," Ralene explained, "Jesus didn't go with the flow, so why should His followers?"

The conversation was simple, and yet, inexplicably, unspoken volumes were understood by all three of them.

"I see you've moved, sir." The waitress's abrupt manner demanded a quick reply.

"Yes ... is that all right with you?" Luke's warm smile and mannerly demeanor had their effect.

"Why, of course it is. Would you like more iced tea?"

"Yes, I surely would," Luke responded. He quickly handed her a crisp five-dollar bill for her trouble. Her face exploded into a warm, ear-to-ear grin. She turned and headed at a brisk pace for the kitchen.

Casey watched appreciatively and smiled to herself. *It's amazing*, she thought, *what a little kindness and recognition can do.*

Before anyone offered more conversation, the waitress reappeared with a pitcher of tea, which she set in the middle of the table. "Anything else for you folks? We have some fresh baked pies today."

"No, thank you, not today anyway," Casey said wistfully. She and Ralene couldn't afford to indulge in luxuries such as pie. She glanced at Luke. His clear, blue eyes were fastened upon her, and she squirmed uncomfortably. Why did she feel like he knew everything about her? It was definitely one of the most thrilling, yet strangely unnerving, experiences she had ever had. She heard herself address him in her most matter-of-fact tone. "Mr. Solomon ..."

He held up a hand. "Please, Casey, if you don't mind, just call me Luke." He smiled knowingly at her, and she felt herself begin to unravel.

"I'm s-sorry, Luke," she faltered, "I was just wondering, I mean, where did you come from, and do you attend church somewhere, and..."

Casey's interrogation was suddenly swallowed up by Luke's laughter. His eyes twinkled with amusement. After a few moments, however, he grew strangely somber. Both Casey and Ralene watched him keenly.

"Ladies, may I assure you that I have an honorable source and, secondly, that I have attended countless churches over the years." Suddenly both ladies knew this intriguing stranger would never divulge details about his life. They fell into a contemplative silence. Just who was he anyway?

"Don't worry about me," Luke said amiably. "What's important here is you two and what you've been through and where you are today."

"Why?" Casey blurted impulsively. She felt tears sting her eyes. "Nobody much cares where we've been, what we've suffered, where we are, or where we're going for that matter!"

"God does." Luke's words pierced her aching heart. It was true; she knew it was. But why was it so hard to believe?

"Casey's been through a lot," Ralene finally spoke up. "You see, Luke," she cupped her hands around her coffee mug and leaned forward, "when God put our little ministry together, He knew we were both terribly naïve and inexperienced where the church system is concerned." She paused for a moment. Luke silently nodded. She continued, "Oh, we knew our God, knew His Word, and were gifted in many ways. But, nevertheless, we knew it wouldn't be an easy road. However, we just weren't at all prepared for the incredible obstacles we would face in the church! Not the world, understand, but the church! And by that, I mean the church system, not the Body of Christ!"

"I understand," Luke commented softly.

Encouraged, Ralene continued, "You see, we simply want to be the salt and the light in this dark world. We want to see souls saved. We want to see Christians discipled to be followers of Jesus Christ. We want to see people win! We want to redeem the time!"

"That's right!" Casey interjected.

Ralene took a sip of coffee, looked at Luke to ascertain if he was truly interested, then, satisfied that he was, she continued. "Naturally, we felt the first place we should go was the local church. To make a very long story short, we have been through more battles with so-called Christians than we ever have with the unsaved of this world. Some churches have allowed us to work among their ranks, but when they saw that the people were being set free and sending others our way, they quickly shut us down. The church system can't afford competition. It wants to be served rather than to serve!" Her voice had risen and several people glanced their way.

"All we want to do," Casey explained, "is to carry out the work Jesus gave us to do. But, when you're a woman, and a single one at that, and you don't have a big income, a big name, and a big following, people don't take you seriously."

Luke sipped his tea in silence while his solemn eyes communicated deep understanding. Both Casey and Ralene believed with all their hearts that God had sent someone who understood their plight to listen, even if for only an hour.

Ralene smiled faintly. "Luke, you see, we do realize that God has called us to go through this process so that we can have the honor of experiencing the sufferings of Christ in a deeper way. It's just that we get so sick and tired of banging our heads against a wall!"

Finally, Luke spoke. "You have spoken truth, both of you. God knows your faithfulness, hard work, distresses, disappointments, and times of discouragement. He knows Satan has repeatedly tempted you to compromise, but He also knows you have steadfastly refused to do so. Ladies," Luke's twinkling eyes hinted at an undisclosed secret, "you will reap if you do not faint. Your labor is not in vain in the Lord. It matters not that you are not known among men, that your ministry and service to the King of kings is not among the giants of Christendom today. Jesus is concerned over one lost sheep, and it is a great honor to be entrusted with even one of His sheep. Therefore, do not fret or question where God has placed you. God knows your needs, and He will be faithful to meet them. You are precious in His eyes. What matters to Him is your love for Him above all else."

214

Casey's eyes were wide. How did this man, whom neither one of them had ever laid eyes on before, know where they had been? One thing was sure: Just being able to talk freely about their challenges and disappointments without being put down was uplifting and refreshing. She felt renewed hope and energy flooding her soul.

Neither Casey nor Ralene could explain afterward exactly what happened next. All they could remember were the blood-curdling screams of the victim in the parking lot adjacent to the café.

Luke automatically stood to his feet while Casey and Ralene nearly tripped over each other getting out of the booth and to the door. Shoving through a group of startled on-lookers they raced to the side of a woman who lay dazed on the pavement. Quickly kneeling beside her, they helped her sit up. Blood oozed down the side of her head, and one blackened eye was beginning to swell.

"What happened? Tell us what happened!" Casey urged. Someone offered a towel to Ralene, and she pressed it gently on the woman's head wound.

"He," gasped the shaken woman, "my husband ... hit me ... knocked me down ..." She began to cry.

"Is she okay?" asked one of the concerned on-lookers.

"Yes, I'm okay," answered the woman as she struggled to her feet. Not willing to get involved, people began shuffling away in different directions, some returning to the café while others got into their cars and pulled out of the parking lot.

"Where is he?" Ralene held the woman's arm, making sure she was strong enough to stand on her own.

"Gone. He's gone. He ... he left me. I'll not see him again, I'm sure," she stammered.

A look passed between Casey and Ralene. "What's your name?" Ralene asked.

"Nita. Nita Perez."

"Come with us," Casey said, "into the café. We'll get you something to eat and drink."

"Oh, but I couldn't do that!" exclaimed Nita. "I mean, you are both so kind and all, but ..."

"Do you have family or friends around here?" asked Ralene.

215

"No. You see, we were traveling through ..." she swayed, and Ralene tightened her grip.

"Let's go inside," Ralene said as she began moving toward the café.

Once inside, both Casey and Ralene furtively glanced around for Luke. "Where is Luke?" Casey finally asked.

"I have no idea," Ralene answered. "I thought he followed us out of the café."

"Well, the booth is still empty, so let's sit there again and wait to see if he shows up," suggested Casey. Disappointment registered on her face.

Ralene and Casey made their way to the empty booth, where they insisted Nita order whatever she wanted from the menu. Reluctantly, she accepted their offer and then, at their gentle urging, revealed the story of her life. It was obvious she was alone, broke, and totally at the mercy of strangers. In unspoken agreement, Casey and Ralene knew God had entrusted Nita to them to be cared for and ministered to even though they had never experienced the luxury of financial security themselves. Somehow God always brought in just enough.

Casey stared out the window at the lengthening shadows. What an eventful day this had turned out to be! Hadn't she and Ralene, just that morning, felt as if God had no more use for them; that there was nothing left for them to do?

Suddenly she caught a movement out of the corner of her eye. How could it be? But, yes! There it was again, among the shadows from the tall shrubs that bordered the parking lot. It had to be him, but she couldn't be positively sure. She blinked, straining her eyes, forcing them to see into the darkening hedges.

Ralene abruptly stopped talking to Nita as if she, too, was suddenly aware of an unseen presence. She stared in the direction Casey was looking. At the same instant, they saw him. A smiling Luke Solomon, standing tall and dignified, lifted his hand in salute. Then, they watched in amazement as his image blended into the dusky shadows and completely disappeared.

"Whoever he is," Ralene said in a hushed tone, "I have the distinct feeling we'll be seeing him again."

7

THE ANOINTING

"The show is about to begin," the announcer spoke into the microphone as the camera crew flashed a shot of the enormous stadium in the background. A faint smirk tugged at the corners of his mouth as he fought to maintain an unbiased pose. He squinted into the camera. "As you can see, ladies and gentlemen, once again the 19,000-seat auditorium is packed in anticipation of the, uh, well-known evangelist from the Middle East."

Unseen by human eyes, Maschil stood on a grassy slope that extended to the edge of one of the massive parking lots that surrounded the impressive structure. He gazed with sympathetic interest as several groups of hopeful parents, pushing their invalid children in wheelchairs, entered the building. Next a chartered bus wheezed to a stop near a side entrance. Maschil watched the bus driver as he stepped down and then turned to offer a helping hand to the elderly people who carefully negotiated their way down the bus's steps to solid footing on the pavement.

The sooty gray shadow came without warning. Maschil stood motionless, waiting. Finally, it spoke. "They'll get their money's worth, you know." Maschil stood unflinchingly and ignored the evil presence. "Let's face it, Maschil," it sneered, "all of them love my doctrine." Deep, rumbling laughter forced its way into Maschil's mind. It echoed and shimmered down his body, reverberating and exploding until it finally crackled into silence. He maintained his silence.

"Oh, Luke Obed Solomon," the voice taunted, "are you going to join the crowds? Are you going to watch what I can do through one little puffed-up heretic?" The hideous laughter repeated itself.

Maschil slowly turned and looked into the glowing green eyes of the hooded figure. "You could do nothing if God Almighty did not allow it." He watched the reptilian eyes narrow into slits. It took a step backward and stood rigidly as if waiting for orders to unleash the sword hanging at its side.

"Go ahead, Baalis," Maschil said steadily, "you already know what the outcome will be." He turned back to the scene below. The parking lot was full to capacity, and most of the people had entered the coliseum. It was time for Luke to make his appearance.

"I'll be back, Maschil," hissed Baalis. "We are not through with you yet." Maschil's alert eyes watched the powerful warrior demon withdraw to his destination within the crowded building. Spontaneously the arena burst with thunderous applause. The show had begun.

"I want you all to know," shouted the medium-built, dark-haired speaker, "that I had a new revelation!" The noise was deafening as the crowd clapped, cheered, and whistled. "And," he screamed into the microphone, "do you know why I have a new revelation?"

The 19,000 enthusiastic devotees shouted, "Why?"

Luke squirmed uncomfortably in the narrow seat. At least he was sitting on the aisle. That way there was only one adoring worshipper seated next to him. Luke noticed that the woman was probably in her early thirties and obviously too caught up with the hype to notice his quiet demeanor.

"I'll tell you why! Are you ready?" Again, the crowd erupted into a frenzy of shouting and clapping. Everything inside of Luke wanted to run, to escape from this hell on earth. What was wrong with these people anyway? Couldn't they see that they were being systematically brainwashed? That all this imposter was after was their money while Satan stole their souls?

The speaker was pacing the floor, working up his audience. Luke smirked. The guy was a pro, no doubt about it.

"I, uh, I get revelations because I have a greater anointing!" He screamed into the microphone. "Did you hear me?" He began to wave his hand, pointing at different people in the sea of adoring faces. They screamed, yelled, whistled, and clapped. Luke literally gripped the armrests on either side of his chair. He had to sit this out. It was part of the assignment.

The speaker began to do a little jig. The crowd members went wild. Finally, after they quieted down again, he lowered his voice as if to impart a great secret to a select few. "The anointing, oh, oh," he took out a handkerchief and wiped his forehead, "uh, the anointing, it comes when you have Kingdom order!" The spellbound audience yelled their agreement. Luke wondered if there was a single person there who knew what "Kingdom order" even meant.

"You see, I mean, I can't even begin to tell you," he swaggered a little as if to intimate that he was getting "drunk in the Spirit," "I have never, ever felt the power of the Spirit more in my entire ministry!" He staggered around the platform until the crowd quieted. "Let me tell you people!" His voice rose to a shout, "If you don't learn how to tear down the traditions," he stomped his foot three times, "yes, if you don't learn how to tear down those traditional strongholds, then you ain't never, and I mean never, ever goin' to go on to the next dimension of anointing!"

Luke gritted his teeth as the woman next to him jumped to her feet, clapping and applauding with everyone else. *This is horrible! What can I possibly do here? Lord?*

The word that came was clear: *Wait.*

"Excuse me," said the woman next to him, "but are you alright? I mean, you don't seem to be feeling very well. Do you want me to pray for you?" Genuine concern reflected in her soft blue eyes.

"Oh, no thanks. I'm fine, thank you." He smiled. The last thing he wanted was for some deluded soul to lay hands on him. She kept staring at him, puzzled. "It's just that I have never actually sat in a meeting quite like this one before," he explained. "I mean, there are so many people here."

She smiled understandingly. "Oh, I see. Well, after you've heard Brother Rhodocus a few times you get used to his style. You'll see! This is real revival!" She turned back to face the stage.

Half an hour passed as Brother Rhodocus praised himself for his great anointing, his long periods of fasting, his great ministry, and his

219

superior knowledge. After that, he spent another thirty minutes deriding the churches, pastors, and others who did not agree with his new revelations. "I say," he shrieked, "to hell with them all! These doubters, God will get 'em!" The crowd now resembled a well-heeled wolf pack on the trail of blood. Finally, the time came to take the offering.

"Okay," ranted Brother Rhodocus as he paced the platform, "now I want you all to understand that this is God's ministry!" More cheering. "Good!" shouted Rhodocus. "Now that we have that established in everyone's mind, let me tell you that if you withhold from this ministry, you are withholding from God! And, if you withhold from God, you will be cursed! Cursed! Do you hear me, people? Cursed! I say it again, cursed! Now," he panted, "I want every one of you, dear brothers and sisters, every one of you, do you hear me? Every one of you to be blessed! I want you to have the fullness of God!"

He threw his arms back and the crowd roared their agreement. Luke watched out of the corner of his eye as dozens of trained ushers seemed to materialize out of thin air. Each had a large bucket for the offering. Contemporary music began to play. Soon the crowd began clapping and stomping to the rock beat. As the offering swept toward the back rows, those in the front began jumping to their feet, dancing and swaying to the music.

"Excuse me." It was the girl next to Luke again. "Aren't you getting it yet?" She patted his arm and then withdrew her hand, embarrassed. "I mean, doesn't anything move you?" Her eyes searched his face.

"Yes," he answered. He fell silent, and waited.

Finally, she spoke up. "Okay, like what?"

"Reverence."

She bit her lip. "Reverence?" Her eyes were troubled.

"Yes."

She jerked her head around and stared at the stage, but her eyes were focused on something that had been jarred in her memory.

Suddenly the music stopped. The girl sullenly watched Brother Rhodocus step to the edge of the platform. His penetrating eyes scanned the audience as if he were searching for something, for someone. "I can feel it!" His abrupt scream caused many people to jump visibly in their seats. "There is someone here who is coming against this ministry—against me!" He began pacing and pointing randomly at the crowd. "Let me tell you, brother," he sputtered, "let me tell you sister, let me tell you whoever you are, you're coming against God!" A low moan rippled through the startled people. "I want to warn you that this," he held up the finger he had been pointing with, "this is the very finger of God!" He wiped his face with his dingy handkerchief and replaced it in his jacket pocket. "Now that we all understand that," he forced a smile, "I feel, oooh, I feel the spirit movin'!" He began to tremble.

Luke bolted upright in his chair, his eyes riveted to a place just above Rhodocus's head. It couldn't be ... but it was. "No," he whispered under his breath.

"Yes!" mouthed Baalis as he disappeared into Rhodocus's trembling body.

"Aaaah, yessss!" Rhodocus screamed. "Here it is!" He loosened his necktie and then began clawing hastily at his jacket. He half doubled over, and his breath came in short pants. "God is here! I feel him; I hear him; I've got his power, and it's coming through for you, and you, and you ... for all of you!" He swung his jacket crazily over his head. Around and around it went as Rhodocus's eyes gleamed with a strange light. "Catch it, catch the spirit!" he shouted.

What happened next both surprised and horrified Luke. The entire audience collapsed in their seats. Those ushers who had been standing along the exits and aisles likewise fell to the floor. Then, without warning, the girl next to him toppled into his lap.

"No!" barked Luke into her ear as he gently tried to lift her into a sitting position. Her eyes were closed and she appeared to be in a coma. "Corine, snap out of it, in the name of Jesus!"

He gently shook her until she opened her eyes. They were dully focused on something unseen.

"How did you like that little trick, Maschil?" the voice sneered. Luke smelled the horrible sulfuric stench of Baalis, but said nothing. "She's mine, you know, Maschil." He threw back his head and roared with laughter. "You'd like to save them all, wouldn't you?" He giggled insidiously. "But you know the rules. Humans have their own free will, and all these people have chosen ME!" He spat out the words menacingly. "Now, get out of here and leave the girl to me."

221

"Stand aside!" Maschil ordered as he lifted the semi-conscious woman into his arms.

Baalis placed a greenish hand on his sword's handle. The fires of hell reflected in his eyes. "Make me!" he challenged.

"Glory to the Lord Jesus Christ, King of kings, Lord of lords," Luke began to sing under his breath. "All honor, glory, praise, and worship to Him who alone is worthy!" He held the young woman close and began walking up the aisle toward the exit.

"You won't get away with this!" screamed Baalis in a rage. He shook his fist at the retreating angel. "We will meet again, Maschil, and on that day ..."

Luke carried his new acquaintance out of the building and into the twilight. He spotted a park-like enclosure where they could find a place to rest and remain undetected by the throngs of people when they finally began to make their way out of the building.

"Umm," the girl's head rolled from side to side on the wooden park bench. "What happened?" She was suddenly wide-awake. "Where am I? What are you doing ... are we doing ... here?" Her eyes widened in fear.

"Please, Corine, let me explain ..."

She gave a small shriek and drew back. "How did you know my name? I never told you my name ... did I?" A slight frown etched her smooth brow. She ran her fingers through her tousled light brown hair.

"How I know is not really important," Luke said softly. "It's just that, well, you see, you needed help."

"Help? Did I faint or something?"

"Well, it's more like you were in a trance."

"A—what! Don't you even know about being slain in the spirit?"

"Yes, I know all about the Spirit," Luke said softly. His smile was contagious, comforting. She visibly relaxed.

"But, but," she stammered, "how did you, uh, carry me past the guards?"

"Easy," Luke said with a grin, "they were all asleep on the floor."

"Oh ..." her voice trailed away.

"Do you remember what I said about reverence?" She nodded. He continued, "Reverence, true godliness, integrity, and truth, are essential if a person is going to know the real Jesus and be able to discern what is of God and what is not of God. God is holy. God is a Spirit, and they that worship Him must worship Him in spirit and in truth." He hoped beyond hope that she would understand what he was trying to say in the short time he had left.

Part of her wanted to run, to escape from this stranger, and yet, on the other hand, her heart urged her to stay. "You remind me of someone ..." her voice was soft, distant.

"Your dad, perhaps?" volunteered Luke.

She caught her breath and her eyes widened. "How do you know about my dad?" Before he could answer, she pointed an accusing finger at him. "He sent you to spy on me, didn't he? He's the one behind all of this. You ..."

"Corine," Luke interrupted gently, "No." His eyes locked on hers, and she found herself unable to look away. "What do you see, Corine?"

Her lips trembled. She gasped weakly, "Love, truth, wisdom ... I see heaven! Oh!" she buried her face in her hands and wept.

Luke waited for the sobs to subside, then gently lifted her face and wiped the tears away with his fingers. "Are you ready to tell me about it?" he asked.

Corine stared at her hands folded in her lap. "He warned me," she began quietly, "I remember it all now. It comes back to me." Tears began to course down her cheeks. "Papa is a preacher, you know, plus he writes books about cults and false prophets and such." She sniffed and Luke handed her a clean handkerchief. "Thanks," she murmured. "It was all right for a while, but you see—what's your name?" she interrupted herself.

"Luke."

"Oh, well, Luke, okay, um, I was happy at home until I met Star. She started taking me to a bigger church in the city than the one Daddy pastors. It was so different. I mean, all the kids loved it. It was *alive!* We no longer sang those old hymns and stuff. We got to sing lots of new, upbeat choruses and dance and wave banners and such. We didn't have to listen to the same old dead, boring sermons about sin and grace and hell and all that. I loved being able to express myself!"

223

She looked up at Luke, who was listening attentively. He nodded, and she continued, "It was so much fun being with Star. Star had been a drug addict but now she said she was getting high on Jesus. She took me to Jesus marches and to hear all kinds of exciting speakers."

"Like Brother Rhodocus," Luke interjected.

"Exactly! So, you do understand?" Corine's blue eyes searched Luke's thoughtful face.

"Oh, yes, I do understand." Luke shifted his weight on the hard bench. "You found a way to escape from discipline, accountability, and responsibility. You found a way to rebel against everything your godly parents tried to teach you and still have a form of 'religion,' except this time it allowed you to appease your flesh, your rebellion, and your emotions. In other words, it suited your purpose, not God's."

Corine gasped. His truthful words stunned her into an uncomfortable silence. In her heart she knew he was right.

"What about the child you carry?" She gave a little shriek, but before she could speak, Luke continued. "Star told you that abortion is okay, didn't she?"

"Yes, but ..."

"Do you really want to continue on this destructive path?" Luke asked gently. She could feel his clear blue eyes probing the depths of her soul. *Just who is this Luke anyway?* she asked herself. *Never mind, Corine,* she self-admonished, *make a decision.* "No," she heard her voice answer. She couldn't remember opening her mouth, but there it was again: "No."

"Come then," Luke stood and offered her his hand, "I'll walk you to your car."

"Oh, my purse ..." Corine momentarily panicked.

"Right here!" Luke produced her purse from under the bench.

She reached for it. "Thank you. Really, Luke, you have no idea how much you have helped me ..." her voice faltered as she gazed into the blue depths of his eyes. She marveled at the wisdom, peace, and love she saw there. She had never seen anyone quite like him before. She thought of Brother Rhodocus's dark eyes filled with an eerie sort of mean and angry fanaticism. She shuddered involuntarily.

"Luke, all of a sudden, I see ... I see how deceived I allowed myself to be. I truly want Jesus to forgive me and take my life!"

He grinned and fell behind her as she threaded her way through the maze of parked cars. She could hear his footsteps lightly crunching on the blacktop behind her. "Oh, there it is, over there!" She pointed toward a silver Taurus. "Luke," she began as she dug in her bag for her car keys, "will I see you again? I mean, can we get together some time to talk?" Her searching fingers located the elusive car keys. "I so much appreciate all you've ..." she stopped in mid-sentence, eyes wide, keys dangling from her hand. He had simply and silently vanished into thin air.

8

THE SILENT LISTENER

A polished silver coffeepot towered over a mountain of giant poppy seed, chocolate chip, banana nut, and almond muffins. Another elegant carafe brimming with hot water sat next to it. A dainty imitation silver basket offered a variety of exotic teas that would cheer the heart of the most avid tea connoisseur. A sparkling imported crystal vase overflowed with an assortment of fresh flowers that competed with fine China cups, a sugar bowl, and a cream pitcher for first place in the nostalgia department.

Luke smiled to himself. He preferred to work, as he did this day, invisible and undetected. Being too involved with human beings could get complicated.

"Hey, Michael! Are we still on for golf this afternoon?" A tall man in his thirties and dressed in a three-piece suit entered the cheerful room. Luke noted his permed blonde hair, large diamond ring, and manicured nails.

"You bet, Albert," Michael said as he shook his hand. "I can't wait to show you my new set of golf clubs." Michael laughed as he followed Albert into the room. He was shorter than Albert. His dark features and olive complexion revealed his Jewish heritage. He, too, was dressed in a suit. A diamond tie tack glittered brightly from his expensive silk tie. Both men helped themselves to coffee and muffins.

A short, well-dressed, middle-aged woman with slightly bulging eyes and sporting a large nametag with "Ethel" printed on it bustled into the room and handed each man a sheet of paper. "Good morning, pastors. Here is today's schedule for the TV interviews." Her smile revealed an uneven row of teeth. "As you can see, the other guests haven't arrived yet."

The men nodded and she left the room.

"Say, Michael, you have quite a thing going on in your church, I hear," Albert said as he lowered himself on to the expensive sofa. Michael sat in an ornate chair next to the couch. He nodded in reply as he washed down a bite of muffin with his coffee.

"Yeah, man," he replied as he rubbed a napkin between his hands. "It's really phenomenal; no kidding. We are running three services now, so we're planning on expanding the church to seat seven thousand at a time ..."

Albert whistled under his breath. "That's terrific, Michael. It's goin' great guns down at my church too. Problem is," he shuffled his feet and grinned at Michael, "we're having a problem with the parking lot. It simply can't handle all of the traffic anymore."

"Boy, that can be a bummer," Michael sympathized. "What do you foresee, Albert? Think you'll have to relocate, or will the city allow you to build a parking garage next to the church?"

Luke watched Albert stare into his half-empty coffee cup as if the answer lay on the bottom. "Well," he began slowly, "I'm thinking we need to grab that seven acres that's come up for sale down the road about a quarter of a mile from our present location. Then we can build a larger sanctuary and parking lot," he set his cup on the mahogany coffee table and waved his hands in the air, "and build a school too!"

Michael slapped his knee, "Way to go, Albert! Think your board will go along with your idea?"

Albert leaned back against the sofa and grinned. "Believe me, Michael, my board is always behind whatever I want to do. They know I'm an apostle, and besides that, I have booked a series of meetings with a certain Prophet Black. I'm thinking of asking him to be our house prophet."

Just then a trim brunette entered the room. Michael and Albert both stood to their feet. "Hi, Honey," Michael grinned at his wife. "Lila, you remember Apostle Albert from Miracle Mountain Fellowship in the southeastern part of the city?"

She tossed her head and flashed a smile at Albert. "Of course I do! It's so nice to see you again. I've been chatting with your wife in the powder room. She's borrowing my makeup artist."

Albert raised his eyebrows slightly as she hastily explained, "I can't stand the way they make you up here at the studio, so I brought my own makeup lady."

"Oh, um, very good!" Albert mumbled. His eyes lingered over her soft curls and accentuated eyes and lips. She was a looker all right, totally stunning in her white brocade dress. No doubt about it, that Michael was a lucky man. Besides, hadn't he heard that she always was in agreement with everything Michael said when they hosted the TV interviews? Always smiling, always nodding submissively. If only his talkative, feisty wife would show him as much respect. It would certainly make him look better in front of the other pastors.

Albert reluctantly tore his gaze away from Lila and helped himself to another cup of coffee. He always looked forward to these times in the "green room" before the TV taping got underway. The coffee was terrific, the muffins out of this world, and the titillating conversations with fellow pastors gave him a sense of belonging. Yes, being the pastor of a very large, growing church had its rewards besides the incredible salary and benefits he received.

Ethel burst into the room again followed by three single women and an elderly gentleman who shuffled shyly between a middle-aged married couple. Luke immediately recognized them all. They were all doing their best to disguise their nervousness.

"Okay, Pastor Cohen," Ethel smiled at Michael. "These are the people you and Lila will interview today. As well as Pastor Albert, of course, whose wife Tessie is, um, along, er, I mean, here too." She nodded briefly in Albert's direction, then continued "These two ladies, uh Ralene and Casey, have their own ministry, and Dixie here is our singer, and Mr. Jordan has a testimony to give." She took a deep breath and glanced in the direction of the couple who had entered the room with Timothy. "These are friends of, um, Mr. Jordan. They are here for moral support."

After introductions were made, she whirled on her heel, nearly colliding with Albert's wife, who had walked in behind her. "Oh sorry," squealed Tessie. Ethel grimaced slightly, lowered her head, and stalked out the door.

Christians are such an interesting bunch, Luke mused to himself. He focused his attention on Timothy, who stood silently in the middle of the room while the others stood in line for coffee, tea, and muffins. *Timothy Jordan!* Luke was elated. Timothy, the first human contact he had met on this unique assignment! How good it was to see him bathed, clean-shaven, and dressed in a gray suit. Luke could tell Timothy felt awkward and out of place as he waited for his turn at the refreshments table. Finally, Michael and Albert approached him, shook hands with him, and asked him a few courtesy questions about himself. Luke noted that Timothy seemed overwhelmed by the two well-to-do men and appeared hesitant to offer much more in the way of conversation than was necessary. Timothy found an empty chair next to Gladys and Gerry. Luke recognized them as the couple who had taken him into their home.

Eventually Michael and Albert teamed up in an empty corner and exchanged information and tips about their investments in the stock market.

Meanwhile, Ralene and Casey talked politely with the soloist. Luke concluded that the "professionals" had duly snubbed them. Tessie and Lila hovered next to the table in animated conversation. It became increasingly clear to Luke that things were not as they appeared to be on the surface and that there was most assuredly more than one reason he had been given this assignment.

Ethel poked her head through the doorway. "Okay, Pastors, Lila, and Dixie, please follow me, and, uh, you too, Tessie." She called back over her shoulder, "The rest of you can watch the first interview on the TV over there on that wall."

Everyone's attention turned to the small screen as the daily program's theme song announced the show was about to begin. Suddenly Dixie began singing to a blaring tune with a rock beat. Everyone's eyes were glued to the TV as Dixie blasted the audience with "I'm rockin' and walkin' with Jesus, Ooooh, yeah! Every day it's this way—ooooh yeah! He's a comin' to go a rockin' and a walkin' with me!"

Luke shuddered. He longed for the beautiful worship of the courts of heaven. He wondered how humans could possibly connect a Holy God

229

with such a pagan racket. Finally it was over, and he noticed the obvious looks of relief from everyone in the small room.

Ralene and Casey looked at each other in undisguised disgust. Timothy saw them and the corners of his mouth turned up slightly in a knowing grin. Gladys and Jerry sat staring at the floor, obviously shaken by the fleshly spirit that threatened to engulf the uncomfortable space.

"… and our first guest is Apostle Albert, and his wife, Tessie." Michael's cheerful voice snapped everyone's attention back to the TV screen. Michael, with Lila at his side, shook hands with Albert and Tessie, who took seats opposite from them. Albert's eyes, Luke observed, lingered too long on Lila.

"So, uh, Apostle Albert," Michael began the interview as the cameras rolled, "tell us what God is doing at Miracle Mountain Fellowship."

"Oh, let me tell you, brother, God is on the move. Yes He is!" He flashed a toothy smile at Michael. "We've got real revival, don't we Hon?" He glanced over at his wife. Tessie flipped a runaway strand of blonde hair back from her eyes, and gushed, "You betcha! It's really exciting and it's sooooo much fun!" Albert jumped in before Tessie had time to run away with the conversation. "I've never seen anything like it before!" Without another word to Tessie, he managed to keep her quiet by describing how the Spirit was moving in all three services, how the people were responding with laughter and were being set free to dance in the Spirit, and that all kinds of miracles and healings were taking place.

Throughout the interview, Michael deftly steered the conversation into all the "right" channels to grab the attention of the viewers. He knew that most of them had been groomed by a steady diet of "Christian" entertainment, and anything that fell short of the entertaining format could result in loss of viewers. All the while Lila, with a fixed smile on her face, nodded and looked adoringly at her husband. Everything about her gave the appearance of the perfect submissive wife.

Meanwhile, in the green room, Ethel motioned for the two women ministers to prepare for their interview. "As soon as Apostle Albert leaves the set, then you two go in and they'll put on your mics."

Luke watched Albert, once he passed the cameras, give a thumbs-up sign to Michael. He grabbed Tessie by the arm and ushered her down the hall to the reception room and out of the building. He wanted to get her home as fast as fast as possible so he could change into his golfing clothes and head out to meet up with Michael.

Meanwhile, Dixie belted out another jazzy number as the two women were wired for sound and brought fresh glasses of drinking water. Dixie finally wrapped up her number and stepped down as the ladies were introduced on camera.

"So," began Michael while Lila struck a reserved pose, "I understand you two ladies have a ministry that is quite unique and that you have written a book about relationships. Is that correct?" He forced a smile.

Ralene spoke. Her intelligent hazel eyes looked straight into Michael's brown ones. "Yes, we have. The book reveals how people get into cycles in their relationships and how to break those destructive cycles."

"Can you tell us how you came by this information in the first place?" Michael asked. Lila's eyebrows arched quizzically as if to silently reinforce her husband's question.

"God gave it to me," she replied straightforwardly. Michael's stunned countenance dissolved into incredulity.

"God?" His voice was edged with doubt. Mockery glinted in Lila's eyes. Luke found it all very interesting. Gladys, Jerry, and Timothy appeared to be simultaneously holding their breath.

"Yes, God," Ralene stated matter-of-factly.

As if suddenly realizing that millions of people who actually believe God still speaks to people would be watching the program, Michael regained his composure. "Ah, of course, God does, uh, speak to different people in different ways." As if on cue, Lila smiled at her husband and nodded.

The remainder of the interview went smoothly as both women exalted Christ and talked about the root problem of pride in people's lives, the need to deny self and follow Jesus, and how He is the one who sets the captives free, heals the broken-hearted, and gives sight to the blind. Luke noticed that the phone counselors were kept busy during the entire interview. As their short time together drew to a close, Michael assured Ralene that he would schedule her into his church to hold a seminar.

Luke shook his head sadly. He knew that Michael's enthusiasm was a sham and that he had no intention of booking Ralene and Casey in his church. *One more mark against his record,* Luke thought to himself, *for lying.*

Then it was Timothy's turn. Gladys and Jerry put their arms around him and prayed for him, rebuking fear and assuring him that Jesus would give him the words to speak. The next thing he knew, he was being escorted by Ethel to the speaker's platform.

Michael seemed visibly relieved to be rid of the two women when a disgruntled Timothy sat down opposite him. At least here was another man, and in spite of his timid demeanor, perhaps the interview could be steered in a more appropriate direction.

He was dead wrong.

"Jesus sent an angel," Timothy declared, his wrinkled face beaming under the lights. "Yes He did! He reached down from heaven and picked me up right out of the miry clay." He raised his hands heavenward, "Oh, Lord Jesus, I love You. You've made a new man outta me! You've given me new life! I praise Your holy name."

Lila's mouth hung open while Michael shuffled uncomfortably on the couch. He leaned forward, trying to capture the old man's attention, but it was no use. Timothy's face reflected the glories of heaven as his eyes focused on something no one else could see. Everyone was stunned.

Tears began to course down his cheeks as he unintentionally ran away with the interview. "I was a no-good bum, livin' on the streets of the city, eatin' out of garbage cans. I was a drunk. I hated everybody, includin' God. I hated myself. But Jesus ..." he faltered momentarily. "If it wasn't for Jesus, I'd surely be burnin' in hell by now!"

Lila closed her mouth and bit her lip. Michael stared helplessly at the camera crew. They were all crying. Except for Apostle Albert, this just had to be the worst bunch of "professional" interviews he had ever been involved with. Would it never end?

Michael turned back to face the old man and found a finger pointing straight in his face. He heard Lila gasp.

"Preacher," Timothy found a boldness he never knew existed, "you need to get on yer face before the Lord God Almighty! You and your fancy lady there!" His eyes fastened on Lila's painted face. "Yer so busy bein' professional an' buildin' a kingdom here on earth when there's folks jus' like me livin' on the streets of this here city with no hope at all. All of 'em, hell-bound. Don't you care about that? Jesus does!"

Silence.

Lila glanced furtively at her stunned husband. She had never seen him without a good comeback. She cleared her throat as she caught a glimpse of Ethel and the station manager in the background waving their arms frantically in the air. She stammered into the uncomfortable silence, "Um, well, er, Mr. Timothy? I mean, Timothy, we're so glad that God stepped into your life. Yes, that's what it's all about." She ever-so-slightly nudged her shocked husband.

He must need resuscitating, she thought.

"My husband and I, why, of course we're very concerned about the deplorable conditions of this city—what I mean is, we know that something needs to be done about it." There! She had covered for them both—or had she?

Timothy was in charge. "If yer so concerned, ma'am," his tone was serious but carried a note of sweetness, "where were you when I was lying in the gutter in my own puke?"

Lila visibly recoiled. Michael opened his mouth but shut it again. It was as if he was struck dumb.

Meanwhile, Luke watched with satisfaction as the two women, who had returned to the green room, along with Gladys and Jerry whispered joyful exclamations of "Hallelujah" and "Praise the Lord."

Then the bomb hit.

"Do you really know Him?" Timothy pleaded. "Really love Him with all of your heart, mind, soul, and might?"

Silence.

"Let me tell you my testimony," he glanced at the clock. He had three minutes. It was enough. "When I was a little bitty laddie, my daddy disappeared and my mommy married a preacher. He had a big, successful church. He made lots of money. But when my mommy wasn't lookin', he was doin' terrible things to me. Things a body shouldn't talk about, ya know. So when I got old enough, I left home, and I left that man, and I left his church … and I left God. I ran away from all of 'em. I hated 'em all!

233

Michael and Lila resembled two wilted flowers leaning against each other for support. Timothy continued, "I lived in hate my entire life. Oh, I jumped a steamer and traveled the world and had plenty of adventures, mind you, but no fancy preacher ever came up to me an' told me about the love of God. Then He outright sent an angel and then brought Gladys and Jerry the same hour to take me into their home."

Michael sighed. Thankfully time was running out and he could go play a round of golf with Albert and forget the whole miserable morning. Or could he?

"Now I have a question for you, pastor." Timothy leaned forward, his penetrating eyes searching the depths of Michael's soul. "If I had come into your fancy church when I lived on the streets—you know, all smelly and all—what would you have done?"

Michael cleared his throat. "Um," he looked up at the clock and then hastily announced, "well, brothers and sisters, this has been a most interesting day today. We trust that you have enjoyed all of our special guests," he smiled into the camera as he wrapped up the program, "and may God bless you until we meet again!"

He grabbed Lila by the arm and ushered her out a side door that led to the reception room. "Get your purse," he hissed through clenched teeth. "We're out of here!"

Luke watched with joy as Gladys, Jerry, Timothy, Ralene, and Casey made plans to have lunch together.

The last thing he heard as he left the studio was, "Let's go talk about Jesus!"

9

THE PROPHET

He was short and stocky, and every eye in the crowded room was riveted on his face. The heavy hush of expectancy was a tangible thing that seemed to suck the air out of the small space. No one moved; no one spoke.

Luke wrestled uncomfortably within himself. *I hate being in the presence of demons!* Yet he knew this was an assignment of utmost importance. He must not allow his revulsion to surface in any manner. Caution and diligence must be foremost in his mind.

It had not been an easy thing to accomplish, gaining entrance to this secret gathering. The Christian who so generously offered his home for a meeting place had met Luke in a natural foods co-op. They had struck up a conversation about the benefits of certain herbs. That topic led to the current government interference with natural remedies. From there the dialogue easily swung to the Patriot movement, and eventually the subject of spiritual matters surfaced.

Luke smiled to himself as he recaptured the scene in his memory. The friendly man had introduced himself as Ernie Bjornson. With a little prompting on Luke's part, Ernie had finally opened up and proceeded to share his enthusiasm for a certain prophet he and his wife had met.

"This man is a prophet to the nations," he said with pride.

"There are many false prophets in the world today." Luke's gaze was solemn.

"Oh, yes, but," Ernie contended, "this man is a *true* prophet! He has gone all over the world to different nations and prophesied to presidents and kings!"

235

"I would like to meet this man."

"Well, if you tell me where I can reach you, I'll ask the prophet if it's okay for you to come to one of our weekly prayer meetings that are held in our home." His blue-gray eyes sparkled.

"Father!" the prophet's sharp voice snapped Luke back to the present. "We are about to come into Your presence, Lord. Grant that we may be worthy to approach your throne. Grant that we may be worthy to establish Your Kingdom on earth. Grant us Your protection as we tear down the enemy's strongholds. Bring down our enemies that we may go forward, bringing the warning to all nations! Amen."

Luke felt the penetration of steely gray eyes. In return, he looked past the prophet's gaze to the mocking familiar spirit positioned directly behind him. It acknowledged Luke's presence with a sneer and then resumed its concentration on the group of devotees seated around the speaker.

"Judgment is coming to every nation on earth," the prophet warned. "We must repent. We must preach repentance. We must lay aside all that is not reality and all that is vain. We must repent of our pride."

Luke surveyed the somber faces around him. Each listener was as still as carved granite. The prophet rubbed his hands together slowly as his eyes moved from face to face. He reminded Luke of a spider carefully spinning its web around one victim at a time.

"God is bringing judgment against the churches, for they are of the Babylonian system." His cold stare lingered on Luke, and he knew the prophet was straining to detect any resistance. All the prophet saw, however, were clear blue eyes calmly gazing at him.

"The time has come to fast like never before and to pray like never before. God is raising up prophets and apostles for a strategic reason. We are being positioned to lay the foundations for a new era altogether; foundations for the dawning of a new Kingdom age. We are in the throes of the birthing of a whole new order—a whole new dispensation! We are going to establish the fullness of the Kingdom of God on earth!"

Luke watched the familiar spirit whisper in the prophet's ear. Then, without warning, the prophet jumped to his feet and began pacing in front of the astonished group.

"There is someone here, tonight, in this very room, who would betray this ministry!" His eyes gleamed with a strange darkness. "You need to know and never forget that this ministry is the most important ministry on the earth today! God has entrusted me with His warnings to the nations! If you choose to walk out of this ministry, you will be cursed!" His eyes narrowed to slits. "I repeat, if you have made a commitment to this ministry, then you are bound by covenant to remain with this ministry. No one who leaves this ministry will be blessed!" He stopped pacing and glared over the heads of the people as if seeing into the distant future.

"God has told me that only a blood-washed, blood-soaked people who are real Christians, not the hypocritical, self-righteous, self-taught, self-educated fool who spreads his own dogma today, will reign in the new Kingdom! And God wants you to know that all those who do not keep God's holidays, laws, and Sabbath will be removed when His fiery wrath falls." He took his seat and scanned the motionless faces before him.

Luke cringed. He had not encountered love since the prophet had begun his indoctrination speech. He glanced at Ernie, who was nodding in agreement. Everyone in the room appeared to be in a breathless trance state. The prophet continued to hammer his dire warnings. Fear wrapped its ugly tentacles around the hearts of the men and women, squeezing and snuffing out what little life, hope, and joy they had left. Luke struggled against the angry fire that threatened to engulf him. Surely God wanted more of him than to remain a passive onlooker!

"We," the prophet's voice exploded into the silent room, "are the Elijah Company! We are preparing the way for the Lord! We are to preach repentance to the nations!"

Another forty-five minutes passed as the prophet angrily spewed forth his perverted doctrines. After that, another twenty minutes were spent listening to him pray. Luke concluded that this was, indeed, an extraordinary "prayer meeting," for the only one who prayed was the prophet. At the conclusion, Luke breathed a sigh of relief. It was finally over.

He was dead wrong.

"Help me!" shrieked a tall, thin man in his twenties. "I need to repent! Oh God, I repent!" He fell to his knees and began sobbing uncontrollably.

The prophet walked up to the prostrate man, laid his hands on his head and said, "Father, this man has come before you to repent. Everyone needs to repent!" he shouted.

The man screamed and rolled over on to the floor. "I repent, I repent," he screamed uncontrollably. The rest of the group suddenly became animated and gathered around him, extending their hands and praying loudly in tongues. Luke desperately wanted to vanish, but he could not. His orders plainly stipulated that he must ride it out. Luke wondered how the sinless Son of God had borne the sins of all mankind.

Ernie stepped up beside Luke and laid his hand on his back. "Oh, Lord," Ernie prayed, "thank you for your anointing tonight. Thank you for convicting us. Thank you for your warnings." He opened his eyes and searched Luke's face. Luke returned his gaze. How could he warn this sweet, sincere man that he had been subtly and systematically brainwashed? That he was supporting and propagating a dangerous cult? That his beloved prophet was a wolf in sheep's clothing? That after all of his living had gone into the pockets of this imposter, he would be cursed, condemned, and cast aside like a worthless piece of garbage?

Luke fascinated Ernie. He drew him aside as the melee quieted down and asked him what he thought of the meeting.

Luke responded with a question. "Why is my opinion important to you?"

"Because the prophet is looking for qualified men to help his ministry expand around the world."

"And just how does he propose to bring his message to the world?" Luke's broad smile was contagious. Ernie visibly relaxed.

"Radio, videos, Internet, social Media, churches and crusades."

"Um-hum," Luke turned and purposefully strode to the refreshment table. He poured himself a cup of raspberry punch. Suddenly Prophet Black was at Luke's side. "Haven't I seen you somewhere before?" He squinted up at Luke. "I don't know; have you?" asked Luke. He smiled knowingly.

"I guess not," said the prophet. "But there is something about you that seems familiar." He turned away and joined a married couple who were deep in conversation about the difference between the law and grace. Luke listened as the "prophet" began to expound why Christians need to keep the law if they are to be holy before God.

Luke turned away, sickened.

"There's just so much the prophet is teaching us, Luke." Ernie was at his side again. "I'll tell you what. Why don't you come to the prophet's crusade this weekend. It's at the Center, you know, close to City Park."

Luke forced a weak smile. He had his orders—he would be there.

10

THE PLAN

It was three o'clock in the morning. Ominous black clouds hung over the sleeping city. Somewhere a dog's howl echoed through the manmade jungle of cement, brick and metal. Luke shivered.

He pulled the collar of his long overcoat up over his ears and then shoved his hands deep into the side pockets. He had no idea how long he had been pacing back and forth in City Park. His troubled thoughts drove him like the stiff breeze on the bay drove the sleek sailboats.

Why, why, why? The unanswered questions buzzed through his troubled mind. *Why did a sincere Christian like Ernie fall for the lie? Why couldn't he see through it? Why couldn't all those people in the crusade tonight see where Prophet Black's teaching was leading them?*

Luke stopped his pacing and looked up at the glowering sky. For a moment he thought he saw a giant net being lowered to the earth. Fashioned of pure evil, it descended lower and lower. Far off in the distance he watched two scaly hands masterfully working the encroaching trap.

Luke shook his head, blinking rapidly. Once again, he squinted up at the sky. Billowing gray clouds filled his vision. Then, something began to glow. Had moonlight found a weakness in the heavy curtain?

He gasped. Whatever it was, it wasn't moonlight. It appeared in an instant and then vanished. But the hideous image was etched into his mind.

Luke groped behind him in search of the familiar park bench. His fingers touched the cold metal railing as he stumbled backward onto the worn wooden seat. He couldn't tell if his eyes were open or closed—all that filled his vision were two repulsive, slanted yellow-green eyes with glowing red pupils.

"Lord Jesus," he cried out loud, "Lord, Jesus!" The eyes faded from sight.

"Luke!" The familiar voice startled him.

"Pirathon!" Luke jumped to his feet. "Am I ever glad to see you!"

The two angels exchanged warm smiles. "You did see what you saw, Luke. I just thought you should know that."

"Thanks, Pirathon. For a moment there, well, I wasn't too sure ..." Luke sighed.

"I know, Luke." Pirathon quickly glanced around the park. "It's still lurking around here."

"It is, isn't it?"

Pirathon shrugged and turned back to Luke. "This is a hard assignment. Everywhere you turn it seems that God's people are falling prey to the enemy."

"I just don't understand it, my friend," Luke said solemnly. "Ernie loves God. His family and friends do too, but after what I witnessed at the crusade this evening with 'the prophet,' it's hard to fathom."

"Our Creator forewarned the people, Luke." Pirathon's sweet countenance reflected heaven's glory. "You and I have seen a lot through the centuries, Maschil," he said, reverting to Luke's angelic name. "We have witnessed 'kingdom rise against kingdom' as Satan's armies have fought against God's faithful ones."

"Only this time," Luke interjected, "Satan knows that his time is short and his tactics have grown even more subtle. I'm so glad you came, Pirathon."

A shrill voice interjected, "I'm not!"

Luke and Pirathon turned as one to face a tall warrior demon. Luke stared into the reptilian greenish eyes with the red pupils.

"It's Ra-Dan!" Pirathon's voice was barely audible.

The demon, dressed from head to toe in black war gear, threw its head back and laughed. "What's the matter with you two sweet little angels?" Another burst of hellish laughter. He took a step closer. Luke and Pirathon held their ground. "Humph," snorted Ra-Dan, "you two little wimps. You had to choose to follow Him!" He sneered and a stream of foul breath erupted from his nostrils. "I, Ra-Dan, chose to follow Lucifer, the light-bearer! And I, Ra-Dan, will rule and reign with him right here on this earth!"

Luke and Pirathon looked sideways at one another. Ra-Dan's boasting was futile. Both angels knew Satan was a hard taskmaster. And both angels knew the final outcome of planet earth.

The demon began waving his scaly arms in the heavy night air. "You!" he shouted at Luke. "You want to know, don't you? You want to know what's happening to God's little flock! Well, I'll tell you, Maschil. It's no secret anymore, but the people want what's being offered. They are ready for the final course. They have been carefully prepared all these centuries for this hour!" He beat the air with his fists as if delivering the final knockout punch to an invisible foe.

Luke and Pirathon remained silent, watching, waiting. God had surely allowed Ra-Dan to confront them with his boastful ravings. Luke was aware that the answers to his questions were going to come straight from hell itself. He was all ears.

Ra-Dan's lips curled gruesomely. His eyes narrowed to slits. "It'ssss like thissss," he hissed. "Soooo easy!" He crooned.

Luke raised his eyes skyward. *Get on with it, will you?* he thought to himself.

"The Plan!" snapped Ra-Dan suddenly. "You two know The Plan, don't you now?" He began to bounce from side to side. "The Plan that worked so well in the Garden of Eden! *That* little Plan! It has always worked with mankind! Never fails!" He snorted in derision and took another step toward Luke and Pirathon.

"That's far enough, Ra-Dan," Pirathon commanded. The demon hesitated, then stepped back.

"If you have something to say, then say it!" Luke ordered.

Ra-Dan's eyes glowed with hatred. "All right, here's The Plan, but you two can't stop it. No man, no angel can stop it! It's even in His book. It is all laid out. The 'falling away from the truth in the end days,' and we are the ones who are bringing it to pass!" Pride vibrated through his tall body.

"So?" Luke asked.

"What do you mean, 'So'?" the irritated demon snarled.

"The Plan?" Luke asked.

"Ah, yes, The Plan," hissed Ra-Dan. "It's like this. Working through the esoteric cults and secret societies," he squinted at them hoping for some indication, if ever so slight, that they were impressed. When he saw nothing but revulsion, he continued, "such as the Illuminati, the Brotherhood, and the Templars, or Freemasons, you know, the lodges, we have successfully maneuvered mankind into our web of intrigue. Regardless of what religion they belong to, mankind has always had a weakness for being his own god. Mankind craves power and control. It can all be traced back to the Garden of Eden."

"We know that," stated Pirathon. "So, what's The Plan?"

"I'm getting to that!" snapped Ra-Dan. "All of you angels put together can't stop us from taking over the earth! We have infiltrated His last bastion on earth! His beloved church!" he sniveled.

Luke felt sick to his stomach. Was he ever going to have his questions answered? Why didn't God just tell him directly instead of allowing this insidious demon to bring the 'news'?

Ra-Dan drew himself up and glared at his audience. Finally, as if forced by an unseen power not his own, he continued, "Christians today," he grimaced at the word 'Christians,' "want their ears tickled. They are sick and tired of what He calls 'sound doctrine.' They don't really want the truth!" He snickered. "They want to be entertained, they want fun, they want to have religion without paying a price! It's that simple, you see. They are chasing after and believing *our* doctrines!"

Doctrines of demons, Luke thought to himself.

"You know, Satan is clever," he gloated. "He has always been able to appear as an angel of light. In these times, people want to have religion, but they also want to be their own god. They don't want to sell out completely to *Him.* They are tired of waiting for something to happen. They want to establish the Kingdom on earth *themselves.*" Ra-Dan folded his arms and rocked back on his heels.

"So, what's The Plan?" prodded Luke.

Ra-Dan curled his lip in a sneer of disgust. "You don't get it, do you? It is *us,* working behind the scenes, telling the weak, undisciplined, carnal *Christians* that they can *take the kingdoms of this world for Christ.* Our workers, that is, familiar spirits, are breathing false prophecies into the

243

false prophets all over the world. *Christians* love it! Ahaha, ouuuu do they ever love it! They are running to and fro to get a prophecy and to experience lying wonders! They are flocking to meetings where they can experience what they think is the *Spirit!*" Ra-Dan's mocking laughter reverberated through the thick darkness. "You'll surely see them while you're here visiting our planet, Luke!"

Luke winced. He glanced at his motionless friend. Pirathon's expression remained unchanged, but his eyes never wavered from their focus on Ra-Dan.

"Laughing, writhing, hissing, barking, howling, clucking," Ra-Dan nearly doubled over with laughter. "So many demons finding fleshly dwelling places! What a clever deception. And then those nice little deluded people carry *us* back to their friends and families and churches. Laying on of hands is a wonderful way to share their *spirit* you know! These silly people call it 'The Impartation!'"

Suddenly Ra-Dan's tone changed as His words tumbled over one another in an explosion of fury. "The Plan is simple. The latter-day apostles and prophets are helping to usher in the one-world religion. They already operate with an anti-Christ spirit. Their pride and the pride of their victims give great momentum to this worldwide movement. People want unity! People want power! People want to be part of 'The New Thing!' And they will do anything to bring about so-called world peace, even it means turning over their minds to ussssss, and a bloody revolution to cleanse the earth." He rubbed his reptilian hands in glee. "We have great numbers against a little remnant. Consider those fanatics who worship the Mesopotamian moon god, Allah. Oh we are using them, those terrorists," he hissed. "They are working for us—they don't know it, but their agenda to torture and kill every Jew, Christian, and non-Muslim on the face of the earth simply serves our purpose of rushing the nations into a world-police state that will eliminate any religion that dares to declare that there is only one true way. And you know what that means!" He fearlessly sneered at the two angels of God. "It won't be long now. That little remnant is going to be wiped off the face of the earth."

Ra-Dan took a menacing step toward Pirathon and Luke. "Back with you!" Pirathon ordered. Ra-Dan hesitated and then sullenly retreated to his former position.

"Ah, little Lukie," Ra-Dan turned his full attention to Luke. "You are here on this stupid mission. What a waste of time when you could have been part of the rulers of this world!" His eyes glowed with contempt. Luke held his peace. Ra-Dan continued, "The Plan always works, he boasted. First, we plant seeds of doubt in people's minds about God and about His Word. Then we carefully work to undermine the meanings of words. Our apostles and prophets reinterpret the words of the 'old order' into new meanings for the 'new order.' Since people are always looking for some new revelation or new teaching, it's as easy as that," he snapped his greenish fingers, "to replace their old way of believing with the new way of thinking—a totally new world view." A low rumble in his throat bubbled to the surface and morphed into a distorted chuckle. "The Plan, aha, yesss, it always works! Just alter their consciousness, strip them of critical thinking, change their perceptions and mindsets … then you have them, just like that!"

Luke stole a look at Pirathon. He had assumed a defensive stance, legs slightly spread, arms folded. Suddenly Luke understood that it was no accident that Pirathon was there. Ra-Dan was a powerful demon. God had sent Pirathon to make sure Luke's mission wasn't delayed in any way.

"Christians!" Ra-Dan spat contemptuously. "They love to play church! It makes them feel good about themselves!"

"Not always," Luke interjected. "Not when their pastor stands on the Word of God and challenges them with it. God has His people who love the truth even when it convicts of sin. Not all of God's people are worldly."

Ra-Dan momentarily looked as shocked as if Luke had taken a poke at him. He quickly recovered, however. "Aaauugghh! Only a few, Lukie boy. Wake up! We have most of them." He shook his fist.

"God always has had His remnant who love Him and serve Him, Ra-Dan, and you know it." Luke's voice rang with authority.

"Well, listen to this!" Ra-Dan hissed vehemently. "God's so-called people love miracles and signs and wonders. They seek them, you know! So, we produce them! Weeping statues, visions in the clouds, gold fillings in their teeth through our knowledge of alchemy, and gold dust in their churches! Our angel came and prepared our way through that William Branham. He was one of our best workers! And now" his voice rose into a high-pitched shriek, "we even have the 'deep state' globalist world planners sacrificing to us in order to gain technology that humans have never even dreamed of before. Who do you think gave them the ability to create flying saucers, alien robots, clones, genocidal plagues, direct energy weapons, and those mysterious lights that can cause a commercial airliner full of hundreds of people to simply vanish into thin air?" He paused as if waiting for a violent reaction. When none came, he sneered at them, his dark eyes widened into a grotesque and horrible glare, "You both know," he bragged, "just who those sweet, innocent sacrifices are don't you? Let me tell you the gory details of what takes place in the tunnels we control under the whole earth..."

"STOP! NOW!" Maschil and Pirathon each held up a hand to silence Ra-Dan.

Luke and Pirathon exchanged solemn glances. A sudden gust of wind swirled through the gloomy park, scattering leaves and particles of dirt. The temporarily silenced Ra-Dan frowned at Pirathon, and then turned his attention back to Luke. "Don't you see, Luke? *He* gave mankind freedom of choice, free will. That is all to our advantage, you know." Insidious laughter gurgled into a low snarl. "Once humans give their minds over to delusion, it's easy for us to brainwash them through our teachers."

"False prophets, false apostles and false 'anointed ones,' or 'little Christs,'" Luke whispered more to himself than to Ra-Dan.

"Exactly! Maybe you're not so dumb after all," mocked Ra-Dan. "Even *He* said that if a human refuses to receive love for the truth then *He* Himself will send such a strong delusion that those truth-hating, vulnerable individuals will believe a lie. All we have to do then is provide the lie! Ouuuu it's so simple!"

Luke suddenly felt sick to his stomach. Wishing Ra-Dan would evaporate into nothing, he retorted, "Is that all, Ra-Dan?"

"Almost. I have to make sure you understand The Plan. We are proud of The Plan, and guess what? Neither you nor all those 'patriots' or 'white hats' or whatever else they call themselves who think they are going to usher in a thousand years of peace on earth, can stop us. We have the upper hand because we have convinced most of deluded mankind that good is evil, and evil is good! You two certainly have to know by now that all through the centuries it has remained the same. Simply tempt mankind in one way or the other to be a god. Tempt his mind! Promise him divine wisdom, knowledge, and illumination into the mysteries of the Universe! Tantalize his emotions with powerful sensations and illusions that are so seductive that he cannot resist. Convince him he is part of the elite! Trip him up with fear and guilt, luring him away from *His* grace so he will gladly run back to dependence on his own works and goodness under the Old Law. That way, the poor victim will unknowingly exchange his freedom for a curse!"

"Enough! It is enough!" Luke pointed a finger at Ra-Dan.

"Aw, come on, Luke," Ra-Dan drew back in mock terror. "You don't want to hear about all the bloodshed that's coming when our Kingdom is in place? You don't want to hear about how all those *Christians* who refuse to submit to the apostles and prophets will be hunted down and eliminated by those who think they are doing *Him* a favor? When the real rulers of this world, working through "social justice" and revolution produce the antichrist, they will take those pathetic, so-called apostles and prophets along with whatever remnant of Christians and Jews are left and put them into concentration camps to be terminated in one great blood sacrifice to the ruler of this world—Lucifer!"

"Be silent and GO!" Pirathon and Maschil ordered in unison. The reaction was instant. In one violent swish of wind, he was gone.

Luke blinked. One minute he had been faced with a hideous emissary of Satan, and the next minute his adversary had vanished. He turned to Pirathon, who stood sedately by his side.

"Any more questions, Luke?" His voice was hushed and low. Luke caught the unmistakable note of sorrow in it.

"No."

247

11

ACCIDENT?

The small motor home careened around the hairpin curve, nearly colliding with the guardrail. Amber held her position behind the wheel of the runaway vehicle. Her foot was jammed so tightly against the brake pedal that her leg felt stiff as a log. Blurred images of the jagged cliff and crashing surf below the corkscrew road flashed across her vision.

She gritted her teeth and intensified her grip on the steering wheel. *"Jesus! Help me! Jesus!"* her mind screamed a silent plea for help.

The grade became steeper, forcing the runaway RV to greater momentum. "Oh God!" Amber screamed as she tried to maneuver the bucking Winnebago around the sharp curve.

"Noooooo ...." Her terrified scream became a tangible thing, hanging motionless in space.

Everything from that point on somehow appeared to be in slow motion—crashing through the guardrail, becoming airborne, tilting toward the relentless sea, falling downward, the deafening sound of metal crunching against jagged rock, the acrid smell of smoke, cold seawater, the rush of darkness. Somehow, in her semi-conscious state, she imagined a pair of strong arms carrying her to the shore followed by nothing but swirling darkness.

A moan escaped Amber's lips as she slowly moved her head from side to side. She tried to open her eyes, but her eyelids refused to obey. Where was she? How long had she been here?

Her mind seemed to still be screaming, *"Jesus! Help me! Oh, Jesus!"* She could hear the surf swishing against the sand somewhere in the distance, and then the unmistakable gurgle of water rushing back to sea.

"Over here!" a male voice called. "Quick, bring the oxygen!" Then once again, everything went black.

"Amber, Amber, can you hear me?" The soft, familiar voice faded in and out of Amber's mind. She tried to speak, tried to move, but her body refused to obey. "Amber, it's Ellie. Can you hear me?" She felt someone pick up her hand and gently squeeze it.

"It may take her awhile to regain consciousness," a strong male voice stated matter-of-factly.

"Doctor?" It was Ellie's voice. "Is she going to be all right? I mean she's not paralyzed or anything is she?"

"No, no nothing like that. It's just that, well, she is very fortunate to have even survived such a horrible accident. We will never know how she even managed to get out of the surf and up onto that stretch of sandy beach. It's going to take time for her body to recover from such a shock." He shook his head and walked out of the room.

Amber moved her lips. "Ellie?" she whispered. "Ellie?"

"Oh, Amber! I'm right here! Can you hear me?"

"Yes," Amber managed weakly. She willed her eyes to open and they reluctantly complied. They briefly glanced at her friend's concerned face, and then fluttered shut again.

"Where am I? The brakes," Amber tried to explain, "they—they—weren't there, Ellie. No brakes." She sighed weakly.

"That's strange," Ellie said more to herself than to her friend. "John just checked that RV over from top to bottom. The brake fluid and all was A-okay."

"Someone ..." Amber's voice trailed off. Ellie waited in suspense. Amber had something to tell her, and Ellie would wait all night if she had to. She had her own suspicions, but she kept them to herself. She brushed back a strand of dark brown hair from Amber's forehead.

"Someone," Amber began again, "... something was out there."

"Out where?" Ellie gently prodded.

"The night before I left ..."

"It's okay, Amber. Don't push yourself!"

"I have to tell you, El ... somebody was in the dark ... at night ... I heard somebody out by my RV ... I remember now ... I heard something drop in the driveway ... like ... *clink* ... like a wrench or something. I ...

249

I didn't think it was important ... but the neighbor's dog was barking and barking ..."

Ellie's dark brown eyes widened at the implications of what Amber was trying to tell her. If she understood it right, this had been no accident. Someone had deliberately drained the brake fluid. Her mind whirled. Could enough of the unfortunate Winnebago be recovered for an investigation to be done?

"Ellie, where are you?" Amber's eyes were tightly closed, but her voice was stronger.

"Right here, my friend. I am right here."

* * * * * * *

"The most terrible thing happened to one of the women who used to be part of our group," Ernie explained to Luke after the meeting with Prophet Black in Ernie's home was over. Luke was relieved that the four hours of repetitious teaching had finally drawn to a close. Ernie's eyes narrowed as he continued his explanation. "She was going on a little trip in her RV to minister to some friends and she lost control of it and went off the coast highway. But God gave her a second chance, and somehow she managed to get to the beach where someone found her and called 9-1-1. She gets out of the hospital tomorrow."

Luke's blue eyes fastened on Ernie's serene countenance. "Second chance, Ernie? I don't understand ..."

"Ah, Luke!" exclaimed Ernie as he poured himself a cup of coffee. "Amber used to be part of our group here at the house. She's been a friend of ours for years, you know, and so we assumed she'd fit in when we met the prophet and started having meetings here."

"Fit in?"

"Well, you know, we thought she'd see how anointed he is and get a burden for his ministry. After all, this ministry is vital to the future of this whole world."

"How so?"

"Come on, Luke!" Ernie studied Luke's face over his coffee cup. "You've been to a couple of meetings and you attended the prophet's crusade! Surely you realize it's vital that the nations of the world hear the warning ... the message to repent."

"Of course," Luke said evasively, "repentance is necessary for true salvation, but what has that got to do with Amber's 'second chance'?"

Ernie sighed and set his half-empty cup on the counter. Rubbing his hands together absent-mindedly, he pursed his lips together as if he was in deep thought. Finally, he moved toward Luke, took him by the arm and steered him to one of the oak chairs that circled the heavy oak dining table. "Here, Luke, take a seat and let me explain something to you."

Luke obliged his host and then waited quietly for Ernie's explanation.

"I am going to be perfectly honest with you, Luke. If Amber had drowned or died as a result of this accident, I fear her soul would've been lost."

Luke raised his eyebrows, but he remained silent.

"Amber could have had a place in this ministry, Luke, but she refused the prophet's covering. On top of that, she began to question his anointing and his authority."

"Oh? How?"

"She said he wasn't scriptural." Ernie shook his head and gave a short chuckle. "The problem is, Luke, Amber was brought up under the old system. For God's Kingdom to be established on earth the old foundations have to be done away with and a new foundation laid." He glanced at Luke to see if he followed. He deciphered Luke's thoughtful countenance as an encouragement for him to continue. "Amber began gathering up all kinds of articles, books, and documented information from the old order, plus scripture, of course, and gave them to the members of the group, including myself. Try as we might, we could not educate her as to the true meaning of scripture which has been wrongly taught in the Babylon church system for two thousand years! She refused to learn!"

Refused to deny the truth, Luke thought to himself.

"So you see Luke, Amber was unteachable. She was rebellious against the authority of the prophet, who, by the way," he lowered his voice to a whisper, "is also an apostle. So, she left prophet's ministry! And, as the prophet always tells us, 'Anybody who leaves this ministry is leaving the truth and will be cursed.' Now do you understand why Amber's soul is in jeopardy? She must repent, humble herself, return, and submit to the prophet's covering."

"Then you do not believe the blood of Jesus is enough for salvation?"

Color crept up Ernie's neck and flushed his face. "Luke, you have to understand that Christians must keep the Law! The church is the commonwealth of Israel, but they have forsaken their Jewish roots, and God is going to pour out His wrath upon them if they do not repent! Keep coming to the meetings and you will learn!" He stood abruptly and walked into the living room where the prophet and several members of the group had gathered together.

"So you see," the prophet explained to his eager listeners, "this is what happens to people who come up against this ministry! They are cursed!" A unanimous sigh of agreement filled the room.

Luke walked quietly to the door and slipped out into the moonless night.

* * * * * * *

"Hello! I didn't see you come in." Amber turned and smiled at the tall stranger with the clear blue eyes.

"How are you feeling?" he asked with a smile.

"Very well, considering," she replied. "Who are you anyway?"

"Luke. I am a friend."

"A friend?"

"Let's just say I heard about your accident."

A slight frown creased Amber's brow. Caution crept into the brown eyes. "Who?" It was more of a command than a question.

"Ernie."

Amber turned her face to the opposite wall. "I'm tired. If you don't mind, I'd like to sleep now."

"Amber." The way he spoke her name stirred something deep within her. Where had she heard her name spoken in this manner before? She closed her eyes. It had been recently, but where? When?

"You've suffered a terrible injustice."

252

She turned toward him, now fully alert. Perhaps he wasn't another indoctrinated member of Prophet Black's group. She asked, "What do you know?" Before he could respond, she said, "There's something about you, something strangely familiar, you know something, don't you?"

"I know that you love Ernie and his family with the love of the Lord God. I know you care about all the members of that cult that meets in their home. I know that you'd give your life to see them wake up from their spiritual slumber of death."

Unbidden tears pooled in her eyes. "Yes," she whispered, hoarsely. "You know it's a type of Manifest Sons of God cult? That he's a false prophet? That some of what he preaches, especially about the church system, seems right on but there is a very evil spirit in him? Of course you do!" She waved her hand helplessly in the air. "Can you help them somehow?"

"No."

"Oh, Lord!" She fell back on the pillow. Tears escaped from underneath her closed eyelids and trickled down her flawless complexion. He gently caressed her cheek and wiped the tears away. She opened her eyes and looked up into his face. Compassion and sorrow mingled with love poured from his eyes into the depths of her soul.

"Amber, God has given every human being that has ever been born freedom of choice. He has provided His Word, His Son, and His salvation. Ernie and his friends have made their choice. They have chosen to follow a hireling shepherd."

She began to sob. He sat beside the bed and took her hand. "Pray, Amber. Pray for them. Never give up fighting for them in prayer."

"I know," she stammered, "I know." She began to relax. "Where do I know you from?" Her eyes searched his face.

"The accident."

"The accident?"

"Amber, you will never be able to prove it was not an accident. Neither will you be able to prove it was an accident."

She sucked in her breath. Her eyes widened. "You, you are an angel, aren't you?"

253

He smiled.

"You! You're the one who carried me out of the water to the beach! I remember now!"

He stood to his feet, still smiling. He lightly brushed his hand across her hair. "You need to know," he said as he walked to the open doorway, "Ernie had nothing to do with it."

"Luke ..." she called after him.

He turned and gave her one more smile. Then he was gone.

12

THE FUNERAL

Shivering mourners silently gathered around the flower-laden casket as the darkening sky rumbled in anger. Torrents of rain pounded the flimsy canopy that had been erected over the final resting place of Ron Greeley. An unexpected gust of wind threatened to wrench umbrellas from numb fingers. The canvas canopy flopped wildly in the wind, adding a cacophony of angry notes to the mournful scene.

Pastor Gladstone cleared his throat and began reading the familiar words of Jesus in a loud voice. "Let not your heart be troubled: ye believe in God, believe also in me."

Maschil's presence was neither seen nor felt by the miserable band of people who had come to pay Ron Greeley their last respects. The inclement weather as well as strained relationships added to everyone's misery. It was obvious that Ron Greeley's mourners distinctly fell into two camps.

Maschil surveyed the first group. There was Amber, still weak from her terrifying ordeal in her RV, and her friend, Ellie. He watched Ellie take Amber's arm in a gesture of protection as well as comfort. He knew that Ellie's concern went far deeper than merely protection against the gusty wind. Ellie's mechanic husband, John, stood behind the two women with his head bowed in open grief. Next to him stood Ralene and Casey, faces grim.

His gaze swung past the coffin to the opposite cluster of shivering humans. Ernie and his attractive wife stood to the side of the prophet.

Maschil's keen eyes recognized those that huddled close to the prophet as his confused and faithful adherents.

Ron Greeley's two older brothers and their families quietly tried in vain to console Ron's weeping mother as well each other.

It was an interesting and strained situation.

A potluck was to be held at Ernie's home after the funeral. Once there, several of the early-comers thankfully sipped hot coffee as they gathered around the wood stove. Even though they spoke in hushed tones, Maschil heard every word.

"What a miserable day!" exclaimed a short, gray-haired woman to the group in general.

"Yeah, a terrible day for a funeral," a stocky woman in her mid-forties replied. "Poor Ron! He was only thirty-one."

Everyone murmured in agreement.

Ernie and his wife, Kate, bustled from kitchen to dining room, setting up chairs, plates, silverware, napkins, and drinking glasses.

The prophet, who had made himself at home in the living room, was surrounded by half a dozen adoring disciples who hung on his every word.

"Is there room in here for us?" asked a short woman who was followed by the wood-stove group.

The prophet extended his hand in welcome, and then half turned and squinted back toward the kitchen where familiar voices could be heard. The other group had arrived.

Ernie and Kate, gracious as always, welcomed Amber, Ellie, John, Casey, and Ralene into the warmth of the family room.

"We brought a casserole that needs to be warned a bit," Casey said to Kate with a grin.

"Ooouu, it smells delicious," Kate said as she took the dish and placed it in the oven. "Would you like a cup of tea?"

Casey nodded. Ernie had already poured steaming hot coffee into several mugs for the others who had quickly occupied the spaces vacated by the women from the prophet's group. Ellie and Amber set salads on the countertop.

I know I'm supposed to be here, but the question is, why? Maschil thought to himself.

"Because you will learn about extremes."

He smiled. *I think I know a lot about extremes, Lord. I've been watching people for centuries.*

"Listen."

"Poor Ron," whispered Ralene. "He would be alive today if he hadn't gone to such extremes."

"What happened exactly?" asked Amber. "I was in the hospital when he, um, when he was committed to the psyche ward."

"Yeah, just what did happen to Ron?" Ellie said hoarsely. "John and I thought he was part of the prophet's group. How come they didn't keep an eye on him?"

Casey and Ralene quickly gave each other a knowing look and then stole a glance toward the kitchen. Satisfied that Ernie and Kate were busy carving a lamb roast and mashing potatoes, Ralene confided in hushed tones, "For one thing, Casey and I aren't part of this group, but we used to be close to Ernie and Kate. As for Ron, we've known him for about three years. We met him in a missionary school where they train short-term missionaries for overseas work."

Casey noticed Amber's eyebrows lift in question and she quickly interjected, "The teachings there were somewhat similar to what is taught here."

"Oh," Amber said weakly.

"Go on; tell us what you know about Ron," John urged.

Ralene set her empty coffee cup down on the kitchen table. "Okay, you all know the Sonship and Latter Rain dogma about extreme prayer and fasting, right?"

All heads nodded in unison. She glanced towards the kitchen. Satisfied that no one was listening, she continued. "Ron became caught up with the current river of revival and doctrines of the Manifest Sons of God, which, as you know, has developed along the same lines as the Latter Rain stuff. He began to attend all the big revival meetings and conferences and such. Eventually he became thoroughly convinced that he needed to give himself over to long periods of fasting and prayer."

"Of course," Casey interrupted, "you all know Ron from the prophet's group, where he was bombarded with the extreme emphasis on repentance."

"What's wrong with repentance?" John asked. Maschil watched Ellie poke him in the ribs with her elbow.

"Good question," Ralene smiled. "There's nothing wrong with that unless you forget to preach Christ and His forgiveness."

"Oh, right," John grinned and grasped Ellie's fingers in his motor-oil stained hand.

"This extreme teaching is part of the Manifest Sons of God stuff," Casey whispered vehemently. "They believe if all the nations on earth repent, then God won't pour out His wrath and they can institute their Kingdom rule *before* Christ returns. In fact, they believe that they must take over the earth so that He *can* return."

"Whoa!" exclaimed John. "What about the reign of the antichrist?"

Ralene replied, "They don't believe in him. They think the antichrist is lawlessness."

"What about Ron?" whispered Amber. Her watchful eyes fastened on the activity in the kitchen.

Ralene sighed, "Ron wanted to serve God so badly. He was always trying to be worthy you know. Well, some months ago, he met this unsaved woman in his workplace. He was very attracted to her and tried to share the Lord with her. Well, one night at a church meeting one of those false prophets came up to Ron and told him that he would marry this woman and that they would go off to the mission field together."

"No kidding!" John shook his head in disbelief. "Go on."

"So Ron took that as a real word from God and he approached her about it. She flat refused to consider having anything to do with him, and he was totally devastated! Well, from then on, he really went downhill. He felt like a total failure, that he had failed God. He began fasting for forty-day periods at a time because he felt so unworthy. Pretty soon he had no appetite whatsoever and his electrolytes caused strange sensations in his body. Whenever anyone did manage to coax him to eat something, the electrolytes began tingling in his legs. He believed demons were attacking and biting him. So, he refused any food because of his fear that they would attack him. He became a walking skeleton. It was horrible!"

Tears formed in Casey's eyes as she explained, "Ralene and I had counseled him from time to time that his bottom-line problem was pride.

His pride wouldn't allow him to believe that he could make a natural, human mistake, so he tried to 'pay' for his failure through extreme fasting and prayer.

"We repeatedly explained to Ron that Jesus shed His blood for all of our sins and that there is nothing that we can add to what Christ did for us on the cross. We told Ron that all of our righteousness is as filthy rags and that we can't atone for our sins, mistakes, and failures by fasting, prayer, through good works, or by trying to keep the law. We warned him that his insistence on punishing himself was actually a denial of the free gift of eternal life God offers to all those who trust in Jesus. We also told Ron that it was his pride that kept him from accepting God's grace. But he refused to listen. He actually believed he was too good of a Christian to have carnal thoughts and desires for an unsaved woman. He continued to starve himself until he was too weak to walk, talk, or think straight. When we paid him a visit and saw his condition, we looked up his brothers' phone numbers and alerted them to the danger Ron was in. Poor Ron couldn't even see by then! He kept telling us the lights were all out and it was dark when it really wasn't. We stayed with him until his older brother came and had Ron admitted to the hospital."

"Come and get it, everybody!" Kate's voice rang through the house. "Everybody grab a plate and dish up in the dining room."

"Let's go somewhere after we eat," whispered Amber, "so we can finish this conversation." She raised her eyes and met Kate's questioning stare.

"Okay," everyone quietly agreed.

"Where?" Casey asked.

"Denny's, on 5th," Ralene suggested. Heads nodded in agreement.

"Are you coming?" Kate asked with a crooked smile.

"Here we are!" Casey said enthusiastically. Maschil watched as the little group began inching its way toward the kitchen. The aroma of freshly baked bread, lamb roast, lasagna, and apple pie wafted through the house from the noisy dining room.

Ralene and Casey led the way to the food-laden table, followed by Ellie and John. Amber slowly entered the room and reached for a plate, eyes lowered. She could feel the bold stare of the prophet as he stood at the far end of the adjoining living room.

Ernie approached Casey and Ralene. "I see you girls remember Amber from the couple of times you came to the prophet's meetings here." He smiled cordially toward Ellie and John. "It's nice to have you folks here, but it's too bad it's under such sad circumstances. I'll introduce you to the folks gathered in the living room. I want you to meet the prophet," he said proudly.

Ellie's hand poised in mid-air with a forkful of salad. She glanced nervously at her husband. He winked his encouragement at her and continued filling his plate with a variety of mouth-watering food. Nothing, not even a false prophet and a room full of adoring adherents could squelch his appetite. Reassured, she smiled and slightly shook her head.

Maschil watched everyone settle in the spacious room. He listened to simultaneous conversations between people who gathered in small social groups. He smiled to himself. There were three distinct congregations of people in Ernie and Kate's home. Ron's family, each struggling with their own pain and grief, huddled together for mutual support in the far corner. The prophet and his disciples spread informally across the room as if it was their own property, and in a way it was. After all, Prophet Black had claimed Ernie and Kate's home, property, bank account, retirement funds, time, plans, goals, and lives as his own. Neither of them any longer had an independent thought. Everything came under the control, or covering, of the prophet.

Finally, there was the little band of believers who sought to cling tenaciously to the truth and to their beloved Jesus regardless of the cost. Maschil knew it was a lonely walk for these pilgrims treading through territory ruled by the "god of this world."

Ernie and Kate flitted from group to group. They chatted amiably with their deluded friends and the prophet whom they adored, then moved to Ron's distraught mother, brothers, and their families. Kate and Ernie offered words of condolence and hope, assuring them that Ron had "given his all to the Lord." Maschil caught the look of dismay, then disgust, on Casey's face. She had plainly overheard the conversation.

"Ah, Amber," said Kate. She somehow managed to squeeze in between Amber and Ellie. "It's so good to see you! And you do look good considering the terrible accident you had!" She patted Amber's arm.

In spite of the obvious sincerity of Kate's friendly overtures, Amber paled. *If only these people knew the whole truth,* she thought glumly to herself. She had always loved Ernie and Kate, but once they had "turned off their minds" as she called it, their friendship had been strained. Amber had done everything in her power to warn them of the intentions of the false prophet who had slithered into their lives and hearts. Every warning had fallen on deaf ears. Every scrap of printed evidence of this horrible heresy had slipped unseen before blind eyes. She sighed.

"Are you okay?" Kate's eyes filled with genuine concern. "Can I get you something, a drink of water perhaps?"

Amber's eyes filled with tears. She bit her lip and nodded. As Kate rose to fetch the water, Amber sensed the intense stare of the prophet upon her face. Suddenly she felt as if her very breath had been sucked out, leaving her faint and dizzy. Tentacles of fear clawed at her mind and heart, threatening to strangle her into extinction. Jumping to her feet, she nearly upset her plate of uneaten food. "I, uh, excuse me," she blurted to Kate who approached with a glass of ice and water. "I have to leave!"

Startled, Kate set the glass on a table and followed Amber to the door. "Are you sure you'll be okay, Amber?" She watched Amber retrieve her purse and coat from the guest closet. "Yes, I'll be fine—I'm just, tired, that's all!" She began backing out the door toward the driveway. "Thank you, both of you. I love you!" With a sob she turned and ran toward her car.

"That's odd," Kate muttered to herself as she returned to her guests.

Maschil watched the prophet position himself next to Ron's grieving family. He took the broken-hearted mother's hands gently in his own, looked deeply into her red-rimmed eyes and spoke in low tones. She began to visibly relax and eventually she smiled weakly. "So you see," he said, "your son was truly an overcomer and gave his life to bring God's kingdom to earth."

Meanwhile, after politely extending parting words of comfort mingled with sorrow to Ron's grief-stricken family, Ellie, John, Casey, and

Ralene made their way to the door. Ernie helped retrieve their coats, all the while talking rapidly about how he and Kate would be traveling throughout Europe holding crusades in the coming months. "We sure miss Amber and wish she'd return to the meetings," he said with a shake of his head. A slight frown creased his brow as he looked at Ralene and Casey. "You two should reconsider giving up that struggling ministry of yours and come work with us. You need a good covering!"

Casey bit her lip in an attempt to stifle the torrent of words that rushed to the surface. *Covering! The only time covering is mentioned in the Bible is either in reference to a woman's hair, or an evil covering over the earth!* Her mind screamed in protest. *And our ministry wouldn't always be on the ragged edge if people like you would give to us like you give to that phony in the living room!*

Always calm, always wise, Ralene tipped her head and looked Ernie full in the face. "Ernie, we love you and Kate, but God has given us our ministry, however small it may be, and we have to be faithful with what He has entrusted to us."

Ernie nodded. "Well, I suppose you're right, but we sure could use some good counselors."

****

Denny's was always a favorite meeting place for those who wanted to linger over endless cups of coffee or tea. Maschil watched Amber wave from a table in the back of the room as Casey, Ralene, John, and Ellie entered the restaurant. Once comfortably settled, Amber, now composed, leaned toward Ralene. "Tell us about the hospital, Ralene. Is that when Ron died?"

"Not exactly," said Ralene. "He actually cooperated with the doctors and nurses as well as his family because he wanted out of that psyche ward very badly!"

"When then?" Amber questioned.

Ralene's lips pressed together in consternation. "Well, as you know, he believed every word Black said. He became obsessed with trying to be holy, and so as soon as he was released from the hospital, he went back to fasting."

262

"Ah, that's what he was doing when I was still hospitalized," Amber said thoughtfully.

The little group lapsed into silence as the waitress deftly refilled half-empty coffee cups.

Casey sighed and then said, "Ron starved himself to death trying to atone for his own failures, trying to become holy. Friends, there is a name for it, and it is 'holy anorexia.'"

Unseen and undetected, the angel of God slipped away into the night to contemplate the dilemma of fallen mankind and of those who had been offered the greatest Gift of all time, and yet, somehow, still missed it.

13

MOUNTAIN RETREAT

Luke's strong fingers tightened their grip on the steering wheel of the bucking Jeep Cherokee. He grinned to himself and thought about the difference in modes of transportation between angels and men.

He preferred being an angel.

The rutted gravel road suddenly topped a rise and curved sharply to the left. Luke slammed on the brakes, causing the rented Jeep to fishtail to the right in a cloud of dust. He straightened the steering wheel and pulled the vehicle to a jerky stop. Setting the parking brake, he opened the door, climbed out, stretched, and squinted into the shimmering sunrise.

"This is nice," he muttered to no one in particular. His keen eyes swept the broad expanse of sky, then slowly lowered to the jagged mountaintops that reached up to greet the pastel dawn. Farther down, his vision adjusted to the forested foothills that still lay asleep within the embrace of purple shadows. Finally, his gaze rested on the fertile valley floor. It was dotted with an occasional sprawling ranch. A ribbon of water that resembled liquid silver lazily twisted its way through the verdant pastures, completing the tranquil scene.

Luke leaned his arm against a pine tree and sighed. The fragrant air caressed his senses. He closed his eyes and listened to the *tap tap tap* of a red-winged woodpecker. A breeze playfully whirled among the tall trees, rustling leaves and causing a half-fallen tree to creak and groan. Then silence.

Thank you, Lord. I am so thankful to be out of that city for a while. Luke opened his eyes and watched the cool shadows shrink before the advancing blanket of warm sunlight. He had never liked the confinement of noisy man-made cities, and when this new assignment had come he inwardly rejoiced.

It was infinitely easier to sense the presence of his Creator in nature. He leaned back against the rough bark of the giant pine and closed his eyes. A squirrel chattered noisily overhead, and a sassy blue jay screeched a reply. A golden shaft of sunlight found its way through the tree branches and caressed his serene face with warmth.

His reverie was suddenly shattered by a high, thin, nearly imperceptible whine. "Hello, Luke. We know why you're here!" it taunted. "What do you think you can accomplish? It already belongs to us!"

Luke's blue eyes flashed as he pushed himself away from the tree. He could see no one, nor did he expect to. He knew the unseen, yet very real, source of that mocking voice. The battle lines were being drawn. It was time to go.

He brushed pieces of bark off of his blue jeans and red plaid western shirt. Climbing into the Jeep, he quickly glanced in the rearview mirror, checking the winding road he had just traveled. Sure enough, a cloud of dust half way up the mountainside betrayed the presence of another vehicle. Undoubtedly, the occupants were heading to the same destination Luke was.

He shook his head. *No use eating their dust!* He told himself grimly as he turned the key. The engine roared to life. Slipping the brake off, Luke carefully maneuvered the Jeep around the sharp curve and began descending into the canyon below.

The drive through the narrow, rocky canyon was a pleasant one for Luke in spite of the nagging doubts that assailed his mind. Obviously, this was one assignment the enemy was unusually agitated over. If it got too tough, perhaps Pirathon would be sent to assist him.

A weathered, wood sign caught his attention and Luke braked to a stop. Squinting through the dust, he read aloud, "Rocky Canyon Ranch and Christian Retreat." A painted red arrow pointed to a one-lane trail to the right. Luke turned off the road and slowly followed the rough road for another mile before it widened into a spacious parking lot. He turned into the first empty parking space and jumped agilely out of the vehicle. What he saw next was so unexpected that it nearly took his breath away.

Perched on the side of a slope, under an enormous outcropping of solid granite, was an enormous pole lodge. Several cabins and other buildings were scattered throughout the campground. A small, graceful waterfall plunged down the side of the cliff and splashed into a crystal-clear creek about fifteen feet wide. Off to the left of the lodge a couple played an intense game of tennis while several youngsters tossed baskets on the basketball court. To his right he could see an enormous swimming pool and beyond that, up past the guest cabins, Luke saw the stables, corral, and a couple dozen well-groomed horses.

Another structure was still under construction, which Luke figured to be the chapel. All in all, it was an impressive operation.

"Greetings! You must be Luke Solomon!" He turned to face a medium-built, middle-aged man whose gray eyes melted into his face when he smiled. "I'm Jeremiah Delaney." They shook hands. "I'm so glad you could join us for the weekend, Luke. We have a very special group coming all the way from Denver. It should really be something." Luke followed Jeremiah to the lodge. "Come on and let me show you around."

Jeremiah was obviously proud of the retreat he had built from money he had inherited from a rich relative. Luke listened attentively as Jeremiah enthusiastically shared the story of how a woman in his church had a vision for a Christian retreat in Rocky Canyon and how God was going to perform mighty signs and wonders there. Even though the vision had not originated with Jeremiah, it was plain that he had literally adopted the prophecy as his own and taken up the challenge when he found himself unexpectedly wealthy.

"Signs and wonders, huh?" Luke spoke softly. Jeremiah thumped him on the back and grinned broadly.

"You bet! Just wait until you meet Mick Bain and his wife, Heather. Talk about anointing! Man, you've never seen anything like it!" He opened the main door to the lodge and gestured for Luke to enter.

Luke's gaze took in the heavy pine beams and pillars, pine tables and chairs, and serving counter. It was a magnificent building, no doubt about that. Jeremiah beamed proudly. "Come over here, Luke, and check out the kitchen."

Luke allowed himself to be led through the pantry, underground storage for food and supplies, and then followed his eager host up a flight of stairs to the sleeping quarters. Bunk beds with bright green bedspreads lined the new pinewood walls. Jeremiah watched Luke's expression as they went from room to room.

"And this," Jeremiah announced as they entered a spacious room with commanding views, "is where we presently hold meetings until the chapel is completed."

Luke nodded. Two teenagers were busy setting up folding chairs in a semi-circle. Jeremiah suddenly exclaimed, "They're here! Come on, Luke. I want to introduce you to the Bains." He briskly walked toward the stairway.

Jeremiah hurried down the stairs, across the dining area, and out the door. He squinted into the bright light. "Greetings, Brother Bain and Sister Heather! I'm so glad you arrived this early!" He gave each a warm hug. "I want you to meet Luke Obed Solomon, who has come to visit us this weekend. Luke wants to witness the power of our meetings. Isn't that right Luke?" He turned to face the tall visitor.

Mick Bain's dark eyes narrowed to slits as he forced a smile and grasped Luke's hand. Luke firmly closed his hand around clammy, slender fingers. Bain slightly shuddered and suddenly withdrew his hand. He turned to his wife and hoarsely whispered through gritted teeth, "Let's unpack our things before it gets hotter, darling, and then perhaps we can find some time to rest a bit."

"Oh, yes, by all means," Jeremiah chimed in. "Just make yourselves at home. In fact, if you want to drive right on up to that two-story little condo," he pointed to a wood structure nestled among some pine trees, "you can unpack or rest or do whatever you wish." He looked nervously at his watch. "Lunch is served at 12:30 and dinner will be at 6:00."

Luke watched the tall, dark-complexioned man assist his well-groomed, blonde wife into their car. *Well, Lord,* he thought to himself, *this should be interesting tonight. Very interesting indeed.*

"Luke?" Jeremiah questioned, "would you like me to direct you to your cabin now?"

"Yes, please, I would appreciate it very much." Luke turned to face Jeremiah. Was that caution that flickered momentarily in Jeremiah's veiled eyes? What did he suspect?

"Um, just go back out this way," Jeremiah pointed back toward the narrow entryway, "and then drive on back through the trees toward the corrals. But, before you get that far, you'll see a one-lane road off to the right. Follow that and you'll come to the cabins. I reserved number one for you because it's the most private and has the most shade." He grinned mechanically as he handed Luke a key. "Let me know if you need anything. I have to help get lunch ready." He turned abruptly and disappeared through the lodge door.

Luke quickly settled into his temporary living quarters. He was thankful for the relative privacy the small cabin offered. Sighing, he swept the crisp checkered curtains aside and peered through the window. For a moment he thought he saw a shadowy figure slip behind a giant ponderosa pine. Blinking to clear his vision he continued to stare at the place where he was certain he saw something move. A breath of air gently swayed the narrow limbs of smaller trees and bushes sprawled between Luke's cabin and the huge tree. Still nothing. Luke sighed and turned away.

Running his fingers through his thick hair Luke looked around the cabin. His gaze swept over a double bed, small bathroom with a shower, kitchenette, table, two straight-backed chairs, couch, rocking chair, and an end table with an old-fashioned lamp on it. Everything looked rustic, but Luke knew it was brand new. Jeremiah's pride in his accomplishment was obvious. But what kind of a Christian camp was it anyway? A tinge of fear began creeping up his spine.

"No!" Luke's tone was firm. "No!" He lowered his voice even though no other guests had taken up residence next to cabin Number One. "You spirit of fear you are rebuked. Get out of here, Satan! Bow the knee to the Lord Jesus Christ!"

The strange sensation immediately left.

"I wonder what on earth is going on around here," he mumbled to himself. He walked over to the couch and sat down. As he settled himself to get comfortable, he heard a rustling sound under the cushion. He quickly stood to his feet and slightly lifted the cushion. He cautiously ran his hand under it, when abruptly his searching fingers brushed against the slick covers of two magazines. He pulled them out and sucked in his breath.

"Ah," he said quietly, "this may be a key." His eyes quickly scanned the covers. "'The Voice' and 'Dominion,'" he read aloud. "What telltale titles!" He lowered himself onto the couch. Turning the magazines to the back covers, he saw that the address labels contained Jeremiah's name and address. No doubt about it. Those magazines belonged to this place.

Glancing at his watch he noted that he had nearly two hours before lunch was served. Two hours to piece together the real purpose for this camp.

****

"Heather! Quit pacing back and forth and sit down!" Mick scowled angrily at his agitated wife. "Everything is going to be just fine! Once the meetings start, nothing can stop them."

"I know Mick," her mouth drooped into a slight pout while her fingers twisted nervously at her wedding ring, "but there's just something about that man, whatever his name was, that makes me nervous."

"That's obvious," Mick said sarcastically. "Come here, baby, and sit by me." He patted the empty cushion next to him. She gave him a weak smile and plopped down beside him on the couch.

"Just look at this spread," he grinned broadly as he opened the magazine he had been reading to the centerfold. "There we are, honey, under the bright lights." Heather squirmed uncomfortably. Mick scowled at her. "Look, look at this! What a shot. Here you are, right in the front row with Mason," he tapped a picture of a man in a wheelchair, "and here I am on the platform with Apostle Perry Flynn! This magazine goes to millions ... are you listenin'? ... millions of people!" He glanced over at his wife. Her eyes were staring into space. "Aw come on, honey, don't worry!" He tossed the magazine aside and put his arm around her. "The power is with us!"

"I just don't know anymore, Mick. It's not right—and besides, it's beginning to scare me. In fact, it scares me a lot anymore."

"Nonsense! People love the excitement, Heather. They love the signs and wonders. They love the music! Why not give 'em what they want?"

She shrugged off his arm and stood wordlessly to her feet. Wrapping her arms around herself, she walked to the window and focused on the cascading waterfall.

"Okay!" Mick snapped irritably. "What do you expect me to do? Quit? After all these years of building this business?"

"It's supposed to be a ministry, Mick."

He swore. "Heather, listen to me!" He jumped to his feet and began pacing the floor. "People *want* to give us money! They *want* to see the supernatural. Don't you think it's better, if they are going to throw away their dollars, that they throw it our way instead of wasting it someplace else?" His temper began to rise. "Look, Heather," he swore again, "which mansion do you want to give up? Perhaps you'd rather have me sell that stable full of purebred Arabian horses you're so fond of? Or maybe I should sell the yacht?" He watched her face pucker.

"Oh Mick!" She turned to face him, fighting back the tears. "Let's not fight anymore, please." She walked into the bathroom to retrieve a tissue.

"Of Course, Honey," Mick called soothingly after her. *Good old Heather,* he thought to himself. *Her insatiable desire to be needed and loved always gets the best of her.* A crooked smile played across his lips. *Besides, Heather loves being rich ... almost as much as I love being powerful.*

It had been nineteen years ago at a healing convention that Heather and Mick first met. She had just turned twenty. He was twenty-two. Her eyes full of stars and her heart yearning for romance and adventure, Mick had totally swept her off of her feet.

Mick sang and played the keyboard in those days as he accompanied a famous Word-Faith preacher around the country. Eventually Mick was granted opportunities to share with the audience. It soon became apparent that he was a perfect carbon copy of the original in every way. As soon as he and Heather were married, he began holding his own meetings. Heather's good looks and professional singing ability doubled the crowds. Life was good.

As time went on, however, Mick realized that the type of business he had chosen for himself was extremely competitive. His former teacher had tripled his following in a few short months because of an increase in prophetic utterances and accompanying signs and wonders. Mick decided it was time to step up the program. He enlisted the best marketing geniuses he could locate and within six months his "ministry" was launched worldwide via satellite television. His schedule was full three years in advance, and with the help of a ghostwriter, Mick managed to publish seventeen sensational books that were in continual demand.

At first Heather had been disturbed and somewhat embarrassed by the obvious thread of error and unscriptural teachings contained within the pages of her ambitious husband's books, but eventually she shrugged off his deviations from truth and joined him in the book business. She gained her own following after writing a book on spiritual warfare for women in which she outlined the importance of spiritual dancing and flag waving in order to knock demons out of the air. Her latest book reassuring wives that any type of sensual pleasure their husbands wanted to engage in was "holy" was an instant success.

She always backed Mick up in public and played the role of the submissive wife. *After all,* she mused, *that is what the Bible demands of women … isn't it?*

****

Luke's eyes narrowed as he read an article about revival in America. Half a dozen colorful pictures showed a smiling Mick Bain as he stood on a platform in front of thousands of worshippers. His arms were raised and a strange light appeared behind his head. Another photo featured Mick standing between two women who claimed to have received gold fillings in their teeth in one of his meetings. Still another picture showed Mick baptizing a man who appeared to be screaming. Luke looked closer at the man's eyes and shook his head in recognition of the demon that seemed to stare blankly back at him.

Luke flipped the page and scanned a list of Mick's books. He grimaced as he read, "My Date in Heaven", "Our Daddy Loves You",

"Never Be Sick", "Visions of Revival", "Taking the World Back from the Enemy", "Power for the Hour", Hi There, Holy Spirit", "The Overcomer's Manual", "We Are God's Gods", "God Wants You to be Happy," "Money in Your Mouth: Speaking Blessings into Existence", "Kick That Dirty Devil", and "Move Over, Elijah." Luke sighed and picked up the other magazine.

One thing for sure, Luke thought to himself, *Prophet Black would thoroughly denounce this guy as a phony, but the sad fact is, he's just as dangerous and maybe even more so because he knows the psychology of subtle brainwashing and control.*

The cover of the second magazine depicted a space-age type of glass building with a glowing cross on the peak. What appeared to be personalized UFOs zoomed overhead while others were in the process of landing in a multi-colored parking lot. The artist had depicted people of all ages streaming into the building. Their sensuous, tight-fitting clothes resembled something out of a science fiction nightmare. It was impossible to distinguish between males and females. Revulsion swept through Luke and he shuddered. He read the caption audibly between clenched teeth, "The Global Church of the Future." Then something caught Luke's eye. Barely visible, yet deliberately painted in as an extension of this futuristic church building was a tiny mosque! He held the magazine at arm's length and gasped at what began to emerge from the cleverly painted scene. His keen eye outlined the shape of a towering mosque that overshadowed the entire picture, dwarfing the global church in its shadow. Its subliminal message was subtle and insidious, and Luke wondered how any publisher that claimed to be Christian could reproduce such a surreal and blatantly anti-Christian painting on the cover.

Luke felt his stomach turn. He stood to his feet and paced around the small cabin. No doubt about it, Satan was a mastermind at marketing. What was happening to God's church? Hadn't Jesus proclaimed that even the gates of hell could not prevail against it? Perhaps the end of the earth age was closer than Luke or the other angels knew. After all, mighty and powerful as they were, there were certain things known only to God. He returned to the couch, picked up the detestable magazine and forced himself to read every page.

Luke was so engrossed in an article on how the prophecies in the book of Revelation had already been fulfilled that he nearly missed the shadow that suddenly passed across the window, momentarily blocking the sunshine. He jumped to his feet and in two steps was at the door. Yanking it open, he stepped out on to the small wood porch. Shielding his eyes from the bright sunlight, he carefully scanned the forest. Someone, or *something*, had definitely walked right past his cabin. But where was it?

He let out a ragged breath. His senses told him that something evil was definitely lurking around this camp. He could feel it. Every nerve was on edge. His ears strained to hear the slightest noise, but all was calm as death. Even the birds were strangely still. Nothing moved, not even the smallest insect. *It's as if the entire world stopped breathing, moving, existing.*

Luke visibly jumped when the sharp clang of the dinner bell rang from the lodge, signifying lunch was about to be served. He absently wondered how many more guests had arrived. Basically, he didn't look forward to meeting them.

Twenty minutes later those who had arrived in time for lunch were gathered in the dining room. Luke positioned himself at the end of the room where he could observe most of the diners. From what he could gather, most of them were from a church located several miles from the camp. The women slightly outnumbered the men, but that seemed to be the norm in any Christian gathering Luke had attended. The men, Luke noted, were amiable enough, laughing and talking among themselves. One tall man in particular seemed to draw considerable attention. They called him Abel. His wife, Evelyn, was equally popular with the women.

Jeremiah flitted through the dining room, introducing people to one another and making sure everyone had enough to eat. He looked in Luke's direction once and nodded, but other than this brief recognition, he kept himself busy elsewhere.

"Well, if it isn't Abel!" Luke listened to Mick's loud greeting. "Abel, brother, I haven't seen you in months!" Mick crooned as Abel quickly stood to his feet. They shook hands. Luke didn't miss the mutually secretive look that both men exchanged as their eyes briefly locked.

Abel motioned for Mick to sit next to him and grabbed an empty chair. Luke watched as they put their heads together in deep conversation. He wondered at the intensity of their exchange.

"Okay, everybody!" Jeremiah tapped a spoon on a small saucepan. The noisy buzzing subsided. "I just want to welcome you to Rocky Canyon Ranch! We're looking forward to having a wonderful time of refreshing from the Lord tonight! Dinner is at 6:00, and the meeting follows with Apostle and Prophet Mick Bain and his lovely wife, Heather!"

Loud applause followed. Luke glanced over at Heather's strained countenance as she tipped her head and forced a broad grin. Luke sensed that there was an emotional war going on inside of her.

Luke sipped the last of his lemonade and then silently exited through a side door. *Lord God,* he thought, *this is going to be some meeting tonight! And I don't think I'm going to enjoy it one bit!*

****

The rest of the afternoon was uneventful for Luke even though on more than one occasion he felt an invisible presence hovering nearby. He went for a long walk and marveled at the beauty of God's creation, then returned to the cabin. By the time the dinner bell echoed through the trees, he was actually glad for an excuse to escape the oppressive confinement of the small cabin.

The crowd had doubled since noon, and the din throughout dinner dragged on Luke's nerves. Soon enough, however, most of the people expectantly made their way to the lodge. Whatever was supposed to take place was about to begin.

Luke looked up in time to see Jeremiah staring at him and he smiled. Jeremiah nervously responded with a quick grin and then joined Mick and Abel with their wives as they made their way to the meeting area.

The plush room was already set up, complete with modern sound equipment. Luke noted that Mick's team, which had arrived after lunch, was efficient and organized. As the musicians, including Heather and Evelyn, quickly took their places, Luke headed for a seat in the farthest corner of the room. He already knew the first hour or so would be an intense, ear-splitting experience of worshipping the worship.

And so it was, until …

"GOLD!" screamed Abel, "Oh, Brother Mick! You're covered with glory dust!"

The crowd went wild. "The Lord is with us!" shouted Mick as Abel laid face down on the floor. A few others joined him. "The glory cloud prophesied by Brother Branham has descended tonight!"

Mick turned and nodded at Heather, who began to pound out, "We've Got the Power" on the keyboard. "God is honoring us tonight, brothers and sisters! The time has come that the sons of God are being manifested throughout the earth! God's kingdom is being taken by violence! The age of the fourth reformation is being birthed! Do you hear me, people? The church is giving birth to a new age where the apostles and prophets shall rule and reign over the earth!" Some people shouted, others sobbed hysterically. Luke watched as most of the people, with arms raised, swayed to the beat of the music. Heather led the musicians into a medley of upbeat, repetitious choruses while Mick continued to work up the crowd.

Jeremiah, standing in rapt attention in the front row, turned his head slightly and caught Luke out of the corner of his eye. He frowned and turned away to face Mick. Something was definitely different about this guy. Jeremiah shivered involuntarily. Luke must be a spy, not a reporter as he had assumed. He tried to recall previous conversations with Luke, but the noise dissipated his thoughts. He vowed to himself to find out if it was the last thing he did.

Everyone in the first five rows suddenly dropped to the floor as if leveled by an unseen hand. Luke stiffened when a dark shadow hovered over the lifeless forms. "You!" he whispered as the grotesque band of demons took position and possession. As if on cue, every one of the prostrate people began to manifest in one accord. Luke's eyes widened as they barked, howled, growled, hissed, shrieked, screamed, writhed, and foamed at the mouth.

"The Holy Spirit's come upon us!" Mick's voice rose above the chaos. He stooped down and laid hands on Abel. "Brother, receive, I say, receive the blessing of the Lord—a new impartation in authority and power! Receive the spirit of prophecy!" He stood to his feet as Abel lay face down on the floor, sobbing. "That's it, brother; let it come!"

275

Luke watched the pandemonium around him. Some were clapping and swaying, others jumping up and down, but all were caught up in the hypnotic choruses—all that is, except for three people in their early twenties. Luke watched as the two men and one woman bolted and ran for the exit. Luke sprang into action and followed them.

"I'm outta here!" exclaimed the tall man in the lead. It seemed to Luke that his sandy hair was literally standing on end. *And with good reason, too,* he thought.

"These people are insane," gasped the woman as she clutched her purse to her side. "I'm scared silly!"

"Hurry up," growled the shorter man who brought up the rear, "or I'll run right over you two." They disappeared through the exit leading to the stairway.

Luke wove his way through the jumble of gyrating bodies. As he reached the door, five women, staggering like drunken sailors, blocked his way. He stood and watched in dismay as the terrified threesome tumbled down the stairs, tore across the dining room, and made a mad dash to a blue pickup. By the time he worked his way around the women, ran down the stairs, and leaped around the tables and chairs in the dining room, it was too late. The three panicked visitors piled into the pickup on top of one another and frantically gunned the engine to life. With tires squealing, they disappeared down the dirt road in a cloud of dust. He knew that the departed threesome were unsaved and that they had come hoping to find answers for their lives. *How grieved the Holy Spirit must be*, he thought to himself. Dejected, he turned from the doorway. Everything inside of him screamed in protest, but he had to finish this unpleasant assignment regardless of how he felt about it.

"It's too bad they didn't stay for the impartation." Luke whirled to face Jeremiah, who stood above him on the landing. Luke remained silent. After a long and uncomfortable silence, Jeremiah slightly grinned. His cold gray eyes narrowed to slits. "You were coming back to the meeting, weren't you, Luke?" It was more of a statement than a question.

"Of course," Luke's deep voice was calm. "I just wondered if your three guests were all right." He grinned at the irony of his words. They certainly were in far better shape than the hysterical crowd upstairs. He slowly climbed the stairs until he faced Jeremiah. He noticed color begin to creep up Jeremiah's neck and flush his cheeks before he turned to lead the way back into the chapel.

Heather, perspiring and red-faced, was still pounding out choruses, but Evelyn was moving from woman to woman, laying her hands on each of their heads, praying loudly for them. Her hands vibrated uncontrollably. Luke stiffened as several of the women screamed, threw their arms up into the air and fell over backwards. He noticed that their eyes rolled up into their heads before they collapsed on the floor. A surge of red-hot anger began to explode within his body. He clenched his teeth.

Suddenly he felt strong hands on his shoulders. "Luke," Mick spoke close to his left ear, "God wants us to pray for you, brother!"

"That's right," echoed Abel, who stood to his right. Luke cast him a sideways glance. The demon in Abel's eyes mocked him. "You need an impartation of the Spirit, Luke!" His lips curled into a sneer. Their grip on him tightened. Luke tried to step backward, but he bumped into Jeremiah, who stood directly behind him. Jeremiah suddenly moved around to face him, obviously relishing Luke's discomfort.

"Now, Brother Luke," he drawled, "we'll give you something you'll never forget—no, not ever!"

14

THE SWORD
OF THE LORD

The room momentarily swayed as Luke tried to focus on Jeremiah's glinting eyes. The power emanating from the three men who surrounded him was feigned. And Luke knew all too well exactly where that power originated.

"Almighty God," Luke whispered a prayer, "strengthen your messenger!"

Jeremiah gasped audibly as Luke's blue eyes met his. He tried to tighten his grip on Luke's shoulders, but a mighty, unseen force pressed against his chest, driving him backward. At the same time, both Mick and Abel found themselves propelled away from either side of Luke. Abel, against his will, crumpled to the floor while Mick staggered a few feet but somehow managed to remain upright. He pointed an accusing finger at Luke. "You!" he sneered, "You're a spy! A spy sent in to discover our liberty in Christ!"

Heather's fingers unexpectedly lifted off of the keyboard in the middle of a rousing chorus. An eerie silence descended upon the crowded room. Her eyes were fastened upon her glowering husband. Heather slowly rose and inched her way along the wall until she reached the exit. There she stopped, waiting, watching.

Luke, eyes lit by holy fire, took a step toward Mick. "No! No! Get away from me! Don't you touch me!" Unbidden words, like bullets, spewed forth from Mick's gaping mouth. "This is my hour, *not* yours!

God will curse you for coming against His anointed! Do you hear me? How dare you come against the anointed of the Lord!"

A low rumble issued from the crowd, but quickly faded. Every eye was riveted on the two figures, but not one person moved. Mysteriously, their racing hearts and gasping lungs and become entombed within stone limbs and bodies. Luke glanced at the jumble of motionless humanity and breathed a silent prayer of gratitude to God.

Jeremiah struggled against the faceless pressure holding him captive. Tormenting questions raced through his mind. What would people say about Rocky Canyon Ranch? What would happen to his reputation? What could he do to get rid of this man who called himself Luke Obed Solomon?

Jeremiah rolled his eyes toward Abel, hoping that somehow, he could manage to lay hands on Luke and propel him out the door. But one glance at Abel dispelled that idea. Disgust momentarily surged through Jeremiah at the sheer panic registered on Abel's immobilized features. If anybody was going to throw Luke out, it would have to be him or Mick, but try as he might, his body simply refused to respond to his brain. He felt short-circuited even though he knew his useless limbs were not paralyzed.

As Luke slowly advanced, Mick backed himself into a corner. His lips curled as he hissed into Luke's face. His eyes bulged with venomous hatred, and his fists clenched in warning.

Luke spoke, his voice low. "The Lord rebuke you, Satan." The authority of that one statement hit Mick like a physical blow. He sucked in his breath and doubled over. Mick groaned helplessly as his knees buckled. He slid down the wall where, as if in slow motion, he curled up into a ball.

Authority and power flowed from Luke as he turned back to face the ashen-faced crowd. "You came for an experience," he spoke softly. "You came for a touch from the Lord." Some managed to groan. "Some of you came to see physical healings." A few moans ascended to the vaulted ceiling. "You came for revival!" Muffled acknowledgement rolled through the still figures. A muscle twitched in Luke's jaw. "But all of you came for yourselves," he thundered.

Silence.

Luke moved to the front of the chapel and stopped. Bulging eyes stared at him unblinkingly. Mouth grim, eyes aflame, he spoke. "You call yourselves children of God, yet you do not know God! You have literally prostituted your souls to the spirit of the world, as you support wolves in sheep's clothing, whose business is merchandising the things of God to build up their own worldly kingdoms at the expense of your souls. You worship idols of your own making!" People gasped, but were helpless to move. Frozen into position, they had no alternative but to listen to the tall stranger who faced them.

"Let me name some of your idols!" He roared in indignation. "You worship what you call worship, yet it is pagan to the core! Nothing about it glorifies a holy God, but everything about it appeals to your flesh. Your so-called dancing before the Lord is a flimsy excuse to satisfy your craving for spiritual experiences and to arouse carnal appetites." In vain they tried to shut out Luke's voice and his piercing, searching eyes. His words cut like a two-edged sword.

"The revival you seek has become an idol in itself—an idol much sought after to grant you thrills and satisfy your insatiable desire for entertainment. You come near to God with your lips, but your hearts are far from Him. You flatter with the cheap words of your mouth, but in your heart you burn with lust, greed, and hatred for all that is pure and holy!" He looked toward the ceiling for a moment and then continued. "Oh, foolish people! You chase after lying signs and wonders such as so-called gold flakes and fillings. You swoon when a feather falls from the sky, claiming it's from angels. You run to and fro around the world with your ridiculous, demonic 'trance dancing,' 'cross pollination' heresies and doctrines of demons."

Luke paused, letting his words sink in. "You think that anything supernatural is from God whether it lines up with His Word or not! And all because you do not have the love of the truth in you! No, the truth insults your religious sensitivities! It insults your pride! It throws light on your spiritual darkness and reveals the intents of your heart!"

A smile played on the corners of Luke's lips. The atmosphere was intense, suffocating. He knew if God's power had not come, had not immobilized the people, he would be physically attacked.

He raised his arm and swept the room with his hand. "You're addicted to Satan's lies because he tells you what you want to hear. You think God has touched you because you laugh hysterically and cannot stop! You think the Holy Spirit is manifested because you sound like a bunch of animals. The Holy Spirit is just that ... holy! You have deluded yourselves! What you are manifesting are demons!" He let his words sink in for a moment. "You need to repent and renounce the demons you have invited in!" A low, menacing growl rumbled through the crowd. It reminded Luke of an earthquake deep within the bowels of the earth.

Luke pointed at Abel. "This man has told you that Evelyn is the wife of his youth, that she is God's will for his life. All of you know that Abel left his first wife and three young children to marry Evelyn, his mistress, because she carried his child! Yet not one of you who call yourselves Christians ever rebuked him for his sin! That is because if a pastor, a leader, can get away with adultery and lies and sin, then so can you also have a cloak for your sins!"

The crowded room grew dusky with hatred. Luke watched a dark mist descend over the stricken men and women. He slowly shook his head.

Luke glanced sideways at Mick. Seeing that he remained curled up on the floor, he continued. "This false prophet," he nodded toward Mick, "feeds you spiritual poison straight from the pit of hell! His power comes from the deceiver, from the occult!" Luke heard a collective gasp. "Mick is another one of your idols that you have chosen over the real Jesus, who is God incarnate!"

The scream was collective. It echoed throughout the camp, ricocheting through the trees. Every demon in Rocky Canyon Ranch reacted to the name of Jesus, God incarnate.

Mick suddenly uncoiled and struck at Luke's leg, but Luke, quick on his feet, sidestepped him. Several of the people who previously had been writhing, foaming, hissing, and making animal noises began slithering like a ball of snakes around the room. Heather screamed and disappeared through the exit.

Luke watched Evelyn make her way to Abel, who had managed to struggle to his feet. He was still in a daze. She pulled him by the hand through the open doorway. Luke listened to their muffled footsteps as they stumbled down the stairs.

Luke turned back to face Jeremiah, but the place where he had been struck motionless was vacant. He sensed a movement behind him and ducked just as a piece of firewood flew past his head. Whirling, he grabbed Jeremiah by the arm and flipped him to the floor. Uttering profanities, Jeremiah lunged at Luke's legs, but instead he ended up grappling with the dazed and confused Mick.

"Where'd he go?" Mick gasped. "I swear, he was right here, between us! We almost had him!"

Jeremiah's gray eyes filled with terror. He grabbed the front of Mick's shirt. "I knew it!" He whispered hoarsely, "I knew there was something different about him!"

"What do you mean, Jeremiah?" Mick eyes narrowed accusingly. "Why did you invite him here anyway?" Anger boiled to the surface. Before Jeremiah could defend himself, Mick jumped to his feet, dragging a protesting Jeremiah with him. "This is all your fault, Jeremiah Delaney! You're supposed to screen the people who come out here! Now look at the mess you've made of my meeting!" He cast a furtive glance around the room. It was in total pandemonium. People were screaming, weeping, hissing, moaning, and laughing hysterically while some were singing at the top of their lungs, off key.

"He was a reporter!" Jeremiah said lamely.

"Reporter my eye!" Mick let go of Jeremiah's shirt. "Reporter for whom?"

When Jeremiah didn't answer, Mick swore. "That's just what I thought!" he growled. Mick brushed off his sleeves, straightened his jacket and looked around the room for Heather. "Where is that woman? Why isn't she at the keyboard?" Anger flushed his cheeks. *I don't have time to run around the camp looking for her right now,* he thought to himself, *but I'll find her, and when I do, she's going to pay.* He took a deep breath and then calmly walked up to the microphone.

"Good people," he crooned, "please, please let's just take our seats and let the Spirit calm our hearts. We've suffered a grave injustice tonight by a false prophet." Shouts of agreement split the suffocating air. People began groping their way to their chairs. "While this has been a most terrifying and disgusting experience for all of us, my beloved," his smile was dazzling, "let us remember that God isn't going to allow anything to happen that is beyond His control." A few people clapped their approval.

"In fact," he beamed, his confidence bolstered by the crowd's eagerness to agree, "this has been a good lesson for us all. A lesson I trust we shall not soon forget!" The people cheered in unison. Mick went on, "Did not Jesus Himself tell us that in these last days there would be false prophets and false Christs? Did He not warn us that the time would come when we, who love the truth, would be persecuted and even put to death?" Loud applause followed.

Mick's eyes darted to the corner of the room where Jeremiah leaned against the wall. His eyes were shadowed, his expression fathomless. Mick swallowed and turned back to the eager faces before him. "We have to expect that Satan will attempt to destroy this New Thing, this great end-times revival!"

Several people shouted "Amen!"

"Are we going to let the enemy come into the camp and steal from us? Are we going to let Satan walk right in and deceive us through lying signs and wonders?" The crowd went wild. Mick watched Jeremiah smirk in admiration. There was no mistake about it; Mick had charisma. "Now, I don't know about you people, but I came here to meet with God!" Mick shouted. "Let's get on with it! The Spirit is not through with us yet; in fact, He's just begun."

****

The sound of cascading water splashing against the rocks offered a backdrop for crickets and other creatures of the night that busily filled the balmy air with their own unique blend of noises. Puffs of wind rustled the pine needles of the giant trees that stood as dark silhouettes against the light of a half-moon. It was a tranquil scene.

Heather gasped in fright as she heard a twig snap somewhere behind her. She let out her breath as Luke stepped into the clearing. Moonlight outlined his handsome features. He smiled reassuringly at her. She turned back to face the trailing waterfall. Tears sparkled on her cheeks.

"I'm sorry to startle you," Luke said gently, "but we need to talk." When she remained silent, he continued. "You love Jesus," he stated matter-of-factly, "and you want to serve Him with all of your heart."

She uttered a soft cry. "Yes," she whispered.

"Mick has sold his soul to Satan, hasn't he?" Luke prodded.

"Yes."

"You're afraid, aren't you?"

"Yes!"

"Your parents know, Heather."

She whirled to face him, eyes wide. "How do you know that?"

"What is important right now is getting you out of here. You can stay with them. They'll help you."

"I can't, I mean, I can't just up and leave Mick! I mean, he'll be so angry ..."

Suddenly an eerie howl from the chapel reverberated through the forest. The chilling sound, a chorus of many voices, repeated itself. Heather hugged herself and shivered.

"It's time to leave!" Luke reached out to take her arm. She hesitated. He moved a step closer and offered his hand. "Please, Heather." She stood for a long moment, held captive by the indescribable look in his clear eyes.

Suddenly she sparked to life, and looked up into the night sky. "Thank You Jesus, my Lord!" she exclaimed and then submitted to Luke's guidance. He led her back through the forest to the condo she and Mick shared.

"Can you pack your belongings in a hurry?"

"Yes, I'm sure of that," she whispered breathlessly.

They reached the small clearing and Heather stepped past Luke to insert the key in the door. She had barely taken two steps inside of the door when suddenly Luke brushed her aside and lunged through the doorway.

Heather screamed.

It was at least ten feet tall and shrouded in black. Its red eyes glowed underneath the black hood, and its claw-like hands clutched a raised dagger. It meant business.

Luke dodged the first slash and turned to face his attacker. "I want the woman," it hissed.

"No!" Luke jumped back, avoiding another attempt to stab him.

"She's mine!" the thing warned.

"No!" Luke argued as he moved around the room cautiously.

"I said she's mine!" It lunged. Luke's feet slipped on the braided rug, sending him sprawling on the floor. The hooded figure landed on his chest. "Aha, Lukie boy," it sneered, "you lose this time!" It raised the dagger high and then plunged it downward, barely missing Luke's throat as he rolled to the side, knocking the killer backwards against the couch.

"Lord God Almighty! Send help from the Sanctuary!" Luke panted, dodging another rush by the enemy.

Heather's eyes widened. From her viewpoint outside the doorway all she saw was a blinding light that filled the small room. Shielding her eyes against the brilliant glare, she tried in vain to see Luke, to see anything that would give meaning to the strange scuffling sounds she thought she was hearing.

"It's about time you got here, Pirathon," Luke wiped his face on the back of his sleeve.

Pirathon grinned broadly. "You need to know that this place is well guarded, my friend! However," his eyes twinkled, "the guards have been temporarily detained, so you should be able to get out of here without any more problems."

"Praise God Almighty!" Luke said.

As quickly as it had come, the light faded. Heather blinked. Luke was standing calmly in the middle of the room, head tipped with a jaunty grin on his face. "Well, Heather, are you going to just stand there all night, or are you going to come in and pack?"

She shook her head slightly. Was she imagining the incredible battle that had just taken place? Perhaps her nerves were so shot she was hallucinating.

"Hurry," Luke urged, snapping her to attention.

Heather walked shakily into the small bedroom. Her eyes darted around to make sure nothing was lurking in the corners. "I can assure you, everything is okay, but we must hurry," Luke warned.

Eight minutes later Heather and Luke unlocked the doors to his rented Jeep Cherokee. He threw her luggage in the back compartment and then settled her in the passenger seat. He stuck the key in the ignition and started the engine. "Wait here, Heather. I'll get my stuff. I won't be but a minute."

He entered his cabin. A gasp escaped his lips. The place had been thoroughly ransacked. The only thing that seemed to be untouched was his thick leather-bound Bible on the counter. He grabbed it up with one hand and scooped up his jacket off the floor with the other. He ran out the door to the waiting vehicle. Jumping in, he shoved it in gear and stepped on the gas.

The cabin exploded into a fiery inferno just as the Jeep careened around a thick stand of young pine trees.

Heather's face blanched in sheer terror. Her tongue stuck to the roof of her mouth and she felt faint. "Here," Luke offered her a drink from the canteen he had left in the Jeep. Her fingers trembled as she fought with the cap. Finally it gave and she pressed it to her lips.

"Pray," Luke ordered, "out loud!"

"I ca-ca-can't!" she stammered.

"You have to!"

Tears rolled down her cheeks. "I've, I've sinned too much, Luke! You just don't understand!"

"Jesus will forgive you, Heather. He knows you have always loved Him in your heart, even though you walked a long, crooked path away from him after you married Mick." He tossed her a reassuring smile and then turned his attention to the road. The headlights bobbed and flickered as he sped down the bumpy dirt road. *That highway should be coming up soon*, he thought to himself. He glanced in the rearview mirror. The churning dust rose into the still night air, hanging like a cloud before sifting back to earth. *No headlights. So far so good.*

"Pray, Heather!"

She choked back a sob, "Lord Jesus, please forgive me! Forgive me, Lord! Forgive me!" she buried her face in her hands. Luke sighed in relief. Satan wasn't going to have an open door with her any longer. "Lord, grant us safety. Oh God, please have mercy upon us and send your angels to protect us as we go from this awful place!"

Luke grinned to himself and slowed to a stop as they approached the paved road. A rabbit, trapped by the glaring headlights, sat straight up in front of them. Abruptly it spun around and dashed into the safety of the bushes.

"Well?" Heather questioned, her eyebrows raised. "We turn left here, don't we?"

"Yes, that's the way we all came in, but I'm afraid we're going to take the long way out and turn right. Just to be safe." Looking back to make sure no one followed yet, Luke turned right. He hit the gas throttle, and the vehicle speeded up the narrow, winding road. Fifty feet later they were deep within the rocky canyon, hidden from view.

"Who are you?" Heather turned and stared at Luke. Lights from the dashboard outlined his barely visible masculine profile.

"Luke Obed Solomon."

"I mean," she quizzed, "just who are you really?"

"That answer isn't good enough for you, Heather?"

"No, it isn't. There's definitely something about you ..."

"Hang on!" Luke thundered as he swerved around a buck. "That was close!"

The road twisted and turned through the narrow gorge then began to seesaw its way up a steep mountainside. Luke saw a turnout and pulled into it. Switching off the headlights, he shoved the gearshift into park and set the emergency brake. He peered through the windshield, then pointed through the fading moonlight toward the canyon floor. "Down there! Look!"

Heather sucked in her breath sharply as she rose from her seat for a better look. Headlights from two vehicles could be seen far below on the Rocky Canyon Ranch road. They stopped when they reached the main road. Luke and Heather stared in silence until they finally turned left. She let out her breath. "Oh, thank You, Jesus!" she exclaimed.

Luke waited until the vehicles disappeared around a sharp bend before switching on his lights and pulling back onto the road.

"Where does this road go?" she asked.

287

"According to the map, it takes us down toward the river, and from there we can get you to the airstrip for a flight to Jamesville. Your parents will be waiting for you."

She cocked her head. "Just how do you know so much, Luke? How do you know they'll even take me back?"

"Let's just say that I'm a servant of God and the Lord tells His servants what they need to know. Now, why don't you just lean back and get some rest. We have a long trip in front of us."

"Okay, but before I do, I need to tell you something important." He nodded, and she continued. "In the meeting tonight, when you were preaching," she hesitated, then sucked in her breath and continued, "I saw the sword of the Lord come down."

Luke smiled to himself. "And?" he questioned, his voice low.

"That's when I made the decision to separate myself from all that's phony and, regardless of the cost, come back to Christ." Unbidden tears filled her downcast eyes.

Finally, he spoke. "I'm really glad Heather. More than you'll ever know."

15

BETWEEN A ROCK AND
A HARD PLACE

The smiling waiter seated the stylish, middle-aged woman at a view table and handed her a menu. She smiled up at him. He momentarily wondered at the sorrow reflected in her warm, brown eyes. "And, you are expecting someone?" he asked.

"Yes ... a Mr. Solomon. Would you kindly direct him to this table when he arrives?"

He nodded. "Coffee today?"

"Yes, please, with cream." She turned to study the tranquil waterfront scene. Several fishermen expectantly cast their lines over a worn wood railing at the end of the ferry dock. Waves gently licked the pebble-strewn beach. Seagulls floated serenely on unseen currents of salty air, scanning the water's surface and shoreline for scraps of food. Soft, puffy clouds dotted the pastel sky. Yes, it was an unusually beautiful day.

The waiter returned with a pot of steaming coffee and cream. "Thank you," she murmured absently as she surveyed the tall, blonde man who entered the dining area. He seemed to know exactly where he was going without asking for directions and headed straight for her table.

"Serena Temple?" His blue eyes twinkled a thousand smiles.

"Yes," she looked up at him, "and you are Mr. Solomon?"

He nodded and slid into the booth seat opposite her. "Please call me Luke." He glanced out the window. "It is beautiful, isn't it?" He studied her profile as she watched two excited fishermen struggling with their wriggling catches. Her platinum hair softly framed her oval face. Her only jewelry was a pair of delicate silver earrings that matched a fashionable pin on the lapel of her navy blazer.

"Um-hum. I love it here." There was a distinct note of sadness in her voice.

"Me too," he replied. Regardless of the toll the fall of man had taken on earth, there was no denying the beauty that still remained. Truly, all that God created was good. He picked up the menu and studied it for a few moments. He knew Serena was surveying him with interest and wanted to give her time to collect her troubled thoughts.

"Aha!" he exclaimed, pointing at the open-face, fresh crab sandwich smothered in cheese sauce. He peeked at her over the top of his menu. She lowered her eyes and quickly scanned her menu even though she already knew what she wanted.

The waiter returned to take their orders. "Madam," he tipped his head and smiled warmly. "Are you ready to order?"

"Yes, please. The seafood salad special with house dressing."

He turned to Luke. "Sir? What will you have today?"

"Grilled crab sandwich with cheese sauce, side of green salad with Russian dressing, and coffee, please."

"Ah," the waiter nodded approvingly. "Excellent choices—both of them."

After he had retrieved their coffee and bustled to another table, Luke cleared his throat and addressed Serena. "I so appreciate your willingness to meet today to discuss CKDZ radio station. I am most interested in knowing how to become a guest on the popular Sonny Star talk show. I feel I have certain areas of expertise that would greatly interest the listening audience." Her soft lips curved into a smile. She decided she liked this Luke Solomon, whoever he was. There was something different about him, some intangible quality that warmed her heart and somehow made her feel safe. And God knew she hadn't felt safe for a very long time. She folded her fingers on the table edge and leaned forward. "Pardon me, Mr. Solomon, but you seem to be naïve concerning the world of Christian radio."

"Please call me Luke, and yes, I have to admit, my interests have been concentrated elsewhere lately."

She tipped her head. "Oh?" She was too polite to press him for an explanation, and he didn't volunteer.

The waiter returned to refill their coffee cups and assure them that their lunches would soon follow. Luke studied her with appreciation. In spite of the fact that her eyes were pools of sorrow, there was no undercurrent of bitterness or anger. Her countenance was soft, almost glowing with the light of Christ. She carried herself well and exuded good manners. All too often women in Christian work were plagued with a religious spirit and mountains of pride.

"Here we are," the waiter smiled as he placed their lunches in front of them. "Can I get anything else for you?"

Serena and Luke exchanged looks. "No, thank you," they said in unison, followed by soft laughter. They shared a few moments of relaxed silence. The lunch was delicious and each seemed lost in thought.

"Let me explain," Serena broke the silence in between bites. She took a sip of coffee and continued. "It's my job to sell advertising spots. This is how the radio shows are financed."

He nodded. "I understand. You need sponsors."

"Yes." She studied his face and wondered just what he was really after. Her keen intuition coupled with years of experience told her that Mr. Solomon wasn't interested in buying radio time or advertising. She was certain he was not going to be the answer to her mounting financial difficulties. Yet, somehow she knew this wasn't going to be a waste of her time.

"Mrs. Temple, it is 'Misses,' isn't it?" His impish smile caught her off guard.

"Yes, it's 'Misses.'" She took a breath and hesitated. It would be so easy to spill her guts, to blurt out the whole sordid story of her past, present, and seemingly hopeless future to this amicable stranger. Then, without warning, a rush of fear swept through her like a cold December storm. She felt herself whither and quickly withdrew behind an icy wall of safety.

Luke felt it as well and veered off the course he was taking. "Look at those crazy seagulls," he chuckled. She turned to follow his gaze. On the beach several gulls, intent on stealing what one of their flock carried in his beak, squawked and bullied the lone bird until it took flight.

Frantically it circled above the shimmering water seeking a place of refuge in which to devour its find. Other gulls, hearing the commotion, joined in the attack. It wasn't long before the beleaguered bird lost control and dropped his morsel into the water. Instantly the screeching flock dove in after the prize. Luke and Serena watched as the battle intensified between the feathered mob. Meanwhile, the loser flew toward the end of the pier where he helped himself to bits and pieces of fish bait laying on the sun-bleached planks.

Serena laughed. "It looks like number one seagull came out ahead after all."

"Just like you will, Serena."

She turned to face him. His fathomless blue eyes plumbed the depths of her soul. Suddenly her brown eyes brimmed with unbidden tears. She stared into her half-eaten salad.

"I'm curious," he spoke at length, "about your job, how it's going."

She sighed, relieved. At least he wasn't probing into her private life. Not yet anyhow. But she had a queasy feeling that would soon follow. On the other hand, she was in some way strangely happy that perhaps today would be the day in which she would be set free from all of the nightmares that had plagued her for so long.

"Mr. Solomon, er, Luke," she said with resolve, "my main goal is to serve the Lord Jesus Christ. I am going to be very honest with you." She smiled to herself. What good would it do to try to hide anything from this perceptive individual? "Right now my job is in jeopardy because I refuse to sell advertising spots to promote and sponsor the Stanley Stewart talk show." She watched him raise his eyebrows and continued. "Mr. Stewart has preempted Sonny Star five evenings a week." She shook her head sadly. "As you probably know, Sonny has been very popular with the people for over eleven years. He is a no-nonsense, true-blue Christian who doesn't hesitate to make waves by exposing false teachings, false prophets, and the growing apostasy in America. He talks about controversial issues such as abortion, sexual immorality, human rights, euthanasia, capital punishment, drugs, gangs, and other issues of vital interest in our society." She paused as the waiter refilled their water glasses. "You see, Luke, he is faithful to also give the Gospel, often."

Luke sipped his coffee and smiled encouragingly.

292

"I have no problem with signing up sponsors for his program. However, two months ago our radio station changed hands, and we have a new station manager." She paused and looked into Luke's face. He watched her face pale as she revealed the inner workings of Christian Radio Station CKDZ. "He is not a Christian!" she rasped. Color flooded her cheeks as anger bubbled to the surface. "In fact, one of the reasons he cut Sonny back and replaced him with Stanley Stewart is that Stewart is liberal, tolerant, and politically correct." She leaned toward him. "To be perfectly frank with you, the new station owners are actually part of the Emergent Church Movement. Perhaps you are aware that this movement is subtly replacing the true commission of the Church with a compromising worldly mixture of tolerance or political correctness. Such tolerance makes people comfortable in their sin, while leading the professing Church into a one world religion."

Luke's eyes narrowed in consternation. During his entire earthly assignment, he had found few true men and women of genuine faith and integrity. The situation on planet earth was far worse than he had previously imagined it to be. Church after church was nothing more than a façade for fallen man's insatiable lust and moral compromise to justify and gain power and riches. Most of the churches Luke had visited were in the extreme, and none of these portrayed the true character of God or the real Jesus, let alone presented the life-changing Gospel. Many preached a Hollywood style, entertaining, easy-believism, watered-down version of the Gospel that contained no convicting power. He observed that the members of this type of church attended out of habit like brainwashed zombies going through their religious motions. Other churches were steeped in doctrines of demons, filled with gross error. He knew that those who insisted on drinking from these poisoned waters would be eternally lost. However, to bring these two diverse camps under one delusional canopy for the sake of peace and ecumenism, the Emergent Church developed from the faulty foundations with its McDonald's-like environment. It touted how it did away with the old-time religion in order to usher in the new to attract more people of the world to a new more tolerable religion. He shuddered to think of the unholy agreement that is actually prostituting souls in the name of Jesus.

"Luke?" Serena's inquiring voice snapped Luke to the present.

"Sorry, Serena," he said apologetically. "I was just thinking about how typical this scenario is these days. What a tragedy!" He pressed his lips together and searched her face. Convinced that she trusted him, he said, "So let me guess what is happening with your career. The pressure is being put on you to secure advertisers to keep Stewart, and others of his ilk, going strong, regardless of whether or not they are true to God and His principles."

"Yes, you've got it." Her voice was grim. "He is pressuring me to get more sponsors for a man called 'the prophet'—Prophet Black. He's nothing but a Manifest Sons of God heretic, who could easily cause those who are vulnerable and innocent in the Church to reject the fundamental Christian faith with a substitute belief system that will best serve their purpose!" she blurted.

"I know him."

"Oh ..." her voice trailed away. Perhaps she had gone too far, said too much.

"Don't worry, Serena," Luke said. "I know what the man is."

They spent the next few moments in silence, finishing their lunches. Serena asked, "Just what can I do for you, Luke? Are you sure you want to meet Sonny?"

He leaned back in his chair. "For starters, allow me to pay for our lunches and then come sit outside for a while. I know you have time today, and it's a beautiful day!"

Serena, usually composed, was taken aback. *How does he know my schedule?*

"Good!" He smiled as he put a generous tip on the table. "It's settled then!" "Thank you, Luke. That was very kind of you." She felt dazed, as if she had suddenly been plummeted into a surreal world. Nevertheless, once outside the crowded restaurant, she allowed Luke to guide her along a narrow, paved pathway that led to several wooden benches facing the bay. Other than an elderly couple who sat at the far end of the row of weather-beaten seats, the private alcove was deserted.

"I want to know if you can speak to Sonny about interviewing me on one of his live call-in shows," Luke said as he sat down.

"Oh?" she queried, sitting next to him. "What is the topic you wish to discuss?" Before he could reply, she added, "Sonny has a way of throwing curves at you, you know." She smiled in amusement.

"I know he does, but that's fine with me."

"You seem very confident."

"The Lord will tell me what to say."

The reverence in his voice stilled Serena's jangled nerves. She closed her eyes and concentrated on nature's medley of sounds—the distant droning of an outboard motor; the methodical gurgle, swish, splash of the waves; the birdcalls of the busy gulls; and over it all the occasional laughter of the fishermen on the wharf. *Oh Lord, she silently prayed, it's been so long—the battle never seems to end. Oh, Lord Jesus! I need you to comfort me!* Her fingers trembled as she brushed unbidden tears from her cheeks.

"Yes," she whispered, eyes still closed. She tipped her face toward the sun's warm rays. "I'll speak with Sonny first thing tomorrow morning. I'm sure he'll be delighted to have you as a special guest on his show."

"Thank you, Serena." His voice was low and barely audible. "You do know, don't you, that you only have another month on this job."

She sighed. "Yes, I suspect that is true."

He paused, waiting for her to communicate the horrible burden she carried. It was now or never.

Finally, she spoke. "I need this job, Luke. You see, I can't lose my home ... can't let anything happen to me ... my daughter ..." She buried her face in her hands.

"Serena," Luke soothed. "God knows all about it. He has something better for you."

She tried to compose herself. Retrieving a tissue from her purse, she dabbed at the corner of her eyes and forced a faint smile. Her brown eyes focused on a full-to-capacity ferry boat that plowed heavily through the water. *That's just how I feel. Trying to make headway against the current.*

"I must have a job that honors Christ and at the same time pays well, Luke. I have to try and keep my house."

"And?" Luke queried.

"Michelle, my daughter, lives with me."

He smiled at her knowingly. His blue eyes probed her soul. Suddenly she knew he knew. And she had to let it all out.

Relief swept over her beleaguered soul. Later she would admit that there was no rhyme or reason to it; in her humanness there was no understanding of it or words to explain it. But she knew in her innermost being that she could trust this stranger and that God had sent him at just the right moment. "Michelle has a six-month-old baby boy, Ryan." She smiled at the thought of him. "He's adorable, but you see, Michelle isn't married."

"I know."

"Why do I believe you do?" She paused, as if trying to prioritize the jumble of memories, thoughts, and facts that surfaced in her mind. "Michelle is a good girl," she said more to herself than to him. "But after what happened to her, she went off the deep end. Looking for love!" She fought back tears of anguish.

"That isn't at all unusual," he said gently.

"I know, but you see, it wouldn't have happened if I hadn't married Brian."

"You can't blame yourself for trusting him."

"No, I suppose not. I was innocent, gullible. I thought that he was God's answer to so many of my problems after what happened to David."

"Would you care to go back to the beginning, when you and David vowed to serve God together?"

She squinted up into his intelligent face. *How does he know about David and me? Who is this man anyway?*

"Serena, you can trust me." A smile played around the corners of his mouth and his blue eyes twinkled with joy.

"Yes, I believe that, Luke." She grinned at him. He made her want to laugh in spite of the pain in her heart. This day, this hour, this moment was a divine gift from God, and she didn't want to lose or misuse it.

She sighed and closed her eyes. "David was the most committed, loving, kind Christian you could ever meet. He was handsome, intelligent, and godly. I loved him deeply. When we finished our training to be missionaries in Africa, we married and immediately flew to Kenya. Michelle was born a year later. There we served the Lord for five years together. Our daughter adored her daddy." Her voice broke. "He was so good to both of us. Then," she drew a deep breath, "then on a flying mission his small plane crashed and both he and the co-pilot were lost."

Luke whispered, "I am so sorry, Serena. Only God knows why these tragedies happen. His ways are past finding out."

"Yes, I know." She lapsed into silence for a few minutes before continuing. "I brought Michelle back to the States and remained unmarried for ten years. We attended the Woodside Baptist Church up on Manzanita Hill." He nodded knowingly, and she went on. "That's where I first became acquainted with Brian. He is a very well-known evangelist, worldwide. But Woodside Baptist was his home church. When his wife suddenly died, he didn't travel as much because he was needed at home by his teenage son and daughter. To make a long story short, he began courting me, and the next thing I knew, we were married." Her involuntary shudder did not escape Luke's notice.

The elderly couple stood to their feet and shuffled past Luke and Serena. She waited patiently for them to pass. Satisfied they were out of earshot, she said, "Brian and his family are very well-known, Luke."

"I understand, Serena. This is strictly confidential. It's between you and me and God."

"Very well." She forced a grim smile. "I believed he was a man of God, Luke. I believed he was like David. I believed he would take care of us. But I was wrong!"

"And Michelle paid the price, didn't she?"

Serena's eyes widened. "How did you know that?"

"It happens more often than you would ever want to know, Serena."

"They *both* molested her! The father, *my husband*, and his son!" She bit her lip, fighting to control her churning emotions.

Luke produced a large handkerchief for her, which she thankfully accepted.

"When I finally found out what was going on, I immediately took Michelle and left! I filed for a divorce and brought charges against Brian and his son. But no one believed me, Luke! Brian had made such a name for himself that everyone thought I was fabricating the story to bring down his ministry!"

"And both you and Michelle suffered terrible persecution from the church."

"Yes ... and then Michelle walked away from the Lord. She went crazy, and I couldn't control her. I took her to a dozen counselors, but it did no good. She stayed out late at night and then ..."

"She became pregnant with Ryan."

"But thank God, she didn't murder him through an abortion! I never could have survived if that had taken place."

"And now you need a secure job that enables you to support your daughter and grandson. But you can't conceive of working outside of service to Christ, who is your first love and commitment."

"Thank you." Her simple response spoke volumes. Suddenly her burden lifted. Renewed hope surged through her heart. God was here. He knew. He understood. And somehow, He would see her through.

Luke stood to his feet and offered her his hand. Together they watched the over-burdened ferry pull up to the dock. Once secured to the ramp, the crew signaled for the foot passengers to disembark. Then followed the cars, pickup trucks, campers, logging trucks, and even a half dozen motorbikes.

Serena tilted her head and sniffed the salty air. The ferry, once unloaded, remained docked until another load of passengers and vehicles filed on board. *Lord,* she prayed, *help me to safely dock in Your harbor, where I can unload my burden. But dear God, help me to leave it there and not take on another load like this ferry boat! Help me to be a fishing boat, fishing for lost souls. So be it!*

16

LIVE

"In just a couple of minutes my special guest and I will be discussing problems confronting Christian churches today. But right now, here's a word from our sponsor." Sonny flipped a switch and grinned at Luke, who sat perched on a stool opposite his host. "I have a feeling this is going to be a lively interview!"

Luke adjusted his headset and listened to the upbeat commercial. Thoughts of Serena flashed through his mind. Wherever she was, he knew she would be tuned in to the program. He nodded at the short, fair-haired host, whose slight build denied the smooth, deep voice that had made him the most beloved Christian talk show host for miles around. Looks could be deceiving.

Sonny studied his calm, unruffled guest. People who had never been on a live radio program were usually fidgety and nervous. Luke, however, sat straight and poised as a marble statue. A tingle of anticipation shot up Sonny's spine. This might be one of his best interviews yet. "Ten seconds and you're on. ... Three, two, one ..."

"Good morning one and all! This is your host, Sonny Star. If you were tuned in last week, you may recall that my special guest today was scheduled to be Pastor Horatio from the Happy Church. However, Pastor Horatio can't be with us today, but I do have with me in the studio Mr. Luke Obed Solomon. Luke tells me he has been visiting our area for the past few months and he has made some very astute observations. So, to begin with, Luke, tell me what your overall impression is of the churches in this area."

Leave it to Sonny to get right to the point. "First of all, Sonny, thanks for having me here today. To answer your question in detail would take more than our allotted time, but let me say this: It all boils down to a few C's."

"C's?" Sonny prompted. "Like the letter C? What do you mean, Luke?"

Without missing a beat, Luke stated, "Careless, compromising, commercial, competitive, contrary, covetous, comfortable, controlling, cultic, cold, and Christless." Sonny's eyebrows shot up in surprise, but he met Luke's gaze with a sudden flash of understanding and appreciation.

In Sonny's lively imagination he could hear the collective gasp from radio land. "Well, folks, you just heard some strong words. Before we take your calls, I am going to give Luke an opportunity to explain these C's for us. Meanwhile, grab your pen and paper and write down this number: 789-7770. Okay, Luke, explain for us just exactly what you mean."

"I'll be happy to, Sonny." He grinned broadly at the host, whose eyes were alive with excitement. "Careless means indifferent. There is indifference among Christians today, Sonny. Isaiah 47:8 says, 'Therefore hear now this, thou that art given to pleasures, that dwellest carelessly, that sayest in thine heart, I am, and none else beside me; I shall not sit as a widow, neither shall I know the loss of children.' But I tell you," Luke's tone was somber, "the church is given to pleasure, entertainment, and carnal pursuits in the name of Christ while countless millions are perishing and on their way to hell."

Sonny cut in, "So, Luke, what you're telling us is that most Christians today are neglecting their salvation."

"Yes, and not only that, but they are indifferent to truth—to the reality of the risen Christ, His soon return, and the fact that they will be required to give an account of their lives."

"In other words, Christians need to take stock, examine themselves, and ask God to show them where they are spiritually? That they may not be where they think they are?"

"That's right, Sonny. They need to be conscious of redeeming the time, for it is short."

"As our Lord said, 'Watch and pray,' and," he added, "this carelessness is a sign of the Laodiceans, wouldn't you say so, Luke?"

"Yes. The Laodiceans gauged themselves by the world. They did not recognize that they had come into agreement with the ways of the world through compromise with its values, making them complacent or indifferent to the righteous ways of God. When you come into agreement with the world, you commit spiritual fornication. Such spiritual harlotry or prostitution will cause people to become spiritually dull towards the profane, thereby, allowing that which is holy to be redefined according to worldly standards."

"Would redefining holiness allow the professing Church to use worldly methods and means to attract people with a promise of a more liberal or friendly environment?" Sonny asked, giving a broader platform for Luke to address the more controversial issues confronting the Church.

"Exactly! And this leads us to commercial, Sonny. The organized church system has become very commercialized. The bigger churches are organized and run like a corporation with no resemblance of the New Testament church whatsoever. Their goal is making money instead of disciples of Jesus Christ, and this goal requires large numbers of members. Instead of lifting up Christ, the churches have become competitive, while immerging into a lifeless system that will lose all autonomy as it merges into a one world religious system."

"The fourth C is competitive," Sonny interjected.

"Yes, you're right," Luke said. "They employ expensive marketing techniques to promote their churches through endless entertainment programs and such. Also, you would be shocked at the psychological methods that are used to gain control over the people in order to bring about unity. It is not the unity of the Holy Spirit, but unity under the control of the leadership."

Sonny shook his head, and uttered one word: "Propaganda!"

Luke took a deep breath and spoke into the microphone. "There is no genuine regard for the poor, the single women, fatherless children, or the lost. Missionaries and ministries that do try to help in these areas are financially starved out. You know, Sonny, people who get caught up in all the hype of this type of church are blinded by church pride. It is simply a type of religious sub-culture that has nothing whatsoever to do with real Christianity."

"I know what you mean," Sonny lamented sadly. "This briefly takes care of four of Luke's C's—careless, compromising, commercial, and competitive. What's the fifth one, Luke?"

"Naturally this leads us to covetousness, which is idolatry. One of the doctrines of demons that is so popular within Christendom today is the one that promises wealth and health for those who learn how to 'positively confess' and who send their money to the wealthy wolves among the flock. This covetousness quickly deteriorates into all-out greed. Large sums of money go into the pockets of those who are already extremely wealthy while struggling missionaries, the poor inside the church, and others in need are grossly neglected. By the time a person degenerates to this state, he is demonized."

"Whew!" Sonny exclaimed, shaking his head. "Well, folks, are you still with us? If so, Luke is about ready to explain the sixth C!"

"Most of the churches I have seen are comfortable. Not that all churches have padded pews and such, but they are comfortable in their religious traditions and their ingrown social clubs. They have become a social sub-culture with their own language and mindsets—you know, like an elite club where people can go to feel good. They don't want to be stirred out of their comfort zone. In other words, they don't want to pay the price to be a Christian; they don't want to pick up their cross and follow Jesus. So," Luke hesitated, "… Jesus is not their Lord, and they are not saved. They are on their way to hell."

Sonny sucked in his breath and leaned back in his chair. Wide-eyed, he asked Luke, "Are you telling us, Luke, that these people who believe they are saved are actually lost?"

"Yes, I am, Sonny. According to the Bible, they are not true believers. Consider Jesus' warning as recorded in Matthew 25 and specifically verses 45 and 46: *'Then shall he answer them, saying, Verily I say unto you, Inasmuch as ye did it not to one of the least of these, ye did it not to me. And these shall go away into everlasting punishment: but the righteous into life eternal.'* Saving faith obeys the Lord and produces good works. A person with saving faith produces fruit. True salvation is the result of God's grace, and it results in good works."

"And, number seven?" Tension strained Sonny's usual mellow voice. He leaned back in his chair and stared at Luke in open amazement. In the back of his mind, he wondered if this Luke person was suicidal. Surely, he wouldn't survive if he continued his list of C's.

As if reading his mind, Luke grinned at him reassuringly. "Sonny, number seven is controlling churches. Leadership is always sorely tempted to lapse into some means of controlling the flock so it can have assurance of income, church growth, loyalty, and success. They see nothing wrong with this because they tell themselves a certain amount of control is necessary for the protection of the flock. Of course, this is merely a justification. Eventually this control becomes witchcraft, which is the essence of control. People unconsciously slip into a deluded state where they are made to feel guilty if they do not live up to the teachings and expectations of the leadership. This control can cover a broad spectrum, such as financial control and manipulation, church attendance, religious duties, keeping the law, and so forth. People under controlling churches experience fear, intimidation, guilt, anxiety, and depression."

"And the next C?" Sonny's tone was low, serious.

"Naturally the issue of control slides into the area of cults as well as the occult. But controlling churches are not the only churches that are cultic today. Now, I am not speaking of the obvious cults out there such as the Mormons, Jehovah's Witnesses, Seventh-Day Adventists, Unity, Universalism, or the Jesus Only people, but of what has infiltrated, and in some instances, taken over the church."

"Such as?"

"Popular doctrines such as positive confession, which is faith in faith; the dominion and restoration beliefs; Kingdom Now; the New Thing; the New Wine; Replacement Theology; the New Paradigm; the "laughing revival;" so-called "territorial warfare" and "spiritual mapping;" Jewish Roots Movement, which involves keeping the Old Testament feasts and Law; and the latest seeker-friendly churches that are soft on sin, as they do away with fundamental Christian principles to make the church environment more attractive to the world, along with signs and lying wonders, just to name a few."

"Can you be specific about the signs and lying wonders?" Sonny prompted.

"Glory dust, feathers supposedly falling from Angels, seeing angels in the clouds, gold fillings, the Impartation, so-called visions of Jesus, trips to heaven, and a myriad of other false manifestations that people believe are from God. And," Luke held up a finger to signal his host that he had one more statement, "not to mention an overabundance of false prophecies, visions, dreams, and 'new revelations,' and that includes automatic writing and channeled messages from demons that are purported to be actual conversations with God, or Jesus, all of which can be blasphemous. This dangerous flood of unholy books, videos, movies, and so-called "revelations" do not line up with scripture and are of the wrong spirit."

Sonny held up a finger, but before he could say anything, Luke continued, "Then there is the music! Music is a hot issue today, especially in the seeker-friendly, non-denominational, 'neutral' 'relationship' based churches. In the "New Thing" churches, the people worship the worship, Sonny, and most of it is pagan."

Sonny grinned, gave Luke a thumbs-up and said, "Would you briefly explain 'pagan' for us, Luke?"

"Sure. 'Pagan' means sensuous. Simply put, what the church deems 'new' is nothing more than the 'old' paganism. This includes the loud, ear-splitting music with a hypnotic beat, vain repetitions, jumping up and down, and other actions that have been employed for centuries by pagan societies in their demon worship."

"Wow! Okay, folks, hang on to your hats because we have two more C's to go right after this short break." Sonny rattled off the commercial like the pro he was, but Luke knew his mind was racing from what had been sent out over the airwaves this day on his weekly program.

Sonny adjusted his headset. "For those of you just tuning in, this is the Sonny Star program and my guest today is Luke Obed Solomon, who has been giving us a brief overview of some of the problems within the modern church. So far, we've briefly touched on careless, compromising, commercialistic, competitive, covetous, comfortable, controlling, and cultic. What else do you have for us, Luke?"

"Cold!" The word sliced like a frozen knife through the airwaves. Then it seemed to point an accusing finger of ice at the shocked listeners. "In fulfillment of New Testament prophecy, the church today lacks love—genuine, unfeigned love for God, Jesus, the Bible, for one another, and for the lost."

Luke's abrupt halt jolted Sonny into action. "So, Luke, that brings us to the final C, which is ..."

"Christless!"

Luke watched Sonny's face blanch, then flush a bright pink. "Christless?"

"Allow me to explain, Sonny. If Christ is the Head and the Church is His body, then shouldn't the Church resemble the Head?"

"Yes." The talkative host seemed to be at an unusual loss for words.

Luke knew that time was ticking down. He only had a few precious minutes left. Taking a deep breath, he "grabbed the verbal ball," and ran with it. "For all of you listening who aren't afraid of the truth, let me ask you some questions. First, how does the professing Church resemble the Lord Jesus Christ today? Is this visible church lifting up a standard of holiness? Or is it profane, full of perversion of every kind, such as perversion of the Word of God, doctrinal perversion, sexual perversion, and the like? Can you honestly say that the church draws the world to Jesus Christ? I tell you *no*! It draws people to itself because it has compromised the Gospel by looking, sounding, tasting, smelling, and feeling like the world. Is the power of the Gospel evident in the church, or is the so-called fleshly 'power' in today's lukewarm church from another spirit? Is God glorified in most of today's churches, or is man exalted? Tell me, if Christ is the true Head of most of today's so-called Christian churches, then why isn't the church obedient to God, abiding in the Vine, bearing good fruit, and practicing good works? Why aren't Christians willing to lay down their lives for one another, as Christ laid down His? Why aren't they self-sacrificing? Is it because they are spoiled, self-centered, selfish, and self-serving? Tell me, if you can, why so-called believers live totally for themselves and are not willing to die to the self-life and separate from the influences of this present age so that they might live? How can the church claim to have Christ in its midst when it is full of loathsome pride and sin, which God resists? How is the church like Christ when it has lost both its salt and its light?"

Sonny held his breath. His entire being seemed to vibrate with excitement. This is what he had longed to shout to the world on program after program, but hadn't dared. This one broadcast summed up the entire reason for his existence and purpose before God. He was utterly speechless.

Luke rescued the stunned talk show host by calmly interjecting into the microphone, "Actually, all of these can be summed up in one word."

Sonny suddenly seemed to recover and said, "Okay, let's have it!" He watched the board light up indicating there was a full round of callers, just waiting to rip his guest to shreds. "What is that one word, Luke?"

"Corrupt."

It was a small word, but it hovered heavily over every listener. Sonny sighed deeply and then pushed the first button.

"Caller number one. Hazel, you're on the air!" Beads of perspiration dotted his face. None of his listeners would forget this day!

"Hi, Sonny. This is Hazel. I try to listen to your program often. I just want to say ..." the elderly caller hesitated momentarily. "Well, at first I was very angry when I heard Mr. Solomon, but you know Sonny, I've served the Lord for many years as a missionary overseas and I have to admit, the American Christian church does, as a whole, fit this description. Not all of them though. But it's very discouraging to be so far from home, working in a foreign field under terrible circumstances, sometimes pressed in on all sides by the enemy and knowing you could die there ..." There was a slight pause, and everyone in the studio knew the caller was crying silent tears. "It's heartbreaking beyond description to see starving children and orphans that are forced to sell themselves just for a crust of moldy bread and then come home on furlough, turn on the television, and see certain so-called prophets and evangelists raking in millions and millions of dollars to heap upon their lusts!" She stifled a sob. "Anyway, let me just say that most American Christians have no idea what it really means to lay down their life for Christ."

"Thanks for calling, Hazel; we know where you're coming from."

"You're welcome."

Sonny pushed the button for caller number two. "Hello, Claude, you're on the air."

"Oh, okay. Hey, ah, Sonny. I listen to your program a lot ya know…"

"Glad you do, Claude. What's on your mind today?"

"Well, ah, ya know I don't agree with your guest. No, ah, I don't agree at all."

"Would you like to tell us why, Claude?"

"Well, ya know, ah, I've been a Christian for many years, and I, ah, belong to this church ya see. And, ah, I go every Sunday when I can ya know. And, ah, our pastor says if ya wanna get to heaven, then all ya have to do is to say that prayer, ya know, the one ya say when ya ask Jesus to be your Savior."

"Okay, Claude. Just what don't you agree with specifically?"

"Ummm, well that there's anything wrong with the church. I mean, I think he's got a grudge against the church or somethin' because I believe we're gonna see a great big, world-wide revival soon!"

"Thank you, Claude." Sonny disconnected the line. "Let's hear from Luke about the revival for just a moment. Luke?"

"Of course, Sonny." Luke's clear blue eyes seemed to gaze into eternity as he spoke into the microphone. "True revival begins with genuine repentance. What most people call 'revival' today is not real revival in the biblical sense. There may be some worldly sorrow, but what most people are seeking is a religious experience. In fact, the Bible clearly reveals that in the end times the world will be extremely evil, Christ's followers will be persecuted, scattered, and hard-pressed, and that it's questionable if real faith will be present when Jesus finally returns."

"Whoa!" Sonny exclaimed. "Look at those phone lines. All right, caller number three … Cynthia, isn't it?"

"Yes, I'm Cynthia and I just want to say that I agree with Luke to a point, you know, about the pastors who are Pharisees, but what I want to say is, Christians do need to keep the Law, the Sabbath, and the Jewish feasts."

Sonny's eyebrows knotted together, giving his pale face a comical expression. "Please explain what you mean, Cynthia. I guess I'm confused by the term 'Pharisees.' I thought the Pharisees were the very ones who demanded that the Law be kept."

"What I mean by the Pharisees is that they think they know it all when, in fact, they don't! If they were in God's will, then they'd know that Christians today do need to obey the Ten Commandments, the Old Testament Laws, and get back to their Jewish roots."

"Very interesting, Cynthia. Luke, would you care to respond?"

Luke grimaced slightly. "What you're saying is, Cynthia, that Christians are careless about keeping the Old Testament Law ..."

"Precisely!" the caller agreed.

"This is one of the problems I have found in the churches," Luke said. "Christians are careless about their relationship with Christ but not about religious duties, whether it's the Old Testament Law or some other set of religious do's and don'ts. You see, Cynthia, there is a vast difference between Israel and the Church. God, through Moses, gave all of the Old Testament laws and ordinances to the children of Israel. The church didn't come into existence until Pentecost. According to Colossians 2:14, Christ blotted out the handwriting of ordinances that was against mankind, which were contrary, and took them out of the way, nailing them to His cross. When I say that Christians are careless, Cynthia, I'm not talking about the need for them to come under the bondage of the Law, but I am saying that they have left their first love—Jesus Christ. After all, Jesus declared that His followers were to keep the first two commandments, to love God and to love your neighbor as yourself, which is the fulfilling of the Law. On the other hand, many Christians today are careless because they believe that since they are saved by grace, they don't have any responsibilities towards God so they can think, say, and do whatever pleases them. This is not what the Bible says, and in fact, if you carefully study the Sermon on the Mount, you will see that Christ expounded the spirit of the law rather than the letter of the law. So therefore, anyone who is truly born again will actually go beyond keeping the letter of the law because he or she will be enabled, through the indwelling Holy Spirit, to keep the spirit of the law as well."

"Well," Cynthia responded tersely, "I don't agree! We need to do more than that. We need to keep the Jewish feasts, and the Sabbath, and study the Torah, and ..."

Click.

Sonny grinned at Luke, "Hi, Harry. Welcome to 'Live.'" *Whew!* Sonny thought to himself. *This Luke guy just dropped a bomb.*

"Uh, yes, Sonny," a pleasant male voice responded. "I just want to say that in many ways I agree with Luke, but churches do need money with which to operate. The church I go to is in the process of an enormous building program and, well, who is going to pay for it? I mean, we're building a gym for the kids, a game room, and a swimming pool. We have a huge chapel project going where people can buy crypts and niches for their deceased loved ones, and it's being elaborately decorated. What's wrong with that?"

"Well, what do you say Luke?" Sonny's face literally beamed. He was eating it up.

"What is the purpose of the church, Harry?" Luke asked. Without waiting for a response, he continued, "Does the Church exist for itself, or is it supposed to be the salt and the light of the world? How can the Church fulfill the Great Commission of Christ and reach out to those who need the Gospel if every cent is designated to these types of building programs that do nothing to further the Kingdom of God? Jesus said, 'Let the dead bury the dead.' And, Harry, think about it. How many people are there around you who struggle just to make ends meet, to feed their children, to keep on top of the rising cost of living?"

"Uh," Harry stammered, "I sort of get your point, Luke, but our church has a food bank, and I know some folks that the church has helped with their electric bills and stuff."

"Let me ask you this, Harry. Did your church expect those people to pay the church back?"

"Well, I dunno ..."

"You know they expect it to be repaid, Harry."

"Well, all right, I suppose so, but wouldn't the church go broke if all we did was help people?"

"What do these verses mean to you, Harry?

309

But whoso hath this world's good, and seeth his brother have need, and shutteth up his bowels of compassion from him, how dwelleth the love of God in him? My little children, let us not love in word, neither in tongue; but in deed and in truth. The liberal soul shall be made fat: and he that watereth shall be watered also himself. He that hath a bountiful eye shall be blessed; for he giveth of his bread to the poor. He that hath pity upon the poor lendeth unto the LORD; and that which he hath given will he pay him again. Whoso stoppeth his ears at the cry of the poor, he also shall cry himself, but shall not be heard."[1]

Click.

"It looks like Harry's off the line," Sonny grinned wryly. "Time for a quick message from our sponsor."

Luke suddenly caught a glimpse of Serena as she passed by the soundproof window. Her face was pale and drawn as she glanced his way. A brief smile of recognition played across her lips. Then she turned and disappeared through the doorway leading to the front office. *I've got to find her after this talk show is over with,* Luke told himself.

"Okay, Lucille, you're on the air," Sonny leaned forwardly expectantly.

"Hi, Sonny. I listen to you every week if I can," the terse female voice stated matter-of-factly, "but this is the first time I've ever called. I just want to state I don't know who on earth you are, Mr. Solomon, but I have never heard such a bunch of hogwash in all my life! Really! Who do you think you are to get on the air and bash the church? We are experiencing revival at our church! People are just starting to open up now in our worship services, dancing, banners, and victory shouts for at least two hours every Sunday morning! Sometimes we don't even have a sermon it's so wonderful. The young people are flooding to our church and are entering into spiritual warfare and intercession like never before. We know that we shall overcome! That we shall take over the kingdoms of this world before the Lord comes! People like you, Mr. Solomon, will fit

---

[1] Proverbs 11:25; 19:17; 21:13, 22:9; 1 John 3:17-18

into God's kingdom and come into submission to the apostles and prophets, or, or ... else!"

"Do we have a reply, Luke?" Sonny asked.

"Jesus said in Matthew 7:21-23,

> Not every one that saith unto me, Lord, Lord, shall enter into the kingdom of heaven; but he that doeth the will of my Father which is in heaven. Many will say to me in that day, Lord, Lord, have we not prophesied in thy name? And in thy name have cast out devils? And in thy name done many wonderful works? And then will I profess unto them, I never knew you: depart from me, ye that work iniquity.

The key is, Lucille, does Jesus know you? Are you doing the will of the Father?"

Click.

"Well, it appears Lucille is off the line, so on to our next caller. Hello, Laurie, you're on the air."

"You, Mr. Solomon, are preaching 'another gospel!'" The loud female voice made Sonny wince. "If everybody would carefully listen to your words, you are saying that we must make Jesus our Lord in order to be saved! This is heresy, I tell you! You are a heretic! You're preaching Lordship Salvation! I know a heretic when I hear one! You need to repent because I happen to know that for us Gentiles, we don't have to repent because that is *works*. We don't have to do any good works because that is *works*! We don't have to make Jesus Lord because that is *works*! We are saved by faith. Period. We do not have to DO anything!"

"According to scripture, Laurie, you are the one preaching 'another gospel'. True saving faith results in salvation plus works. James 2:24 tells us that 'A man is justified by works, and not by faith alone.' Why did the Apostle Paul warn the Thessalonian Christians to obey the Lord Jesus Christ so that they would not pay the penalty of eternal destruction in 2 Thessalonians 1:8 and 9? Jesus commanded people to both repent and believe the gospel. Check out Luke 24:47, Acts 26:20, John 5:29, and Mark 8:34-38. In fact, a careful reading of the entire New Testament outside of your doctrinal frame of reference will indeed reveal to you that you are in error!"

"You are wrong, wrong, wrong, and a heretic!"

Click.

Sonny grinned at Luke as he punched another button. "Hello, Dino, you're on the line."

"Uh, yeah, hi, Sonny. I enjoy your program."

"Thanks Dino. Glad you're with us."

"Okay, but I do want to say something to Mr. Solomon."

"All right, Dino, go ahead. You're on the air."

"Fifteen years ago I was into drugs, rock music, and witchcraft. You know, all that stuff."

"I know," Luke said softly.

"Well, I met this guy on the street who talked about Jesus all the time, so I ended up going to church with him one Sunday. To make a long story short, I knew I was a hell-bound sinner, and when the invitation to receive Christ was given, I gave my life to Christ. I have to admit I truly repented. And I also knew that Jesus had to be my Lord as well as my Savior. Well, I stayed at that church for the next ten years, during which time I got married and had two kids. But do you know what?"

"Tell us, Dino."

"Stuff started happening, like more so-called Christian rock instead of the reverent music and worship that they had when I first went there. Then these prophets started coming to our church after the first pastor left and we got this new pastor, you see. They began telling the people that we had to lay a new foundation and that God was going to do a new thing. You know, that sort of stuff that you see on TV and hear about all the time."

"I know."

"At first, I just ignored it or excused it, but then one day the Lord opened my eyes to the awful truth! A subtle change had come over the people. They no longer lifted up Jesus as the solution. They no longer loved one another. They started arguing and bickering. Many people left. My wife got heavily involved with this group called the 'Handmaidens of the Lord.' She began to change towards the children and me. She got downright militant after a while, and I could see that cold glint in her eyes that so many of the people in the church now had.

Everybody was talking about the 'Elijah Company' and 'Joel's Army.' To make a long story short, an angel-of-light spirit had completely taken over the church that once loved Christ! The Lord showed me that I couldn't change it, that I should flee that place ... that He would guide us to a real fellowship of true believers. But when I confronted my wife, she ..." Dino's voice broke. He took a deep breath and choked out the words, "she left me. She took our children and left. She said that I was rebellious and in sin because I wouldn't submit to the apostles and prophets that had come in to our church."

"I understand."

"It hurts so much! Satan has come in and deceived so many people. I don't know who you are, Mr. Solomon, but I know in my heart that you're of God and that what you've said today barely scratches the surface of what's happening to the church and to Christians. What's happening today has just got to be the falling away from truth spoken of in scripture. I'm glad that Sonny had you on the program today."

"Thanks so much for calling, Dino, and for your words of truth." Luke's eyes locked with Sonny's. The talk show host was obviously in total agreement with Luke and Dino. *Praise the Lord!* Luke thought.

"Time for just a couple more calls," Sonny announced. "Okay, Chet, you're on the air."

"Hi, Sonny. I have a question for Mr. Solomon."

"Okay, Chet. Shoot."

"Mr. Solomon, aren't you afraid of touching God's anointed? I mean, we're told in scripture not to touch God's anointed. I don't know, but I'd be really careful if I were you."

"Thanks Chet, I'm glad you brought that up. That term is a popular one today and is used extensively by the false prophets who wish to remain above close scrutiny by watchmen who question their motives and unscriptural teachings. They have taken a verse out of context from the Old Testament that true Bible scholars know means something entirely different. In the Old Testament only the prophets, priests, and kings were anointed for service. God told the people that they were literally not to *kill* the prophets, priests, or kings that had been anointed with oil for their particular positions. False prophets of today coin this term as a means of threatening discerning believers from exposing their

313

unfruitful works of darkness. Ironically, these so-called anointed leaders are not of God, nor are they anointed, but rather they are the false prophets and Christs, or anointed ones, of these end times. Jesus strongly warned against them."

"Wow! I didn't know that! Thanks!"

"Thanks Chet. Okay, our last caller today is Pastor Horatio, from the Happy Church! You're on the air, Pastor."

"Hi, Sonny. My how I do wish I could've been there today as we had planned. I got to listen to most of the program. I have to admit your guest is contentious, bigoted, opinionated, and dogmatic. He sure has a lot to learn! But we'll all forgive him." He gave a deep, guttural laugh. The grave, monotone voice continued, "Oh well, on the other hand, I think it's good for the people to have a contrast, you know, between those who are negative and those of us who are positive. After all, we know that Father loves everybody and that since Jesus died for everybody, everybody is going to be happy in heaven someday with Father! Ah, yes, even those who rebelled with poor Lucifer are all going to be redeemed, so I will conclude by saying that we all need to just love one another and be content that Father wants us to be happy!"

"Pastor Horatio," Sonny interjected, "this is called Universalism. For all of you folks out there in our radio audience who may not understand what Universalism is, bottom line it's the belief that the church has been misinformed for the past two-thousand years and that there is no literal hell. Universalism has been on the rise lately, along with all of the other latter-days doctrines of demons."

"Well!" sputtered the pastor, "You better go re-read your Bible, Sonny, because it doesn't say what you think it says!"

Click.

"Okay, friends, that's all the time we have for today! Thanks for tuning in, and be sure to listen next week. My special guest will be," he glanced at a scrawled message on a pink slip of paper, "uh, my special guest will be Prophet Black." Sonny scowled at the paper and crumpled it in his fist. "God bless," he said crisply as he looked at the control room. He took off his headset and shook his head. "I used to be able to pick my own guests," he muttered unhappily, "but since the new management ..." He looked up at Luke. His lips twisted into a wry smile.

"But I've got to admit, you're one of the best I've ever had in the studio." His eyes twinkled. He rose and extended his hand. "I don't know where Serena found you, Luke, but I'm mighty glad you were here today. God bless you!"

"Thank you, Sonny. He does. And the same to you, too. Keep the faith, Sonny, no matter what." His eyes held a solemn warning that didn't go unnoticed.

"It's going to get that tricky, is it?"

"Yes, but God has you here to speak the truth as often as you can to as many people as you can. And you know that."

"Yes, I do," he whispered wearily, as the receptionist opened the door and handed him a telephone message. He glanced at it and then smiled at Luke.

"Serena is waiting for you in the Corner Café down on 4th and Main. She says she needs to talk ..." His voice trailed away as he watched Luke pick up his jacket. There was something so indefinably different about this man. Where had Serena said he was from?

"Luke, I do appreciate what you shared today. It was very interesting indeed, and I loved it. Perhaps we'll meet again?"

"Perhaps."

"I'm sure many people who tuned in today are hoping you will soon go back to wherever you came from." He tipped his head and studied Luke's glowing countenance.

"In that case," Luke's smile revealed an even set of teeth, "they won't be disappointed."

Sonny watched the lone figure as he disappeared down the long hallway and into a waiting elevator. "I wonder just where that is," he whispered to himself.

17

THE PLOT

Upon entering the Corner Café, Luke immediately spotted the conspirators huddled together in the booth behind Serena. He knew she was unaware of the dangers lurking next to her, but not wishing to cause alarm, he grinned broadly and slid into the booth to face her.

"Thanks so much for taking time to come down here," Serena said. "I know you're a busy man." She raised her eyebrows questioningly.

"No problem, Serena. In fact, I was hoping to find you today to thank you for putting in a good word for me with Sonny and to ask how you're doing. You seemed a bit distraught when I saw you pass by the window in the studio."

She dropped her eyes. "I *was* distraught, Luke, but I'm okay now."

"Are you sure about that?"

She gave a slight sigh, and then smiled at him. "Yes, I'm sure about that. It's going to be okay. I did lose my job at the studio, and that's what I wanted to tell you. I won't be there anymore."

"I'm sorry to hear that, but surely it must be God's will for you. He has something better planned for your life."

"You sound so confident of that ..."

"Coffee?" the busy waitress interrupted Serena as she stood poised with order pad and pen.

"Yes, please, and the tuna special for me," Serena said.

"The same here, and please put both on my tab," Luke said absently as his eyes wandered past Serena to the three men sitting directly behind her. One with bushy, unkempt brown hair sat with his back to

Luke and Serena. The two men facing Luke forced themselves not to look directly at him. One of them was tall and muscular with dark eyes that reminded Luke of a warlock. The other was stocky, wore a crew cut, and was covered with tattoos.

Serena seemed not to notice Luke's interest in the people behind her and continued talking. "I have friends, really good friends who love the Lord, who are helping me through this time. They are a couple of single ladies who have a powerful but much overlooked ministry. You wouldn't know them, I'm sure, but they are helping me financially."

Luke's lips curved into a knowing smile, but he remained silent. He knew that Casey and Ralene had promised to help Serena even though they barely made it themselves from month to month. It was gratifying for him to pause and reflect on true believers. He had found so few in his brief earthly mission.

"The final straw was that awful so-called prophet. He is nothing less than a wolf in sheep's clothing!" Serena looked wide-eyed at Luke. "Oh, I'm so sorry. I shouldn't have said that. I shouldn't talk about ..."

"No, Serena, it's quite all right. I do know who that man is, and yes, you're right. So tell me what happened."

"I soundly refused to locate sponsors for him! He came into the studio, and instantly he and the new owner hit it off."

"Deep calls to deep," Luke said under his breath.

"Exactly! Well, then I was immediately assigned to go out and get sponsors for his newly-acquired radio spot." She leaned forward and lowered her voice to a whisper, "I just couldn't do it, Luke. That man is awful! He's of the devil! A genuine false prophet if ever there was one!"

"It was a set up wasn't it?"

Serena's brown eyes widened with sudden understanding. "Oh, oh, I see now. They *wanted* to get rid of me because I wouldn't play their game and compromise the truth!"

"Exactly."

The waitress returned with their lunches, refreshed their coffee and busied herself at the booth behind Serena. After the waitress left, Luke picked up snatches of the tense conversation. "Joel's Army..." "Time for action..." "Submission to the apostles and prophets..." "New paradigm..." "Purging the earth..." "Fundamentalists..." "The old order."

317

"Luke," Serena broke into his concentration. "I heard your interview with Sonny today. It was wonderful! Just the kind of stuff Sonny likes! And I don't worry about them taking Sonny totally off the air because he's been there too long and people love him and his live talk show. But today was the best he's ever had. But..." her eyebrows knotted into a slight frown, "aren't you afraid for yourself? I mean, some of those callers were quite upset!"

"There's no doubt about that, my friend," he grinned at her. "But I'm not worried about any physical violence if that's what you mean."

"Yes, that's exactly what I mean," she said solemnly. "Last year Sonny interviewed my friends, Ralene and Casey. Well, they got on the subject of hell. It was a terrific interview, but some of the callers became quite militant and nasty. After that, unsigned letters with no return addresses began showing up in their Post Office Box. A couple of people even threatened them over it. Can you imagine?"

"Yes."

Serena folded her napkin and leaned forward, "Would you excuse me for a moment? I have to go wash my hands."

"Of course." He watched her disappear into the lady's room.

He wasn't the only one who watched her.

Luke's keen hearing tuned in to the conversation between the three men. "Thar she goes," hissed crew cut.

"Aw, she'll be back, Irv. We'll be in the parking lot before she leaves," said the tall man.

"Are you sure this is gonna work, Eby?" asked bushy brown hair.

"Leave it to me. We get two birds with one stone this way. When I get through with the little lady, she'll wish she wasn't such a goody two-shoes."

"But that guy with her, Eby...I mean, he's pretty big."

"Losin' yer nerve, Harvey? There's three of us, remember? Besides, I'm bettin' he's that dude that we just heard on the radio. We take him out too, and we get a double bonus."

"I get her first, Eby," the one called Harvey whispered hoarsely.

"Shut up!" Eby's dark eyes narrowed to slits. "We have to take care of the big guy first, then you'll wait yer turn!"

Luke thoughtfully sipped his coffee. These three men were no problem for him, but what *possessed* them could prove to be a challenge. He lifted his eyes and stared into the air above their heads. The assembly of dark, grotesque demons jeered back at him.

It was clearly the time to ask for reinforcements.

"Luke?" Serena's soft question snapped his focus back to the material realm.

"Yes?"

"You looked so strange a moment ago—like you were seeing into another dimension or something."

"Haven't you ever seen things that weren't visible to others?" he asked nonchalantly.

She gave a short laugh, "Well, yes I suppose I have on certain times when the Holy Spirit has shown me something."

They lapsed into a comfortable silence, enjoying their meal. Afterwards, as they lingered over a final cup of coffee, the bushy-haired Harvey suddenly rose from his seat behind Serena and ambled into the men's rest room.

"Let's go, Serena!" Luke said in hushed tones. He quickly slid out of the booth and waited for her.

Serena looked startled, but she grabbed her purse and followed him to the cash register where He handed the ticket and a fifty-dollar bill to the cashier. He watched Eby and Irv out of the corner of his eye. They were clearly agitated and he knew he would have to move quickly. Meanwhile, the cash register drawer jammed. In frustration, the cashier ran to get the manager but by this time Eby and Irv were sliding out of their booth.

Oblivious to all that was transpiring, Serena moved around from behind Luke and walked toward the exit. "There's a book in my car that I forgot to give you." She disappeared through the door before Luke could stop her.

Forfeiting his change, Luke whirled to follow Serena but suddenly a heavy weight clipped his knees from behind. He crumpled helplessly to the floor. By this time the manager had returned with the flustered cashier. He hovered over Luke, trying to help him to his feet but Luke shook him off. "It's okay! I'm okay! Keep the change!" He jumped to his feet and charged out the door leaving the stunned manager and cashier staring after him.

He frantically scanned the shady parking lot for any sign of Serena or the two men who had followed on her heels. Trees and shrubs separated the parking lanes, making it difficult to see clearly. As he jogged toward the farthest corner of the crowded lot he caught a glimpse of Eby slipping into the back seat of a blue Chrysler Sedan. But where was Serena?

"Keep movin' smart boy!" he felt the hard jab of a pistol against his ribs. Harvey had come up noiselessly behind him. "Over there, to the car," he directed.

Luke fought the urge to flatten Harvey before he knew what hit him. But first, he had to get to Serena.

Then he saw her. She sat behind the wheel of her car. A gun was held to her head. Irv sat in the front beside her with his finger on the trigger.

"Get in the back or she loses her brains," Harvey ordered levelly. Luke complied and Harvey followed him into the crowded car. Luke found himself pinned between Eby and Harvey. It was not a good time to take them on while Irv had a gun on Serena.

"Well, well nice of you to join us," Eby mocked. "You make one wrong move and your lady friend gets it," he snapped his fingers in Luke's face. "Poof! Just like that, she's gone." He leaned back and spoke to Serena. "Okay Sugarplum. Nice and easy. Pull this car out and head for the freeway. North!" Turning to Luke he said, "I don't believe we've met. I'm Eby, that there is Harvey and the executioner in the front is Irv. Now, just who are you?"

Luke remained silent. He knew that as long as Serena was driving, Irv wasn't going to shoot her and jeopardize their lives.

"I asked you a question," Eby snarled. "Who are you?"

"Who do you think I am?"

"I think you're that big mouth who was just interviewed on the Sonny Star program."

Luke's calm blue eyes stared straight into Eby's dark eyes. To Luke they resembled the bottomless pits of hell itself. "What if I am?" he said quietly.

"Aha! I thought so! Boys, we have the distinguished honor of having Luke Obed Solomon with us today! This is gonna be a very special treat for the boss!"

"Luke?" Serena's soft voice seemed to float on a sea of masculinity.

"Shut up and drive!" Irv shoved the pistol into her waist.

"It's okay, Serena." Luke reassured her. "Don't be afraid. Remember, greater is He who is in you than he who is in the world!"

Eby's exhale resembled a hiss. "You two have had it!"

"Would you like to explain to the lady just what this is all about?" The controlled tone of Luke's voice unnerved Eby.

"Sounds like Lukie already knows about the purge, Eby!"

"Shut yer mouth, Harv!"

Luke watched Serena's face in the rearview mirror. In spite of their circumstances, she was amazingly calm. He knew that the Comforter was giving her the peace that passes all understanding.

"Take the Sandy Beach exit!" Irv ordered Serena.

"Going to your underground tunnel?" Luke asked lightly.

Shock and disbelief flooded the faces of the three men. "Just what *do* you know?" Eby rasped. Perhaps this Luke character was part of the counter intelligence. Perhaps, instead of them setting the trap, they had been trapped themselves. Panic surfaced and his mind began to spin out of control.

"I've known your boss's boss for a very long time." Luke stated flatly. He watched Eby's face pale.

"You're just bluffin'!" Eby's voice was strained.

"Really?" Luke asked pleasantly. Eby was definitely unnerved. "Then, tell me if you can," Luke leaned back nonchalantly against the soft gray upholstery, "why he can't explain to you the whole picture every time you ask him?"

"How did you know that!"

Luke smiled knowingly. "You see, the mastermind of the Plan is not that little man, *the Prophet*. You so-called "reapers" are nothing more than hired killers who are being used to help him and other ranks of that fanatical Joel's Army to purge the earth. Then the new order can be put into position. Believe me, in the end, both you and your prophet and the duped "Joel's Army" all will face the mastermind's firing squad! You

321

won't even be so fortunate as to end up in one of the concentration camps! Luke watched Serena's eyes widen in surprise.

Eby wiped the perspiration off of his forehead with the back of his hand. Irv and Harvey lapsed into an uncomfortable silence. Finally, Harvey spoke, his voice a raw squeak. "Eby, what if that's true! I mean, what if we're just being used!"

"Shut up Harvey! I'm trying to think!" Eby glared at Luke. "Okay, boys let's not lose our nerve. Sure, we're being 'used'. We're being 'used' to do the Army's dirty work of helping to reap, uh, purge the earth. We get paid for a good cause. We botch this job and we don't get paid! So, we're goin' through with it, ya hear?"

Harvey and Irv mumbled under their breaths. Eby stared out the window for a moment, then ordered Serena to slow the car as they crossed over a narrow bridge. "Okay, sister, turn right onto that dirt road."

"What? There's hardly any road there at all…"

"Just do as I tell ya!"

Serena yanked on the wheel. The car plunged onto a rutted, dirt road. Undergrowth of elderberry bushes, blackberry vines, alders, and other vegetation slapped at the windshield and sides of the car. Luke saw her grip tighten on the steering wheel. He knew once they entered the cold, paved, underground labyrinth that her chances of survival were slim.

"Serena!" he suddenly shouted, "STOP!"

As she hit the brakes, Luke jammed his arms to each side, knocking Eby and Harvey unconscious. Irv, meanwhile, slammed against the dashboard, but managed to keep his grip on the pistol. "I'll shoot her!" Irv threatened shakily.

"Oh really?" Luke leaned over the seat.

"Get away from me or I'll shoot her I tell you!"

"What if my friend outside this car kills you first?"

"You don't fool me Solomon! That's an old trick!"

Irv heard the door behind him open, but it was too late. Invisible fingers wrapped around his neck, choking him into unconsciousness. Serena screamed and fainted.

Luke reached over the seat and snatched the gun out of the stricken man's hand. "Pirathon, my friend," Luke grinned. "What took you so long?"

"You should know the answer to that! The hierarchy has declared all-out war on you. But the Commander of the Hosts of the Lord has dispatched more warrior angels until you get out of here!"

"Let's take care of these guys," Luke said. Together they carried the unconscious forms into the forest and laid them against a fallen tree. "The Insiders are using every means to bring in Satan's one-world government and religious system," Luke said more to himself than to Pirathon as he quickly bound the men's hands with their leather belts. He frisked them for weapons and found four knives and two more handguns. He tossed them into a nearby swamp.

Pirathon spoke. "The enemy has managed to alter nearly every person's world view. Only those who remain true to God and His Word will be able to discern the truth. There is only a remnant, Luke."

"I know."

"The ancient Templar Brotherhood-Freemasons, Illuminists, along with the Whore riding the Beast have successfully infiltrated the church through the various so-called 'Christian' movements. By brainwashing the people to believe that the church is Israel, or that it is the church's responsibility to become seeker-friendly, or that it must take dominion of the earth, the global Planners have subtly convinced so-called Christian leaders that it is God's will for the church to "reap the earth".

"In other words, kill everyone who will not comply with their plan…will not fit into their kingdom, new order, or movement, right?"

"Right."

"I fear a terrible bloodbath will occur. Many more martyrs for us to escort Home."

Pirathon extended his hand. "I must leave you now. I look forward to the day when you return, Maschil," he whispered.

"It won't be long…"

Luke returned to the car. In actual time he had only been gone for a few seconds. He walked up to Serena's still form and slowly moved his hand over her face, causing a deep sleep to come upon her. Then he gently moved her to the passenger side of the car so he could slide behind the steering wheel. He turned the key and the engine purred to life.

When she awoke, the trees and shrubbery of the Corner Café parking light were bathed in the red glow of the setting sun. She ran her fingers through her hair. Suddenly she gasped and bolted upright in the car seat. *I'm in my car. In the Corner Café parking lot. What am I doing here? Where's Luke? What on earth happened…?*

She noticed that the doors were locked, the key was in the ignition, her purse on her lap. But there was something else she had to do…what was it? Oh yes, the book! She had a special devotional book for Luke! She had put it right there…It was gone.

18

THE UNKNOWNS

"Good morning; it's good to see you again." The enthusiastic greeter pumped Luke's hand warmly. "It's Luke, isn't it?"

"Yes. Luke Solomon."

"Well, Luke, we're all glad you could make it again today."

The white, overcrowded little church sat nestled among tall evergreen trees. Mist from the nearby river rose in steamy swirls as if trying to embrace and kiss the pale glow of the distant sun as it melted its way through the thin blanket of fog. Birdsong filled the damp air, occasionally silenced by the racking caws of sassy crows, seemingly intent on drawing attention. All in all, it was a picture-perfect postcard scene.

The ancient boards creaked under Luke's feet as he made his way across the back of the church, but no one seemed to notice. After all, the squeaks and groans of the worn, oiled wood blending in with the happy chatter of young and old had been a part of Greenwood Glen for nearly a hundred years.

He edged his way through the smiling faces to a vacant spot in a pew in the next-to-the-last row. As he settled himself on the well-worn smooth bench, the church bell rang its solemn call to worship.

An expectant hush fell over the friendly congregation.

Luke smiled to himself. *At last, I've found a real Christian church!* This was Luke's second visit. From his usual post in the city, he had had to drive forty-five minutes on the freeway and then another 20 minutes down a narrow country road. But it had been worth it.

It had been five weeks since the radio interview with Sonny Star. Most of the Christians who had heard the program went on with their lives as if they had never been challenged to think outside of their well-worn platitudes, doctrines, and creeds. Luke Obed Solomon had almost been forgotten, but not quite.

Pastor Brownstein's twinkling eyes and sweet smile warmed the hearts of his congregation as he invited them to stand for prayer. He watched the tall blonde man in the back of the church stand and reverently bow his head. Pastor Brownstein was a regular listener to the Sonny Star program and had listened to the invigorating discussion the day Luke had been the featured guest. But he had no fear of Luke or cause to worry because Pastor Brownstein knew the Lord and the Lord knew him. And while he would have liked to corner Luke for stimulating conversation and fellowship, Pastor Brownstein knew that the time had not yet presented itself.

The congregation fused into one standing body of believers as it sang "The Old Rugged Cross." Luke sensed the mingled emotions of every person in the room. In his mind's eye he saw multiple colored threads representing each soul flowing and blending into one beautiful pattern of unsurpassed design and beauty. This was true unity in the Body of Christ. Each person considered others better than him or herself and selflessly sought to pour out his or her life to the Lord as a living sacrifice for the benefit of needy hearts. Love radiated beyond the walls of the aging wood church and touched heaven.

Luke trembled. The sweet yet powerful presence of the Holy Spirit swept through the sanctuary. Faces glowed, hands raised in adoration, tongues sang in purest praise to the One who is worthy. And suddenly everything within Luke Obed Solomon cried out to return to the glories of Heaven.

Pastor Brownstein's sensitivity to the Holy Spirit had taught him that neither he nor any other person in the congregation should ever interrupt the Spirit's leading during worship. He had faithfully taught the people entrusted to his care how to discern the moving of the Holy Spirit. Now, like a finely tuned stringed instrument, the worshippers allowed the Spirit to lift them into the throne room of God. Luke listened to muffled weeping, sighs of repentance, and adoration blended with joyous notes of praise.

No one knew or cared how long hearts were joined in the flow of worship. Finally, a holy hush settled over the congregation. Pastor Brownstein stood reverently, face lifted upward, eyes closed ... waiting ... listening.

The gentle voice of a woman spoke in an unfamiliar language. The strange yet beautiful words poured forth like liquid gold. As soon as her words died away, a strong masculine voice gave the interpretation. Luke recognized him as one of the church elders. "Behold, you have bought from Me gold tried in the fire and are clothed with white raiment. Your eyes have been anointed with eye salve so that you are able to see with the Spirit. I know your works. You have kept my word and not denied My Name. Your hearts have been purged from sin and darkness by My blood. But I tell you today, remain in My word; worship Me in Spirit and in truth for Satan is sending one into your midst who is seeking to draw you away with enticing words and strange doctrines. Watch and pray, I tell you, and remain steadfast in the faith."

A low rumble echoed through the room. Pastor Brownstein nodded for the congregation to be seated. His brown eyes reflected grave concern under the slight furrow that had formed between his dark eyebrows. "Brothers and sisters, we have just heard from our Lord and Savior. This is a most solemn warning and to be taken seriously. The Lord has told us to watch and pray. And that we will do!" He stepped down from the low platform, turned to face the pulpit and lowered himself to his knees. The people followed his example as some bowed while others kneeled or lay prostrate in the isles. Voices joined into a single prayer that ascended to heaven.

No one paid attention to the creaking boards in the back of the church. Luke tilted his head back as he stepped into the glowing sunshine and inhaled deeply of the pungent air. The smell of damp earth and composting leaves mingled with the sweet aroma of cottonwood trees. He strolled down the path leading to the river's edge. Of all the places he had found himself while on this assignment, this was his favorite. The rustic church with its jaunty steeple, the rolling green pasture land, the crooked fences and lazily flowing river provided a serene refuge from the discordant noises of traffic, jets, trains, whistles, and sirens, not to mention the cramped misery of multitudes of people. Luke nearly laughed out loud as it occurred to him that if he had been born a human being instead of being created by God as an angel, this is the very spot he would prefer to live.

Lost in his own musings, Luke started at the smiling figure stationed underneath a towering evergreen. A disturbed squirrel angrily chattered somewhere overhead.

"What are you doing here?" Luke whispered.

"Two reasons, my friend."

"Two reasons?"

"Yes, two."

"Do tell me then!" Luke urged as Pirathon turned and led the way to a small thicket hidden from view of the church.

"The warning, Maschil." Pirathon's demeanor was suddenly grave.

"You mean to the church just now?"

Pirathon nodded. "Yes. He is coming here." A chill tingled its way up Luke's spine and momentarily sickened him.

"Prophet Black?"

"Yes." Pirathon's usually calm features appeared taunt, guarded.

"When ... how?" Luke's lips pressed together in silent determination.

"Soon—that's all I know." Pirathon turned to leave.

"Wait! Tell me the second reason you are here."

Pirathon's eyes twinkled knowingly as they met Luke's in mutual affection. "This world," he paused and waved his arm as if to embrace the idyllic scene, "is not your home any more than it is theirs." His clear eyes glanced towards the church.

"I know," Luke said as he followed Pirathon's gaze. "They are sojourners, pilgrims, citizens of Heaven. Just passing through—the unknowns ..." Suddenly the air swirled around him. He turned back to Pirathon, but the angel had passed from view.

"I don't understand yet why I was led here," Luke spoke into the blue sky. Silence answered him. "I wonder how that false worker is going to try to deceive these sheep! They truly love God, and they know Him! They love and care for one another, which is rare," Luke mused to himself. "These people live separated, holy lives, they know their Bibles, walk in obedience and ..."

"Exactly!" the voice slurred behind him.

"What!" Luke whirled, expecting to see the thick darkness of a warrior demon. Instead he found himself squinting into light so brilliant it momentarily blinded him.

"Remember me, Machil?" the voice taunted.

Luke's mind spun dizzily. He fought against the energy draining from his human body as he struggled to stand. Everything within him wanted to flee, to run, to escape from this all-consuming power before him. *Jehovah God, the Great I AM!* Luke's inner cry for help exploded from his tortured mind. The impact was instant.

"Aaaahhh—no!" screamed the evil one.

"Yes!" Luke's mind shouted. "The Lord Jesus Christ rebuke you, Satan!" Luke watched the dazzling brightness evaporate into the air. He heaved a sigh of relief. There was no doubt about it; Satan himself had targeted this precious body of believers.

Luke stood for a moment, staring at the place that had been vacated by the devil. As he watched, an eerie shape began to form. *Here we go again,* Luke thought.

"The light bearer is gone, Maschil," the demon reflecting the false light sneered. "But I am consigned to this place, and I will carry out what I have been sent to do! You cannot stop me. It is so decreed." It snickered.

"Very well then," Luke said in an even tone. He turned and made his way back to the narrow trail that led to the church. He paused outside the door and listened to the message.

By the time the message ended, Luke knew that Prophet Black would finally meet his match in Pastor Brownstein, and that somehow, in spite of the intense evil that preceded Prophet Black and the destruction that followed him, God would have the final say. God always used Satan's evil tactics for His own ends, turning all that was meant for evil into good. But just how that could happen in this situation was beyond Luke's comprehension.

19

KINGDOM AGAINST KINGDOM

Three weeks had passed since Luke's encounter with the demon at Greenwood Glen. They were exceptionally wonderful weeks. Seven souls had found Jesus as their personal Lord and Savior in that three-week period, and fifteen people had been baptized by Jesus with the Holy Ghost and fire. Twenty-six people had been water baptized in the river.

Luke smiled to himself as he sat in his usual place toward the back of the church. He could easily surmise that nothing from the realm of darkness could come against the Greenwood Glen church and that the ugly encounter was only a figment of his imagination. But he knew that wasn't true. It was only a matter of time.

His attention was drawn to a group of new Sunday visitors who filed quietly through the open door and made their way to the front of the church. He instantly recognized Casey, who was in the lead, followed by Nita and then Ralene. Nita's glowing appearance was a sharp contrast to the pathetic state she had been in when Casey and Ralene had first met and rescued her in the café parking lot. Jesus had certainly set Nita free to be all that she could be in Him.

Luke visibly started when out of the corner of his eye he caught sight of Ellie, John, and Amber, who happily slipped into the pew behind Casey, Ralene, and Nita. Cheerful greetings were quietly but exuberantly exchanged. "I love the spirit in this place!" Casey whispered to Amber. "It's so good to be in God's presence!"

"I know!" Amber responded with a grin. "I'm sure if it's anything like we've heard, it will be well worth the long drive out here. I'm glad we could all get together today," she added.

A slight frown creased Luke's brow as he mused on the irony of this particular little band of Christians' showing up in Pastor Brownstein's church in light of the gloomy warning he had been given. Why had they seemingly been led of the Lord to show up at this particular time?

He didn't have long to wait for an answer to his unspoken question. A dark figure approached the doorway and halted momentarily, blocking the light. His shadow seemed to throw a cold chill over the crowded sanctuary before he slowly made his way across the back of the church. He was followed by a small clump of devotees who, with bowed heads, kept a respectable distance.

Luke's body tingled with electricity as the leader brushed past him. *It's him!* Luke thought to himself. And, even though he had been forewarned, the unbidden words pounded in his brain. *How could Pastor Brownstein let this monster into his church? How could this discerning pastor let a ravening wolf into the midst of his flock?*

Luke watched in amazement as Prophet Black stepped up onto the platform where Pastor Brownstein, grinning broadly, shook his hand and motioned for him to be seated next to the pulpit facing the congregation.

Luke glanced toward the other side of the room and noted the shock and dismay registered on the pale faces of Casey, Ralene, Ellie, John, and Amber. "What on earth is that heretic, that false prophet, doing in this church?" whispered Casey to Ralene. "We heard that Pastor Brownstein was a true man of God!"

"Shhhh ..." Casey hushed her. "We don't know why he's here. Maybe Pastor Brownstein doesn't know anything about him ... yet! We have to give this pastor a chance. Pray"

"If I'd known that *that nut* was gonna be here, I'd have stayed home!" John growled under his breath to Ellie. She patted his arm and smiled warmly up into his face. "I know, Dear," she said, "but remember, God is in control."

"There's Ernie and Kate!" Amber whispered to Ellie. "Over there, look!" She nodded her head toward the front row on the opposite side of the church.

"Kate looks awful," muttered Ellie as she grabbed a hymn book and stood to her feet with the rest of the congregation.

"… that is page 243 in the red book," Pastor Brownstein said with vigor. "'I Love To Tell The Story of Jesus and His Love.' Do you love to tell the story?"

A joyful chorus of voices responded, "Sure do!"

Luke stood with the rest and watched from his vantage point as the eager worshippers sang their hearts out to the King of kings. Prophet Black sang with vigor and conviction and from all outward appearances was a genuine New Testament saint.

The sweet presence of the Holy Spirit filled the sanctuary. Luke noticed that Pastor Brownstein seemed especially happy today. *If only he knew,* Luke thought to himself, *what I know.*

After the worship service, the pastor opened in prayer. Then he turned toward Prophet Black and nodded for him to join him behind the pulpit. "Brothers and sisters," Pastor Brownstein said enthusiastically, "we are honored this morning to have a very special guest. Prophet Black! He comes very highly recommended from Pastor Albert of Miracle Mountain Fellowship."

If Pastor Brownstein heard the faint collective gasp uttered from Casey and the little group of first-time visitors, he paid no attention. "I met Pastor Albert on my last trip to the city. Prophet Black will be sharing with us what God has shown him about these last days in which we live. And," he said as he stepped down from the platform and sat in the front pew, "I believe we all need to pay close attention."

Luke shuddered as the stocky prophet scanned the congregation and then gave a tight-lipped grin. His steel-gray eyes glinted through half-closed lids. "Praise the Lord!" His voice cut through the thick air like a well-honed knife. "I said, 'praise the Lord!'"

A few shaky "Amen's" were uttered.

Again, Prophet Black stated, "I said, 'praise the Lord!'"

"Amen!" shouted Ernie and Kate in unison. Like well-trained dogs the handful of Black's devotees echoed their enthusiastic response and shouted, "Praise the Lord!"

The little congregation at Greenwood Glen Church was not used to being primed, pumped, and prodded. Its members had always been taught that they should respond to the Holy Spirit, not to man's manipulation. Luke watched confusion enter like a ghostly blanket of swirling eddies and whirlpools. It descended upon the unsuspecting people and covered them like a giant spider web.

"Stand with me as we praise the Lord!" Prophet Black commanded as he opened a hymnbook. "We need to praise the Lord!"

Luke watched Casey and Ralene struggle to their feet. "We already had worship!" stated Casey to Ralene. "And, it was good!"

"Well," Ralene said under her breath, "apparently he wants to start over and run the whole show."

"This is going to be exhausting!" complained Casey. "I want to leave, right now! The guy is possessed!"

"Shhhh! God has us here for some reason!" Ralene reprimanded her friend.

"Oh, I never thought of that!" mumbled Casey resignedly.

Prophet Black gave them a warning glance and then resumed his loud singing and pacing back and forth across the front of the church. Luke was glad that the short man couldn't see past the standing congregation to where he sat in the back with crossed arms. *Why does it always have to be like this here on earth? Any spiritual oasis of truth, beauty, and love always seems to be a special target for the enemy. Eventually such places will be systematically hunted out, infiltrated, defiled, and destroyed. How that fallen angel and his hordes hate the Almighty Creator and those who love and worship Him!*

Pastor Brownstein stood and enthusiastically sang along with Prophet Black. After all, he firmly believed that the old hymns were essential for a Christian's solid foundation and faith. But, after half an hour dragged on to forty-five minutes, the pastor's broad shoulders began to sag. Several of the older members of the congregation, along with the children, quietly sat down. Luke watched Casey, Ralene, and

Nita sink into the pew, followed by John, Ellie, and Amber. A heavy weariness settled over the once-expectant gathering.

What subtlety, Luke thought to himself. *What a two-pronged method to take control over people. First, you get them to believe you are of God because you adhere to the anointed old hymns with their scriptural truths. Then you push it to extremes so everyone is too tired to think critically.*

"Oh, Father!" Prophet Black intoned as he positioned himself behind the pulpit. "We repent of our wickedness! We repent of our sins! Because of our pride and rebellion, you are about to judge this wicked nation! Fire! Fire! Fire! I see fire falling from heaven upon this ungodly nation!" He banged his fist on the pulpit.

"Amen!" shouted Ernie and Kate in unison. A low rumble of "Amen's" followed.

"I have a prophecy for America! There shall be earthquakes, floods, plagues, tornadoes, hurricanes, rioting, looting, burning, and an increase in crime!" He paused to let his words sink in. "Unless America repents, there will be nuclear war on our soil!"

Another round of "Amen's" sounded from Black's followers and a few members of Greenwood Glen who in good conscience knew that this was the ugly truth.

"We are guilty of the blood of the innocents! We are guilty of the worst kind of lewdness from child pornography to harlotry to sexual perversions of every type imaginable! And I do mean sodomy!" He pounded on the pulpit with a clenched fist.

Luke observed most of the congregation nodding in agreement. He knew that what Prophet Black had said to this point was technically true. How could it be otherwise? Didn't the Holy Bible warn of such judgments upon the ungodly, and hadn't America stepped over the line many years ago with its covetousness, greed, and idolatry? What Luke had seen in the churches during his time on earth was appalling to him. The so-called Christian church, with very few exceptions, had little in common with the believers of the New Testament pilgrim church.

Luke's brain seemed to split into two directions. Part of his mind listened to the warnings that Prophet Black was firing off at the congregation while the other part analyzed the plight of the modern church. True, there was a form of godliness, but the power was denied. *The power is in the Gospel*, Luke thought. He didn't personally understand all of the ramifications of that since he wasn't a redeemed human, but he knew wherever the Gospel was not fully preached, that church was powerless. *That was it! The Gospel! Prophet Black never preached the Gospel! He may be right on as far as God's judgments, which anybody could read about in the Bible, but he never lifted up Christ! Repentance, yes—Christ, no!*

Prophet Black's voice broke through Luke's thoughts like a jackhammer. "Repent! God is saying that if America heeds my warning and repents then His judgment will not come. God is telling me right now that if the church in America repents, then America will be spared! God is telling me that you people of Greenwood Glen must repent! You need to stir yourselves up and fall down and cry out to God in true repentance!" He began pacing back and forth across the front of the church, muttering under his breath about all of the false prophets he had encountered. He then launched into a thirty-minute detailed overview of all of the prophecies that he had given to leaders of nations around the world and how they had come to pass. It appeared as if he had an impeccable record as a true prophet of God.

Luke felt an oppressive heaviness pressing against the congregation from all sides. The people sat rigid with fear. Horror and hopelessness filled their eyes, and some were softly crying. Luke couldn't see Pastor Brownstein's face, but he sensed a growing agitation. He watched him shift his weight and throw his arm across the back of his pew. His fingers began drumming on the worn wood.

"The church today," Prophet Black thundered, "has failed to keep God's laws! This means that the church must return to her Jewish roots and keep God's Sabbath, God's laws, and God's feasts!"

Waves of shock rippled through the tense crowd. Keep God's laws and His feasts? What could this possibly mean?

"After all," he lowered his voice, "Jesus said that if we love Him, then we will keep His commandments!" He paused to let the well-known scripture take effect, and then in a threatening tone he said, "It's a fact, ladies and gentlemen, that those who fail to keep God's feasts are in

335

rebellion and lawlessness, which is the antichrist spirit! This means that they are not truly born again!"

What happened next took everyone by surprise. In one movement Pastor Brownstein jumped to his feet, pointed straight at the prophet, and commanded, "You lying spirit! I rebuke you in the Name of Jesus Christ!"

The startled congregation stared wide-eyed as Prophet Black crumpled to the floor behind the pulpit. Ernie, followed by two elders, hurried up the steps and knelt down beside the still form. "He's dead, he's dead!" Ernie cried hysterically. "The prophet is dead ..."

"No, he's not dead," one of the elders stated flatly. "Here, help me get him up."

"Take him to the prayer room in the back," Pastor Brownstein ordered tersely as he took his position behind the pulpit. "Dear people ..." his voice broke. Tears streamed down his cheeks. "Please forgive me ... oh, God! Forgive me." He took out a handkerchief and wiped his face. "I am so sorry that I ever exposed you to this ... this ... fake!"

"Amen!" Casey shouted.

Ralene grinned. *Leave it to Casey*, she thought to herself.

"That's right!" John said as he stood to his feet. "Pastor, we're just first-time visitors here this morning, but now we know that God had a purpose for bringing us here today. At first we were all sorry we chose this particular Sunday to visit, but God directed our steps, for which we praise His name!"

There was a murmur of agreement. Pastor Brownstein nodded for John to continue. "You see, we're from the city and we know all about this so-called prophet because we have had experiences with him in the past. We've been sitting here, praying for you and this congregation all morning. And, Pastor Brownstein, you are right on!" He sat down and gently squeezed Ellie's hand.

"Well, I am out of here!" Kate mumbled. She glared at John and the others as she snatched up her purse and Bible and stomped out the back door. She fully expected the others of Prophet Black's group to follow, but they remained motionless as if frozen to their pews.

"Church," Pastor Brownstein's voice broke, giving witness to his stricken heart, "we need to call a special meeting to bring truth and understanding to what was said here today and to what has just taken place. Right now, though," his eyes, filled with tears and compassion, swept the upturned faces, "you are all very tired and deserve to go home and rest. But I would very much like for you to come back tonight at seven o'clock so God can move amongst us and minister to us and ..."

His sentence was cut short by the piercing, blood-curdling scream from the prayer room. The scream descended into a snarling roar that tore through the little church like a banshee and ricocheted through the trees of Greenwood Glen. The prayer room door crashed open as Prophet Black dashed through it with Ernie and the two elders in pursuit. Pastor Brownstein, momentarily stunned, quickly jumped off the platform and joined the chase.

Luke was already stationed at the back door of the church. Prophet Black charged towards him and hissed, "Out—out—out of my way or I'll ..." he shoved Luke, knocking him backward, and ran down the road toward the river.

"No! No! Oh, no!" yelled Ernie in hot pursuit. "Prophet Black, stop! Stop!" The two elders along with Pastor Brownstein trotted behind Ernie. Kate followed at a distance. The other members of Black's group finally stirred themselves and fell into line behind Kate.

The amazed congregation filed out of the church and began walking towards the river. Not one of them had any desire to go home and miss whatever was about to transpire.

"Judgments of God!" screamed the prophet as he began to hurl curses into the air. He somehow managed to stay ahead of his pursuers. "God will destroy you all! God will cause this river to become a mighty torrent of destruction upon you because you refuse to obey Him!" He had reached the narrow bridge that spanned the deep, flowing river. "Stop!" He held up his hands in warning. "Don't come near me!" He began backing toward the center of the bridge.

Everyone halted at the edge of the bridge except Ernie. "Prophet Black," Ernie entreated, "Wait for me! I am your disciple! I'm coming, too!"

"Noooo!" wailed Black. "You are a fool! You are going to die like all the rest of them! You have no idea who I really am! You don't know the signs! I tried to teach you, but you have too much of the traditions of men in you to be of any use to me! Stay away from me! I don't want you to defile me! You need to repent! I am the prophet to the nations!"

Ernie dropped to his knees and held his head in his hands. "Oh, Kate!" he yelled. "What is happening? Kate?"

"I'm here Ernie, and I'm scared. He's lost his sanity!"

"Kate! I believed in him! I gave him everything! Our home, our bank account, my retirement, all gone! I gave him ..."

"Look!" a voice cried out, "Look on the bridge! There's that fellow, what's his name? Oh yes! Luke Solomon, on the other side of the bridge ... how in the world did he get over there? He's walking towards Black."

Pastor Brownstein stepped around Ernie's prostrate form and began slowly walking across the bridge toward the prophet. Black held out his arms as if to hold the pastor at bay. "No! You hireling shepherd of Greenwood Glen, don't you come near me! Stop—not one step closer!" Still facing the slowly advancing pastor, he began to back up. "I know who you are," the voice growled.

Pastor Brownstein's tone was dead even. "I know who you are, too."

"Don't you come near me!" it hissed.

"Jesus is Lord!" Luke's voice rang out in the crisp air.

Prophet Black whirled to face the tall figure walking toward him. "You!"

"Yes."

"No! No! It's not my time!" Black screamed. He gripped his head in his hands and began weaving back and forth. His face contorted until he was unrecognizable. Suddenly his tortured screams erupted in a foul stream of profanities.

"Enough!" Luke commanded. "May the curse you just pronounced on this group of Christians return on your own head." His eyes swept past the writhing figure and met Pastor Brownstein's. In a moment of brief understanding, something profound and deep passed between them. "He's not the last, you know—there are others."

Pastor Brownstein nodded his understanding, and then extended a hand toward Prophet Black.

"AAAAAUUUUGGGGHHHH! Don't touch me, you pig!"

Even though every eye was riveted on Prophet Black, afterwards, in the retelling of that eventful day, no two people could agree over the exact details of what happened next. But they all vividly recalled that there was a frightful, horrible noise like a freight train roaring past, followed by a few seconds of eerie silence, and then a huge splash.

Rescue teams were called and sent out. They searched for two weeks and then gave up. No body was ever recovered.

Some said that the false prophet catapulted over the railing alone. Others said that he grabbed the tall Luke Solomon and forced him off of the bridge. A few argued that the short man was no match for Mr. Solomon. One person insisted that he saw them wrestling and that they both fell off the bridge. Another said that she saw Luke back away from Black, who then hurled himself into the whirlpools under the bridge. Two children insisted that they saw Luke Solomon evaporate into the mist. Pastor Brownstein, on the other hand, refused to say anything.

The identity of Mr. Luke Obed Solomon would forever remain shrouded in mystery to the folks of Greenwood Glen.

20

THE GATES

The little church at Greenwood Glen was packed to overflowing the following Sunday morning. Pastor Brownstein stepped up behind the pulpit and watched the animated conversations taking place. He knew that everyone had either a question or a comment, or both on their minds.

"Good morning, everyone," he said with a smile, trying to make his voice heard over the din. His brown eyes maintained their usual twinkle in spite of the weariness he felt. Everything about him exuded an air of calm, confident authority. He kept his dark brown hair short and neat, and he was always careful to dress in a way that honored the Lord. He loathed extremes, and avoided over-dressing like "those fancy CEO pastors" in the big city churches, and he also avoided stepping up to preach in a rumpled shirt, sloppy T-shirt, or casual pants. He said once that he'd rather be hog-tied to a pole and tossed in the river than wear men's cropped pants.

"Let's open in prayer." The hushed congregation reverently stood with bowed heads as their beloved pastor interceded for them, their community, the nation, and for the peace of Jerusalem. He ended by asking the Holy Spirit to impart into every heart that which the Lord wanted them to understand.

"Praise the Lord!" he emphatically said with raised hands. "You may be seated." He waited until the people were settled, then declared, "God has done great things! He has done great things in, through and for us beyond our understanding because He is faithful and His love for His people knows no bounds. The events that took place here last Sunday give us cause to humbly consider what we take for granted, what we think we know but probably don't—at least not to any great extent—and to seek the face of God more fervently and more often. It should also serve as a warning, especially to those who, for one reason or another, have little, if any, fear of God, for the Bible tells us that 'The fear of the Lord is the beginning of wisdom' and God knows that we all need wisdom!" Several heads nodded in agreement.

Pastor Brownstein paused as his eyes scanned the people before him. His lips curved into an impish grin. "If anybody here believes that they don't need wisdom, please come see me after the message because I'm interested in why you think you don't, plus, I would love to shake the hand of the wisest person here."

A ripple of laugher rolled through the church. "Today the Lord has impressed upon my heart to first discuss what is on all of our minds and hearts, openly share the Word with one another, and then land on the runway of love, joy and faith in worship to our wonderful Lord and Savior.

He glanced over the congregation and was encouraged by the open and pleased looks beaming back at him. "Seriously, the Lord has put it upon my heart that I need to talk to you today about a couple of topics, one being angels. Hebrews 13:2 tells us, 'Be not forgetful to entertain strangers: for thereby some have entertained angels unawares.'"

He caught the sound of a few surprised folks sucking in their breath, while some whispered to each other. "I think by that response," he grinned at them, "we're all pretty much on the same page, as they say these days."

A low murmur of "Amen's" rumbled through the crowd. "First, let me state that I am not here to try and convince you one way or the other, or to get you to agree with me on what I personally believe. The safest and best way to study this subject, as with any other biblical topic, is to prayerfully go to the Word of God for the answers. And, I'm glad to see you all brought your Bibles with you."

He paused to take a sip of water, cleared his throat and continued. "I know that most of you are already familiar with the Scriptures we're going to look at together this morning, but instead of glossing over them because we may assume that they were written for another people living in another time and place, or written for those down the line who will follow us, let us take a more careful and clearer look at them as pertaining to you and me right now!" He paused for a few seconds, hoping his words were 'sinking in' and smiled to himself as he saw Casey and Ralene exchange knowing looks.

Pastor Brownstein lifted his Bible and held it up. "This is God's Word, it is living, it is holy, it is truth and it is powerful. Satan, the world, communism and all the other "ism's," cults and religions hate it, but the children of God love and cherish it. In it the mention of angels occurs almost three-hundred times. That God created them, and the fact that they are real, is undebatable. We know from Scripture that Lucifer, who became Satan, wanted to be God and led one-third of the angels into rebellion against God. We do not know all the details of his expulsion from heaven to earth, but we do know that his fall was prior to his entrance into the Garden of Eden and thus, as you all know, caused the fall of man. I would suggest that you all pursue a serious study of this subject in the coming days. *A Survey of Bible Doctrine* by Charles C. Ryrie may be helpful to you."

"Now," he grasped the edges of the worn wooden pulpit, slightly leaned forward and lovingly scanned the eager faces before him. "Let's get right to the point of what many of you have on your minds. Was Luke Obed Solomon a man, or an angel sent by God for a specific purpose?" *I wish I had a camera right now,* he thought as everything from incredulity, amazement, consternation, thoughtfulness, curiosity and joy registered on people's faces. "Just as I thought," he said. "The souls of all of us have been stirred by his presence among us."

The wide-awake congregation watched their pastor as he stood motionless, holding his Bible close to his heart, with eyes closed, and lips barely moving. After a few moments without moving from his position, he prayed aloud. "Lord Jesus, thank You for every precious soul here this morning. Thank You for your loving care of us, Your flock. Thank You for protecting us from a ferocious wolf, from Satan's beguilements, wiles, and destruction. Thank You for sending Your servant, Luke Obed Solomon at just the right time. Whether he was an angel from You, a messenger from heaven or not, we cannot prove one way or the other, nor should we try because the truth is, You do all things

342

well, and Your will has been done in this small church for which we are eternally thankful. Now, Lord, I ask that the Holy Spirit will guide, teach and touch each of us, and Your servant as I lead these precious sheep into some rocky pastures and steep places this morning. Praise Your holy name! Amen."

He looked at the faces before him and warmly smiled. "For the next few weeks, we will be taking a more in-depth look at the subject of angels, their purpose, their assignments from God, their ranks and battles with the fallen angels as well as recorded visitations from heavenly angels to people in the Bible. We will also hear testimonies of people who know they have had an encounter with an angel, as well as look at both modern and historical accounts from different Christians. It should be an exciting and interesting journey for all of us to take together, so please write down your thoughts, any experiences you may have had yourself, as well as any questions you may have. And, please don't exclude your children from the discussion because they often have encounters with angels themselves, but don't know how to express it to others. Also," he held up a warning hand, "please, oh please do not become unbalanced and obsessed with angels as some have done and gone off the deep end into error!" A low rumble of agreement flowed through the congregation.

"Good! Now," he took a deep breath as if preparing to take a high-dive into a pool of ice, "I am going to make a sharp turn onto a controversial road that more and more Christians seem to be detouring onto." The relaxed muscles in his face visibly tightened as his tone grew gravely serious. It was obvious to most of the people that he was not comfortable with what he was about to divulge. "There is a very strong, yet subtle, deeply-rooted wild vine creeping, for the most part, undetected into the midst of God's church—which I'll refer to as His vineyard. I am not speaking of just our little church here, but throughout the world."

Casey's eyes widened and her pulse quickened. *I think maybe I know where he's heading, and if so, it might upset some people in here.* As if reading her thoughts, Pastor Brownstein's eyes locked on hers for a moment. Then he turned to God's "vineyard" and quoted Philippians 2:8-11, "And being found in fashion as a man, he humbled himself and

343

became obedient unto death, even the death of the cross. Wherefore God also hath highly exalted him, and given him a name which is above every name: That at the name of Jesus every knee should bow, of things in heaven, and things in earth, and things under the earth; And that every tongue should confess that Jesus Christ is Lord, to the glory of God the Father."

"While I'm reasonably certain that everyone present today is familiar with, and believes these verses and looks forward to that great and glorious day, there nevertheless is, as I just mentioned, an insidious wild vine that is creeping throughout God's vineyard, seeking to pervert the truth, and this is one of the verses that is used to promote it."

Every eye was riveted on Pastor Brownstein. He looked over the heads of the people and implored, "If you have become unwittingly entangled in what I am about to say, please hear me out. This vine is a lie that, although it may appear harmless on the surface, once you follow it down to its very roots, you will begin to understand how satanic, blasphemous and insidious it really is."

The pastor watched people begin to squirm, and he wondered if he heard right from the Holy Spirit about "grabbing the bull by the horns." He would have preferred to "grab the bull by the tail" and then work up to the head instead. He took a deep breath, and plunged in. "The name of this vine may not be too well-known by many Christians, but it's one of the many "isms" that has a powerful, beguiling spirit behind it that novices and those who are unskilled in the Word, and even more mature Christians find quite pleasant, tantalizing and even hopefully probable."

A thick blanket of silence descended over the people. Pastor Brownstein reached for the water glass, took other sip of water, slowly set the glass down, studied the people for a moment, then solemnly said, "I realize that we have gone over the 'doctrines of demons' and a host of other 'ear-tickling' doctrines throughout the years, but at what point can we honestly assume that we are informed and wise enough to ignore the perilous times we are living in, and Satan's never-ending wiles to bring about a one-world religion that will deceive the nations?"

Judging by the restlessness of the congregation, he knew he had to "grab the bull by the horns," spit it out, and hang on. In a terse voice he slowly said, "What I'm talking about today is called Universalism, and it is mostly spread by fictitious, Scripture-twisting books, novels, videos, music, false prophets and," he paused, "the globalists and New Age.

The response was immediate. Casey and Ralene said a hearty, "Amen" at the same time. Now that the silence was broken, others added their "Amen's." Encouraged, the faithful pastor explained, "There are varying beliefs in Universalism, but what concerns us is 'Christian Universalism' or 'Christian Reconciliation' which also believes that there is no eternal hell, and that all mankind will eventually be saved. Some even believe that Satan and the fallen angels will be saved based on the Scripture that every knee shall bow, and every tongue confess that Jesus is Lord." He watched the different reactions to this statement. Some faces remained thoughtful while others, with raised eyebrows, gave evidence of questions that needed to be answered.

"Does anybody have a question?" he asked. "If so, please raise your hand."

"Yes, Pastor," a woman said as she raised her hand.

"Very well, Lilly. What is your question?" He beckoned for her to stand.

Rising to her feet, the middle-aged woman explained, "I have always hated the idea of eternal judgment, and so it seems to me, if everyone is going to bow to Jesus and confess Him as Lord, then why shouldn't they be allowed into heaven?"

"Thank you, Lilly. That is a very good question," he said, then glancing around the sanctuary he asked, "Who would like to answer that question using Scripture?"

"I will," said an elderly gentleman in the back of the room.

"Thank you, evangelist Gladstone," the pastor said.

The elderly man stood to his feet, squared his shoulders, and took a deep breath. "This verse, in context is about glorifying God, the one true God, Creator of heaven and earth and all that is within them." His voice was strong and deep. "It is a verse that makes it clear that the Victor is Jesus Christ, and when the battle is over, every knee, whether in heaven, or earth or in hell under the earth will confess that there is only one Lord of all and that is Jesus Christ.

"This is what happens after a battle, folks! The defeated and conquered people, after any battle, must confess that they lost the victory and their foes won. Think about it, God's people, both Jew and Gentile have been in a battle for centuries! This verse certainly doesn't mean, folks, that those knees and tongues confessing that Jesus Christ is Lord are connected to hearts that love Him, or that suddenly their names are going to appear in the Book of Life! The Bible is clear that only, and I do mean ONLY those whose names are written in the Book of Life will inherit eternal life. Revelation 20:15 says, 'And whosoever was not found written in the book of life was cast into the lake of fire."

He remained standing, head bowed as he wiped a tear from his cheek, and then he said, "Listen to Revelation 21:7 and 8, then try to show me that this is not the plain Word of the Lord concerning God's just judgments; 'He that overcometh shall inherit all things; and I will be his God, and he shall be my son. But the fearful, and unbelieving, and the abominable, and murderers, and whoremongers, and sorcerers, and idolaters, and all liars, shall have their part I the lake which burneth with fire and brimstone: which is the second death." He closed his Bible and sat down.

Everyone sat in silent thought for a few minutes. Finally, a teen age girl nervously stood to her feet. "May I say something?" she meekly asked the pastor.

"Of course, you may Susan. What's on your heart?" he asked with a smile.

"Well," she began, "um, well, I have this friend at school who says she's a Christian, but she can't come to church with me on Sundays because her family is always busy or going somewhere. I talk to her a lot about Jesus and stuff, but she says if God is love, then surely Satan could be saved if he repented. She got that idea from her cousin who doesn't believe in hell. In fact, he's a Universalist and told her the Bible wasn't translated correctly. What should I tell her?" She sat down and looked around hopefully for an answer

Ralene stood to her feet, and Pastor Brownstein nodded for her to go ahead and respond. "Susan, you need to point out to her that the Bible tells us the fallen angels such as Satan, who was created as Lucifer, but became the devil when he chose to rebel against God because he wants to be God, have no place for repentance. Furthermore, they are already judged. Hebrews 12:17 tells us even

Esau, who sought a place of repentance with tears, could not find it. Judas, who betrayed Jesus, repented out of guilt but not true conviction and Jesus said 'woe to that man who betrays the son of God.' Why would He say that if there was a place of repentance for him?

"In Daniel 12:2 that those who sleep or have died shall awake some to everlasting life, and some to shame and everlasting contempt. Jesus clearly brings this same scenario out in John 5:21-29. It is clear that not all will experience heaven's bliss."

She took a deep breath and continued, "When it comes to Satan, John 16:11 tells us that as the prince of the world, he has already been judged. Revelation 14:11 plainly states, 'And the smoke of their torment ascends up for ever and ever: and they have no rest day or night who worship the beast and his image, and whosoever receives the mark of his name.' This refers to Satan and those who worship and obey him.

She flipped the pages in her Bible to the Old Testament. "In Isaiah 45:9 the Lord is telling Satan, 'Hell from beneath is moved for thee to meet thee at thy coming: it stirs up the dead for thee, even all the chief ones of the earth; it has raised up from their thrones all the kings of the nations.' I hope you'll have your friend read the whole chapter because it is crystal clear that Satan and those who fight against God and hate Him, and never repent will never be forgiven. According to Psalm 89:34, and other verses, all that is prophesied in the Bible is established in eternity, and will come to pass in time. God said that He would not alter the things that have gone out of His lips. The bottom line is, Jesus said, 'Repent, or perish!'" Several "Amens" were uttered as she sat down.

Then Casey stood up, and the pastor beckoned for her to speak. "Jesus did not die on the cross and shed His blood for Satan, or for fallen angels, or for any other creature. He died for fallen man because Adam was made in His image. None of the angelic beings, or any other creation was made in His likeness. God is holy, and God is just. All His works are done in righteousness, and it would be outside of the character and attributes of God for Him to pardon from the judgment and justice the most evil, vile, profane, unclean, and wicked beings who hate Him.'"

She tapped the Bible she was holding, "This is God's Word and it holds people accountable. The bottom line is, when it comes to

Universalism and all the other 'isms,' people just flat out don't want to be held accountable for their sins. In other words, they call God a liar, that He doesn't mean what He tells us in His Word! And that includes all the prophecies from cover-to-cover concerning Satan's fiery future and all those who serve him!" She abruptly sat down and hoped she had said enough to convince those who were teetering on the fence to get into the Word and embrace the truth for the sake of their own souls.

"I see our new sister, Carol sitting in the second row has something to say," the pastor said. "Please share with us what your thoughts are."

"I just have one question for you all, and it's this: If it's true that everyone, whether saint or sinner who ever lived will be reconciled back to God because of His great love, then why did He send His Son to die for sinners? If that's true, then Jesus wouldn't have had to come, right?"

Pastor Brownstein's face broke into a large grin. "That's a great question! Does anyone want to comment on Carol's question?

"Hallelujah, praise the Lord!" a middle-aged, heavy-set man literally hopped to his feet. "Thank you, brothers and sisters, for putting my mind at ease over this Universal stuff! I just want to say that I'm fairly new here, and my name is Randy for those I haven't had the pleasure of meeting yet. But today, many of you have greatly helped me out of the confusion I've been in for some time over this very issue. And, I can also say that thanks to all that's been said so far this morning, that it has definitely inspired me to do a thorough study of the Bible from Genesis to Revelation. There's just too much unbiblical stuff floating around out there these days to remain as ignorant as I have been about the Bible!"

As he sat back down, several hands reached out and patted his back, arms and shoulders while showering him with words of encouragement, including an invitation for lunch after the service. He blushed at the outpouring of understanding and love, and happily accepted the invitation. As the pastor watched his little flock display love for one another, which was a weekly occurrence, his heart swelled with joy.

"Does anyone else have something to say concerning what the Bible says about eternal punishment?" Pastor Brownstein asked.

"I do!" a young boy's voice rang out from the back of the church.

"Is that you back there, Daniel?" the pastor asked with a grin.

"Yesssir! It's me and I have a verse to read. Can I read it please?" The eight-year-old boy looked anxiously at Pastor Brownstein.

"Why yes! Of course you can! Why don't you bring your Bible and come up here by me, and read what you have for the whole church?"

"Yessssir!" Daniel solemnly said. "Here I come!" He looked back at his smiling parents, slipped out of the pew, and marched to the front of the church. The kind pastor positioned the boy close to him, and told him to read "real loud."

Daniel opened his Bible to the place where his bookmark was and said, as loudly as he could, "I am reading from Matthew, chapter 25, verse 41 what Jesus said, because it's in red and it says, 'Then shall he say also unto them on the left hand, Depart from me, ye cursed, into everlasting fire, prepared for the devil ad his angels." He glanced up at the pastor, and whispered something in his ear. Pastor Brownstein nodded his head 'yes'.

"So," Daniel turned and said to the people, "Jesus told the sinners to go away from Him into everlasting hell, and besides that," he pointed to his Bible, Jesus said that hell was made for the devil and his angels!" Before Daniel could say another word, the people clapped for him. But instead of closing his Bible and stepping off the platform, Daniel politely waited until it became hushed, and then he blurted out, "So I have a question for you. If Jesus said everlasting fire was made for the devil and his angels, did He really mean that, or was He lying?"

Tears came to the pastor's eyes as he thought to himself, *Out of the mouth of babes! Praise You Lord!* He laid a hand on Daniel's shoulder, leaned down and quietly said, "Well said, Daniel! You are a good disciple and will make a fine preacher of the Word someday."

Daniel grinned up at him with shining eyes, then turned and quickly walked back to sit with his parents.

Pastor Brownstein's voice choked with emotion as he addressed the congregation. "Unless there are any more comments or questions, let's just spend some time praising the Lord!" He waited a few minutes to give people an opportunity to share their thoughts, but it was apparent that the question about Universal Reconciliation and the subject of hell had been settled, at least for the time being. Everyone knew that the pastor was always available for the people if they had questions, concerns, prayer requests, or needed help with other matters.

As the pianist began playing "How Great Thou Art," and the people joined in song, Pastor Brownstein thought he heard a familiar voice, a strong celestial voice like that of an angel, saying, *"I will build My church, and the gates of hell shall not prevail against it."*

Epilogue

Maschil rejoiced to be back in the realms of glory and away from the turmoil on earth.

Pirathon, (or Prince) who had watched the final scene at Greenwood Glen between Luke Obed Solomon, Pastor Brownstein, and Prophet Black, was happy to accompany Maschil on his return journey.

Neither angel would ever forget the moment when, hidden from human eyes, four snarling demons dragged the raving prophet to hell.

Pastor Brownstein started a series of discernment classes for his own benefit as well as for the members of his congregation. Much to his surprise, many of the prophet's former devotees, including Kate, attended these special classes, and they also faithfully attended every Sunday.

Ernie, faced with bankruptcy, left Kate and disappeared. Some said he moved to South America to make a new life for himself, but no one knew for certain.

Books By Jeannette Haley

Books co-authored with Rayola Kelley:
Hidden Manna (original)
The Many Faces of Christianity (Volume 6)
Post to Post 3: Meditations Along the Way
Post to Post 4: Inspirations Along the Way

Other Books:
Rose of Light, Thorn of Darkness
The Pig and I
Reflections of Wonder (Devotional)

Children's Books:
Little Stories for Little People
Traveler's Tales
The Adventures of Zack and Mira
The Adventures of Paul and Dana:
(A House on the Beach)
The Monster of Mystery Valley

www.ingramcontent.com/pod-product-compliance
Lightning Source LLC
Chambersburg PA
CBHW071159020726
47502CB00002B/469